"If *Hannibal* didn't fill your serial killer fiction needs, give this one a look... It surpasses *Hannibal* in action."

—*San Antonio Express News*

"[A] slick, grisly page-turner...An abundance of old-fashioned fright."

—*Publishers Weekly*

seek...........find............kill

TURN THE PAGE FOR MORE PRAISE . . .

CATCH ME

A. J. Holt

St. Martin's Paperbacks

CATCH ME

Copyright © 1999 by A. J. Holt.

The verse by Antony Jay on page 22 is reprinted by permission of the author.

Library of Congress Catalog Card Number: 99-22063

ISBN: 0-312-97130-3

Printed in the United States of America

St. Martin's Press hardcover edition / August 1999
St. Martin's Paperbacks edition / February 2001

St. Martin's Paperbacks are published by St. Martin's Press, 175 Fifth Avenue, New York, NY 10010.

10 9 8 7 6 5 4 3 2 1

This one is for Tony,
With love and gratitude

PROLOGUE

She watched as his hand edged toward the scissors at the edge of the light green felt blotter on the big desk that stood between them.

"Don't do that," she said.

The psychiatrist looked at her and at the gun in her hand that was pointed at the middle of his face. His hand moved away from the scissors. A small hand, but strong-looking, with tanned fingers and pink nails, manicured with perfect little white half-moons. A murderer's hands.

The scissors. Something is wrong with the scissors.

"Why are you doing this?"

"Because you're Christie."

"That's not my name."

She nodded toward the computer on the stand to the left of the desk. "It's the name you use when you're talking on that." She took a breath and let it out slowly. "As in John Reginald Christie."

A light came on in the psychiatrist's eyes. A frightened light. "He was a serial killer. In England."

"Good for you."

The light in his eyes intensified and the fear turned into horror. "I know who you are now. You're the one they've been calling the Ladykiller. The one who's been . . ."

Jay didn't want to hear it. She let herself close her eyes for a few seconds, then opened them and put a finger to her lips. "Don't say another word, Mr. Christie."

He tried to keep his voice calm. "My name isn't Christie. My name is George Spenser. I'm a psychiatrist."

"I know who you are and I know what you did. On June

14, 1993, you murdered a man named Martin Shook in North Beach, Maryland. You took him down to Daniels Creek and you put a bullet into the back of his head. Then you used the saw blade from a Swiss Army knife to amputate his penis and testicles. A year and a half later you did the same thing just outside Canton, Ohio, to a man named Wayne Rifendefer. In November 1996 you stepped things up a little with a twenty-six-year-old drifter named Jack Andrews. You shot him, castrated and emasculated him, and then you sliced off his nipples as well. The cops found him wrapped up in a blanket at a rest stop outside of Palmdale, California. He was missing both legs below the knee and his head. There's probably been a lot more, but those are the ones you boasted about to Ricky Stiles and all your pals on the Net."

"I don't know what you're talking about! This is insane!"

"That's one word for it."

The computer is wrong, too.

This doesn't feel right.

The psychiatrist glanced at his watch. She smiled. "Expecting someone? It's Friday. You always close up early on Fridays so you can beat the traffic down to your place on the shore. I'm your last appointment for the day." She let her finger tighten on the trigger of the 9 mm automatic. "I'm your last appointment, period, doctor."

The watch.

It's a Tag Heuer.

Not that, stupid! It's on his right wrist.

So what?

"Why are you doing this?"

She knew he was playing for time, trying to keep her talking. She blinked, trying to keep the fatigue at bay for just a little while longer. He was the last. After this she could rest, sleep for a thousand years and pray that she wouldn't dream.

"I'm doing this to prove to myself that God is still in his heaven, and to prove that sometimes the bad guys really do get punished."

You're so full of shit, Jay. That's not why you're doing this at all.

Shut up. Shut up, shut up, shut up!

"You're making a terrible mistake," said the psychiatrist.

Wrong. All going wrong.

Oh Christ, look at the phone. It's on the wrong side of the desk.

She glanced down at her own wrist, the one holding the gun. Her right wrist. No watch. The watch was on her left wrist. Her hand was shaking now. A feather touch was all it was going to take. A breath on the trigger and it would be over.

So easy.

No.

Shook, Rifendefer, and Andrews had all been shot once with a .38 caliber revolver from about a foot away, the bullet traveling slightly upward from right to left, lodging behind the victim's left forehead. The evidence of the castration was equally specific; the sawing motion through the flesh was from right to left, indicating that the Swiss Army knife in all three cases had been held in the murderer's right hand.

Those are left-handed scissors.

The mouse for the computer is on the left side.

The computer's to the left of the desk and the phone is on his left as well.

Right-handed people wear their wristwatches on the left wrist.

Oh, Jesus. He's left-handed.

She swallowed, willing the hand holding the gun to remain absolutely motionless. "Pick up your pen."

"What?"

"Pick up your goddamned pen!"

Losing it. I'm losing it.

Hold on. We can get out of this. We can back off. It's not too late.

Oh yes it is.

The psychiatrist reached out to the pen set that stood at the outer edge of the desk and she watched, hypnotized, holding her breath. He used his left hand to pluck one of the pens from the holder and stared at her. "Now what?"

She nodded toward the pad of lined paper on his blotter. "Write something."

He did, his left hand curling into a familiar, cramped fist, turned inward. The same fist Colleen Hicks, her best friend in grade six, had used. She was left-handed, too. The psychiatrist finished his demonstration and turned the pad around so she could see.

> Now is the time for all good men to come to the aid of the party.
> The quick red fox jumped over the lazy brown dog.

Perfectly legible. No right-handed man could do that with his left hand.

She read the handwritten lines, then looked up at the man. "I almost killed you," she said softly. She forced herself to lower the gun, ease her finger back off the trigger.

So close. So terribly close.

"I'm sorry," she said, realizing even as she spoke that the words wouldn't mean anything to anyone but her. "I'm so sorry."

ONE

"Your father was Charles Manson?"

"Correct."

Total fruitcake.

"Your mother was one of the Manson family members?"

"That's right. Mary Jane Shorter. My father called her Starr."

"That's not what your file says, Billy."

"Then the file is wrong."

His name was William Paris Bonisteel and in his thirty years of life on the planet he had murdered at least twenty-three people, usually in a complex ritual of simultaneous suffocation, disembowelment, and rape, inevitably leaving a trail of taunting evidence that baffled half a dozen police forces until the various links in the chain were put together by rogue FBI agent and computer expert Jay Fletcher, better known in the popular press as the Ladykiller. The tabloids had given William Bonisteel a nickname, too; a perfect fit considering his occupation and his gory sexual proclivities.

Billy Bones.

The psychiatrist looked up from the file and glanced at the young man seated across from him. Billy was dressed in hospital whites and expensive-looking leather slippers. Dark-haired and almost angelically handsome, he smoked a cigarette calmly, looking totally at ease.

"According to your file, you very much objected to the nickname given to you by the press. Billy Bones. You also used another name when you communicated by computer with your friend Ricky Stiles."

"Christie." Billy nodded.

"The British serial killer."

"That's right."

"You have a thing for names then."

"You could say that. I should have been given my birth father's name, or my birth mother's."

"There's no record at all of who your birth parents were."

"I was a ward of the court, just like the rest of them."

"Them?"

Too Freudian for words. Jesus.

"Charlie's kids. The files were all sealed by court order in 1971." He leaned forward and gently tapped his cigarette onto the edge of the heavy cut-glass ashtray that sat on the psychiatrist's desk. "Not too bright, Doctor." His voice was still calm. "I would take about ten seconds to bash your brains in with that ashtray. Maybe less."

The psychiatrist smiled. "Not your style, Billy."

To prove his point the psychiatrist turned slightly behind his desk and glanced out the window. The days of Bedlam and Cuckoo's Nest were long gone; Spring Grove Hospital Center, an annex to the University of Maryland Medical Center, was a pleasant group of three-story buildings set in a campus-like setting on the outskirts of Catonsville, Maryland, about twenty miles west of Baltimore. It was the logical jurisdiction for Billy since Maryland was where he had committed his last crime before being apprehended.

There were no dank basement corridors lined with open cells, nor was the hospital run by a single institutionally deranged idiot out of Dickens. The psychiatrist smiled; the Spring Grove Hospital was in fact run by a *committee* of institutionally deranged idiots. He turned back to the file. Billy was crazy as a loon, of course, but at least he had some of his facts right.

"Your adoption file says your name was William Paris."

"That's the name they gave me. I went into the system as a John Doe, just like all the rest of them."

The model sociopath. An answer for everything.

Born in December 1970 of unknown parentage, Billy had been taken into state custody in March of the following year, his file sealed by order of the Los Angeles District Juvenile Court. There was a small addendum to the original case-worker's notes that said Billy's only possession other than a very dirty set of clothing had been a crumpled postcard of the Eiffel Tower—hence the name William Paris.

According to a series of later notations made by a long list of state-employed medical personnel, Billy was generally in reasonable health although prone to various respiratory ailments. He also appeared to be autistic and was completely mute until the age of seven when he suddenly began speaking in fully formed sentences. An evaluation at that time showed Billy to be extremely bright, but even then there were the first signs of problems ahead; according to file entries made over the next three years, Billy was a bed wetter, a pyromaniac, and was suspected of having tortured, killed, and mutilated several domestic animals.

Just like Jeffrey Dahmer.

At the age of ten these activities appeared to cease and for the next two years Billy was the ideal orphan boy. On his twelfth birthday he was given a second evaluation and came up with an IQ score of 165, easily putting him into the genius category. Eight months later, in October 1980 he was adopted by George Bonisteel, a rural high school teacher, and his wife, Emilia, an elementary school teacher and an amateur weaver. For the next six, uneventful years Billy Paris, now William Paris Bonisteel, lived with adoptive parents in the bedroom community of Santa Clarita.

According to a previous interviewer's notes, Billy had mentioned that the distance from his family home on Walnut Street in Santa Clarita to the infamous Spahn Ranch at 1200 Santa Susana Pass Road in northern Los Angeles—where he had supposedly been conceived by Manson and Mary Jane Shorter—was exactly 9.78 miles. The interviewer checked and discovered that Billy was correct. Pursuing the young man's well-formed delusion, the interviewer further discovered that Billy was an encyclopedia of information about the Tate-LaBianca murders and actually referred to Charles Manson's first child as his half-brother. Manson's only legitimate progeny, Charles Manson, Jr., was born in 1956 during his brief marriage to a waitress named Rosalie Jane Willis.

The interviewer also thought it was instructive to note Billy's choice of mother for his delusion—there was no doubt that Mary Jane Shorter, dark-haired and starlet beautiful, was easily the most attractive of the family members, and physically wasn't a bad match for Billy himself. Shorter, never indicted, vanished shortly after the trial, and her last known address had been Lynden, Washington. Seventeen years old at the time of the Tate-LaBianca killings, Billy's "mom" would now be in her mid-forties.

"You like to get the details right, don't you, Billy?"

"In my profession it's a requirement."

Slaughtering is a profession? Like being a CPA?

"You mean your work at the museum?"

Billy smiled, crossed his legs carefully, and puffed on his cigarette. "Of course," he said, a twinkle in his eyes. "What else?"

After graduating from William S. Hart High School in Santa Clarita with the highest SAT scores the school had ever seen, Billy had his choice of any university in the country. He chose to go to UCLA, where he majored in chemistry and biology, receiving a bachelor's degree in science three years later. A month before graduation both George and Emilia Bonisteel died in a motel fire in Hawaii, where they were celebrating their twenty-fifth wedding anniversary.

Billy used the resulting inheritance to pay for a postgraduate degree in anthropology and for several elective courses in medical illustration at Columbia University in New York. He followed this with a Ph.D. from Georgetown University in Washington, submitting a brilliant thesis on the identification by both computerized and physical means of the skeletal remains of a young woman who had died in a hotel fire in New York in the early 1920s.

Just like mom and dad.

Of the fire's twenty-three victims, she was the only one whose body had neither been claimed nor identified, and it had been assumed at the time that she was either a vagrant or a prostitute. The articulated skeleton of the woman had been used as a teaching tool at Columbia for decades.

Using a computer program he had designed himself and a cast of the woman's skull, Billy eventually matched her with a passport photograph, identifying the skeleton as nineteen-year-old Bridget Coffey, a mail-order bride from County Mayo in Ireland. Waiting for her husband-to-be in the small hotel after a steerage-class Atlantic crossing, Bridget had been trapped in her cupboard-sized room by the raging fire that swept through the hotel.

By the end of his thesis William Paris Bonisteel had not only identified the woman, he had also managed to track down the name and descendants of the man who'd brought her across the seas to meet her fiery death.

The thesis was a tour de force and earned Billy not only his Ph.D. but also a position at the American Museum of Natural History in New York. He was twenty-six years old and his new job solved a problem that had been bothering him for the better part of ten years—how to get rid of the bodies.

After his arrest Billy described his first "real" killing to the court-appointed psychiatrist as a bungled mess, not much more sophisticated than his cat carvings and rabbit mutilations. According to his story, the victim, "harvested" in 1987, when Billy was seventeen and just beginning his first year at UCLA, was a nineteen-year-old co-ed named Susan Bryant.

Billy picked her up one evening at a Baskin Robbins on Washington Boulevard in Marina Del Rey, offered her a ride back to her dorm, and instead knocked her unconscious, took her north toward Malibu, detoured up Surfview Drive, then dragged the bound and gagged young woman into the woods of Topanga State Park.

Under cover of darkness he raped Susan several times, then simultaneously suffocated her by cramming dirt into her mouth and eviscerated her with the hooked blade of a linoleum-cutting knife. With his trophy taken, Billy then loaded the corpse into the trunk of his car and drove around for an hour trying to decide what to do with it. Eventually he dumped the corpse into the community recycling depot in the play yard of Marquez Avenue Elementary School, only a few blocks away from where he'd taken Susan into the woods.

According to later interviews, Billy was astounded that he hadn't been arrested then and there, considering the over-whelming amount of forensic evidence he'd left behind, from clotted blood in the trunk of his car to semen in a variety of bodily orifices, real and invented.

On the other hand, no one remembered what the good-looking guy at Baskin Robbins had been driving when he left with the girl, other than the fact that it was Japanese and dark blue; the young man who'd actually served Billy and Susan was short-sighted and had forgotten his glasses that shift; and as luck would have it, no one recalled seeing a blue Japanese car pulling up to the school on Marquez Avenue.

Along with enough serum DNA to convict him a dozen times, Billy also left fingerprints all over Susan's body, her clothes, and the vinyl covering of her purse. At seventeen, however, Billy had never been fingerprinted and thus there was no existing file on him in any of the databanks available at the time. The case was back-burnered and eventually for-gotten. Billy had managed to get away with murder, but only just.

He continued to get away with it as the years passed, re-fining his techniques with each killing and learning from his mistakes, but he knew that the human remains he left behind were his great vulnerability. Without the corpus delicti there was, effectively, no crime at all, and without the crime there could be no punishment; a goal longed for but never achieved. Until, with seven deaths to his credit, he was given a job at the American Museum of Natural History in New York.

There were two methods of removing the flesh from a body at the museum: bacterial maceration—a nice term for letting flesh rot in a tank of tepid water—and the use of Der-mestid beetles—tens of thousands of them. Both methods of so-called osteological preparation were easily available to Billy, as were convenient walk-in freezers to store the dis-membered bodies of his victims until he was ready for them and marvelously designed, hermetically sealed shipping containers of various sizes, complete with official American Museum of Natural History/Smithsonian Institution labels. Billy also had free access to the museums's UPS and Federal Express account numbers, so shipping the bodies was not only efficient but economical.

With the body parts shipped to himself and safely within the museum, Billy spent many happy overtime hours letting his ever-hungry beetles methodically destroy the evidence of his crimes, stripping an entire body down to bone and gristle within a day or two, and down to virtually nothing at all in a day or two more. The few greasy scraps left after the Dermestids' feast could be flushed down the men's room toilet across the hall from his lab. Perfect place, perfect job, perfect crimes.

Perfect death.

The psychiatrist looked up from the file folder in front of him. "You call the murders you committed 'perfect deaths.' "

"That's right."

"Why?"

"Because that's what they are," Billy answered. He was starting to look a little annoyed and the psychiatrist knew that he wouldn't be able to stretch the interview out much longer.

"I don't understand."

Billy sighed and leaned forward to stub out his cigarette. "Ordinary death is a random event, a fundamental expression of chaos. For example, Princess Diana is killed in a car accident in Paris that involves the juxtaposition of hundreds of elements at a specific place and time, a jigsaw puzzle in four dimensions that no one could have foreseen or prevented. Just as easily one or more elements could have kept the accident from happening at all.

"Dodi Fayed says to Diana, 'Let's stay here tonight,' and they simply go up to their suite at the Ritz. Or they choose a different car, a different driver, a different destination involving a different route. Random death—hit by a bus while crossing a street, struck by lightning, a heart attack from out of nowhere, a blossoming cancer that consumes a person in days. The fate that awaits almost all of us."

"But not your victims," said the psychiatrist, suddenly understanding.

Billy nodded. "I choose the victim, the time, the place, the way. I know who is going to die and how and when. Perfect death. No randomness, no chaos, no fractal plane or Mandelbrot."

"I see."

"No," Billy said, shaking his head and smiling. "I really doubt that you do." Fractal geometry, invented by the Polish mathematician Benoit Mandelbrot, dealt with the mathematical chaos of the physical, like coastlines, clouds, mountains, and even galaxy clusters.

There was a pause before the psychiatrist spoke again. "You've volunteered for our brain research program at the National Institute of Mental Health." The NIMH project in Washington was trying to discover the neurological and perhaps chemical reasons for violent crime.

"That's right. I presumed this was the screening interview."

"It is," said the psychiatrist. "That's why I'm here."

"What would you like to know?" Billy asked. The smile was back, but there was something wrong with it. The psychiatrist shifted uneasily in his chair. There was a faint sense of threat that he couldn't quite put his finger on.

"Well, for one thing, how did you hear about it?"

"They let me work in the library here. They say it's good therapy."

"So you read about the project?"

"Yes."

Liar.

"Why exactly did you decide to volunteer?"

Billy shrugged. "I want to help."

No. I want to get out of here.

And kill again.

TWO

She basked in the flaring white heat of the furnace, twisting the pipe deep into the glowing pool of molten glass to make the gather. When she had the size she wanted, she pulled the pipe out of the furnace in the swift single motion she'd learned, then turned just as quickly, lowered the pipe, and puffed hard to expand the small bubble of air in the center of the gather. She watched carefully as it blossomed into a near perfect sphere at the end of the five-foot-long blowpipe.

Turning back to the superheated chamber of the glory hole next to the furnace, she reheated the glass, withdrew, then rolled the sphere into the three lines of powdered color she'd already arranged on the steel surface of the marvering table next to her bench. She reheated a second time to fuse the swirls of bright color into the glass, turned again, and this time sat down at the bench, the pipe resting on steel supports bolted to the seat. Rolling the pipe to keep the cooling glass from slumping downward, she slid her other hand into a large asbestos glove, took a pair of the foot-long, tweezers, and dipped them into the large cask of water to her right.

After the glass air-cooled to the right temperature, she dribbled a line of water across the neck of glass between the blowpipe and the piece, listening to it hiss and crackle for a moment before she tapped the jacks sharply across the end of the pipe, cracking the finished paperweight into her asbestos-covered palm.

She ducked under the blowpipe, crossed the shop to the annealer, and levered it open. Turning her face away from the heat, she pushed in the paperweight, arranging it beside the two dozen others she'd made that day. The operation over, she closed the annealer, stripped off the glove, and went to the open shop door. Robin Kayter, the forty-something owner of the glass shop, handed her a mug of non-alcoholic beer and toasted her with a mug of his own. His hair, once black as pitch, was streaked with gray, but he still wore it rock 'n' roll long, tucked under a Grateful Dead bandanna when he worked. She plucked her sweat-soaked T-shirt away from her skin. The evening breeze was a blessing after the constant heat of the furnace, the cool air scented with sea salt and pine.

"Not bad." He grinned. "We'll make a blower out of you yet."

"Not bad! That's twenty-three I've done so far."

"Twenty-three in four hours. Call it seven an hour to be generous. We wholesale them at fifteen bucks a piece. That's about a hundred bucks an hour, gross, say seven hundred a day if you take an hour for lunch. Net after expenses you're looking at maybe two hundred a day. Not much to split between you, me, three assistants, and that snake of an accountant who comes down from Fort Bragg once a month." He snorted. "And that's still not including our pals at the Internal Revenue Service."

She drained her beer gratefully and laughed. "I thought you were an old hippy. Haight Ashbury, Be-ins, and beads. You sound like a business school grad."

"Hippies grow up," he answered. "The ones who didn't are either in jail or in mental hospitals."

"Or running hot shops up the coast in Mendocino," she teased.

He teased back. "Teaching slowpokes like you."

"I guess that means you think I'm not fast enough." She smiled.

"No." He smiled back. "It means you're learning. You love it enough, you'll get it eventually."

"I love it enough," she said carefully, and he nodded.

"I know. I can tell." He reached out and put one hand on her shoulder. "But go home now." The hand squeezed.

"So you can do some real work, I suppose?" She handed him the empty beer mug.

"No," said Robin. "So I can do the books."

"Tomorrow?"

"First thing." He nodded. She took a step forward, put one hand on his chest, kissed him lightly on the mouth, and whispered a quick "thanks" in his ear. Then she turned away before either one of them said or did anything more. She headed off across the yard and down the road without looking back, even though she knew he was watching her. She could feel the familiar squeezing tension in the small of her back and the little ripples of heat that ran around under her belly, turning as molten as the glass.

Tempting.

Too soon.

Are you nuts? It's been a year and a half.

A year and a half ago her name had been Jay Fletcher, an FBI special agent and computer expert who had stumbled onto an Internet bulletin board for serial killers called Special K. Taking matters into her own hands, she had begun hunting down the murderers herself, killing four before she almost cold bloodedly murdered a fifth, and, as it turned out, totally innocent suspect.

The near-miss had been the wake-up call she needed, and after some long and complex negotiations, the woman they'd called the Ladykiller quietly struck a deal with the FBI and Justice Department. In return for handing over all the data she'd collected on Special K, including a complete list of its subscribers, Jay Fletcher was given full immunity for her previous crimes on the understanding that she would disappear into the Federal Witness Security Program administered by the U.S. Marshals. As far as the rest of the world was concerned, Jay Fletcher would cease to exist. They threw in her FBI pension and a lump-sum payoff to sweeten the pot.

Jay agreed to the terms, and while her new identity as "Carrie Stone" was being created, she briefly and anonymously took part in the investigation that led to the arrest and conviction of Billy Bones. Not a bad swan song for a "retired"

FBI agent, and the only thing that irked her was the fact that the good-looking Billy had hired a hotshot, Dershowitz-style lawyer who turned Billy into a media sensation and managed to get him off by reason of mental defect. Jay would have much preferred to see the son of a bitch strapped down to a gurney with a hypo stuck in his arm, or better yet with a few hundred thousand volts zapping from one ear to the other.

On the other hand, Billy's brief rise to *People* magazine fame and CNN stardom easily overshadowed the Ladykiller's moment in the spotlight, and Jay Fletcher sank below the surface of the media ocean with barely a ripple. The day after Billy's trial ended, Jay Fletcher's name was scrubbed from every federal database, her Social Security number was voided, and her membership in the Witness Security Program given a coded number known to fewer than half a dozen people on the planet. A week later, Carrie Stone resurfaced in Mendocino, California, and began a new life.

Reaching the end of Lake Street, Jay paused for a moment to watch the sunset splash of colors streak and blur across the distant horizon. A hundred yards away she could make out the edge of the cliffs that fell steeply down to the sea, and she could hear the comforting pound of the surf echoing up from the narrow stony beach far below. Smiling, she turned away from the sound of the sea and the colors of the sky, going up the short walk to the little house that had been both sanctuary and home to her for more than a year now.

Like the rest of the buildings in Mendocino, her house looked as though it had been transplanted from Cape Cod or Nantucket. It was a small, clapboard cottage with plain wood floors, lots of windows, and an upstairs master bedroom that looked out over the sea. It had belonged to the two young men who'd run the local video store, but when one died of AIDS, his partner couldn't bear the thought of living in the house any longer and put it up for sale.

She'd bought it furnished, using up most of her lump-sum hush money from the Bureau, but she'd slowly added her own touches, including a sprinkling of dark-varnished rattan furniture that took her back to her childhood in Wisconsin, a ghastly grand piano someone had painted green with added sixties-style flowers that looked as though they belonged either on a VW bus or the bottom of a bathtub, and a big stuffed chair almost as ugly as the piano but wonderfully comfortable and perfect for late night reading beside the Craftsman-design tiled fireplace.

A single northern California winter taught her that wood floors are freezing cold first thing in the morning, and she'd searched out more than a dozen throw rugs at the local craft stores, littering them like brightly colored stepping stones throughout the house. Her only concessions to being part of a larger world were the telephone, a very high-end computer set up in her tiny downstairs "library," and the outsized Trinitron TV and satellite dish that had come with the house.

Climbing the stairs, Jay began stripping off her clothes, then jumped into the shower. She stood under the lukewarm spray, letting the gushing water rinse the salt sweat from her chest and belly and back, hoping that it would wash away the tense hot feeling in the pit of her stomach as well.

The more she thought about it, of course, the worse it got. Whatever was going on between her and Robin was getting worse—or better—with each meeting. She was beginning to hate the fact that the best clothing to blow glass in was a cotton T-shirt. Within twenty minutes it was sticking to her like glue, and Robin had given her plenty of admiring looks since she'd begun taking lessons from him a few months ago. The attention was nice, but it wasn't doing much to ease her frustration.

She let out a long bubbling breath and bent her head, letting the water slam into the back of her neck.

So sleep with him. He wants it and so do you.

She thought about what that would mean. Lust would shift and change as easily as the sunset sky, moving from sex to intimacy. Fair questions asked and no other option open to her except to lie. She was already doing that a little, going along with the background story they'd given her at Justice. Recent widow, no children, living abroad for years to explain the lack of friends and phone calls. Too close and he'd see too much, and she'd have to give him truths instead of lies, and then it would be all lopsided.

He'd try to understand the anger that had driven her to do what she did, the need she'd felt to even the odds, to take back a little for all the victims and all the pain. He'd try to understand, but he wouldn't even come close and, when push came to shove, he'd lie beside her in the dark and, touching her, know that he was touching death.

Jay turned her face up into the spray, feeling little needles of it etch into her eyelids. Here she was, no more than simply horny for him, thinking all these thoughts, bringing herself up to the edge of tears. What would it be like that first time together in his bed or in hers? What would she be thinking in that last second as he entered her and it was all too late?

Mistake, mistake, mistake.

That's what she'd be thinking, and in her head she'd see the little movies playing just the way they did sometimes when she was sleeping. Movies filled with blood and pain and numbing horror. Chains of fear and fury and memory that sometimes took her back to her high school days at F.D.R. Consolidated in Tomahawk, Wisconsin. Back to the night she'd been raped by Robby Rawlins, remembering the sweet-sick stink of the rum and Coke she'd vomited, remembering the shame and the horror of it all, the end of everything.

But it hadn't been the end of anything, of course. That had just been the beginning of the secret and the lie that she'd never revealed to anyone except her mother. Seven weeks after the rape, there had been no way to avoid the truth of what had really happened that night and still she said nothing, but by the third month panic overcame the fear and she told her mother she was pregnant.

Jay bent and turned off the tap. The drumming water stopped and there was nothing but a dripping silence. She pushed back the frosted glass door, stepped out of the shower, and grabbed a towel.

Don't think about it. Don't think at all.

Her mother never really talked about it, but somehow she

managed to make all the arrangements on her own, and one afternoon in late August they'd climbed into the station wagon and started the long drive north to Sault Sainte Marie and the abortion clinic on the Canadian side. She spent a day recuperating in a motel room on the shores of Lake Superior, and then they went home to Tomahawk.

All the secrets were like open wounds, and all the lies, like bandages covering them, hiding them from view because they were the kind of wounds that never really healed. How could you bring all that to a man, a lover, even a friend? At least there was an easy answer to that question—you didn't. You kept away. Stayed numb.

That was best for all concerned, wasn't it?

She dried herself, looped the towel onto the door hook, and went out into her bedroom. It was done in cool blues and greens with an old iron bed, her fat old chair beside the double dormer window that looked out to sea, and a trio of small rag-rope rugs scattered across the pegged board floor. She reached out and pulled open one of the windows, letting the breeze blow across her, breathing in the sea-tang again, feeling her nipples harden and her breasts goosebump in the chill, knowing that right now there was nobody who could see her from here to China unless it was some kinked-up shiphand out there on a freighter with a very powerful telescope and some obscure fetish involving white ladies on the near side of middle age who'd obviously been through the wringer a couple of times.

It was getting dark now, so if he was out there he'd need infrared as well. Jay smiled at the thought of her demon peeper dragging all his equipment up on deck, trying to explain to the first mate just what in hell he was doing. She checked herself out in the ghostly reflection coming back from the windows. What would the deckhand see if he really was out there looking? She'd trimmed a few pounds in the past year or so, putting herself back on a jogging routine like the one she'd been used to back when she was working at the Bureau in D.C.

She'd also been doing a little martial-arts stuff one or two evenings a week at the community school, topping it off with the whole foods, fruits and nuts and berries diet that was hard to escape in this part of California. Sudden cravings for a burger and fries involved getting into the old Volvo wagon she'd bought along with the house, then booting it ten miles up the coast to Fort Bragg for a cruise along the South Main Street strip. She poked and prodded a little. The smallish breasts were still full enough to suit her ego, and they hadn't started to sag, or at least not so you'd notice, and where most people had love handles she had muscle and sinew.

The body was hers, but the rest of it was invented. More lies to foist on Robin if it ever came to that. The shaggy shoulder-length hair was hers, but the color was an easy-to-do mix of a couple of Lady Clairols to get an auburn that was a long way from her natural mouse color and the eyes were a cheat as well: Part of the deal with Justice involved a trip to an ophthalmologist and a prescription for tinted contacts. Once blue, now green, they went with the hair, but even she wasn't really used to them staring back at her from the mirror.

She closed the window and turned away, crossing the room to the louvered doors of the cupboard that took up the whole sloping side wall. She shrugged into a dragon-printed kimono she'd picked up on a trip to San Francisco and then went downstairs. If she was going to be mature about all this and not get involved with Robin, she deserved a bonus for her ascetic life. Burger King was too far away, but she had a frozen pizza in the freezer that would have to do for now.

"Screw sex," she muttered under her breath, and headed for the kitchen. She nuked the pizza, flipped it onto a plate, then went out onto the side porch to watch the sun finish setting. She ate, bare feet up on the worn old railing, staring out over the sea to the Technicolor horizon.

It's all bullshit.

She wanted to sleep with Robin because she hadn't had real sex for a year and a half, but she didn't want to sleep with him because she knew how disappointing it would be. He'd be more than solicitous of her needs; he'd make sure there was lots of foreplay and he'd be romantic all over her, and that was all well and good but he'd also be a total wimp about it. There'd be no strength or power; there'd be nothing even close to the furious magic of the sunset she was watching right that minute.

This just isn't working out at all.

None of it. Not California and the Pacific Ocean, not living the laid-back life of the artisan and all the rest of it. And who was she trying to kid? Being raped wasn't the defining moment of her life; it was the single event that had kept her a victim for all those years until the *real* defining moment when she'd tracked down Ricky Stiles and his savage friends, ridding the world of their sick dead eyes and their monstrous acts. Somewhere along that chosen path she'd shed her old life like old clothes, and no illusion manufactured by the U.S Marshals' Witness Security Program was going to change her into something else. She was a wolf in sheep's clothing who was getting tired of living life in disguise. Hunters hunted; they didn't stare at sunsets.

She sighed, stood, and then picked up what was left of the pizza and Frisbee'd it out over the grass, to the edge of the cliff and over, knowing that some ever-hungry gull would probably snatch the high-cholesterol snack out of the air before it hit the surf. Sighing again and wishing that she hadn't been such a good girl and quit smoking, she turned and went back into the house, making her way to the onetime pantry off the kitchen that now served as her "library."

She sat down in front of the computer, hit the Sleep key, and watched as the computer awakened itself and the screen came to life. She frowned, staring at the bottom right-hand corner of the screen; the envelope icon was blinking, which meant she had e-mail, and that was very strange because it was a function of the Internet she rarely used. The only e-mail she ever sent was her once a week check in with the Marshals and the only answers she ever got were the Marshals acknowledging her check-ins. Check-ins were Thursday; acknowledgments were Fridays; and this was Wednesday.

Jay double-clicked on the envelope and waited while the

computer automatically booted itself onto the Net and pulled
up her e-mail program. She clicked "Get Mail" and waited
again. A few seconds later the message appeared:

> So damn your food and damn your wines
> Your twisted loaves and twisting vines
> Your *table d'hôte*, your *à la carte*
> From now on you can keep the lot.
> Take every single thing you've got
> Your land, your wealth, your men, your dames
> Your dream of independent power
> And dear old Konrad Adenauer
> And stick them up your Eiffel Tower.

"What the hell?" Jay stared at the screen. No salutation,
no ending, and the message address was ASCI gibberish—
whoever had sent the poem was computer-smart enough to
hide the originating server. She read through the doggerel
again, trying to get some meaning out of it, but she came up
empty. She had a vague memory from high school about Ad-
enauer but that was it.

Every once in a while she'd had generic commercial e-
mail appear on her machine, usually trying to sell her dirty
pictures from one of the sex Web sites, but the commercial
messages were randomly addressed, no more personal than a
cosmic fax or one of those auto-dialer advertisements on the
telephone. Who would go to all the trouble of sending an
obscure piece of poetry?

Jay dumped out of the e-mail program, picked Bookshelf
out of her CD-ROM rack, and slipped it into the drive. The
message wasn't really poetry at all; it was some kind of political satire, and there was a chance it would be listed in the
Bookshelf dictionary of quotations. She clicked her way into
the program, then started doing word searches, starting with
wines, then going to vines, à la carte, and Eiffel Tower. She
found what she was looking for under "France," second quotation from the top. The quotation was from *Time* magazine
in 1963 and was a commentary on France's rejection of En-

gland's bid to join the European Economic Community. Jay
stared at the name of the author, feeling her heart begin to
pound.

Antony Jay

Jay.
"Oh, Jesus," she whispered. It was too much to be a co-
incidence.
Somebody knows where I am.

"Time for lockdown. You almost done?"
Billy looked up from the computer terminal and smiled.
Dougie, his keep on this shift, was a broad-shouldered jock
in his mid-twenties with biceps that had to come out of a
bottle. Billy's beetles back at the museum would probably
have grown tits after munching on a steroid-flushed specimen
like Dougie.
"One more minute," Billy answered, his fingers flying over
the keys. Dougie was sitting in a chair by the door, tilted
back against the wall, a copy of *Muscle* magazine curled up
in one hammy fist. He had no idea what Billy was doing at
the computer, nor did he care. Dougie's job description was
simple. He was supposed to keep things on an even keel. If
a "client" like Billy started getting noisy or angry or violent,
Dougie was supposed to beat the shit out of him with the
rubber-sheathed baton he carried. He was also supposed to
raise the alarm. All Billy had to do was make sure he didn't
get noisy or angry or violent, a pretty simple quid pro quo
when you got right down to it.
Billy's job at the library was to keep track of the books,
logging in volumes returned and volumes taken out. The majority of his "clients" were doctors and nurses; most of the
patients at Spring Grove weren't big readers. Given the fact
that Billy's crimes had been facilitated by his computer expertise, it had seemed surprising to Billy that they'd let him
get within fifty yards of an electric typewriter, let alone a PC,
and he'd even mentioned the fact to his therapist, the es-

teemed Dr. Hans Shoenauer, who was writing a book about Billy and expected to make a lot of money from his "best" patient.

Shoenauer's logic for letting Billy work in the library was simple enough: the computer terminals there were stand-alone and had no Internet access, and by donating his time and skills, Billy was helping himself therapeutically, not to mention saving hundreds of budget man-hours. Billy had eventually discovered that while most federal penitentiaries banned inmate access to the Internet, only half the state-run prisons had the same rule and virtually none of the mental institutions. He also learned that more than twenty country-wide telemarketing services used inmates at their call centers—all of which were located in the prisons themselves.

Presumably the logic was that since Spring Grove was a hospital, not a prison, it should abide by its own rules and not those of the Federal Bureau of Prisons. Whatever the logic, Billy wasn't about to argue with it, even though Shoenauer didn't know what he was talking about when it came to computers.

The three computers in the library of the Spring Grove Psychiatric Hospital were slave units with no "brain" of their own and no Internet capability, which, on the surface, was grounds for complacency when it came to people like Billy Bones. On the other hand, any slave has a master, and in this case it was the network mainframe of the hospital on Wade Street, which was in turn connected to the Catonsville campus of the University of Maryland, and that computer was connected to the Baltimore campus, which had several Cray supercomputers.

As an added bonus Billy was able to squeeze through an electronic back door into Shoenauer's own computer, allowing him to send updated medication changes to the dispensary at Spring Grove and thus giving him access to any drug he desired. For Billy, or anyone else with serious computer skills, the supposedly brainless little terminal in the library was an open door to the universe.

With the Cray computers, hacking into the mainframe of

the U.S Marshals Service in Arlington had been relatively easy. Since thirteen different government agencies were necessary for the Witness Security Program, there were computer database entry-points everywhere. Less than an hour after Billy started looking he found the Witness Security Safesite and Orientation Center in metropolitan Washington, hacked into the arrival/departure logs, and found everything he needed, from Jay Fletcher's new identity to the name of her case officer within the USMS and her e-mail address.

"We really got to close up shop now." Dougie was climbing out of his chair now, the legs dropping back down on the tile floor with a bang.

"Ready when you are," said Billy. He reached out, turned off the computer, and stood up. He shuffled over to Dougie, his leg chains rattling, and waited while the bulky young man unlocked the door leading out into the corridor.

"Get all your work done?" Dougie asked.

"Just about." Billy nodded, smiling.

THREE

The National Institute of Mental Health's Human Brain Project took up most of the fifth floor of the Neuropsychiatric Research Hospital and Neuroscience Center at St. Elizabeth's Hospital in Washington, D.C. The facility was located on Martin Luther King Jr. Avenue in Congress Heights, on the Anacostia side of the river that neatly severed Congress from its closest constituents.

The NIMH facility had been erected in the late sixties, an eleven-story yellow-brick bunker with tinted windows that you couldn't break or open, a neutral color scheme not even the most sensitive schizophrenic could object to, and some of the best research neurologists and psychiatrists the country had to offer.

Its only physical connection to the much older St. Elizabeth's general hospital next door was a bridge corridor on the second floor with enough electronic and human security to stop anything short of an armed assault by Navy Seals. The only ground-level entrances into the building were through an ambulance loading bay at the rear that was more like a truck-sized air lock, and an equivalent front-door entrance that was a high-tech security gauntlet.

With the exception of a floor full of labs and another floor of PET, CAT, MRI, and any other kind of scanning equipment you could think of, the NIMH clinic was much like any other psychiatric hospital—a maze of corridors, small rooms, and vague murmurings that didn't seem to come from anywhere at all.

Billy Bones' arrival at St. Elizabeth's had come and gone without incident or publicity, which was exactly the way the research staff wanted it. Get him in, give him a day full of interviews, scans, and maybe some drugs, then get him back to Spring Grove with as little muss and fuss as possible. A year from now the Brain Project would publish its findings, and *then* they'd go looking for the publicity. Adding Billy to the project was the kind of thing that could lasso some serious research grants if they played their cards right, but losing it all to the tabloids right now could have exactly the opposite effect. The real money came from being accepted by something like the *American Journal of Psychiatric Research*, not from flogging a few snapshots to the *Star* or the *Inquirer*.

Although straitjackets, hockey masks, and dollies with straps gave a nice visual effect, the reality of transporting patients like Billy was much safer and considerably more in tune with basic human rights: They drugged them up to the eyeballs. William Bonisteel was given an intravenous two-hundred-milligram dose of Haloperidol before leaving his cell in the high-risk wing of the Baltimore hospital and being transported under guard to St. Elizabeth's in Washington, ninety minutes away by ambulance. Haloperidol was a powerful sedative used to handle psychotics, and the dose was aimed at keeping Billy from doing any major damage while moving from one hospital to the other, with an hour or so as a buffer zone.

Among other things, Billy was a trained chemist and he was perfectly aware of Haloperidol's effects on the central nervous system. He was equally aware of how to counteract those effects and did so by using a stolen fifty-milligram rectal suppository dose of a generic methylphenidate usually used for calming hyperactive, self-destructive children and preadolescents. The drug, commonly known as Ritalin, had the opposite effect on adults and was actually a highly effective form of speed. If anyone ever went to the trouble of tracing the meds, they'd lead directly back to Shoenauer.

The rectal suppository was particularly useful since it kicked in quite a long time after the Haloperidol, thus allowing him to present the right symptoms for a thoroughly sedated patient. By the time he was halfway to Washington,

Billy's mind was racing as the Ritalin began cutting in, and by the time they reached St. Elizabeth's he was ready to rock 'n' roll. It was hard to keep a straight face as they slung him, supposedly dozing, into a wheelchair, then took him up to the Brain floor. To keep himself calm, he visualized exactly the effect the Ritalin was having on the reticular activating system in his brainstem, and the sudden release of norepinephrine into his thalamus and hypothalamus.

Life's a slice.

The two heavies who'd accompanied him from Baltimore handed Billy over to the doctors on the seventh floor, then retired to the cafeteria on the St. Elizabeth's side of the connecting bridge. When it was time to take Billy back to Baltimore, the doctors could page them there or in the staff lounge. The NIMH facility was operated under federal security guidelines and the two attendants had followed those guidelines to the letter. For the time being, their responsibility was over, and if Billy ran amok up on the seventh floor and savaged a few doctors and nurses, that was the seventh floor's problem, not theirs.

But Billy was being good as gold. He let himself be interviewed by three different doctors, did a variety of routine psychiatric tests, allowed them to hook up electrodes on some surprising parts of his body, watched "response" videos of people having sex in endless combinations, and gave up five different blood samples. Finally they took him through a series of scanning sessions, and it was during the last of these, the brain MRI, that Billy heard opportunity knocking.

He found himself alone in the MRI chamber with a doctor named Summers, a man in his mid-thirties with thinning, sandy-colored hair and absolutely no sense of humor. Billy tried to engage the man in conversation several times, but Dr. Summers was only interested in going through his list of questions, most of which had to do with the possibility of Billy ruining the whole session because of a forgotten pin in his hip or the chance that he'd recently swallowed enough ferrous metal to do the doctor's beloved cream-colored twenty-ton machine some permanent damage.

Eventually Billy got it across to Summers that answering all the questions was thirsty work, and didn't a cup of coffee sound nice? Summers agreed and left the room, carefully locking the door behind him. He returned a few minutes later with two Styrofoam cups, then went back to his checklist. If the coffee scam had failed to work, Billy would have blamed his small bladder for a trip to the bathroom.

The two or three minutes he'd been alone in the room had given Billy ample time to remove the small paper packet taped to the bottom of his right foot, and when Summers stood up and began switching on the big, tubular machine, Billy dumped the contents of the packet into Summers's cup. The two-gram dose of Gamma-hydroxylbutyrate dissolved without a trace.

The drug, once marketed as a sleep aid and now off the market as a nonprescription medication, was also commonly used to wean alcoholics from their daily dose of liquor and was even easier to get at the Baltimore hospital than the Ritalin. It was colorless, odorless, and tasteless, and it also metabolized in the bloodstream without a trace. The two-gram dose would have left Summers in a deep, dreamless sleep for between four to six hours, but Billy wasn't taking any chances. Dr. Summers collapsed without a sound less than five minutes after drinking his coffee. Billy climbed off the machine, found a box of disposable surgical gloves, and knelt beside the doctor. He pinched the man's nose with two fingers, stuffed a handful of the gloves into his mouth, and waited until the doctor's face turned blue and he died, which took another five minutes according to the dead man's very attractive Rolex.

Knowing that the normal MRI session took between forty minutes and an hour, Billy took his time stripping Summers down to his Jockeys. He dressed himself in the dead man's clothes, including the ubiquitous white coat with its pinned-on security pass and both a wafer-thin cellular phone and a beeper in the pocket. Billy then spent a few minutes going through the doctor's wallet. Dr. Summers's first name was

Ethan; he was thirty-three, and he had several upmarket credit
cards as well as two hundred dollars in cash.

No pictures of a wife or kids, not even a girlfriend and a
trendy address on Church Street Northwest. There was a con-
dom tucked into one of the wallet's side pockets. Ethan Summers was single. He also had a parking pass and the
registration for a 1997 BMW which tempted Billy, but only
for a moment. Cars were too easy to trace, especially a late
model BMW. Better to use public transport even though it
would have been fun to escape in style. More importantly, he
had a receipt from a D.C. computer store for a 56K modem.
The doctor had been into computers.

Satisfied that he knew as much about Summers as he
needed, Billy slipped on the white coat, picked up the doctor's
clipboard, and left the room, locking the door behind him just
the way Summers had when he went to fetch the coffee.

The corridor ahead wasn't empty, but it wasn't teeming
with human traffic either. A couple of nurse types leaning
over the counter of the duty station fifty feet away, a patient
in a pale blue bathrobe being led off in the opposite direction
by a short-coated aide, an orderly with a cart full of big X-
ray envelopes, and that was about it. They'd brought him up
in an elevator, and he knew they were tucked in behind the
nurses' station. Two banks of three, one set for passengers,
the other, larger trio for patients on gurneys. That way would
be the quickest but potentially the most dangerous. All he had
to do was meet one of Dr. Summers's friends getting on or
off and the escape would be over before it had begun.

He turned right instead of left and headed down the dead-
end corridor to the red-and-black Exit sign above the stairwell
doors. Feigning a drugged doze, he'd listened carefully to the
conversation between the men who'd brought him down from
Baltimore and the Brain Project doctors. He knew there was
a connecting bridge between the new building and the old,
and he knew it was on the second floor. Presumably, the
security would be lighter across the connecting corridor than
it would be at the main entrance to the Neuropsychiatric Hospital, and even if it wasn't, there was less chance of running

into anyone who knew Summers in the old building.

The bridge corridor consisted of a pair of full-height turnstiles, one going in and one going out, with a ban-code reader for the clip-on ID badges. Beyond that there was a security guard behind a desk who checked Billy's ID badge a second time and asked him to sign the time log. After that it was a piece of cake. He went out through the front entrance of the old building, turned down Martin Luther King, and strolled the long block down to the Popeye's Chicken and Biscuits restaurant at the corner of Portland Avenue, particularly enjoying the feel of Summers's expensive Nikes. He got rid of the white coat in the dumpster behind the restaurant, picked up a two-piece and biscuit dinner, then zigzagged his way through the rundown neighborhood to the Congress Heights Metro stop. Four minutes later he was riding a three-quarters empty train into the nation's capital, and thirty minutes after that he was letting himself into Dr. Ethan Summers's condominium on Church Street.

By his estimation, the MRI session would have just been ending. The MRI was the last thing on his morning schedule, so time was running short. Billy checked his newly acquired Rolex and gave himself a twenty-minute window.

The apartment was a large one-bedroom with a den, furnished pretty much the way Billy had expected. Black leather furniture in the living room, obviously purchased all at once, a bedroom that could only be described as motel modern, and a predictable kitchen with trendy black appliances. The refrigerator was full of take-out cartons and bags. Dominos, Capitol Hill Pizza, Federal Food Express, Jade Dragon, and some place called Kwan Fo Leung Lin Fo.

Billy turned away from the narrow galley kitchen, crossed the living room, and stepped out onto the balcony. The late Dr. Summers had occupied a seventh-floor apartment with a view looking back over Dupont Circle. Billy checked the Rolex. Three minutes gone and nothing done; less than two years in the loony bin and he was already losing his edge. He could also feel the Ritalin backing off.

Nap time, Billy-boy.

Dr. Summers's den was next to the bedroom and had exactly what Billy had expected—a serious computer setup with all of the current bells and whistles. None of which interested him; all Billy wanted was a bit of quick Net surfing. He booted up the computer, humming a tune from *My Fair Lady*.

All I want is a room somewhere . . .

He'd find what he was looking for, leave a few messages for some very important people, and then he'd be on his way. Smiling happily, he changed his tune as he began to hit the keys. Hoot Gibson or somebody like that.

Back in the saddle again.

At nine in the morning, Pacific time, Jay Fletcher put in a call to the Marshals office in San Francisco and told her case officer about the previous night's message on her computer.

"Someone has figured out not only who I am, but where I am."

"Maybe it's just a coincidence," he said. His name was Ralph Barnes and he was two years away from retirement, filling out his tour by babysitting WitSec "clients" like Jay. He was lazy, yawned all the time, and smoked a good eighty unfiltered Camels a day. His voice had a built-in bubble and wheeze that made Jay mildly nauseated.

"It's not a coincidence."

"Can you tell anything about the person doing the mailing from the return address?"

Jay sighed. Barnes knew as much about computers as he did about the possibility of getting lung cancer.

"There is no return address, or at least none that's decipherable."

"Well, why don't we just calm down and wait this thing out."

"Wait it out? What the hell is that supposed to mean?"

"Whatever you want it to mean," Barnes answered. Jay could hear the yawn behind the words. "E-mailing isn't a crime."

"I'm not talking about a crime, I'm talking about the fact

that your Witness Security Program isn't so secure after all, at least not as far as I'm concerned."

Another yawn and the rasp of a cigarette lighter. Wheeze and suck as he took the first drag of the new cigarette. "I'll let headquarters know about your concerns."

"Do that," said Jay. She hung up the phone. Barnes was an ass.

At ten-thirty her time the little e-mail bell on her computer chimed. Either Barnes had raised some shit or her mystery e-mailer was calling again. She sat down at the machine, accessed her mail and stared at the message.

Hey Ladykiller—
I think we'd better talk things over.

She felt herself go numb, her senses fading into something that was almost a dream.

Run. Someone found you. You can't hide from the monster, you never could.

But there were no monsters anymore; she'd fought them all and won.

There's always one more.

The monster always comes back.

Below the message there was an America On line chatroom address where she and the e-mailer could converse in real time. Mouth dry and heart racing, Jay bailed out of the mail program, went onto the Net, and dialed up the chatroom.

—Who are you?
—**Fear.**
—Whose fear?
—**Yours.**
—How about a name?
—**Rhymes with silly.**

It took her a few seconds but then she got it and her eyes went wide. Jay sat back in her chair, staring at the screen, trying to keep the scream in her throat from rising to her lips.

This was the nightmare, but it wasn't in her dark nights anymore, it had crawled out into the light.

Billy. It has to be. He was the only one good enough with computers to find me.

—Billy Bones?

William Paris Bonisteel. Handsome death. The best student Ricky Stiles ever had.

—My, aren't we smart. Well, so am I, Jaybird. I'm back in the game, and dear lady, I am hot. I've killed another one, and that's just for openers.
—I don't believe you.
—Sure you do.
—I put you away for good. They'd never let you go, not in a million years.
—You might say I took matters into my own hands. His name was Summers and he was a doctor. Snuffed him like a candle. Call Karlson and he'll tell you all about it. I just filled him in, gave him my demands.
—What demands?

Please, let this not be happening. Let this be a dream.

—I told him I wanted you on the case. I told him I'd play fox if you'd play hound.

Norman Karlson was the head of the U.S. Marshals' Fugitive Operations Division in Alexandria, Virginia. She'd met him briefly while going through the whole insertion procedure with Witness Security. She watched the words blink at her on the screen and wondered what idiot had let Billy escape and kill again. She felt the panic rising again and bit her lip hard.

Don't break, don't bend, no fear. Let him see fear and he'll work his way into the wound and then I'll be crazy again and he'll have me cold.

—What if I don't want to play?

Jay gritted her teeth. Back in her old office in the basement of the Hoover Building she'd have been able to trace Billy's computer link in under two minutes, but all of that was in the past. She was on her own. "Shit," she muttered. She only had one telephone line so she couldn't even call out to someone with the trace equipment she needed.

—You have to play.
—Why?
—Because you know I'll play without you, and that means people are going to die. Die mean and nasty. Lots and lots of people, and all because of you.
—I don't make you kill, Billy.
—Maybe not, but you can stop me.
—How?
—Catch me.
—How do I do that?
. . . .
—Tell me how to catch you, Billy.
. . . .
—Billy?
. . . .

He was gone.

She worked her way off the Net, waited until the modem had cleared, and dialed Information for Virginia. Five minutes later she was talking to Norman Karlson at U.S. Marshals' headquarters, and twenty minutes later she was booking her flight east. She packed a bag, thought briefly about calling Robin at the hot shop, then thought again. There was no way she could say anything to him that would make any sense.

Well, it's like this. There's a sick son of a bitch out there who's killing people and unless I catch him he's going to kill a whole lot more people and every step of the way he's going to put it in my face and in my soul. If I don't stop him I'm never going to be any good to you or anyone else, especially not myself, so I'll catch you later, if you catch my drift, pun intended.

No, that wouldn't do.

As she drove north to the little municipal airport in Fort Bragg for her shuttle flight down to Oakland, she wondered how long it would be before Billy killed again, and her foot pushed down on the gas as though it would really make a difference one way or the other. She already knew the answer to her question, it lay in her heart like a dark, cruel flower about to come into terrible bloom. She knew how long it would be before Billy killed again.

Not long at all.

FOUR

"When?"

U.S. Marshal Norman Karlson, Director of Fugitive Operations, sighed and leaned back in his black leather chair. There were three, thick file folders on his desk. "Around noon. He killed a doctor named Ethan Summers, stole his ID and his wallet, and just walked out of the place."

"Shit," said Deputy U.S. Marshal Jack Dane. As one of the senior "bloodhounds" on the Joint Fugitive Task Force, he had a fairly good idea of what was coming. "You want me to handle it, I suppose."

"You suppose right. And fast. This guy's a publicity time bomb and CNN's dream come true. As soon as this gets out the shit's going to hit the Bureau's fan, and then it's going to hit ours unless we can get him back into custody within the next twenty-four or forty-eight."

"Leads?"

"Lots of them. As soon as he left the hospital he headed for the doctor's apartment and started playing computer games again. He left a message on the FBI homepage and he e-mailed me right to this office."

"What was the message?"

"A challenge. Catch me if you can."

"Why e-mail the Marshals? Billy Bones was convicted in a Maryland court. He was never in federal custody. He's not our jurisdiction."

"Yes he is and Billy knows it. The NIMH facility at St. Elizabeth's is legally classified as a federal reservation. He's ours."

Jack Dane looked across the desk and over his boss's

shoulder. The view from the eleventh-floor office of the U.S Marshals Service HQ on Army-Navy Drive looked north toward Arlington Cemetery and the Pentagon, a mile or so away.

The view should have been full of blues and greens but everything was brilliant amber, a result of the bronze-tinted anti-infrared surveillance treatment on the glass. There was also a white-noise generator humming in the ceiling somewhere, designed to prevent laser surveillance. The white-noise generator made it at a little hard to hear, as though you had cotton in your ears.

The irony was that the most likely source of any surveillance would come from the next building over, an identical bronze box that housed the headquarters of the DEA. The other two buildings of the four-cube set held offices of the ATF, the Defense Intelligence Agency, and the National Security Agency—a "cop mall," with everyone wanting to know everyone else's business.

"Why me?" asked Dane.

"Because you're very good at what you do, because you haven't had a partner since Gord Newhouse had his heart attack, and because you're too close to retirement for me to stick you with a new partner."

"You're making me sound like I've got one foot in the grave. I'm only forty-nine, Norm."

Karlson smiled at his old friend. "In this business forty-nine *is* one foot in the grave and you know it, Jack." Karlson paused. "Besides, you hate task forces and group operations."

Jack Dane shrugged again. "I won't argue with that." He looked at his boss. He'd known Karlson for more than a decade and he knew the man had something else on his mind. "There was more to the message Billy left, wasn't there?"

"Yeah."

"Spit it out."

It took a few seconds, but finally Karlson grimaced and let out a long breath. "Jay Fletcher called her case officer last night. Billy got hold of her e-mail address and sent her a message."

Jack Dane stared. "Fletcher? The Ladykiller?"

"That's right."

"Last night? Billy was in the loony bin last night, or am I missing something here?"

"He worked in the hospital library. There was a computer there. From what we've been able to figure out so far, he used it to prescribe drugs for himself, to help him escape. From the looks of the trace we ran, he also managed to get into our files over at the Safesite and find Fletcher, send her a tease. He sent her another message using this Dr. Summers's computer."

"Why get in touch with Fletcher?"

"He wants her assigned to whatever operation we put together to track him down."

"He's nuts."

Karlson laughed dryly. "I don't think anyone would dispute that, Jack."

"*You're* nuts. So is Fletcher. Jesus, Norm! Before she hung up her spurs she executed four people."

"Serial killers."

"Who never had their day in court. She was a vigilante."

"This isn't the time to talk philosophy, Jack. We've got to catch the son of a bitch as fast as we can."

Dane looked at his boss directly. "Why does he want Fletcher?" he asked finally.

Karlson shrugged. "She was the one responsible for putting him away. According to the shrinks, his whole thing is ego. He's smarter than anyone else in the world and he can demonstrate it any time he wants. Fletcher proved him wrong and probably would have killed him if she hadn't turned herself in first. Billy wants a rematch."

"So we pull her out of the Witness Security Program and put her to work? Use her as some kind of bait?"

"That's the idea."

"What if I don't like the idea of working with a killer?"

"I don't give a good goddamn what you like or don't like, Jack. I don't have time. I just want you to do your job."

"So much for me," said Dane. "What about her?"

"What about her?"

"What if she doesn't want to play footsie with Billy? What if she wants to stay retired?"

"It's in her best interests to make a comeback, and Billy knows it."

Karlson dropped his glasses down from his forehead and looked down at the sheet of paper in front of him. He read the last paragraph of the message aloud:

> This is very personal with me, Marshal Karlson. Because of Miss Fletcher I was denied my freedom; now I have regained it and the playing field is level once again. If she is not officially assigned to this case within the next twenty-four hours, I will begin a killing spree of unprecedented proportions. I will also inform the wire services, the networks, and the tabloids of my intentions.

Karlson tipped up his glasses again and looked across the desk at Dane. "He's even threatened to set up a Web site and use it to post digitized pictures of his victims."

"He's blackmailing us. Fletcher plays his game or else he goes public."

"Something like that."

"And you're willing to go along with it?"

"Why not?" Karlson shrugged. "It makes sense. Billy Bones's MO invariably involves computers; that's how he chose his victims before and he'll probably do it that way again. Fletcher's a computer expert. It's a good match." The U.S. Marshal smiled weakly. "How much do *you* know about computers?"

"I can operate an automatic teller machine, that's about it."

"There you go."

"Who's going to know about this?"

"As few as possible."

"What about Main Justice?" Jack Dane asked, using the nickname for the Justice Department's headquarters on the other side of the Potomac. The headquarters office was renowned for having more leaks than a sinking rowboat.

Karlson shook his head. "Nobody. Too risky. They'll have to know about Billy's escape, but not about Fletcher. The Attorney General's on some kind of junket in China for the next ten days, so we can keep her office out of the loop for a while."

"Big risk," said Dane, glad that he wasn't the one taking it.

"Bigger risk to see this thing coming out of Peter Jennings's mouth or as a segment on *60 Minutes*."

"Okay, so we get on it fast. Billy's running; he shouldn't be that hard to track."

"He's got the doctor's ID and credit cards."

"You've got a trace on the cards?"

"Of course, but he's been in Summers's apartment; we know that from the e-mail return address. That means he's got the PIN numbers for the cards and he's probably already jacked them up to the limit with cash advances. Assume he's got traveling money."

"You've got Fletcher's agreement on this?" Fugitive Ops and Witness Security had nothing at all to do with each other, and Dane didn't have the faintest idea of where she'd been stashed when she went into the program. "You really think she's going to cooperate and not go rogue like she did the last time?"

"She called us, not the other way around. Billy's on the loose and he's made it clear that he broke her cover. She wants in, believe me. She lands at Washington National tonight at 7:30. We've booked her in to the Embassy Suites in Crystal City, registered as Kelly Morgan." The name Kelly Morgan would be fresh since presumably she wouldn't want to taint whatever cover name she was using day to day. WitSec would have a purseful of ID and credit cards to go along with it.

"I don't need to know her whole itinerary, Norm."

"Yes, you do." The director smiled. "You're picking her up at the airport."

*　　*　　*

William Bonisteel knew that even without his taunting little missives to the FBI and the Marshals they'd be on top of the good doctor's credit cards almost from the moment they discovered his body. He knew he could charge them up with cash advances with one stop at a bank machine and perhaps even throw in a red herring or two, but more than anything he had to go to ground as soon as possible. It had taken him less than five minutes to find what he wanted on the Net.

With Dr. Summers's computer booted up and online, Billy had done a quick search for home and apartment-exchange services. There were dozens of them all over the world, but he narrowed it down to local D.C. services and finally zeroed in on a company called Capitol X-Change. Once onto their homepage, he hacked into their back files and found a match up. Professor and Mrs. Matthew Bannerman had tried and failed to find a Paris-Washington exchange for a six-month sabbatical and had eventually decided to leave their place vacant and pick up a rental instead.

According to the file, they were now happily ensconced in a lovely two-bedroom on the Avenue Fourcroy only steps from the Champs-Elysées and l'Etoile, leaving behind their equally impressive two-bedroom at the Watergate Apartments. According to the dates, they'd been gone for more than a month. Better and better. Running quickly through the list of amenities the Bannermans had listed, he saw every time-saving kitchen appliance ever invented, but no mention of a security system.

Not surprising. The Watergate was immense, the whole complex covering several blocks along Virginia Avenue with its back to the Potomac Parkway and the river itself. Even ordinary apartment buildings were enormously difficult to hardwire for any kind of really sophisticated system. Even if there were such he could be out of the apartment long before any kind of alarm response. A calculated risk, but one he was willing to take, and in the end, no risk at all.

Getting into the apartment itself was a snap. Once inside the complex he snooped around until he found the maintenance office, used Summers's cellular to call about an electrical problem at the other end of the complex, and waited until the office emptied. He slipped the lock on the office door with a credit card, picked the lock on the gigantic hanging key caddy with a straightened paper clip, and plucked the Bannermans' spare set off its neatly numbered hook. He was in and out of the office in under three minutes.

The Bannermans' apartment was on the seventh floor of the cheaper side of the Watergate with a distant view of the White House and the Mall rather than the much more expensive view of the Potomac and Arlington on the other side. Satisfied that there was no alarm system, Billy gave himself the 25 cent tour.

Rothko in the entrance hall, Maroulis over the mantelpiece of the fake fireplace, and Joseph Solman gouaches in the living room. Hardwood floors with scattered Kirman carpets here and there. Billy didn't waste time actually checking, but the upholstery and the drapery in varying shades of navy and terra-cotta had the crisp, slightly self-conscious look of Ralph Lauren.

The books in the built-in bedroom bookcases were mostly sociology and politics, the books in the living room mostly art. The second bedroom had a loom in it with a half-finished something or other dangling from it in twenty different shades of green. The Bannermans had turned the breakfast nook just off the kitchen into a home office for both of them, and a quick look through the mail and the paperwork stored in a pair of file drawers sketched in the Bannermans a little more clearly.

Matthew was thirty-nine years old, taught political science at Georgetown University, and was using his sabbatical to write a book on the involvement of the French government during the Civil War, particularly their financial interest in the Confederacy. He liked single malt Scotch, called his mother and father in Miami once a week, and spent a fair chunk of change on weekend trips to New York to see Broadway shows.

Susan Bannerman was thirty-three, her maiden name was

Haig, and she had a trust fund that had to be enormous given the size of the interest checks both she and her husband were using to pay for their lifestyle. She took all sorts of classes, called herself both a weaver and a fabric artist depending on whom she was writing to, and had a black, strap-on anal dildo in a plastic bag tucked way in the back of her closet shelf. Matt and Sue were kinkier than the Ralph Lauren Home Collection suggested.

On a more practical note, Billy learned that the plants in the apartment had been removed and were being tended to by a company right in the complex called D.C. Horticultural Boarding Services, and their mail had been redirected to the professor's office at Georgetown University. There were two vehicles in the basement parking garage, his Lexus and her minivan.

The keys to both were hanging on the bulletin board in front of him along with various business cards, notes, and postcards, all layered in an unruly mess that was completely at odds with the rest of the neat-as-a-pin apartment. The bulletin board looked as though it hadn't been picked over for months.

Chaos.

Billy smiled.

Janet Louise Fletcher, aka the Ladykiller, aka Carrie Stone, and now reincarnated as one Kelly Morgan, looked down at the spray of bright lights on velvet that marked Washington, D.C. Once upon a time she'd worked and lived down there, and seeing the city spread out beneath her as the flight headed in was bringing it all back with a vengeance, good and bad.

Mostly bad.

For most of her career the choices had been easy. An FBI agent who specialized in computers didn't get into the line of fire too often, and there were enough good busts to keep the job satisfaction reasonably high. But then it had all started to come apart. Good information obtained badly had led to a walk for a serial killer who should have put in a bag at birth and drowned like a kitten.

Banished to a remote corner of the law enforcement universe, Jay had found a way to track down killers via computer. One thing led to another, and four deaths later she'd found herself in that psychiatrist's office in Baltimore. The man she thought was Billy Bones, until she realized at the last minute. *Oh, Jesus. He's left-handed.*

So close. Too close and suddenly she knew that what she was doing wasn't justice, it was vengeance and vengeance misplaced was no accident, it was murder. She could still feel the pressure of her finger on the trigger of the gun. The single breath away she'd been from crossing the final line, from becoming exactly what she was trying to eradicate.

It had rained that day, and the street outside the psychiatrist's office had been wet. A car went by, wheels making that little hissing sound over the slick pavement. Out in the harbor at the foot of the street, a freighter's horn echoing as it came in to port, and farther still a soft, dangerous rumble of passing thunder. All that, in the split second of her decision, all that would have been the last sounds the man would ever hear.

The wheels of the big jet thumped down onto the runway and she was back in Washington once again. She could feel her heart slowing down as the near hallucination turned back into ordinary memory. But if anything, the urgency she felt was even clearer now.

What was it Billy said to me in his e-mail this morning?

—"people are going to die. Die mean and nasty. Lots and lots of people, and all because of you."

All she had was her carry-on bag—three days' worth of wash-and-wear. She went with the chattering flow of passengers to the exit, stepped off the plane and into the long connecting corridor, then walked a hundred yards to the B section concourse.

She stopped there and scanned the crowds waiting behind the barrier. According to the Witness Security person who'd called her, they'd have someone there to pick her up. Jay almost missed him because of the name change. Her eyes drifted over the guy standing by the exit three times before she realized that the cardboard sign he was carrying that said

KELLY MORGAN in big bold letters referred to her.

Jay wasn't terribly impressed. The man with the sign looked like an aging surfer. Late forties, a little too short for her taste with too-long blond hair turning the color of nicotine. He was tan and weathered like the Marlboro man he probably was and wore blue jeans, cowboy boots, and an old leather jacket—an outfit that was trying to make some kind of statement about aging gracefully and missing the mark by a mile. In his dreams he probably wished he was Wyatt Earp, or maybe even Richard Boone as Paladin, the guy from *Have Gun Will Travel.*

Let's just hope he's just the driver and not one of the people who's going to be briefing me.

She threaded her way through the crowd, reached the man, and held out her hand.

"Hi," she said. She smiled and tried out the new name for the very first time. "I'm Kelly Morgan."

"Jack Dane," the man answered. But he didn't take the offered hand. He just nodded, then tucked the sign under his arm. "Car's a couple of levels down in the parking garage." Then he turned his back on her and walked away.

Uh-oh. Jack Dane was the man Karlson said would be working with me. Gee, we're off to a pleasant start.

Hefting her one small bag, Jay followed him.

He turned left, went through a set of sliding glass doors, and started across the elevated walkway to the parking garage. "You always this friendly?" Jay asked, catching up to him.

"Only when I'm doing a job I really don't want to be doing."

"Karlson said you were the best man he had."

"Karlson's a bullshitter. This is a baby-sitting assignment and we both know it, Ms. Fletcher." He stepped up the pace, the heels of his cowboy boots clicking on the polished surface of the walkway floor.

"I don't need baby-sitting." She'd met this guy before, a hundred times; a Ross Perot chauvinist who had a thing about woman cops. Give him a snowbank and a full bladder and he'd piss his initials in it.

"Call it what you want, Ms. Fletcher. You're supposed to track down Billy Bones and I'm supposed to . . ." His voice trailed off and she saw his jaw set. They reached the end of the walkway and exited onto an upper level of the parking garage.

"You're supposed to what?" Jay said coldly. "Keep me from killing him?"

"Something like that."

FIVE

Billy stood in Susan Bannerman's bathroom and examined himself in the full-length mirror on the back of the door. Sometimes when he did this he wondered if it was an examination to prove to himself that he really existed or an adoration of human perfection. He smiled at his reflection; he wasn't perfect, of course. That would have been a delusion of grandeur, which, thank god, was not one of his aberrations. Perfect no, close, yes.

Not tall, but not short either. A slightly above average five feet nine inches on a slight frame that required care, exercise, and bulking to keep up the swimmer's body look that women seemed to like so much. Enough body hair to define his masculinity, but not enough to repel, all streaming black and wet down his body from the shower, thick and rich like a fur pelt between his legs, a perfect nest for his perfect parts. Good strong legs with muscular calves. Good arches on the feet.

Normal, normal, normal.

Just like he wanted it to be. Except for the face. Face like an angel, that's what his mother always told him.

Which mother was that?

Which angel for that matter?

The problem was, of course, there were a great many varieties when it came to angels, almost as many variations as there were to the human spirit. Good angels, bad angels, even evil angels. Mansemat, for instance, Father of All Evil. Not too far from good old dad's name when you thought about it. Or better yet: "Suddenly, singly, mirrors which reconcentrate again in their countenances their own outflowing beauty." The poet Rainer Maria Rilke had described the process perfectly, which was odd since Rilke had died the better part of seventy-five years ago, which meant of course that they'd never met.

Billy turned his gaze away from the mirror and listened. The CD he'd put on in the living room before his shower was still playing. The Brandenburg Concertos. Angels' music, that was certain anyway, if nothing else was. He closed his eyes and let his head fall back, then lowered one hand and cupped himself for a few moments, enjoying the slightly lifted weight in his palm. He brought the hand to his nose and mouth and inhaled, taking in the fresh soap smell and that faint other scent behind it.

He breathed in again and thought, not for the first time, that it was probably smell more than anything else that had kept him from becoming at least bisexual. The idea of having sex with another man had never disturbed him, but the thought of waking up to that rough, deep, male smell all the time was just too much. A woman's scent, especially a young woman's scent . . . And then he stopped himself, realizing that he was letting his thoughts flow down courses that were bound to bring him trouble.

Instead, he opened his eyes, turned, and left the bathroom, padding back into the big bedroom Susan and Matthew shared. He left the overhead light off; the venetian blinds were open and there was enough of a glow from the late night street to illuminate the room well enough for Billy's purposes. A little nude thought and meditation before the journey began. Ruminations on life choices and a chance to get it all up to speed again. It had been a while after all, and he didn't want to make any foolish mistakes this early in the game.

Fletcher.

How would it have gone down?

She'd made a deal with them before, that much he could be relatively sure of. After the fiasco with Spenser, the Baltimore shrink, running him down had been relatively easy. After the trial she had apparently disappeared into the Federal Witness Security Program.

And now with his call, they'd been resurrecting her, putting her on a plane and bringing her back to D.C. Billy smiled, thinking about that as he stared up at the gloomy ceiling and resisted the temptation to touch himself. She was close, right around the corner; he could almost smell her. He took a deep, lingering breath. He wasn't smelling her; he was smelling his own anticipation, perhaps even a touch of tingling fear.

So what would they do? Assume that he'd do exactly what he had done—suck as much cash as he could from the good doctor's bank account and then go to ground. If they brought her in fast enough she'd tell them that their best bet was in the first forty-eight hours after the escape. While he tried to come up with a plan, they'd be shutting down the entire city. Airports, bus terminals, Amtrak—they'd have it all covered by now. If he'd taken the doctor's Beamer it would have been like hanging a sign on his back saying, Here I Am.

But Jay knew him better than that, and if he'd done things right she'd start to get a sense of the game pretty soon. Tomorrow, the next day at the latest, and she'd be back in the traces, sniffing the scene with whomever they partnered her with, putting more than a profile together, creating the compass needle that would swing to and fro and to and fro again before it settled in the right direction. It might take another body, another scene, or maybe two until she got it exactly, but he had no doubt she'd settle on the right course in the end. Billy smiled again. If she didn't he could always cheat a little and give her a clue or two.

Why am I risking everything?

That was the right question, of course. He knew what Ricky would have done. Ricky Stiles would have slipped away in the night, never to be heard from again. Ricky, his old Internet friend, his only fully realized companion in the darkness, would simply have vanished, then reinvented himself to begin again.

But here he was, about to go head to head with Jay Fletcher, the Ladykiller, the one who'd taken Ricky out, fried his twisted-up old ass as sure as Ole Sparky in that nasty yellow-walled room at Folsom where Billy's father almost wound up before they dropped capital punishment in California.

Dear old dad.

Right from the time he'd figured it out, Billy had followed his father's career with almost obsessive interest. He wasn't the only one; there were at least a dozen different Charles Manson Web sites on the Net, so it wasn't hard to keep track. They'd moved his old man to the psych unit at Pelican Bay State Pen the year before, and there were some people who said that Pelican Bay was state-sanctioned torture, worse than the chair. Billy shook his head against the pillow, feeling tears pooling in his eyes. It was in the blood, cold blood according to Truman Capote. Like father like son. A killing chromosome. The killing gene.

Why, why, why?

He had a raging hard-on now, even without touching, all purple-headed and slick, and he really couldn't have cared less, because it didn't have anything to do with . . . anything really. It wasn't the thought of Jay Fletcher or the doctor earlier that day, so old in his mind that he couldn't even remember his name. No. It was like a teenage boy. You didn't have to have a reason for an erection, it just was. Like him, like Billy Bones, like Charlie's boy.

Like death.

He lay very still for what seemed to be a very long time, letting the past and present and all the possible futures rip and foam and eddy until everything came together in a solid deep green wave within him, rising in his mind's eye until it completely filled his vision, smooth as flesh and heavy as dark metal, but so deliciously soft and vulnerable that even a thought would slip through its surface, swallowed whole.

It was only then that he reached down between his legs and gripped himself so hard that pleasure quickly turned to pain. He squeezed even harder and he felt the wave within him begin to recede, taking the erection with it. He remained still for a long moment more, just to be sure, then swung his legs out over the edge of the bed, sitting up. The Rolex told him it was almost midnight. Time to go.

Let the games begin.

SIX

The day after her arrival Jay Fletcher drove into D.C. with Jack Dane behind the wheel of an unmarked U.S. Marshals' Ford that anyone over the age of twelve would have instantly recognized as a cop car. The outside of the vehicle was bristling with antennas, and the heavy-duty suspension looked as though it had been borrowed from a tank.

For Jay, coming back to Washington was like stepping back in time; she felt physically queasy as they drove slowly past the landmarks that defined her years of living there.

The last time she'd been in D.C. had been for her debriefing after the arrest of Billy Bones and for the closed hearing that had followed. She had almost fooled herself into believing that the past was over and done with, nothing more than bad memories that were already fading.

But it wasn't that easy. The memories hadn't really faded at all, they'd just been covered up, mental dust bunnies hiding under the bed and no broom to sweep them clean. It was all back, fresh as yesterday, dark as blood, cold as death. There was no escaping who and what she was, no believing that she was an apprentice glassblower on the verge of falling in love. She was a killer, and all of his ass-covering euphemisms aside, killing was exactly what Karlson had hired her to do. And that was a problem. Being a bloodhound was one thing, being an attack dog was something else.

No more killing.

But what if it's self-defense?

Don't go down that road, kiddo.

Summers's condo was a squat, ten-story building near Dupont Circle, right in the middle of Washington's trendiest res-

taurant district. Every second car parked on the street was a
Beamer or a Range Rover. Dane squeezed the big Ford in
behind a new-looking Lexus, and they climbed out into the
baking heat of a Washington morning. Jay could feel the sweat
gathering at her temples. This was nothing like the clean,
white heat of the glory hole back at Robin's shop. This was
D.C. in the summertime. It didn't seem to bother Jack Dane
in the slightest.

Jay and the marshal went up to the main door, buzzed for
the manager, and went up to Dr. Summers's apartment. The
front door had been paper-sealed by the FBI and there was a
piece of yellow tape across the door frame that said "Crime
Scene Do Not Cross" again and again.

"When can I take that down?" asked the manager. "It's
bothering the neighbors."

"Screw the neighbors," said Dane. He held out his hand
for the key. "We'll lock up and bring the key back down to
you," said the marshal. It was a dismissal. The manager
opened his mouth briefly, then turned on his heel and went
back to the elevator. Jay and Dane stepped into the dead
man's apartment.

"Being rude, that's some kind of style you have?" Jay
asked.

"I don't do polite very well," the marshal answered. "And
I don't have time for it."

"Be surprised," Jay replied. "Sometimes it makes things
faster."

"If I'd wanted Emily Post I would have picked a copy up
at Barnes and Noble."

"There won't be any physical evidence here," said Jay, as
they walked down the short hall to the living room.

Dane went to the front window and looked down to the
street. He turned to Jay. "Why do you say that?"

"Because he didn't choose the doctor. He just happened to
be in the wrong place at the wrong time."

"A convenience?"

Jay nodded. "That's the way Billy thinks. Opportunity
knocked and its name was Summers. That's why he didn't

try to hide the fact that he was using the computer here."

"He was moving on." Dane nodded.

"Exactly."

"What about the computer? Tech boys at the Bureau want it so they can tear down the hard drive."

"They won't find anything," said Jay, shaking her head. "Billy didn't have time for much. Knowing him, he didn't stay here more than fifteen or twenty minutes, tops. If there's anything useful on the computer it's going to be right near the surface."

"We already know he sent e-mail. What else could he do in that length of time?"

"Find a hiding place."

"How?"

"I'll show you."

Jay turned around and went back down the hallway to the dead doctor's den. She sat down in front of the computer, booted it up, then dropped out of the automatic Windows 98 screen, going back to a C prompt on a black screen. She started hitting keys and the screen filled with arcane lists of letters, words, and numbers.

"I don't understand any of this shit," Dane said, standing behind her.

"You know how to pick locks?" Jay asked, still typing.

"Sure, all you need is a set of picks."

"Same thing with a computer. Nothing special, just a different skill."

"So you say."

The screen cleared, followed by the click, buzz, and dialing sounds of a modem coming online. A few moments later they were staring at the Capitol X-Change homepage. Jay used the mouse to scroll down to the bottom of the page. There was an address and a D.C. phone number. Dane called it and found out what they needed to know.

"According to their records, Dr. Summers's computer was used to check out half a dozen of their listings the day he was killed. He checked one of the listings twice."

"That'll be the one."

"It's an apartment in the Watergate. Supposed to be vacant. The owners are in France."

"He'll be gone by now, but it's worth checking out."

"You really are full of shit, aren't you, Ms. Fletcher." Dane shook his head. "A real piece of work."

"What's that supposed to mean?" Jay asked, staring up at him.

"You're so sure of yourself. You think you know every step he's going to make."

"I know the way he thinks." She frowned. "You have a problem with that, Marshal?"

"I've got a problem with procedure."

"Such as?"

"Such as, I'm a cop, and you're not. Not anymore."

"Do you have a point or what?"

"I've got a point. It's about how we do this thing. About who takes orders from who."

Jay sighed. She'd been here before. Cock games. "You mean we have to have some kind of pissing contest? I'm supposed to defer to the size of your biceps or some other part of your body?"

"No." His lips thinned into a tight line and Jay could see a little worm of vein pulsing high on his temple. "I've been on the job for over twenty-five years. There's a way of doing things. Like I said—procedure. Such as who decides what's worth 'checking out,' as you call it. And how we do it. Backup, stakeouts, security, that kind of thing."

"What's wrong with my procedure?" she asked. "My field of expertise is computers, that's why I'm here. And besides, your procedure wasn't designed for people like Billy Bones, Marshal Dane. Billy's a whole new ball game. He makes up the rules as he goes along, and the thing he likes best in the world is making other people look stupid. Especially people like you and me."

"But you think you're smarter than he is?"

"No, but I understand him. I know what makes him tick." She let out a long breath. "For instance . . . this Watergate address. He knows it won't take me long to track it down;

he knows any commercial aspect of the Internet uses 'cookies,' little markers to identify people using their Web sites. He needed a place to lie low for a while, but he'll be long gone by now, believe me. Stakeouts and backups will just eat up more time. Ours, not his." Jay stood up, putting herself less than a foot away from Dane. "And I thought the object here was to catch Billy, not establish a pecking order."

"I don't give a shit about pecking order. Billy Bones is a fugitive at large. Fugitives think and operate in ways I'm very familiar with. Ways that other people don't think or operate. This is my turf, Ms. Fletcher. I'm not the smartest person in the world. I'm just an old-fashioned retriever dog. Throw a stick, I fetch it back."

Jay smiled to herself. She wasn't buying Jack Dane's "good ole boy" routine for a minute. "William Bonisteel is no stick, Marshal Dane. He thinks Charlie Manson is his daddy and he reenacts the Tate-LaBianca killings as 'homage' every chance he gets. Unlike Charles Manson, Billy has a brain that could give Einstein a run for his money. That's a very scary combination."

"He's still a fugitive."

"No, he's not." Jay said. "He's not running from anything, he's leading us around by the nose. Your boss is right. Billy's the predator, I'm the prey, and the real enemy here is time; the longer we screw around sticking to your so-called procedure, the more people Billy is going to kill."

Jay Fletcher stood in the living room of the Watergate apartment and looked around, trying to sense the presence of Billy Bones and coming up empty. The whole apartment had the chichi feel of *Architectural Digest*; color combinations chosen with a photographer in mind and not a dog hair anywhere. People didn't actually live in places like this; they posed in them.

Jay had agreed to follow Jack Dane's "procedures" to the extent that they'd gone to the resident manager when they arrived. Dane flashed his badge and the man took them up to the Bannerman place, but when they got there the door was already unlocked. The deputy marshal went through a whole gun-drawn, hostile-entry routine and that had been wasted, too. The place was empty and pristine. The only sign that Billy had even been there were the rumpled sheets and crushed pillow in the master bedroom.

Turning, Jay went to the dining nook off the kitchen. She could smell Pledge everywhere; Billy had either wiped the place down for prints or he was teasing Jay with his clean-freak act. She heard the sound of the front door opening and a few seconds later Jack Dane appeared, returning from his trip to the underground parking garage.

"The Bannermans own two vehicles. A Lexus and a Dodge minivan."

Jay smiled. "He took the minivan, right?"

"That's right."

"The Lexus is too noticeable. He won't even use the min-ivan for long. Probably already on somebody's used car lot by now."

"Since you seem to know so much about this guy, how about a best guess on how long he was here?"

"The e-mail went to your boss around 1 P.M. yesterday. He'd want to get off the streets as quickly as possible, so he probably went to ground here by two-thirty, three at the latest. Then he drove out during rush hour this morning."

"Hiding in the traffic in case we were already on him?"

Jay nodded. "Which means he's got about a four-hour head start." She did the figures in her head. "Two, maybe two hundred and fifty miles, maximum."

"Unless he drove to Washington National and flew out," said Dane. "He could be halfway to anywhere by now.

Jay shook her head. "Flying would be too risky. He's driv-ing."

"Where?" Dane's cellular phone burbled. He dug it out of his jacket and flipped it open, listening for a few seconds without saying anything. Then he flipped it shut.

"Anything interesting?"

"Karlson wants us back at headquarters. He just got some more e-mail. Billy's in New York."

*   *   *

William Paris Bonisteel moved slowly through the stark white interior of the Merrick Gallery, a rolled catalogue clasped behind his back. Bannerman's dark Armani suit was a good enough fit, but the shoes were a little small. Stopping to examine one of the pictures on the wall, he made a mental note to pick up a new pair before he paid a call on his next victim.

The picture was a Whistler lithograph entitled *Weary*, depicting a young woman in a chair, her hair spread out around her like some pre-Raphaelite Lady of Shalott. The lithograph was small, no bigger than five by seven, but wonderfully evocative. Billy smiled; the romantic vision of vulnerable womanhood was the sort of thing that made New Age feminists furious; Whistler's women didn't run with wolves, they swooned over love letters and poetry. He let his fingers caress the folded shape of the Benchmade combat knife in his jacket pocket.

How do I love thee? Let me count the ways.

Billy, of course, knew precisely how vulnerable women were; he'd tested that fact regularly and knew that no amount of karate lessons and pepper spray could protect them. In essence, women were all designed to be victims of one kind or another, and they knew it. For Billy, the taking of a man's life was a simple act of slaughter, an occasionally necessary fact of life when funds were low or boredom began to set in. A woman's death, on the other hand, was like the Whistler on the wall—a work of art that perfectly blended skill and talent, leading finally to those last seconds when her soft eyes pleaded in the face of oblivion, then inevitably gave way to acceptance as she took on the ritual role of sacrificial lamb.

He took three steps and paused again. A Venetian scene of a palace by the water, gondolas moving back and forth along the canal. Billy had been to Venice once and had found nothing there; like most of Europe, it lived within its history, weighed down by its past. For him, the entire continent was little more than a down-at-heels social studies theme park whose time had come and gone and would never return.

Out of the corner of his eye Billy saw his quarry leaning

over the plain wood desk at the back of the gallery, apparently
writing a check. Billy took a few more steps and stared
blankly at another Whistler, this one a smoky view of Bat-
tersea at dusk titled *Nocturne*. He listened to the conversation
between his chosen target and the young faux-blond boy on
the other side of the desk.

"Deliver them to Forty-sixth Street; Ken will know what
to do."

"What about the opening?" asked the blond boy.

"I doubt it," answered the older man, combing thick fingers through his gray buzz cut. "I'm tied up at the restaurant
all day and I'm leaving for Rome on the ten o'clock. I'll
barely have time to get home and park."

Home was an apartment in the Clarendon on Riverside
Drive at the corner of West Eighty-sixth Street, and the man
with the buzz cut gray hair was Hunter Connelly, the legen-
dary owner of Hunter's on Broadway and half a dozen more
restaurants of the same name in Boston, L.A., Miami, Lon-
don, Paris, and Rome. A millionaire many times over, he'd
passed on the day-to-day operations of his restaurants to a
son and daughter from his first marriage and now lived in
semiretirement, spending his time hopscotching around the
United States and Europe with residences wherever he had
restaurants. Not bad for a sixty-year-old high school dropout
whose only experience in the restaurant business was a stint
as bartender in P. J. Clarke's, the original template for all
Broadway watering holes.

Connelly finished his business in the gallery and then left.
Billy kept his attention on the Whistler. He smiled at the
gentle scene, pleased by what he'd overheard. It sounded as
though the restaurateur wouldn't get back to the apartment on
Riverside Drive until late afternoon at the earliest; plenty of
opportunity for Billy to run his errands and still get back to
the Clarendon in time to prepare his little surprise. He glanced
at Dr. Summers's Rolex, wondering what Jay Fletcher was
up to and how many of the puzzle pieces she'd put together
by now. He hoped she wasn't being too quick; that would
spoil all the fun for both of them.

Billy went back to the print of the girl in the chair and examined it again, secretly opening the Benchmade in his pocket, letting the ball of his thumb scrape gently across the blade, thinking about how easy it would be to bring out the knife and slash the image of the woman into oblivion. If the little blond gave him any trouble he could be sliced and diced just as easily. It could all be over in a matter of seconds.

Billy closed his eyes for a second, letting the dull sound of traffic outside bring him back to reality again. He stared at the girl in the picture and touched the hidden blade.

How do I love thee?
Let me count the ways.

"He's definitely in New York," said Norman Karlson from behind his desk. The Fugitive Operations Director glanced down at the open file in front of him and then looked up at Jay Fletcher and Jack Dane. "He e-mailed us from the Gramercy Park Hotel."

"What was the message?" Dane asked.

Karlson pushed a single sheet of paper across the desk. Jay picked it up and read it aloud.

"How can they catch me now? I love my work and want to start again. My knife's so nice and sharp I want to get to work right away if I get a chance. Good Luck." She paused and let out a short, hard breath. "It's signed Billy Jack."

"Billy Jack," said Dane. "Wasn't that a movie about some kind of Indian martial arts guy?"

"He's quoting a letter Jack the Ripper sent to Scotland Yard," explained Jay. "Billy was a complete Ripper fanatic. More than two hundred books about the case in his apartment when he was arrested."

"So what's the point?" said Dane.

"He doesn't have one." Jay shrugged. "He's just trying to keep himself amused." She slid the sheet back toward Karlson's side of the desk. "I'll bet there was a second message, though. Something a little more practical, right?"

Karlson nodded. "He wants a direct way of contacting Ms. Fletcher." He stared at Jay. "He wants us to get you a laptop and your own e-mail account. He was very specific about the brand and model."

"Such as?" Jay asked.

Karlson reached down with one hand and came back up with a slim, black case. He laid it down carefully on the desk. "It's an NEC 6260, all the bells and whistles, just like Billy wanted." Karlson cleared his throat. "He also suggested we have it loaded with digital photo software, which has already been done."

"Pretty expensive," said Jay, glancing at the computer. Very sophisticated, a high-tech hound for the hunter; she could feel the old energy beginning to flow.

Back in the big time.

Back where I belong.

"Very expensive." Karlson looked vaguely mournful. "One of those budget overruns that are hard to explain at year-end."

"Not if it gets you results," offered Jay. She gripped the handle of the laptop case and pulled it off the desk. "What about the e-mail account?"

"Already done," said Karlson. "America Online. The address is taped to the inside of the case. Your password is 'Fairy Fay.' "

Jay let out a dry, humorless laugh. "Another idea of Billy's, right?"

"Why, it mean something to you?" Karlson asked.

Jay nodded. "Fairy Fay was supposed to have been Jack the Ripper's first victim. Turns out she never existed. Billy's idea of a joke, I guess."

"Our friend Mr. Bonisteel also attached a picture file to his e-mail message." Karlson took a full-color laser print out of the folder in front of him and slid it across the desk. Jay picked it up.

"It's the bulletin board in the Bannerman apartment," she said. She handed it to Jack Dane. He scanned it quickly.

"I don't see anything. Regular bulletin board junk."

"Billy's giving us a clue," Jay offered.

Dane shrugged. "Obviously. Why else would he send the picture? It's got to mean something."

"You're a U.S. Marshal," said Karlson. "Not a detective."

"I'm supposed to find people who get lost," said Dane. "I agree with the Ladykiller here. Billy's sending some kind of message." He looked over at Jay. "She's the one who keeps on saying this whole thing is some kind of game he's playing out in his head."

"So what's the message?" Karlson asked. Dane shrugged again and handed the picture back to Jay.

"All I can see here are notes, bill reminders, Post-Its, a couple of postcards, just normal stuff," she said. "If the Bannermans are like everyone else in the world, then half the things they've got pinned up are six months out of date." Jay looked down at the picture and pulled gently at her lower lip, thinking. "Maybe you should send a forensic team to the Watergate."

"I thought you were the one who didn't want to waste time," said Dane. "Billy's in New York. We should be, too."

"Agreed." Jay nodded. "But Billy's got something going here. There was no scanner at Dr. Summers's place, but I did notice he had Photoshop installed on his hard drive."

"So?" said Dane.

"It means that Summers probably had a plug-and-play digital camera, and it means that Billy probably took it." She tapped the surface of the laser print. "This is a digital image he bounced from New York."

Dane shook his head. "I still don't understand."

"This is an image of the bulletin board when Billy was in the apartment." Jay explained. "We need pictures of it now, for comparison."

"Why?" Karlson asked.

Dane nodded, suddenly understanding. "Because there might be something missing," he said. "Maybe it's not what *is* there, maybe it's what *isn't*."

"Fits Billy's pattern," Jay agreed. "Most serial killers take trophies. Dr. Summers's wristwatch, for instance."

"He took a trophy from the bulletin board?" Karlson asked.

"Maybe," said Jay. "It's worth checking out."

Karlson sighed. "Which means we're going to have to call the Bannermans in Paris."

"No." Dane grinned, getting up out of his chair. "It means *you're* going to have to call the Bannermans in Paris. Ms. Fletcher and I are going to New York." He turned to Jay. "That all right with you?"

Jay nodded. "On one condition."

"Shoot."

"Don't ever call me Ladykiller again. Not even once."

"Or?" His voice was mocking.

"Or you'll live to regret it."

"Is that a threat?"

"No, it's a promise."

Hunter Connelly sat in the rear of the cab and leaned back wearily against the seat. Once upon a time he'd loved the restaurant business, but now, ironically, it was eating him alive. At sixty, a man as successful as he was should have been thinking of retirement instead of planning to open a new restaurant in Milan. At sixty, you were supposed to look back over your life and relish the fruits of your endeavors, count your blessings, and relax, not hopscotch around the world racking up Frequent Flyer Miles.

On the other hand, what the hell else was he supposed to do with his time? He hated being idle. He could only buy so many prints and paintings, only go to so many Broadway shows and movies, and getting laid these days was like walking through a minefield of sexually transmitted diseases and women who were more in love with his net worth than either his body or his mind.

Except for the restaurants, the best thing in his life was Brittany, his niece, safely squirreled away in a New England boarding school until the raging hormones in her system simmered down. His own kids from his first and only marriage were grown and gone, but for Connelly, Brittany was closer to him than either his son or daughter had ever been, especially since they'd been raised by their mother on the other side of the continent and he'd barely seen them growing up.

Somehow Connelly could see his own youth in Brittany, his own early curiousity about life and love and what made people tick. When the girl's parents had died in a boating accident, he'd taken on the role of guardian with more than pleasure, he'd taken on the job with joy.

The cab pulled up in front of Hunter's on Broadway. Connelly paid the driver, climbed out, and crossed the sidewalk, heading for a three- or four-hour grind with his lawyers and accountants. A week ago he'd thought there might be a chance to visit Brittany at her school in Massachusetts, but now he was going to be lucky if he had time to phone her before he left for Rome. He sighed, dragged open the door, and went into the restaurant.

William Paris Bonisteel sat at one of the tables on the sidewalk in front of the Excelsior Coffee Shop on West Eighty-first Street and looked across the parklike crescent and into the Eighty-first Street parking lot of the Museum of Natural History. From where he was sitting, Billy could see most of the backside of the museum, including the staff entrance he'd once used. That door, however, required a key, and just inside there was a uniformed security guard to check people in and out of the maze of buildings that made up the museum. Nineteen buildings, if Billy's memory served, all of them connected in a half-hidden hodgepodge of tunnels, walkways, and corridors. Nineteen buildings, 750 employees, not counting an on-duty security staff of 200 more, 1,000 volunteers, 17 elevators, 700,000 square feet of floor space, three restaurants including a fast-food emporium called the Diner Saur U.S., and 5.5 million gall wasps, all of them collected by the late sex-researcher Alfred Kinsey.

Home.

Billy sipped the last of his Turkish coffee and glanced at Dr. Summers's pretty watch. Almost two o'clock; he'd have to make his move soon, with or without cover. At that moment three busses pulled into the parking lot, all bearing the name of a Westchester school district. A throng of children disembarked, shooed along by a small platoon of teachers.

Perfect. Billy stood up, crossed the street, and joined them. Four minutes later, effectively camouflaged by the throng of children and their keepers, Billy managed to veer away from the spreading tide of boys and girls on the far side of the Roosevelt Memorial Hall. He took the well-worn stairs down to the basement-level lavatories and pushed through the door of the men's room. Exhibits came and went, but the toilets at the old museum didn't change from one decade to the next.

The room was full of twelve-year-old boys, their loud, laughing voices ringing tinnily off the white tiled walls as they splashed into the urinals, examined themselves in the mirrors over the multiple sinks, and cranked the roller towel for no reason at all except to make noise. Billy smiled, wondering how their mothers would react if they knew who was in a public toilet with their downy-cheeked babies.

Still smiling, he went into the stall farthest from the door and locked himself in. He put down the seat, sat down, and waited. It only took a minute or so for the kids to finish up and then he was alone. He unlocked the stall door and peeked out just to make sure, then locked himself in again, climbed up onto the closed lid, and pushed back a square of acoustic ceiling tile directly over the toilet tank, sliding it back and out of the way.

Blindly, Billy reached up into the damp maze of overhead pipes, his fingers searching for what he knew must still be there. He found what he was looking for and fumbled with the twist of wire until the heavy bunch of keys fell into his hand. A laminated copy of his old security pass was still attached to the ring. He stared at the earnest face on the card. Dr. William P. Bonisteel/Anthropology. The pass was a couple of years out of date, but he doubted that the guards would notice, and the keys would give him access to any part of the museum with the possible exception of the director's office and the supersecret Ivory Vault in the Frick Building.

Billy dropped the keys into the pocket of his suit jacket, eased the tile back into place, and climbed down off the toilet. He unlocked the stall, stepped out, and after a brief check in the mirror to make sure he still looked presentable, he left the men's room. Instead of going back up the stairs he turned right, went down a narrow corridor and through an unlocked door with the words Unauthorized Entry Prohibited stenciled on it. Like most museums around the world, security at the museum was mostly concerned with fire and flood, not thieves or terrorists, and Billy wasn't even mildly surprised to find his entry so unhindered.

The doorway opened onto a second, much longer corridor, this one lined with steam pipes and stapled loops of bundled cable. Following the main corridor for a hundred feet or so, he then turned left, right, and left again, eventually reaching his first objective—the linen storage room, located next to the museum's own laundry facility. With several hundred scientists working within the museum, there was a never-ending need for lab coats, and the museum had long ago given up on having them sent out.

Billy let himself into the room, shrugged on a coat, and clipped the security badge to the lapel. Feeling more like his old self with every passing minute, he strolled down another corridor, plucked a clipboard from its hook on the wall next to the carpentry shop, and continued on his way. He passed the metal shop then turned yet again, finally reaching the big freight elevator at the southeast corner of the main building. He took out his ring of keys, found the appropriate one, and unlocked the gate, then stepped into the cage. He punched the third floor button and the elevator slowly chugged its way upward.

Planning, his old friend Ricky Stiles had once instructed him, was everything. Billy would have been happy to stay at the museum forever, but from the day he began working there he was aware that the odds were against him; eventually he would be caught. On the other hand, the odds were also good that sometime *after* being caught he would find an opportunity to escape, and with that in mind he had prepared for the future, copying every one of his keys, then hiding the keys and a spare security pass in the ceiling above the toilet stall. But that was only the first part of his plan.

Reaching his destination Billy pulled back the cage door

and stepped out of the elevator. He sniffed the air, smiling at the familiar scent of 100 percent grain alcohol. There were several hundred thousand gallons of the fluid on this floor, and the one junior technician who'd been discovered having an illicit smoke a few years previously had been fired on the spot.

In all there were close to a quarter of a million specimens in the Mammalogy storage area, including half a dozen gorillas, several giraffes, elephants Teddy Roosevelt had shot, the mummified contents of a mastodon's stomach, and several hundred varieties of rat. The specimens were stored in various forms—as bones, skins, and stuffed trophy heads, but mostly as "alcoholics," creatures whole or in dissected parts, preserved in alcohol. In the early days of the museum's history the specimens had been stored all over the museum complex, wherever space could be found, which made comparative research almost impossible. Over the last two or three decades, however, there had been a slow consolidation, and by the time Billy had arrived all the specimens had been moved into renovated, spotless rooms on the third floor.

The larger mammals were stored in stainless-steel tanks, while the smaller ones, including the Homo sapiens collection, were kept in various shapes and sizes of glass containers. The very large mammals, including lions, camels, giraffes, and elephants, all dissected and dismembered, were kept in adjacent rooms, stored within even larger steel tanks.

The specimens in the main storage area were arranged in taxonomic, or evolutionary, order, and contrary to popular opinion, Homo sapiens was located in the middle of the phylogenetic tree, not at the top. The first shelves held the most primitive animals, including the duckbill platypus, while the far end was reserved for bits and pieces of the Bovine classification including cows, antelopes, and oxen.

The storage area was empty and Billy headed down the middle aisle in the room without being queried. The small Homo sapiens section occupied only one shelf in the giant room and contained mostly dissected brain tissue and fetuses, some of them almost a hundred years old. Billy knew that the shelf was rarely consulted, since there were far more useful specimens of Homo sapiens kept in the Anthropology section, and like everywhere else in the museum, nothing was ever disposed of on the off chance that some obscure specimen might someday prove useful.

Billy found the right tier in the appropriate aisle, pulled along one of the roller ladders, and climbed up to the single, long, deep shelf of bottled Homo sapiens specimens. The one he wanted had been stored behind a square glass box containing a skinned-out human foot that had once been joined to the ankle of a Bahumba tribesman in the Congo. There was no record of how the foot had been lost or whether its owner had survived the loss, but it had been dissected so many times there was almost no flesh left on the gray old bones.

Billy shifted the Congolese foot to one side, then groped more deeply, pulling out what looked like an outsized Mason jar. Inside the jar was the three-month-old, grossly deformed fetus of what might have become a little girl. The fetus had been removed from the belly of a Japanese woman dying of radiation sickness on the outskirts of Nagasaki in late December 1945.

Behind that jar, hidden in the darkness exactly where he'd left it, was a plain leather wallet. Removing the wallet from its hiding place Billy replaced the fetus, shifted the floating foot back into position, and climbed down from the ladder. He opened the wallet and briefly examined the contents.

Visa, MasterCard, and American Express card, in the name of Thomas George Rawlins, all kept current by computer-hacking funds out of his New York Citibank account in the same name. In addition, there was a New York driver's license, a laminated birth certificate, a Social Security card, two hundred dollars in cash, and finally, tucked into a small inner pocket, a key for a safe deposit box in the same Citibank branch good old Tom Rawlins used for his checking account.

The box contained more cash, Thomas Rawlins's passport, and a second complete set of ID in the name of Paul Sturgis. The Sturgis documentation was all West Coast, and to use it effectively Billy would need to wear eyeglasses and give himself graying temples. The Rawlins identity required a somewhat shorter haircut than the one he now sported and a two-day stubble he already had a head start on.

Both identities had been manufactured quite easily by following the step-by-step instructions in a book he'd purchased in a secondhand store. The book, aptly written by none other than Anonymous, was succinctly titled *How to Create a New Identity,* published by Citadel Press in 1983.

Sighing with something close to regret, Billy slipped the wallet into the inside pocket of his jacket and headed out of the Mammalogy storage area. After one more errand, his work here would be complete and he knew his chances of ever returning were slim. This was goodbye and not just au revoir. Billy found his way back to the freight elevator, passing a couple of self-absorbed scientists in the corridor who were dressed in lab coats identical to his own. He'd never met either of them before. Stepping into the elevator, he pressed the button for the fifth floor—Entomology.

SEVEN

"You don't like flying?"

Jack Dane shook his head and kept his eyes on the road ahead. "Hate it."

They were moving north on Interstate 95 with Baltimore behind them and Wilmington five minutes ahead. The mid-afternoon traffic was moderate, but Jay knew it would get heavier as the day wore on and they neared New York City. Karlson had offered them the use of one of the half dozen small planes the Marshals kept at the FBI airstrip at Quantico, but Dane had declined. According to his math, the flight from Washington to New York would take an hour and a half, but drive time to and from airfields would tack on at least another two hours and probably three. Add it up and you had roughly the same ETA using the interstate. Jay saw the logic, but she'd also picked up on a nervous undertone in Dane's voice.

"Any particular reason?" she prodded.

Dane reached for the pack of Marlboros on the dashboard, shook one out, and lit it. "Yeah," he answered. The marshal puffed on the cigarette but kept his eyes full forward. Jay grimaced. The son of a bitch had been smoking like a chimney for the last hour and he'd never once asked Jay if she minded the secondhand smoke. In fact, she was enjoying the aromatic trickle she couldn't help inhaling, but that was beside the point.

"So?" Jay pressed.

"So what?"

"Marshal Dane's fear of flying. The cause thereof. Idle chitchat."

"I don't like chitchat."

"Neither do I," said Jay. "But as far as I can tell, that's all we've got at the moment. Unless you want to stop at Mc-Donalds or something."

"No."

"Then chitchat away."

"There was an accident," Dane said finally.

"You were in one?"

"Almost."

"Almost an accident, or you were almost in one?"

"Both."

"You'll have to explain that."

"It was an extradition, back when I was in Prisoner Transport," Dane responded, obviously still hesitant. "Long time ago. Ten years now. Federal drug charge. Wall Street asshole who thought he was Al Pacino in *Scarface* or something. Thought he could make more money moving *La Chiva* than selling junk bonds."

"La Chiva?"

"Mexican Heroin," Dane said. "That's where he ran. Mexico. Where I picked him up."

"You were bringing him back?"

"Yeah. Mexico City to L.A. Red eye. It was a DC8 or a 707 or something, I can't remember. Full of people in stupid shirts and big hats. Everyone pissed to the eyeballs but me and the stockbroker."

"And?" Jay saw Dane's fingers tighten on the steering wheel, the knuckles going pale, ten years after the fact.

"And ten feet of the fucking wing blew up, right outside my window. An engine. We dropped about ten thousand feet in five seconds. The whole plane puked. About a hundred and fifty people. There was this sea of it, suspended in midair for a few seconds. It's the thing I remember most. Then the plane straightened out and the puke hit the floor and everybody started screaming except my stockbroker and the only reason he wasn't screaming was because he'd fainted. I thought he'd had a heart attack or something."

"But you made it okay."

Dane turned in her direction for the first time. "Obviously,"

he said. "I'm here, right?" He shook his head and went back
to looking at the road. "I've flown two, maybe three times
since then. I hate it."

"Make the job hard?"

"Not really. When runners run they don't run far, not usually."

"Billy's different."

"So you keep on saying."

"It's true. He's smart, for one thing, which most criminals
aren't. In fact, most of them are pretty stupid, or they
wouldn't be criminals in the first place, right?"

Dane shrugged. He rolled down his window an inch and
flicked out his butt. He reached for the Marlboro pack again.
"Everybody says that," he replied, lighting up. "But that's just
cop bullshit. That, and the crime-doesn't-pay line. The thing
of it is, we only catch the stupid ones, because they're stupid
enough to get caught. The smart ones we never even hear
about."

"Like politicians." Jay smiled.

"Yeah." Dane nodded. "Like politicians."

They drove on in silence. Dane took the 495 exit to bypass
Wilmington altogether, then rejoined 95 on the other side of
the city. "Tell me something about Billy," he said at last.

"Such as?"

"I read the file. A couple of times, in fact. But all that
computer crap gets in the way. I still can't really figure out
how you caught him."

Jay took a cigarette out of Dane's pack and lit it using the
car lighter. She didn't even think about butting this one.
Tucking one leg up under herself, she went through it in her
head again, wondering how much Dane knew, or thought he
knew, about the whole affair. She glanced over at him, then
took a deep breath and let it out slowly. Dane was a prime-
cut chauvinist jerkoff, but they were going after Billy together, so presumably a dose of honesty was required.

"You know about me screwing up?"

"Which screwup would that be?" He looked her way and
arched an eyebrow.

"Don't make this harder than it is," said Jay, drawing in a scratching lungful of smoke.

"The thing with the shrink in Baltimore?"

"Yes."

"Yeah, I know about that." He frowned. "From what I can figure out, you traced Billy back to this psychiatrist's computer; that's why you thought the shrink was Billy."

"Something like that."

"But the shrink wasn't Billy, so what's the connection? Was he a patient?"

"That's what I thought at first, but that wasn't it."

"What was?"

"You know much about Ricky Stiles?" asked Jay.

"The last guy you offed. The one in Vegas." Dane nodded. "More kills than Bundy, Dahmer, and Gacy put together."

"That's right. Among other things, Ricky Stiles designed role-playing games."

"Dungeons and Dragons, that kind of thing?"

"Yes."

"I still don't get it."

"The psychiatrist in Baltimore was doing a paper on identity loss. There was a famous case of a bunch of college kids who got so wrapped up in one of the games that they actually began living them. One of them committed suicide. The shrink was trying to expand on that. He was also into computers so he used his PC to surf the Net looking for games online. He found one designed by Stiles."

"That puts him with Billy?"

"In a way." She paused. "Remember I told you what a computer 'cookie' was?"

"Vaguely. Explain it to me again."

"A computer cookie is kind of like being stamped on the back of the hand when you go into a club. You're marked. In the case of the Stiles game, anyone who logged on had a cookie attached. Using the cookie Stiles could backtrack anyone to their home computer address. It's pretty simple really."

"So this Ricky Stiles character could get into the psychiatrist's computer?"

"Stiles gave Billy the computer address. It was Billy who did the hacking. From then on, he used the psychiatrist's computer as camouflage for his own address. That's what fooled me at first. According to the data I retrieved from Stiles's place in Vegas, the shrink 'looked' like Billy. That's how I made my . . . mistake."

"What happened then?"

"After I gave myself up we went back to the psychiatrist, explained what had happened. He was pretty good about it really. He let us hack into his computer legitimately, and we backtracked Billy to his PC at the Museum of Natural History. The rest you know about."

Dane gave a mock shiver. "The ultimate way for a killer to dispose of his bodies. Bugs and boiling." Human bodies were regularly donated to the museum from local hospitals and because Billy worked in the Anthropology section there was nothing particularly odd about his presence in the Osteology Preparation rooms. It was all gruesomely convenient and there was no real way of knowing how many of his victims were stored in the museum, or even on display.

They drove on for a few more miles and then Dane spoke again. "What do you think we're going to find in New York?"

"Hard to say. Nothing from the hotel, that's for sure."

"What about his old apartment?"

"We cleaned it out long ago. He had to sell it to pay his legal bills. Forget it."

"When a fugitive runs for cover he always goes back to familiar turf. Eventually he'll head for the museum. That's why Karlson organized a stakeout with the New York office and the NYPD."

"It won't work," said Jay. "In the first place, the museum has about twenty ways in and out, and on top of that you'd have to keep an eye on about a hundred thousand people going in and out the doors. Not to mention the fact that Billy would spot your boys from a mile away."

Dane let out a long ragged breath. "Don't you ever have *anything* good to say?" he asked, glaring. "I'm getting pretty sick of all this badmouthing. You badmouth the Marshals, you badmouth the Bureau, you badmouth everyone. You make it sound like you're the only person in the world who's got a chance in hell of getting this bastard."

"I'm not being negative," Jay shot back. "I'm just being realistic." She paused. "And I probably *am* the only person who does have a chance in hell of nailing Billy. That's why your boss dragged me out of my life and into this whole thing." She reached for Dane's cigarettes, found the pack empty, and crumpled it in her fist.

"Jesus! I can't believe this! You've got me smoking again! Goddamn!" She threw the crumpled, empty package onto the floor of the car, then rammed the palm of her hand into the padded edge of the dashboard. "You think I *want* to track down Billy Bones? If you think I'm doing this because I *like* it, you are out of your fucking mind, pal! I'm doing this because I don't have any choice. I'm doing this because the psycho son of a bitch is going to kill me unless we catch him first! You got that!?"

You almost sound like you believe it, kiddo.

You love this shit.

There was a short silence. "You finished?" Dane asked.

"For the moment."

"Good." Dane nodded. He reached over and popped open the glove compartment. It was stacked with red-and-white Marlboro packages. "Help yourself," he said.

By the time they spoke again they were deep in the strip malls and slums of Jersey City, stuck in traffic heading for the Holland Tunnel. By then Jay had smoked her way through almost a dozen cigarettes and any personal guilt about starting up again had already faded, eased out of sight by the steady flow of nicotine in her bloodstream.

"This Charles Manson stuff I read out in the file; anything to it?" asked Dane.

Jay lifted her shoulders. "Billy thinks so. We did some backchecking before his trial. He says his birth mother is actually Mary Jane Shorter. Manson called her Starr."

"Starr?" said Dane.

"Like the old comic strip, not the judge. Manson gave all

his girls nicknames," Jay answered. "Squeaky Fromme was probably the most famous."

"The one who tried to kill President Ford?"

"Yeah."

"Could this Shorter/Starr girl really have been his mother?"

"Maybe." Jay made a seesaw motion with her hand. "The dates fit. Manson hooked up with Mary Jane when she was fourteen. She was one of his favorites. Shorter was almost nine months pregnant when she disappeared during the trial."

"You believe his story?"

"No. Not really. But Billy does."

"Anyone ever tried to track down this Shorter woman?"

Jay shook her head. "Not in any serious way. She just disappeared. She's probably a forty-something housewife by now with a couple of kids and a dog."

"And one hell of a secret she's keeping from her husband," said Dane.

"Everyone has secrets," said Jay. "Some of them are just bigger than others." They were almost at the tunnel entrance, crawling along in the rush-hour traffic, as bad going into Manhattan as it was coming out. They entered the tunnel and slid under the Hudson River, bumper to bumper. Somewhere on the other side Jay knew that Billy Bones was hard at work, plying his terrible trade. A chip off the old block, just like his dad.

Helter Skelter.

His chores at the museum completed, Billy walked a few short blocks to Hunter Connelly's building on Riverside Drive. He was dressed well enough not to attract any undue attention in the wealthy neighborhood, and he walked unnoticed past the Eighty-sixth Street entrance of the Clarendon, reached the corner of Riverside Drive, then turned, frowning and making quite a production of shooting his cuffs and glancing at his watch as though late for an appointment.

He went up the short rise of stone steps to the front door, having learned from his initial walk-by that there was no doorman. He checked the buzzer board and saw that there was an H. Connelly in apartment 504. Billy looked through the glass doors and into the lobby. Two elevators in a short, cul-de-sac corridor with a red-and-black illuminated Exit sign above a doorway to the left. A stairwell.

He trotted down the steps, checking his watch again, then went back up Eighty-sixth Street, turning without pause down a narrow service alley that ran between the Clarendon and the building beside it. The alley did a dog-leg to the left and led back to a small rectangular courtyard.

At the far end of the courtyard there were three large, green plastic garbage bins. The bins were marked Paper, Plastic, and Glass. Half-hidden by the recycling bins, four steps led down to a scarred metal door. Billy went down the steps and tried the door. Not too surprisingly, it was open. So much for security. Billy pulled open the door and entered the building.

A narrow, sour-smelling passage led into the Clarendon's basement. He heard the faint sound of a radio playing and then a distant, phlegm-heavy cough. A janitor. There was a narrow door in the wall on his left with an Otis plaque screwed onto it—maintenance and inspection access into the elevator shaft. On the right there was a dimly lit, open stairwell. Billy took the stairs, climbing until he reached the fifth floor. Using a scarred wooden stop he found on the landing, he wedged open the door an inch or two, giving him a narrow line of sight toward the elevators on the other side of the little vestibule. That done, he went and sat down on the top stair, opened up the fat, old-fashioned briefcase he'd liberated from the Etymology floor at the museum, and took out a copy of *People* magazine. He opened it and began to read. With two working elevators it was doubtful that anyone would have use for the stairs, and a quick glance through the crack in the door would tell him if his quarry had arrived.

Billy managed to work his way through "Picks and Pans" and "Star Tracks" before the elevator opened onto the fifth floor. A well-dressed woman with a cat carrier. He was halfway through yet another article about yet another Hollywood megafilm when the elevator doors slid open a second time. This time it was an elderly, white-haired man with a cane quietly humming "The Pirates of Penzance." Billy went back to his reading, finding an interesting article about Jodie Foster's decision to star in and direct the upcoming film based on the exploits of Jay Fletcher, the Ladykiller vigilante.

Ten minutes later he reached the "Chatter" page at the very end of the magazine, and a few seconds later the elevator stopped a third time. Billy peered through the doorway and watched as Hunter Connelly stepped out into the hallway, looking a little tired after a long day.

Connelly reached the end of the little hallway and turned to the right. Billy stayed where he was on the top stair, giving Connelly a moment to get through his own door. He flipped back through the magazine until he reached the article on Jodie Foster, then carefully ripped out the opening page. He folded the page and put it into the pocket of his jacket.

"What goes around, comes around," he said quietly, then tossed the rest of the magazine into a corner of the stairwell.

Give the guys in Forensics something to do.

Billy reached out, snapped the clasp on the big briefcase, and stood up. He counted to one hundred, added another fifty for good luck, kicked out the wedge under the stairwell door, stepped out into the elevator hall, and headed for Connelly's apartment. He stood in front of Connelly's door, wiggling his toes in the new shoes he'd picked up at a little shop on Columbus Avenue. Much better. He knocked on the door, rapping twice, firmly but not loudly. There was a small glass peephole lens just about eye level. If Connelly checked, he'd see a well-groomed man in an Armani suit carrying a briefcase; not a particularly threatening sight.

Billy put on an extrapolite smile and shifted the briefcase into his left hand. He put his right hand into his jacket pocket and opened up the blade of the Benchmade knife. The door opened. Apparently he'd passed peephole muster. Connelly appeared, jacket off and tie removed. He had his shoes off.

"Yes?"

"Mr. Connelly?" Billy added a nice twinkle to his smile.

"Yes."

"My name is Arthur Bookbinder."

Connelly looked confused and a little irritated. "Yes?"

"From the Merrick Gallery?" Pause, frown, look of concern. "Nobody called?"

"No," said Connelly. He had one hand on the doorframe. Billy could hear *Mishima* by Philip Glass.

Music to die for.

"What's this all about?" Connelly asked.

"Insurance," said Billy. He took a small step forward. "The Whistler prints."

There was a new tension around the restaurant mogul's eyes. Billy almost laughed out loud.

Something's wrong, but you can't quite put your finger on it.

"I've got my own insurance people." Connelly's annoyance was deepening.

Think, Connelly, what's wrong with this picture?!

"I'm aware of that, sir, but I represent the company insuring the prints while they're hanging in the Merrick Gallery. All I need you to do is sign a set of release forms obviating our company from any liability after delivery of the prints." He patted the briefcase. "I've got them right here." He turned up the smile another notch. Connelly stared at him, hesitating.

Last chance, Hunter.

"All right. But let's get this over with. I've got a plane to catch."

Not tonight.

Connelly stood aside and Billy walked into the apartment. Connelly closed the door, slipped past Billy and led the way across the foyer to the living room. Billy caught a short whiff of aftershave. Lagerfeld? At the entrance to the larger room Connelly stopped and turned, finally understanding what was wrong.

"You didn't buzz from downstairs." He was looking a little worried now. "I didn't let you into the building." He took two steps backward into the living room.

"No, you didn't," Billy said. The living room was full of

light, the bare brick walls pale yellow. There was a gray stone fireplace between the two tall windows looking out onto Riverside Drive and the Henry Hudson Parkway and finally the river itself. Lovely.

"Decorate this yourself?" Billy asked, looking around. The painting over the fireplace looked like a Picasso, and not a print.

"Who the hell are you?" said Connelly, voice rising and full of real fear now.

"Please, allow me to introduce myself." Billy put down the briefcase and brought the knife up out of his pocket. He took a long stride forward, his right arm sweeping around in a long arc, the last sun catching the tooth of the blade, turning Billy's swiftly moving hand into molten fire. *Mishima* on the stereo reached its terrible, triumphant climax, and the trembling sound of a thousand birds soaring upward to the heavens filled the air as Billy's blade found flesh.

EIGHT

"You were right," Jack Dane admitted. "There's nothing here." The midsized room at the Gramercy Park looked out over the little fenced-in square of green that gave the hotel its name, but that was the most interesting thing about it. If anything, the room was a little on the dowdy side; clean enough but chipped, worn, and a bit tired. An old lady giving in to the ravages of time.

"What did you expect?" asked Jay. "A bloody message on the wallpaper?"

"I expected something, goddamn it." They'd managed to have the room sealed off before the housekeeping staff got to it, but it wouldn't have made much difference. There was nothing in the wastebaskets, the bed didn't look as though it had been slept in, and the only thing that had been disturbed at all was the bathroom.

It looked as though Billy had shaved and taken a shower. There were towels on the floor, one of the little soap squares had been unwrapped and used, and there was an orange-handled disposable razor on the counter beside the sink. The razor and a few other small toiletries had been purchased at the small kiosk located in a wide corridor off the main lobby of the hotel. The elderly East Indian man who ran the kiosk vaguely remembered someone who fit Billy's description but nothing else. A check of the phone logs came up with only one call—the Internet connection Billy had made to e-mail Karlson at Marshals HQ in Arlington.

"I suppose we could call in a Bureau Crime Scene Unit," said Jay. "But I don't see what good it would do."

"Make work." Dane grunted. "Hair and fibers in the tub

drain that date back to the beginning of time, DNA traces on the skin and hair in the razor that'll tell us what we already know, and Christ only knows what vacuumed up from the wall-to-wall carpet."

Jay sighed. "On the other hand, if we don't call in the CSU it could come back to slap us in the face when and if we catch him."

"There's no 'if,' " said Dane. "Only a 'when.' "

"So you say," Jay countered. "But this isn't giving us much to go on." She shook her head. "Billy's just playing with us."

"And he's the only one who knows the rules to the game," said Dane.

Jay suddenly heard the muffled sound of a trumpet. She went to the window and looked out. The sun was lowering, the trees around the edge of the park throwing deep, heavy shadows. Ghostly in the fading gold light, a black man in a bowler hat and full tailcoat was marching down Gramercy Park North, belting out old Hot Jazz tunes on a gleaming coronet. Behind him, in an even more ghostly procession, came a tall white woman in a bridal gown, fully veiled, followed by half a dozen bridesmaids in pale yellow, a trail of formally dressed ushers behind, and farther back, the bridal party, carrying champagne glasses. There didn't seem to be any groom at all. The procession turned around the park, then went up the steps of an older-looking building across from the hotel, disappearing beneath its canopied entrance. Half a dozen speedwalkers inside the park didn't even look up as the procession streamed by.

Only in New York.

"I don't think there are any rules yet," said Jay, turning back to face Jack Dane. "I think Billy's making them up as he goes along. He hasn't even made his first kill yet."

"You don't count Dr. Summers?"

"No," Jay answered, shaking her head. "Like I said before, Summers just got in the way. To Billy he was opportunity knocking. If the Bannermans had been home at the Watergate it would have been the same thing. You read that e-mail he sent. His knife is sharp and he wants to work."

"You make it sound like finger exercises on a piano."

"Something like that." She waved a hand around the room.
"I think this is where it really starts. This is GO on Billy's
Monopoly board."

"You think he came here to kill someone?"

"Bet on it." Jay nodded.

A cell phone warbled. It was Dane's. He flipped it open,
listened, then flipped it closed. "You were right about the
hotel room giving us jackshit, I was right about Billy coming
home to roost." He shoved the phone back into his pocket.
"That was the museum. They got him on tape."

At the height of rush hour it took them the better part of
an hour to zigzag their way from the hotel to the museum.
Dane took his car around to the back, flashed his badge and
ID to the New York cop at the rear staff entrance, and they
were let into the gigantic museum.

A chatty, chubby-cheeked curator named Andy Blair took
them up to the fourth floor and the Dinosaur Halls. Jay had
a vague childhood memory of giant, gloomy rooms occupied
by dusty, improbable skeletons, but there was nothing like
that now. Glass-floored walkways soared up around the skeletons now and there were interactive computer consoles and
"touch me" displays all over the place. Blair explained that
with the slightly oddball but meteoric rise of dinosaurs' pop-
ularity over the previous ten years or so, there had been a
massive overhaul of the old Saurian Halls and exhibits. *Ju-
rassic Park* had added fuel to the fire, and the Diner Saurus
cafeteria now offered dinosaur-shaped french fries and
chicken nuggets. From the tone of his voice, Andy didn't
approve of either Spielberg's films or the chicken nuggets.
He was after all an entomologist with a particular interest in
butterflies.

"Not much chance of a movie being made about them,"
said Dane.

"Oh, I don't know about that," said Blair. He guided them
around a blank partition hiding an emergency exit and used
a large ring of keys to open the door. Directly in front of

them was an old-fashioned open-work elevator cage. They climbed in and headed upward.

"There's been all sorts of movies about insects over the years." The cage creaked upward and the curator starting ticking them off on the end of his fingers. "*Angels and Insects*, that was just a few years ago . . . too arty for my tastes. All of the *Alien* movies, the ones with Sigourney Weaver— there's no doubt that those things are insects. *The Deadly Mantis*, back in the fifties; *Empire of the Ants*, which was pretty stupid really, and of course the best of them all, *The Fly*."

"You mean, 'Help me! Help me!'?" Jay squeaked.

"Vincent Price." Blair nodded, smiling at the memory. "I'll bet you didn't know the script was written by James Clavell, the man who wrote *Tai-Pan* and all those other novels."

"What about *Arachnophobia*?" Jay offered as the elevator rattled to a stop. "You didn't mention that one."

Blair waved a dismissive hand and shook his head. He pulled back the door of the elevator and clambered out. "Spiders aren't insects." He turned down a narrow corridor and used his keys to open a heavy, enameled metal door.

"Spiders aren't insects?" muttered Dane as they stepped out of the elevator and followed Blair.

Jay whispered back. "Too many legs, I think."

They went through the door and into the first of the insect rooms. There really wasn't very much to see, just row after row of gleaming white cabinets stretching off into the distance.

"Sixteen point five million specimens," said Blair proudly. "Ninety thousand square feet of storage space."

"Maybe what they say about cockroaches eventually ruling the world is true," said Dane.

"They already do," Blair responded blandly. "There's more of them than there are of us, and they've been on the planet a lot longer, too."

"Where exactly are we going?" Jay asked.

"Dr. Korngold's office," Blair answered. "She's head of the department."

Lenora Korngold's office was located in the fourth-floor corner turret with magnificent views up and down Central Park West as well as across the street into the park itself. Except for an ancient desk, a pair of filing cabinets, and a few chairs, the large, high-ceilinged room was awash in bugs. Bugs in mayonnaise jars, bugs in aquariums, bugs in plastic cages, and bugs in shoeboxes, all of them clicking, whispering, hissing, and rustling. There were even boxes of bugs on the windowsills.

Dr. Korngold herself was a wisp-thin woman in her late sixties with steel gray hair, a strong jaw, and raspberry red half-glasses that perched on the end of her patrician nose. Seated off to one side, his hand protectively resting on an audiovisual cart, was a tough-looking man in his thirties. The man was wearing a plain, dark suit, but it might as well have been a uniform—he had cop written all over him. On the cart there was a monitor TV and an industrial strength VCR.

Kenneth Fairhaven, Director of Museum Security, switched on the VCR. The screen flickered and then coalesced into a high-angle view of what appeared to be one of the specimen storage rooms Jay and Jack Dane had just passed through. There was a digital log running along the bottom of the screen and a number-letter code for the location. According to the log, they were watching tape recorded shortly after 2:15 that afternoon. A dark-haired figure entered the picture at the bottom of the frame, and Fairhaven used a remote to freeze the image. He clicked forward a few frames at a time until the figure turned to give a reasonably good profile. It was definitely William Paris Bonisteel.

"What's that in his left hand?" Jay asked.

"Briefcase," said Fairhaven.

"Who the hell let him into the building with a briefcase?" Jack Dane muttered. "Don't you have some kind of bag check or something?"

"Of course," said Fairhaven. "He didn't have the bag when he came into the building."

"There was a briefcase stolen from an office on the third floor," put in Dr. Korngold. Her voice was brittle and precise.

"Presumably that was where Dr. Bonisteel got it."

"You knew Billy?" Jay asked.

"Not on a first name basis," the older woman replied. "He was in Anthropology after all. He consulted with me on a few occasions. Mostly regarding the eating habits of the Dermestid beetle."

Dane grimaced. "Those are the flesh-eating ones?"

"Quite so." Korngold nodded.

Jay spoke to Fairhaven. "Did you backtrack his movements through the camera positions?"

Fairhaven nodded. "We're doing it right now. The cameras are new; they only went in about six months ago, so he probably didn't even notice them." The security man sighed. "Problem is, we've only got them mounted at section entrances, toilet facility entrances, the stairwells, and the elevator stations."

Jay nodded. "In other words, you can tell us where he went but not what he did there?"

"Yeah."

"Where did he go?" asked Jack Dane.

"So far we've backtracked him to the basement-level freight elevator close to the metal shop. From there, he went to the Mammalogy storage area on the third floor, then up to Entomology of the fourth."

"How long did he stay in the Mammalogy storage area?"

"According to the tape, six minutes."

"And up here?"

"Longer. Almost eleven minutes. He probably would have stayed longer if it hadn't been for Dr. Blair here."

The scientist was perched on the edge of a table loaded down with insect cages near the door. He flushed as Jay Fletcher turned in her chair and looked at him. "You were the one who interrupted him?"

"Yes. I saw him taking specimen boxes and putting them into the briefcase. He *looked* as though he belonged there."

"Which way did he go?"

"Past me. Back to the same door I took you both through a few minutes ago. He seemed to know exactly where he was going, so I didn't think much of it at the time."

Lucky he didn't kill you.

"Did he say anything?" Dane asked.

"No," Blair said, shaking his head. "He just . . . left."

"But you *did* raise the alarm," Jay prompted.

Blair's flush deepened. "Not right away." He cleared his throat nervously and shifted on the edge of the table. A box next to his right buttock hissed loudly. "I came here first."

"To Dr. Korngold?"

"Yes. But she wasn't here, so I waited for her to come back."

"You waited?" said Jay.

"Yes." He nodded. "We had some things to discuss about an exhibit. While I was waiting I remembered his face. Remembered who he was. That's when I called Security."

"How long between the time you saw him and the time you called Security?" Jay asked.

"About twenty minutes," Blair answered. He cleared his throat. "Maybe a little longer."

"Jesus!" muttered Jack Dane.

"All right," said Jay. "Have you figured out what he took?"

"He took fifteen examples of Heliconius," answered Dr. Korngold.

"Heliconius?" Jay asked.

"Heliconius is a genus of butterfly," explained the gray-haired woman. "Heliconius cydno, popularly referred to as Longwings and sometimes as Passion Vine butterflies."

"Anything special about them?" Jack Dane asked.

"A number of things." Korngold smiled. "But then, I think all insects are special."

"Any idea why he'd take them?" asked Dane. "Are they valuable?"

"Not in any monetary sense," said Korngold. "I'm not a psychiatrist certainly, but Heliconius has several interesting attributes a man like Dr. Bonisteel might find attractive."

"Such as?" Jay said.

"Heliconius is exceptionally long lived. Most butterflies live for a week or two at the most. The Longwing can live for several months. They also have large brains. They seem to possess something more than simple chemical memory, for instance. In the insect world, the Heliconius is something like an Einstein."

"Anything else?"

"They are deadly poisonous to their enemies," Korngold answered. "Heliconius secretes a form of natural cyanide. Enough to kill anything that tries to eat them."

"Are they native to the United States?" Jay asked.

Dr. Korngold shook her head. "No. South America, Central America, and sometimes as far north as Mexico. They have been sighted in Texas and Florida, but very, very rarely."

"So if he wanted one he'd have to come here to get it," Dane said.

"Basically, yes."

Jay stood up and Dane followed suit. "Thanks for your time," said Jay. She extended her hand across the desk. Korngold shook it firmly.

"Perhaps you could do us a favor in return for our cooperation," said the department head. She gave Fairhaven a quick look.

"If we can," said Dane.

"The fact that Dr. Bonisteel was plying his trade here at the museum caused us a great deal of embarrassment," Dr. Korngold said. "We were hoping that any news of his return might be kept to a minimum."

"Don't worry about it." Jay reassured her. "There's no need to involve the museum at all."

"In fact," added Dane, "we'd prefer it if you didn't say anything about this publicly as well." He glanced over at Blair. "Either of you."

They picked up a cab in front of the museum and rode back to the Gramercy Park in silence. Dane spoke at last. "What do you think about the butterfly thing?"

"I'm not sure," Jay answered honestly.

"A lot of trouble for a few bugs."

"He was after more than just the butterflies," said Jay. "I think they were an afterthought."

"What do you base that on?"

"You read the file. Billy's a planner. He doesn't do anything without a reason. He went to the Mammal storage place first."

"Maybe he was stealing something there, too."

"Or getting something back."

"Such as?"

"Something he stashed before we arrested him. Whatever it was, it was important. Billy is very smart. Scary smart. He knows perfectly well the profiles all say that a head case like him is likely to come home to roost—you said it yourself."

Dane shrugged. "So? He fits the profile."

"And he knows he fits the profile. He'd only come back to the museum if it was absolutely necessary."

"What do you think he stashed? An O.J. kit? Cash, credit cards, passport?"

"Something like that."

"It still doesn't explain the butterflies." Dane shrugged again. "Some kind of thing with the movie?"

"*The Silence of the Lambs*?" She shook her head. "Billy's no copycat."

"Still . . ." Dane let it dangle.

She nodded. "Still . . . You're right, even if it's not that, it must mean something." She let out a long breath and stared out the window. "Whatever it is, I'm sure we're going to find out soon enough."

After slitting Hunter Connelly's throat, Billy Bones relieved the man of his keys, careful not to get his cuffs bloody, called Amtrak for some schedule information, then left the apartment, carefully locking the door behind him. He went down to the Eighty-ninth Street entrance, hailed a cab, took it to the late-closing branch in the Citibank Tower, signed in as Thomas George Rawlins, then emptied his safe-deposit box, retrieving his Paul Sturgis identity. With half a dozen clean, fat, and untraceable credit cards now at his beck and call,

Billy walked over to Madison Avenue and went on a shopping spree. He bought Egyptian cotton shirts from Pinks, a suit at Barneys, another, slightly more casual suit at Armani, then finished up at Bloomingdale's, working his way through the boutique shops until he had everything he needed. From Bloomingdale's he walked over to Rockefeller Center, found a cab, and went straight down Broadway into the Financial District, stopping at Computer World, almost directly across from City Hall and less than two blocks from NYPD headquarters. Using the Tom Rawlins Amex card, he bought a top-of-the-line Fosa laptop and a new Kodak digital camera to replace the inferior ones he'd appropriated from dear dead Dr. Summers and the Bannermans of Watergate.

Shopping completed, he found yet another cab at the Civic Center complex and returned to the Clarendon, letting himself in with Connelly's keys. Once inside the apartment, Billy chose what he needed in the way of accessories from Connelly's bedroom and bathroom, then packed up his new clothes and the computer, using a pair of medium-sized Vuitton suitcases he found in Connelly's closet. Finally, he took a dozen shots of the apartment, packed away the digital camera, and called yet another cab.

By six-thirty he'd reached Grand Central and was enjoying two dozen delicate little Kamamotos on the half shell at the Oyster Bar, washed down with a particularly nice burgundy, which complemented the red-wine vinegar mignonette perfectly.

Chianti my ass.

At seven-twenty he boarded the Metro North train for New Haven and beyond, sat back in his seat, eyes closing as his mind drifted and he thought about the past, the slick taste of oysters still on his tongue.

The dinner party the month after poor Ricky's death had been a great success, laid on, at least on the surface, to celebrate the elevation of a colleague from assistant to full curator, but actually an excuse for Billy to pretend that he was a normal man with friends and social skills that didn't include charring his adoptive parents' bones to ashes.

Prawns with a lemongrass mayonnaise to start, followed
by fresh cod with warm black-olive salsa and roast fennel.
The dessert had been a double chocolate fondue, with white
chocolate as well as dark, mixed with double cream, Coin-
treau dredged into the white, Courvoisier into the dark, with
chunks of fresh pineapple and banana for dipping.

All cooked by the wonderful Gordon, of course, his failed
screenwriter friend who managed a small apartment building
and was steadily drinking himself to death.

By the end of the dinner, the tablecloth was awash in chocolate and his guests were well on their way to being smashed.
The wines had been particularly nice; a Château Le Bon Pas-
teur Pomerol, a 1995 Carmen Reserve Merlot from Chile, and
a Churchill Crusted Port and a box of Dunhill aged Valverde
cigars after dessert. Everyone had taken one, even the girls.
It was fun to watch Audrey, one of the lab assistants, stroking
the long brown cigar in her mouth, her eyes flicking around
the table to see who was watching, and just as funny to watch
Allison, Gordon-the-Drunk's longtime girlfriend, lighting
hers. From what Gordon had told him, the Dunhill was the
only cigar-shaped object that had come near her mouth in
years—not that Gordon had much to offer in that direction,
since according to Allison he hadn't been able to get it up
for the better part of a decade.

Wasn't it grand?

Keeping his eyes closed, barely hearing the train's passage,
Billy let the sounds and tastes and moods of the party wash
through his memory. The best part of all had been the conversation over dessert—serial killers, Jay Fletcher in particular, mixed with dripping chocolate chunks of fruit. Everyone
had opinions about the Ladykiller, but the overall consensus
was that they were all glad she'd escaped the ghastly clutches
of the Federal Bureau of Investigation so the story could con-
tinue.

Kill the bitch, spill her blood!

*Nothing like a bit of Lord of the Flies to set the evening's
tone.*

"The serial serial," he'd joked, and everyone had laughed.

How droll. To sit there with those ineffectual, broken, *small* people, knowing what he knew about them, about Jay Fletcher, about the hot, quick tang of fresh blood, about a whole world just below the surface of this one, invisible, that they could never fathom or understand or even see at all in a million years and more. Like the title of a bad romance: *Secrets and Sinners.*

The train sped on, clicking over the rails, with sunset coming down. Billy got out his cell phone and his laptop, cabled them together, then went online. The bait had already been taken; now it was time to set the hook.

Jay and the marshal had a quick dinner in the hotel dining room, then went up to their rooms to formulate some kind of plan of attack for the following day. Jay checked the laptop and saw the flashing e-mail icon.

Dane snorted, sat down, and lit a cigarette. "Probably Karlson telling us to work harder."

Jay clicked her way into the program and called up the message. "It's from Billy," she said tensely.

"Read it."

—One down, who knows how many more left to go? Up to you, Fairy Fay.

"One down," said Dane. "Shit! He's done it. His first victim."

"There's more." Jay nodded. "A Web site address. Some kind of chatroom. He wants to talk to me." She glanced at her wristwatch. It was almost seven-thirty. "In about two minutes." She looked across the room at Dane. "He has to use a telephone, can we trace the incoming?"

"We can try," said Dane. He jumped up out of the chair and ran from the room. Jay called up the Web site address. It was something called Finders, and from the looks of the homepage it was a noncommercial information exchange for adopted people trying to find and connect with their birth parents. As promised, Billy appeared in one of the Web site's private chatrooms.

—**Been a while, Fairy Fay. You got my message?**
—You've killed someone, and it's not one, it's two.
—**The doctor doesn't count.**
—Tell that to his family.

She remembered Billy's placid, angelic face in the courtroom when she gave her testimony against him, heard herself describing the terrors he'd made his victims suffer before he finally ended their lives, almost as a gift. She'd seen the faces of a hundred killers in her time, but this was the smiling face of hell itself. Talking with him this way was making her physically ill, her stomach roiling, head spinning, but she knew she had to keep him talking for as long as possible.

—**Who have they got to baby-sit you?**
—Nobody.

Billy was looking for a name, an edge, something to work with, and she wasn't going to give it to him. No information at all.

—**They wouldn't let you track me down alone, Jay. Who's there?**
—Nobody.
—**You're not a very good liar, but that's not important.**
—What *is* important, Billy?
—**Making you suffer.**
—How are you going to make me suffer?
—**Your name is going to be the last thing my victims hear before they die. Jay Fletcher, the Ladykiller, let this happen. Jay Fletcher, didn't catch me in time. I'll whisper it to them and then I'll kill them.**

Don't put this on me, you sick bastard; don't you dare put this on me.

—Why waste your time on other people? Why not just
come after me? Or are you a coward?
**—Plenty of time for that. But I'm going to have some
fun first. I'm here for you if you ever want to chat
again. Ta-ta for now.**
—Don't go.
—One more thing:
"Rapt, twirling in thy hand a withered spray,
And waiting for the spark from heaven to fall."
· · · · · · ·

He was gone. A few minutes later Dane came back into
the room, his shoulders slumped.

"No luck," said Jay.

The marshal shook his head. "We weren't ready. Took me
too much time to get through to the phone company, and it
wouldn't have done any good anyway."

"Why not?"

"The son of a bitch was using a digital cell phone. Untraceable. He could have been calling from Timbuktu for all we
know."

Jay dumped the chatroom conversation onto her hard drive
and let Jack Dane have a look.

"He's making this really personal," the marshal commented.

Jay shrugged. "I helped put him away." But she knew it
was more than that, more than just a game. Sifting through
all the material gathered after the death of Ricky Stiles's and
Billy's capture, it became clear that the two men had been as
close as lovers, sharing their deepest thoughts across the Internet, even though, according to the evidence, they had never
met face to face. Jay had stolen that intimacy away, killed his
dearest friend.

Billy wants revenge.

NINE

There was an e-mail from Billy waiting for Jay the next morning:

—Next time maybe I'll clip the ears off.

"Ears?" said Dane after Jay had called him into her room.

"It's another Ripper reference, from one of the letters he supposedly wrote." Jay scrolled down to the bottom of the message on her screen, looking for another chatroom reference. Instead, she saw that there was an attachment to the one-line message. "Pictures," said Jay, pointing to the reference box. "He's using Photoshop."

"Just like you said he would." Dane nodded. "Can you downgrade them or whatever it is you do?"

"Download," Jay corrected. "Yes. It'll take a minute or two."

The pictures were sharp, detailed, and in color. Half a dozen shots of a well-furnished apartment and a single gruesome image of a dead man lying face down in a pool of blood spreading across a hardwood floor.

Nothing else. While Jack Dane called Norman Karlson in Arlington, Jay used her cell phone to bump the images down to Karlson's e-mail address at Marshals HQ, and five minutes later he was examining laser copies of the images.

The director of Fugitive Operations had little of substance to offer in the way of comment or advice beyond the vague promise that he'd have the obscure coding of the originating e-mail address decrypted as soon as possible and an admonition to keep the profile on their investigation as low as they could, at least for the time being. Billy's name would crop up eventually, but Karlson and everyone else involved wanted the lid kept on for as long as possible.

"Big help," said Dane, hanging up the phone on Jay's night table.

"What did you expect?" Jay asked, lifting her shoulders. She was seated at the chipped old desk beside her window. There was a lot of traffic, mostly taxis, feeding off Lexington and going around the little park in a continuous, yellow, honking stream.

"We've got a dead body on the Internet and no way of identifying it," said Dane. "It's like you said, he's teasing us. Last night it's poetry, today it's pictures." He paused. "You find out anything about that quote?"

Jay nodded. "I went out to the Barnes and Noble on Fifth and found a dictionary of quotations. It's from something called 'Scholar-Gypsy' by Matthew Arnold. He's giving us clues."

"I hate fucking clues," grunted the deputy marshal. "Clues are bullshit, like fingerprints. Fingerprints don't catch crooks, they identify corpses. And I'm no goddamned Sherlock Holmes going around telling people what they do for a living by examining the calluses on their fucking pinkie fingers. That's not how you track down a fugitive."

"Okay, how do you track them down?"

"Figure out where they've been and where they're likely to go. Figure out their weaknesses and their fears and exploit them. Squeeze people who know them. Snitches." He lit a cigarette and stared angrily at the image of the dead body on Jay's computer screen. "Not this computer shit."

"Computer shit is where it's at these days," said Jay. She felt for the older man in a weirdly compassionate way. Billy wasn't his kind of fugitive and this wasn't his kind of case. "Billy's leaving us a trail of breadcrumbs. He wants us to find him. When he does, he's going to kill me. It's a pretty simple plan really, he's just muddying the waters."

"I think *that* is more than muddy water," said Dane, pointing at the body on the screen. "I think that is a murder victim."

"The first move in his game," agreed Jay. "He's pretty clear about that. We find out who the dead man is, it gets us closer to him."

"How do we find that out?" Dane asked bleakly. "There he is in plain sight, but we don't have the faintest idea where 'there' is."

"We can make a few assumptions," said Jay.

"You're being Sherlock Holmes now?"

"If you want."

"Which makes me Watson, right?"

"You said it." Jay laughed. "Not me."

"I'll play," Dane answered, his skepticism clear. "For a while anyway. What are these assumptions?"

Jay scrolled through the images, one by one. "It's an apartment," she said.

Dane nodded. "No stairs. Okay, I'll give you that one."

"The apartment is on a corner."

Dane peered at the screen. "Got it. Windows on two sides."

"Check this out," said Jay. She zoomed in on the image, nudging the window to the left on the fireplace into the center of the screen.

"I don't see anything," said Dane, pulling up a chair and sitting down beside her.

"That's the point," said Jay. She made the image even larger. "There's nothing to see. Blue sky, a little strip of green, a little strip of gray, and then more blue, but darker."

"Assume the light blue at the top of the window is sky and the darker blue is water. That makes the green strip a park of some kind."

"How well do you know New York?" Jay asked.

"Not very well."

"There can't be too many places like that."

"Hang on," said Dane. "That little smoke shop stand off the lobby sells maps, I think."

"Coffee too," said Jay. She sighed, then accepted the inevitable. "And a pack of Marlboros."

"Back in a minute."

It was more like ten, but the coffee was from a Starbucks on Lexington and the map was one of those isometric ones that actually showed buildings in three dimensions.

"Thought we could visualize better with a map like that," said Dane, sitting down and popping the lid on his cup. "Almost forgot." He reached into the pocket of his jacket and took out a package of Marlboros, tossing them onto the desk beside the laptop.

"The next time I ask you to buy me a package of cigarettes, don't."

"Right," snorted Dane.

Jay reached out, pulled a cigarette out of the pack, and lit up. Dane sipped his coffee and examined the map. "East River or the Hudson," he said. "Take your pick."

"What do you think?" Jay asked.

"If it was the East River you'd probably be able to see Brooklyn on the other side. And there's not a lot of parks."

"The light isn't right either." She flipped back to the shot of the body. There was a wash of yellowish sun on the wall to the left. "That's late afternoon," she said.

"Which means the window would have to face roughly northwest." Dane nodded. "That makes the dark blue strip the Hudson River."

"Parks?"

"All the way down Manhattan," said Dane unhappily.

"Another assumption."

"What?"

"We assume the dead guy has money." She clicked her way through the images again. "The living room has got to be twenty-feet on a side and the dining room is only a little bit smaller. The master bedroom has its own bathroom, and the kitchen looks like it jumped out of *Gourmet* magazine. It's big and it's expensive."

"Upper West Side," said Dane. He pored over the map again. "Let's say, from 79th Street to 105th. Below 79th it starts to get messy and there are piers and shit in the way. Above 105th and you run into Columbia University."

"Twenty-five blocks of Riverside Drive."

"We'll never cover that," Dane groaned. "Especially not if we have to do it 'low profile.' " He slumped in his chair. "God save me from fucking politicians!"

"I think God *is* a fucking politician," said Jay, and for the first time they laughed together.

Jay took a swallow of coffee then began chewing on the waxed cardboard lip of the cup, staring at the screen. "There's got to be some way we can narrow it down some more."

"How?"

"Elementary," said Jay. "We need an expert, and we need Kinko's."

The Kinko's was simple, the expert a little more difficult. After a call to the New York Public Library, another to NYU, and a third to Columbia University, they eventually found what they were looking for in a man improbably named Dr. Ernl Patrick Funk, an associate professor of architecture at Columbia and a specialist in "named" apartment buildings in New York, particularly those designed and built in the late 1800s and early 1900s. According to the clerk at the Public Library, Funk had four titles in the computer index and a much longer list of publications in the periodical section.

It took a while, but they eventually tracked down Ernl Funk in the flesh, working at a computer terminal in a small three-walled carrel on the second floor of Columbia's Avery Architecture and Fine Arts Library. For some reason, Jay had been expecting a Revenge of the Nerds type, but in fact Dr. Funk was a well-groomed, reasonably ordinary looking man in his mid-thirties.

"Police," he said after introductions had been made. "I don't talk to a lot of them." He paused and smiled. "In fact, I don't talk to them at all."

Jay took the sheaf of color photocopies they'd printed up at Kinko's. "We were hoping you could identify an apartment for us."

"Apartment, or apartment building?" Funk asked, taking the copies from her.

"Either or," said Jack Dane.

Funk went through the pictures, minus the one of the corpse, which they hadn't printed up. "Nineteen hundred to 1910. Looks like it could have been one of the buildings designed by Charles Birge."

"We think it's on Riverside Drive somewhere."

"That fits." Funk nodded. Jay wondered if he was related to the Funk from Funk and Wagnall's but she didn't say anything; he'd probably had enough of that over the years.

The architect went through the pictures again, stopping at the one showing the fireplace flanked by windows looking out toward the Hudson. "Spot anything?" asked Dane.

"Maybe," Funk said. "Let me check with Clio."

"Clio?"

"Online catalogue," said Funk. He glanced at the photocopy again. "That fireplace with the windows on either side rings a bell." The professor worked his way into the computer program, eventually pulling up a floorplan onto the screen. He looked back and forth between the screen and the photocopy, then finally nodded his approval. "Fits the bill." He smiled. "William Randolph Hearst used to live there. Eventually bought the building."

"What building?" Dane asked.

"The Clarendon," said Funk. He used both hands to show them the similarities between the color copy and the schematic on the screen. "Window, fireplace, window, and another pair of windows to the left." He looked up at Dane and Jay. "If you had a view facing to the right, I'm willing to bet it would show pocket doors leading into the dining room, just like the floorplan here."

Jay nodded but kept silent. The view he was describing was the one featuring a body front and center. "How many apartments in the building, do you think?" she asked. Funk checked the floorplan on the screen and counted the number of living rooms. "Five to a floor," he said after a few seconds. He scrolled back to a description of the building at the head of the document. "Nine floors. Forty-five apartments."

"Shit," muttered Dane. Jay knew what he was thinking;

knocking on forty-five doors until you found one that didn't answer was hardly low profile.

"Anything we can do to figure out which apartment we're seeing in the pictures?"

"Sure," said Funk. "It's facing Riverside Drive with a street to the left. The Clarendon is on the corner of Riverside Drive and West Eighty-sixth, and that's what this is showing."

"Nine apartments then," said Jack Dane. "One for each floor on that corner."

Funk bobbed his head, then leaned down and took a very close look at the living-room shot. "It's not very high up, but high enough so that you don't get the other side of Riverside Drive into the frame. No sidewalk."

"What's your best guess?" Jay asked.

Funk shrugged his shoulders. "Third, fourth, or fifth floor. Not higher and not any lower either." He flushed slightly. "Am I being of any help?"

"You have no idea," Jay said, smiling back at him. Not only was Funk cutting down their footwork, he was also helping to keep things low profile.

"I don't suppose you can tell me what this is all about."

"Routine," said Dane. Funk cocked an eyebrow. He wasn't buying it and Jay knew he'd either start babbling about it to his colleagues or start asking questions in the wrong places. She needed the lid jammed on tight.

"Grand Jury," said Jay. "Can't say anything." She put on a brief, official smile. "Don't want to be held in contempt now, do we?"

"Uh, no," said Funk. Jay gave him a nod.

"Appreciate it," she said, trying to imitate some kind of female Jack Webb and keep a straight face.

"So that takes it down to three corner apartments," said Jack Dane. "Now we're getting somewhere."

"How do we find out who lives in the corner apartments?" Jay asked.

"You find out who lives in all of the ones on those three floors," said Dane, in his element now. "One call should do it." He took out his cell phone and dialed. By the time they reached Dane's car parked on 118th Street, he had his answer from the Marshals' New York office in the Federal Building down on Foley Square. They climbed into the car and headed toward the Clarendon. Jay plugged the cell phone into her laptop and the Marshals faxed the list they'd culled from their reverse directory. "So how do we tell which of the three apartments is the right one?" Dane asked as he pulled into a slot on the other side of the street from the Eighty-sixth Street entrance. There was a large wrought-iron canopy over the main doors and the name "Clarendon" carved into the stone above it. "We can't just sit here all day."

"Funk narrowed it down from forty-five apartments to three. Let's not give up now."

"Lead on, Sherlock." said Dane skeptically. "Watson here is all ears."

Jay jumped the digitized pictures back onto the screen while Jack Dane ducked down slightly and glanced up at the gray stone building. "Wait a minute. Check the Eighty-sixth Street view of the living room," Dane asked, keeping his eyes on the building.

Jay did so. "Okay, now what?"

"Zoom in on the two windows."

Jay followed his instructions. "What am I looking for?"

"Tell me what you can see."

"The building across the street."

"Anything else?"

"No." She looked again. "Just the building we're parked in front of right now."

"You see a streetlight? A metal pole, or the light on the top of it, like one of those War of the Worlds monsters? A clam thing."

"No clam thing, no pole," Jay answered.

"Then we've got the apartment," said Dane. He lifted his head and turned to face Jay, clearly pleased with himself. "On three you'd see the pole, the clam is at the fourth-floor level, but on five you wouldn't see anything at all."

"Apartment 504," said Jay, checking the list.

"That's the one."

"I'll be damned," she said quietly. "Not bad, Watson, not bad at all."

"Who you calling Watson, ma'am?" Dane was smiling but there was a competitive edge to it. "And who lives in 504?"

Jay checked the list faxed to her machine by the Marshals. "Somebody named Connelly," she said. "Hunter Connelly."

TEN

They climbed out of the car and headed across the street to the front entrance of the building. "No doorman," said Jay.

"So?"

"How do we get in?"

Jack Dane smiled. "The same way I write up reports," he answered. "Hunt and peck." The marshal went around to the trunk of the car and took out the wheel jack.

"What's that for?" Jay asked.

"You'll see." They crossed the street, Dane with the jack, Jay toting the laptop.

The pair went up the three worn steps to the double doors, and Dane punched buttons until someone buzzed them in. "Apartment 903 is going to be expecting flowers," said Jay, pulling open the door.

"Well, 903 is shit out of luck," Dane answered. They rode the elevator to the fifth floor, took a wrong turn down the corridor, and wound up retracing their steps until they stood in front of the door to 504. Dane knocked. No answer. He knocked a second time, more loudly, and they waited again. Still nothing.

"Now what?" asked Jay.

"Procedure says I'm supposed to find the landlord of the building, get keys, and have the man accompany me into the apartment. Failing that, I'm supposed to call in the locals."

"Lot of time wasted. Lot of profile."

"Right."

"So?"

"Invoke the imminent-danger ruling."

"What the hell is that?"

"Sometimes called 'proximate cause.' If I have knowledge that someone may be in imminent danger of physical harm, then I can enter any premises without want or warrant."

"You should have been a lawyer."

"That's what my old man used to tell me."

"According to that picture, Connelly is a corpse on the floor in there. If there ever was any imminent danger, it's no longer imminent."

"You a doctor? You qualified to write out a death certificate?"

Jay smiled. "No."

"Well, there you go," Dane answered placidly.

"So what do we do? Kick down the door?"

"I think we can be a little more subtle than that." Dane lifted the car jack, turned it sideways, set the base end against one side of the doorframe, and cranked until the head of the jack was firmly pressed against the other side of the doorframe, just above the knob. He jerked the elevating lever back and forth, and Jay heard the wood of the frame begin to creak as the widening jack spread the frame apart. A few more cranks and the door popped open without any difficulty at all.

"You learn something new every day," said Jay, impressed. "Where'd you learn how to do that, Marshals school?"

Dane released the jack. "The mean streets of Cleveland, Mississippi, population fifteen thousand, main industries a nail factory and a place that makes automobile trim." He lifted his shoulders. "I didn't want to make trim or nails, so me and my friends started boosting things out of houses."

Jay reached into her jacket pocket and took out two pair of disposable surgical gloves. She handed a pair to Dane. "Here," she said. "This might turn out to be a crime scene. Put these on." She gave him a sour smile. "Procedure," she added. Dane nodded without answering and slipped on the gloves. He reached into his own pocket and a Colt Mark IV automatic pistol appeared in his hand.

He pushed open the door. They stepped into the apartment with Dane in the lead. He took two steps, then paused, listening, his head cocked slightly, chin up as he tasted the air. "Blood," he said quietly. Dane turned. "Close the door."

Jay did as she was told. "You were a burglar?" Jay asked.

"I wouldn't go that far," said Dane. He took another few steps down the cool, shaded hall. The slick-metal smell of blood was even stronger now. "I was eighteen. I thought of myself as a rebel."

"You get caught?" They edged forward carefully, listening. Dane nodded. "Yeah, by my dad."

"Could have been worse."

"Not really," said Dane. "My dad was the town sheriff. He did me a deal. Go to Vietnam or go to jail. I went to Vietnam." They stepped into the living room. "Shit," said Dane, even though they'd both been expecting it.

The body of Hunter Connelly lay sprawled across the hardwood, feet on a rug, head pointing toward the half-open pocket doors leading into the dining room. He'd bled out completely, a drying, sticky red-brown puddle pooling right until it ran up against the baseboard, following some invisible tilt in the floor. Greenfly maggots were squirming here and there.

"Not a whole lot of imminence here," said Jay.

"No," agreed Dane.

"Not too many maggots yet," Jay murmured, squatting down beside the body. It wasn't her first corpse, but she still had to work hard at keeping her stomach in check. At least the corpse was relatively fresh. In another few hours it would be a white slithering mass, and a few hours after that the room and then the whole apartment would begin to stink as gasses filled the body and fluids leaked from various orifices. "Sometime last night by the looks of it."

"Yeah." Dane was busy scanning the area round the fallen man. Jay stood up.

"How do you think it went down?"

Dane pointed at a streak of blood spatters along the pale yellow wall to his left. They trailed away like an arrow, pointing in the direction of the dining room. "A right-handed stroke with a very sharp instrument. Up close and face to face." Dane frowned. "I don't get it. Why does he let Billy into his fucking living room?"

"Billy's smart." Jay shrugged. "He figured out some way to get into the apartment, some story that was good enough for Connelly to buy."

Dane turned, facing back toward the hallway and the door they'd come through a few moments before. "He lets Billy in, walks down the hall, then just inside the room he turns to say something and the son of a bitch slits his throat."

"Close enough," Jay agreed.

"Look," said Dane, pointing. Jay turned and saw an open, light brown expanding briefcase sitting on the floor, half-hidden beside a telephone table and chair. She went over to the telephone table and picked up the briefcase, looking inside.

"Empty," she said, holding it so Dane could see. "No butterflies."

"Maybe he dumped them."

"I don't think so," said Jay slowly. She put the briefcase down and looked at the body again. "I think we should turn him over."

"All right." He let out a long breath. "Give me a hand."

Jay nodded her agreement and they bent down over the body of the late Mr. Connelly. She gripped the man's left shoulder and Jack Dane levered both hands under the dead man's left hip. He counted off. "On three. One, two, THREE!" They rolled the body over, easing it farther into the living room, away from the largest part of the maggot-speckled pool of blood.

Suddenly the smell of feces and urine was added to the mix, and Jay gagged. She backed away and stood up, turning her head and fighting the rise of poisonous-tasting bile in her stomach. She started breathing through her nose, then turned back to the body. Dane was staring at the eyes.

Etched in slashing patterns of vibrant yellow, deep blue, and orange-red much brighter than the drying blood that ringed the gaping wound in the throat, a delicate spread of wings fanned out across each eye. A long pin had been pushed hard through each butterfly's abdomen, through the victim's closed eyelids, and deeper still into his sightless pupils, turning the two butterflies into a sunset mask.

Jay wanted to look away but found that she could not. Years of working for the Bureau had made her immune to scenes of death or murder, but Billy, like his old friend Ricky Stiles, was cut from different cloth. A liquor-store thief blown away by a clerk with a shotgun under the counter was just a bad guy come to the short, hard end that had probably been his fate from birth; this was something else. This was ritual, purposeful as art. Or voodoo.

"He did this for us," Jay whispered. "This is special."

"Another fucking clue, you mean?" Dane scoffed. "You can buy into this creepo's craziness, but I'm not going to."

"You'd better," said Jay. "It's the only way we're going to find him."

"So you're saying the butterflies have some kind of meaning, some kind of code?"

"I'm not sure."

"What?" Dane said, his tone harsh. "We're going to have to pile up a few more maggot factories like this one before the mystery gets solved?"

"That's how he's playing it," said Jay. "The faster we figure it out, the faster we bring him down."

"He pins a guy's eyes shut with a pair of butterflies, what the hell is that?"

"I'm open for suggestions."

"You're the serial killer expert," said Dane, waving a dismissive hand. "I'm just a dogcatcher." He grunted. "Except this fucking dog's got rabies."

"Serial killers take things, they don't leave things behind." She shook her head and turned slowly, trying to absorb everything in the room, searching for anything that seemed out of place. "Most of what you read about people like Gacy or Bundy or Dahmer is a load of garbage. They don't have some deep-seated need to confess or to get caught. For these people it's an itch they scratch. They've got black holes where their souls should be."

"So all that stuff about leaving clues behind is bullshit?"

Jay nodded. "You bet. There's no such thing as a stupid serial killer. The successful ones are smart." She pulled her Marlboros out of her jacket and lit one with a disposable lighter she'd picked up at the hotel. "Stuffing the pupae of an exotic, easily traceable moth down the throats of his victims was just plain dumb."

Jack Dane looked a little skeptical. "But Billy pinning his victim's eyes shut is smart?"

Jay noticed the tinge of irony in Dane's voice but decided to let it pass. Instead of commenting, she just nodded. "That's right. We're not trying to identify a killer, we're trying to find one. I told you, for Billy it's a game and this is the first move."

"So how do we play?" Dane queried.

"He sent us a bunch of pictures of this place. He assumed we'd be smart enough to figure out where it was. Match those pictures to what you see here and you'll get the next clue."

"So let's start comparing."

They spent an hour, going from room to room, going over everything in detail, zooming in on the pictures when necessary. Nothing stood out until they reached the master bedroom.

It was decorated coolly, the walls here the same pale gray as the fireplace, most of the floor covered by a plainly patterned Tibetan rug, the bed a queen-size with a headboard sprouting built-in night tables. There was a Biedermeier-style desk under the window and three painting on the walls, all in oil. A William Bailey, a Milton Avery, and a Hockney swimming pool.

"Anything?" Dane asked, looking over her shoulder.

"Hang on."

She spent several long moments going back and forth between the computer image and reality. Finally she nodded.

"What?" Dane asked.

She turned and handed him the laptop. He took it gingerly, staring at the digitized image of the room directly in front of him.

"Check the bedside table on the left," Jay instructed. "Is it my imagination, or is it open just a teeny tiny crack in the picture he sent us?"

"I can see a line, yeah." Dane nodded.

"Well, it's completely shut now," Jay responded.

"Which means he wants us to look in the drawer."

"I think so."

Jay put the laptop down on the desk under the window and sat on the edge of the bed. She reached out to the bedside drawer.

Dane's voice stopped her. "Any chance Billy'd do something like booby-trap the drawer?"

Jay hesitated, her hand on the drawer pull. "Nothing in his background," she answered slowly. "Nothing we know about, anyway."

"Just a thought," said Dane mildly.

"You like scaring the shit out of people, don't you, Marshal?"

"I like being careful. I knew a guy from the Miami bomb squad who's minus everything below the belt buckle because he wasn't careful."

"Shit," muttered Jay. He was pulling her chain and she knew it, but that didn't stop the sweat from coming up under her eyes and at her temples. She reached out and pulled the drawer open. It was empty except for a thick, black address book, spiral-bound in red. Jay sat back on the bed and flipped through the tabbed pages.

"There's got to be five hundred addresses and phone numbers in here." She shook her head. "Everything from Stauntons on the Green in Dublin to some place called Red White and Blues in Prague. He's got the number for a cab company in Macao, for Christ sake!"

"If this is a game, then your friend Billy's cheating," said Jack Dane. His cell phone gave a muffled trill and he took the instrument from his pocket. He took the call, wandering out of the room as he did so, leaving Jay in the bedroom with the address book. She bit back her irritation; on the face of it she and the U.S. Marshal were equals, but that didn't stop

Dane from making sure he took the call privately.

She was the wild card in the operation, a potential publicity nightmare if it ever got out that she was a hired gun brought in to go after Billy Bones. All those coy comparisons in the press, all those allusions—"It takes a thief to catch a thief," "Fight fire with fire," "It takes one to know one." In the end what it came down to had nothing to do with a partnership— she was a bloodhound and Marshal Jack Dane was her keeper, the man who held the leash.

Dane came back into the room, running a thoughtful hand through his thinning blond thatch.

"So shy you can't talk to your girlfriend with me in the room?"

It was the marshal's turn to look irritated. "That was Karlson back at headquarters. He tracked the source of the last e-mail message. The one with the pictures."

"And?"

"It was from one of those Amtrak Railfones, using one of Dr. Summers's credit cards."

"They trace the train?"

"Yeah. It was one of the corridor shuttles, met up with the Washington train. End of the line was Springfield, Massachusetts. According to Karlson, the Springfield train connects to the Lakeshore Limited, which could have taken him to Boston in one direction or Chicago in the other." He shook his head. "He could be anywhere by now."

"If he was trying to get away he wouldn't be leaving a trail," said Jay. "He used his cell phone to talk to me in the chatroom, but the Railfone to send the pictures? He *wants* us to track him. The question is, where?" She paused for a moment, thinking it through. "When did he make the call?"

"Ten-thirty-eight last night," said Dane. "The train was leaving some place called Enfield, like the rifle. It's just this side of the Connecticut/Massachusetts state line."

"How many stops between there and Springfield?"

"None."

"So it has to be Massachusetts."

"What has to be Massachusetts?"

"Where he's telling us to go," Jay answered. "Believe me, Billy isn't the aimless type. He made the call when and where he did for a reason."

"More clues," said Dane. "I'm starting to feel like Dick fucking Tracy."

"What's the area code for Massachusetts?"

The marshal turned on his heel and left the room. He returned a few moments later with the Manhattan White Pages from the telephone table in the front hall. He flipped through the information pages at the front of the heavy book.

"There's three of them—617, 508, and 413," he said.

Jay started going through the phone numbers in the spiral-bound book. "You told Karlson about the body in the living room?"

"Yeah. Told us to preserve the crime scene the best we could. Oh, well. He's also going to check with the Bannermans in Paris to see if there's any connection between them and Connelly. He'll also take care of smoothing things over with the NYPD."

"Some Homicide detective is going to be well and truly pissed," Jay commented, flipping another page. "So far no numbers in any of those area codes."

"Maybe it's bullshit." Dane shrugged.

Jay let out a long breath. "Then why call from the Railfone?"

"A red herring? Leading us off in the wrong direction? Or maybe he's not as smart as you think he is."

"If anything, he's smarter than I think he is," Jay answered. She looked up from the address book. "Look, why don't we get the shit out onto the table where we can take a good look at it, Marshal Dane? I'm getting tired of the sniping."

"What's that supposed to mean?"

"I say something, you say the opposite; I take one side of an argument, you invariably take the other. Billy Bones is the enemy, Dane, not me."

There was a short silence and then the marshal spoke. "I do things pretty much by the book, Ms. Fletcher, and you and everything about you are anything but by the book." He shrugged. "I catch bad guys for a living." He shrugged again and let the words hang in the air.

"And under any other circumstances, I'd be one of the bad guys you were trying to catch. So that's a problem?"

"Yeah."

"Well, there's nothing I can do about that now," Jay answered. She squeezed her eyes shut and pinched the bridge of her nose with a thumb and forefinger. Karlson had her roped and hogtied to a Rush Limbaugh clone with a gun.

"We have an idea, either one of us, we discuss it with the other person and we come to some kind of agreement about how to go forward, then we do it. How does that sound?" asked Jay.

"Good enough, but keep one thing in mind."

"What?"

"I'm a cop and you're not, not anymore. It comes down to a life-and-death call, I make it, okay?"

Cock games, Jesus!

"Sure, whatever you say, Jack."

"Good." He slapped the phone book shut, turned, and left the room. Jay went back to the address book. She found it under the M's.

"I've got it," she called. She went back out into the living room. Dane was standing at the window, staring out across the Hudson, his back to the body on the floor. "I've got it," Jay repeated. He turned. "A place called the Blackwood Inn in Blackwood, Massachusetts. He made a little note under the number—$78 PN."

"Per night?" Dane suggested. "A B&B?"

"Maybe." She lifted her shoulders. "Should we call?"

"Is it the only number?"

"I can't find any others with the right area code."

"I say we go up there and cold-call it." He glanced down at the sprawled corpse. "We'll need a picture of him."

"Driver's license?"

"That'll do." Dane nodded. There was a sports jacket draped over the back of one of the chairs in the dining room. Dane left the window and went to the jacket, rummaging around in the inside pocket. He pulled out an expensive-looking red morocco leather case, stamped in gold. He flipped it open and turned it so that Jay could see. "Passport." He closed the document and slipped it into his own jacket pocket. "Must have been going on a trip." Dane shook his head. "I guess he missed his flight."

"I think we're done here," said Jay. "Unless you can think of something else," she added, trying to keep the peace. He smiled thinly at the comment, seeing it for what it was and, by the expression on his face, wondering if she was being patronizing or sincere. He shook his head finally.

"No," Dane said. "I can't think of anything else."

"Okay," said Jay. "I'm going to need to stop at a photo store or one of those big appliance places on the way out of town."

"Why?"

"A video camera I can plug into the laptop. Billy's whole thing is images; I want to see if we can get a jump on him next time."

"You're sure there's going to be a next time?"

"Count on it."

Five minutes later they were back in the car, and an hour and a half after that, video camera packed away in the trunk of the unmarked cruiser, they were sliding onto the Cross-Bronx Expressway, looking for Interstate 95 and the road to Blackwood.

ELEVEN

Her name was Brittany Shields and she was seventeen years old. She was a B-average student, pleasant, a little on the shy side, and thought herself quite plain, which, by most standards, she was. Some people, mostly much older, would search for something positive to say about her appearance and would often comment that she looked very much like a young Sissy Spacek, but Brittany knew better. Sissy Spacek had tits after all.

Her red hair was too bright and tended toward split ends, her cheeks and nose too spotted with freckles, her eyes too pale a green, and her eyelashes so light they always needed mascara. For Brittany the only good thing about being a redhead was the fact that she didn't have to shave her legs as often as the other girls and would never be troubled by bikini-line problems, if by some impossible set of circumstances she ever summoned up the courage to wear such a thing.

On the other hand, plain or not, she was extremely wealthy, or at least she would be when she inherited at the age of twenty-five. Brittany was the only child of Deborah and Charles Shields, of the Shields Development Corporation, which owned and operated seventy-five major shopping mall operations all over the country. Both Deborah and Charles had been killed in a boating accident off Barbados a few weeks after Brittany's fifteenth birthday.

Following the death of their clients, the Shields's lawyers, now Brittany's lawyers, managed to offload Shields Development for a solid profit, then proceeded to sink the resulting cash into a broad-based portfolio of blue chips, mutuals, and bonds, all of which comprised the bulk of Brittany's inheritance and would provide her with a more than comfortable lifestyle for the rest of her life. The lawyers managed the portfolio, but Charles Shields, a lawyer himself, had known the sly and keenly rapacious tendencies of his profession and thus had appointed his sister and his wife's brother as Brittany's actual trustees. The lawyers would grow plump on their fees, billed hours, and commissions, but they would not become obese at Brittany's expense.

Since neither her aunt nor her uncle were able to take Brittany into their homes on a full-time basis, the young woman spent the bulk of her year as a boarder at Blackwood Academy, a onetime boys-only private school in central Massachusetts with an outstanding prep-school reputation stretching back to March 1, 1797, the day Governor Samuel Adams signed a bill granting the school its charter. Steadfastly fighting off the horrors of coeducation for almost two hundred years, Blackwood Academy had finally allowed girls into the school in 1990.

The academy accepted roughly 450 students each year, doubling the population of the town of Blackwood for the fall, winter, and spring terms. The town, almost unchanged since the early 1800s, had long ago given up on marginal agriculture as an economic base and instead had embraced private education as its main source of finance. In addition to the sprawling, red-brick Georgian campus of the academy, there were two junior schools, Bement and Eaglebrook.

Using colonial Williamsburg as its guide, the miniature town, with the help of wealthy and influential Blackwood Academy alumni, had spent decades refurbishing old homes along the majestic, elm-lined "Street," Blackwood's only thoroughfare. Some of them were open to the public during the summer season.

There was only one hostelry in the town, the Blackwood Inn, and most of its income was derived from parents visiting their children. The inn had twenty rooms, all decorated in colonial style, each one bearing the name of someone connected with historic Blackwood. The most famous of these, at least by popular standards, was the Horatio Alger Room.

Alger, author of dozens of rags-to-riches books for children, had never attended the academy, but he had once taught a summer session there in the late 1800s to make a little desperately needed money.

The morning following Jay Fletcher and Jack Dane's discovery of Hunter Connelly's throat-cut body on the floor of his living room, Brittany Shields woke up, groaned, then got up. First a run to help melt off the baby fat, then a piano lesson. Summer hell with only the vaguest hope of something better. Brittany was one of four full-time boarders remaining in Blackwood for the summer vacation.

The others were Alexandra and Michaela Byrne, staying with Mrs. Croft, the Girls' Physical Education teacher, while their parents were on an archaeological dig in Ulan Bator, and Derek Lancaster, who was avoiding his parents' very public separation and divorce by boarding with Dr. and Mrs. Eberling. Brittany, whose parents had endowed a chair in science at Blackwood before their untimely deaths, was boarding at the headmaster's residence, a large, white saltbox that stood just across Albany Road and the common from the large, red-brick and white-columned Academic Building.

Brittany had spent the last two years at Blackwood being shunned by the beautiful Byrne sisters, and for the last two years she had been madly in love with Derek Lancaster. Today, if everything went according to plan, she'd meet up with him on her run, and who knew, maybe sparks would fly. With that small warm hope held safely in her heart, she climbed out of bed and got into her shorts and a Blackwood T-shirt.

She went downstairs, crossed the big country kitchen to the back door and stepped out, did a couple of deep knee bends, then set out on her morning jog. She snorted under her breath; her morning jog, what a crock of shit *that* was. She hated running, loathed track and field, and never in her life had she considered doing anything that athletic on a Saturday. But this was Blackwood, Massachusetts, and Blackwood was a fishbowl. Choose a sport, keep to the sport, or face the wrath of Crafty Croft, the Phys Ed Eva Braun, who had her spies everywhere.

Blackwood was not quite a town, but a little more than a village. It had a grand total of five streets, eight stop signs, and no traffic lights at all. The elm-lined "Street" ran north-south while Island Road, Wells Street, and Memorial Street, ran east-west, joining up with Highway 10 about 150 yards to the east.

The fifth street, Albany Road, bisected the Blackwood Academy campus, virtually dead-ending at the Field and Barton dormitory buildings except for the old farm road that led north beside the woods fringing the Blackwood River. The village was bracketed by two working farms, one to the south and one to the north, and there was open space everywhere, including the campus lawns behind the Academic Building and the sprawling athletic grounds to the south. In Blackwood you could run all right, but you couldn't hide.

Brittany rounded the house and crossed the wide lawn, then headed up the Street under the green canopy of elms, traveling north past the common and the Civil War Memorial, then passing the Brick Church, finally turning west around the little Post Office building and the old Pratt house, heading toward the footpath through the trees that went around the back of the Boyden Library.

It was a classic jogging route, one regularly chosen by Crafty Croft. The usual pattern would be to follow the trees out to the campus lawns, do a couple of quarter-mile circuits, then head back to the barnlike gym building on the far side of Albany Road. She trotted past the south wing of the Blackwood and headed for the anonymity of the trees ahead.

William Bonisteel watched her go, standing at the window of the main floor lounge of the Blackwood Inn, a lovely cup of tea in his hand. The cup was Butani Crane in gold and blue and the tea itself was Twinings; he couldn't have asked for a better way to end a perfect breakfast, and now, right in front of his eyes, the young Brittany, jogging her way to good health.

He knew who it was from the photo he'd taken out of the album in Connelly's apartment, a shot of Brittany and her uncle standing arm in arm in front of the flag- and bunting-draped facade of this very inn. According to the date on the back of the picture, it had been taken during July of the past year, probably the Fourth by the looks of things. In the photograph she was wearing the same Blackwood T-shirt as the one she'd on when she ran past the window.

Billy was well aware that most people would have been astounded by the coincidence of his seeing the very object of his interest, but Billy expected that kind of thing in his life, just as his father had before him. For Charlie Manson, life was just one long set of coincidences that had taken him through worlds of change, out of juvenile nothingness to being, briefly, the most feared and hated man in America. It was a hard act to follow.

For Billy, catching a fleeting glimpse of Brittany Shields was just another ratification of his own philosophy of what he called his special theory of Dark Attractors. In real chaos theory, a "Strange Attractor" charted the trajectory of a system of chaotic motion—everything from dripping faucets to global weather systems. Strange Attractors were used primarily to define general patterns of such movement, since any accurate, detailed charting of chaos was impossible by definition.

In Billy's theory, Dark Attractors were black holes of human negative energy, using their horrifying power to draw in like-minded evil to their cause. There were many kinds of Dark Attractors—groups like the Ku Klux Klan and the IRA which twitched some grotesque mental tuning fork to match vibrations with the most frightful dreams and aspirations of their members. Such members were individuals with the same capacity: Koresh and his Branch Davidians, Jim Jones and his People's Church, Charles Manson and his Family, and Ricky Stiles, of course, who'd made a home for them all on the World Wide Web, bless his black, dead, bitter heart.

And Billy Bones, let's not forget about him.

In the end, it came down to a simple truism that was the very essence of Billy's philosophy—for Dark Attractors, things worked out in the end, one way or another. Billy took a last sip of his tea then turned back to the breakfast buffet on the far side of the room. He sliced a wafer of Edam and lay it across a piece of dark rye, then popped it into his mouth, thinking about the perfect sweep of the knife as it slicked through the center of Hunter Connelly's throat and the look of fear in the man's eyes seeing the vaulting spray of his own lifeblood as it arced into the air.

Billy chewed and swallowed, thinking too about the red-haired girl. He shaved off another piece of cheese and put it on his tongue. The running girl was like one of those little Winston Churchill wordplays: Billy didn't have the faintest idea where she was going, but he knew exactly when she was going to get there. Like everything else at Blackwood, Brittany's days, even during the summer, were scheduled; those schedules were logged in her student file on the academy's computer system, and once there, those schedules were his. He smiled at that, filled his charming cup again, then took it up to his room and began his preparations.

The Blackwood Police Department had once been located in the picturesque, red-brick colonial town hall in the city center but had recently moved to the old Kaiser-Permanente building less than a mile away on High Street, vacated after the huge HMO's merger with Community Health Plan.

Jack Dane pulled his unmarked Marshals car into a visitors slot in front of the sprawling, one-story building, and he and Jay Fletcher climbed out into the sunlight. Jay glanced at the line of white, green-striped Blackwood cruisers parked to their right. "Why is it that the only people who have Crown Victorias are police departments? You never see anyone else driving them."

"Never thought about it," Dane answered, his tone flat. Ever since their bland, Howard Johnson breakfast that morning Jay had been trying to break the newly frozen crust of ice that had formed between her and the marshal, but he wasn't thawing.

"You sure this is the right idea?" she asked as they approached the main entrance to the building.

"We start treading on toes and we'll make more waves than calling a press conference," Dane answered. "You have *no* authority and mine is only federal unless otherwise requested. We need the phone records from that B&B, and the only way we're going to get them is by asking the locals."

Jay shrugged. "Your call." Even with the laptop she could easily have hacked into the local phone company records and saved a whole lot of time, but it would have been totally illegal, unconstitutional, and a whole lot of other things.

Which is what got you into trouble in the first place, remember that.

Besides, Dane already thought of her as a criminal and there was no sense in making things worse. They went in through the main doors, talked to the desk sergeant in the lobby, and were pointed in the direction of the Detective Division in a suite of offices at the far end of the building. There were five desks and four plainclothesmen in the large open room, and an older-looking man in a glassed-in office to the right.

"Help you?" asked a tall, pleasant-faced man rising from behind one of the desks. To Jay, he looked like a kid just out of high school, all arms and legs and lousy fashion sense. The suit was discount-house blue and it looked as though the kid had grown since he bought it.

"Looking for the man in charge," Dane replied, smiling.

"That would be Lieutenant Rawls," the man answered. "Can I ask what this is about?"

Dane pulled out his ID folder and shield. "Bad guys," he said, keeping up the smile. The tall kid in the cheap blue suit sat down, and Jay followed Jack Dane across the main room to the lieutenant's office. Dane showed his tin again, introduced Jay as Kelly Morgan, his "associate," and they sat down. Rawls was in his forties, much better dressed than the kid outside, and had small eyes like a ferret that stared out from behind thick glasses. To Jay, he looked dangerously smart.

"What can I do for you?" he said. There was a distinct Boston twang to the voice. Rawls wasn't a local.

"We're trailing a fugitive," Dane answered smoothly. "He's also committed murder. We'd like to get some phone records from the Blackwood Inn."

Rawls nodded. "Nice place." He smiled pleasantly. "Put my in-laws there once."

"The phone records," Jay reminded gently. Rawls turned his eyes on her and the smile wasn't pleasant at all.

"This is a small town and we're a small-town force—three lieutenants, three sergeants, and twenty-eight patrolmen, which includes the Detective Division." He paused. "But we're not stupid, Marshal, so let's drop the bullshit and you can tell me what's really going on here." The detective glanced at Jay and gave her a long, thoughtful look.

He's made me. The son of a bitch has figured out who I am.

Stop that. You're just being paranoid. He's got some vague memory, that's all.

Dane reached up and rubbed the flat of his hand across his forehead, then scrubbed across the bristle of his cheek. From where she sat, Jay could see a small bundle of veins pulsing at his temple. "We're pretty much on a need-to-know basis on this thing, Lieutenant Rawls. I really would appreciate your cooperation here."

Rawls shrugged. "And you'll get it. Just as soon as you fill me in." He leaned back in his chair.

"All right," said Jack Dane. "Fair enough." He looked at the man closely. "We've got ourselves a runaway killer."

"And he's here?"

"It's possible."

Rawls glanced at Jay. "Anybody I'd know about?" he asked. Jay made a face. The ferret-eyed man was putting the pieces together quickly.

"That's not important," Dane answered. "We just want to catch him, and fast."

The police lieutenant smiled. "Then it *is* somebody I'd know about." He glanced across at Jay again, then turned back to Dane. "Who'd you lose, Marshal?"

"Tell him," said Jay, "Or we're never going to get the

phone records and it's going to be too goddamn late."

Dane let out a long breath. "Billy Bones," he said finally.

"Shit," said Rawls, leaning back in his chair again. "I thought he was gone for good."

"He was," Jay said. "But now he's back."

"And he's in Blackwood?" Rawls looked over Jay's shoulder, peering into the squad room on the other side of the glass. Jay saw a little bit of panic rising in his expression and something else as well. Foxes and hounds Rawls liked the chase and he wanted in on it.

"He's probably just passing through if he's here at all," Dane said, holding up one hand. "Don't get your balls in a knot."

"You want my help?"

"Yes."

"Then make nice," said Rawls. "Tell me about the phone records."

"His last victim had the number of the inn in his address book. Billy made sure we knew about it."

"Then let's go check it out," said Rawls.

Dane frowned. "You're coming along?"

"My fifteen minutes of fame." His smile broadened, but his eyes were flat behind the thick lenses of his spectacles. "And I can probably grease the wheels for you a little bit."

"We're trying to keep this very low profile," said Dane. "No rumors, no boasting, no press conferences."

"I said make nice," Rawls warned. "Trust me, I'll keep it all under my hat."

"Appreciate that," said Dane.

Jay smiled.

Liar. You'll be on the phone to Hard Copy *before the sun sets.*

They went out into the squad room and Rawls stopped in front of the young detective's desk. "These nice people are looking for a bail jumper, Donny," he said, lying easily. "I'm going to be helping them out for a little bit." Rawls rapped his knuckles on the desk. "You hold the fort and if you need me I'm on my cell phone."

"Yes sir," said the young detective.

"Good boy." Rawls nodded. They left the squad room and went down the hall to the main doors. "My nephew," explained Rawls. He smiled again and this time there was a gentle twinkle in the small, hard eyes.

"Little bit of small-town nepotism?" Jay grinned.

Rawls nodded, his expression solemn. "Goes with the incest and the hidden stills in the woods."

"Never trust a cop with a sense of humor," said Jack Dane as they pushed out through the doors and out into the sunlight.

"Why's that?" Rawls asked. They went down the steps and headed for one of the big white Crown Victorias.

Jay answered. "Because it means he's too damn smart for his own good."

"Amen." Jack Dane sighed. Rawls just smiled again.

Jay stopped at the bottom of the steps and turned to Dane. "Throw me the keys to your car, would you?"

The U.S. Marshal dug into his pants' pocket and pulled out the keys. Taking them, Jay went to the trunk and took out the video camera she'd picked up in New York. She slammed the trunk and gave the keys back to Dane.

"What's the camera for?" Rawls asked, looking at it suspiciously.

"Nothing, I hope," Jay answered, and left it at that.

They climbed into the big cruiser and headed back toward town. They didn't go far. Just after turning onto Main Street and the downtown core, the Blackwood police lieutenant swung the boatlike car onto an upward-climbing side street, then veered again halfway up the hill. The neighborhood was mixed residential, medium-sized high-rises looming over clapboard Cape Cods and a few sprawling old Victorian mansions.

The Blackwood Inn turned out to be one of the mansions, a massive old monster of turrets and spires and gingerbread trim, lovingly restored and painted a dark gray with darker blue trim. There was a huge front porch complete with Adirondack chairs and a big, old-fashioned glider. The house was surrounded by sloping lawns and a low, dry stone wall.

"Pretty," said Jay as they turned up the circular drive. "Mint juleps on the porch."

Rawls laughed. "Too far north for that. More like straight gin in a toothglass and conversation about too many big-city types moving in and changing things."

"You sound like you're speaking from experience," said Dane.

"Seven years on the Boston P.D. Met my wife-to-be while she was on a field trip with a bunch of school kids, and I moved down here six months later. That was fifteen years ago and I'm still from 'away' as they call it. I could live to be a hundred years old in this town and it still wouldn't change."

They got out of the car and went up onto the cool porch. Rawls rapped on the screen door and less than a minute later a middle-aged woman with gray hair appeared, wearing an apron, her hands covered with flour. Rawls showed his tin, introduced himself and his companions, and the woman let them into the front hall. Her name was Petra Torrance, and along with her husband, she owned the Inn.

"How can I help you?" she asked, wiping the flour off her hands and onto the apron.

"These people would like to ask you a few questions," Rawls replied. "About one of your guests."

"Is there anything wrong?" she asked. She kept on wiping her hands on the apron even though the flour was gone. She looked nervously back and forth at the three people standing in her hall. "Mr. Torrance is out of town for a few days so . . ." Jay smiled bleakly. She probably hadn't done anything without consulting him for years.

"We're just doing some background checks," Dane soothed. "A guest who stayed here."

"Which guest?" the woman asked.

"His name is Hunter Connelly," put in Jay.

"Sure." The woman nodded. "Mr. Connelly's a regular."

"Oh?" Dane asked. "How's that?"

"Blackwood Academy." The woman shrugged. "He went there a lot."

"He went there." Petra Torrance nodded, smiling.

Jay nodded back. "Yes, so you said."

"No, I mean he *went* there." A tense little smile blinked on and off. "When he was a boy. Now he's on the board of directors, I think." She showed the smile again. "He also gave the kitchen staff at the school a lot of recipes." She shook her head. "I saw the menu once. They even had a dessert cart! Imagine that!"

"So he went to board meetings at the academy?" Dane asked.

Mrs. Torrance nodded. "Yes."

"And that's the only reason he came here?" Jay asked. "To Blackwood."

No, no. Mrs. Torrance replied, shaking her head again. "He comes down to visit his niece."

"She goes to the academy?"

The woman nodded. "That's right."

"Shit," Jay murmured, threading another bead onto the string of thought that had been forming in the back of her mind.

"Is there something wrong?" asked Petra Torrance.

"What was his niece's name?" Jay asked.

The woman shook her head, her hands kneading the towel again. "I don't know."

"Shit," Jay said again.

"You still want the phone records?" Rawls asked.

"Not anymore," Dane answered. "I think we found out what we wanted to know."

"Good," Rawls answered. "Because in that case, I think we should be on our way."

"Agreed." Dane nodded.

They thanked Petra Torrance and left her standing at the screen door, her hands still shrouded in the folds of her apron.

"You think your Mr. Bones is going after the girl?" asked Rawls. They were cutting through a series of side streets, moving at speed, but without any lights or siren.

"It's a good possibility," Dane answered.

"He won't have had much time to prepare," said Jay, speaking from the back seat. "He was in New York yesterday afternoon. He made that call from the Railfone late last night."

Rawls looked at her in the rearview mirror. "You're actually talking to this guy?"

"He's a game player." Jay nodded. "We're his audience."

"You think there's a chance we can catch him?" Rawls asked.

"Pray," said Dane.

The cruiser came to a rolling stop at a major intersection. Rawls checked the traffic in both directions, then swung hard left. He reached down under the dash and hit a switch, turning on the rooftop lightbar but leaving the siren quiet.

"This is Blackwood Road," he explained, dropping his foot down on the gas. "Old Highway Five. Three minutes to the school, maybe less."

TWELVE

Billy Bones lay very quietly, watching the two young people through the binoculars he'd borrowed from the inn. He'd followed the girl at a distance and when she stopped at the small, dark pond in the little clearing he'd moved cautiously around through the trees, flanking her until he found a spot less than twenty feet away from where she sat, obviously waiting for someone else to arrive, arms around her bended knees.

The boy, when he arrived, turned out to be very handsome, as blond as Billy was dark and with a deep-chested swimmer's body. He was the girl's age or perhaps a year older at the perfect time in his life, full of youth and passion and strength and purpose. He didn't know it now, but it would never get any better than it was today with the breeze ruffling the leaves of the birches and the elms, the sun breaking into glittering shards on the surface of the spring-fed pool, and the red-haired girl with him.

Billy was charmed with the boy, almost proud of him. There was no rude fumbling or crudeness about him at all, no sense of urgency even though the girl was clearly as nervous as a frightened deer. He sat down with her, close but not touching, and they talked for what seemed to be a long time. As the moments past the boy moved imperceptibly closer, and eventually he was holding her hand.

He kissed her then and after that things moved more quickly, but still the boy was in control, helping her to take off her clothes, not hurrying, laying her back on the grass still in her panties, holding and caressing her until Billy could hear the deepening rasp of her breathing and through the binoculars he could see the arching of her neck as the boy slid his hand under the last thin fabric, the fingers sliding slowly back and forth.

The boy continued to move his hand, not pressing for any more, his mouth moving from her lips to her neck to her breasts to her belly, then back again, never insisting, always cautious, without pressure, making the pleasure easy to accept.

Oh yes, he's been here before, the little devil.

When the ragged breaths turned into soft moaning and it was time, the boy stood up and stripped off his sweatshirt and his sweatpants, standing above her, waiting for her to open her eyes finally, lift her arms to him, and let her knees fall softly open to accept him as he eased himself down on her and into her in a long, slow movement without any hesitation on his part or hers.

Good for you. Good for both of you.

They began to move together and Billy let the binoculars roam the length of them, watching the honey-tanned, hard, and sculpted muscles of the boy's back move in concert, his shoulders and biceps tense, palms flat on the deep green grass to keep his weight off her except at their centers, his buttocks clenching as he moved, teasing with short, swift thrusts, then changing the rhythm again to an endless stroking that brought her hips higher and higher. Soon she began to buck beneath him, her flaming hair swinging back and forth over the grass, and finally her ankles pounding hard against the base of his spine, her fingers grabbing at his hair and her voice crying out through the trees.

Perfect love.

Billy reached into his pocket, touched the cold blade, and wondered if they knew how lucky they were. He eased himself slowly back into the trees, then stood, turned his back on the idyllic scene and trotted away. Almost time.

Perfect death.

Rawls turned off the two-lane highway, slowing as they came down a narrow tree-fringed street with colonial saltbox houses on one side and a small open field on the other. The street ran for a block, intersecting with a much broader avenue, the trees here huge and ancient, their branches spreading out in a green canopy at least sixty feet above the ground.

"That's it," said Rawls, pointing ahead. On the left there was a large, red-brick building set with a white-columned, Jeffersonian portico. In front of the building there was a half-moon common marked with a dark stone obelisk. The police lieutenant pulled the cruiser up in front of the entrance to the brick building and switched off the engine.

"Let me do the talking," said Rawls. He looked across at Dane and then back at Jay. "This place is very much your dress-for-success establishment, and you two don't really fit the bill." Jay looked down at herself. She'd been wearing jeans and her old suede jacket since leaving California, and Jack Dane was still playing urban cowboy. Neither one of them looked like federal agents.

"Whatever," said Dane, climbing out of the car. "I don't have much time here for protocol."

They went up the steps and into the main building. There were administration offices to the left, empty except for a forty-something man with thinning hair, pecking away at a keyboard. The man was wearing jeans and a Motley Crue T-shirt.

"Dress for success?" Jay said quietly. Dane gave her a quick, hard look and Rawls approached the man at the keyboard. He pushed back from his seat in front of the keyboard and stood up, smiling.

"Help you?"

Rawls showed his identification and the man nodded.

"I'm John Kennaway."

"You work here?"

"Yes. English Master."

"There's no administrative staff around?"

"Like a secretary or something?"

"Office manager?"

"No. Everyone's off for the summer, I'm afraid." Kennaway frowned. "Is there something the matter?"

"We're looking for a student."

"None of those here either," said Kennaway. "Who and why?" he added. His tone was cooling and getting a little defensive.

"We're not quite sure who, but she could be in trouble," Jay said.

"There's no one here." Kennaway shrugged. "What kind of trouble?"

Rawls ignored the question. "There are no students here at all?"

Kennaway crossed his arms in front of his chest. "I'm really going to have to ask you what this is all about," he said. "This is private property." He cleared his throat. "You may not be aware of it, Mr. Rawls, but we have an understanding with your department. There is a procedure, and coming here unannounced isn't part of it."

Jay sighed.

Back in the sixties you called cops pigs and spit on guys in uniform, didn't you?

Pompous ass.

"I'm aware this is private property," Rawls answered. "And I know exactly the procedures I should follow. When a Blackwood kid goes out on a toot or winds up in town doing something we both know he or she shouldn't be doing, I call up the headmaster, we have a little chat, and things get ironed out." He paused. "But you're not the headmaster and this isn't some kid staying out past curfew."

Kennaway flushed and Jay couldn't tell if it was anger or embarrassment. "I'm not aware of any . . ."

"I can call the headmaster if you like," Rawls offered. "I'll even call the fucking mayor if that's what you want. But I really don't think he'd like having his time wasted here on a Saturday." Rawls put on one of his unblinking smiles. "What do you think?"

"There are a few students spending the summer here. I'm not quite sure how many."

"Best guess," said Jay.

"Four or five." He shook his head. "I'm working on my doctoral thesis. I don't really pay much attention."

"How do we track them down?" Rawls asked.

"The headmaster would have them listed."

"Where?"

"Probably in his computer."

"Where's that?" asked Rawls.

Kennaway turned his head and nodded toward a door at the far end of the open office. Jay didn't wait; she brushed past Kennaway and headed for the closed door. "You can't go in there!" said the English Master.

"Why don't you call the cops?" said Jack Dane, following her.

Kennaway turned to Rawls. "This is outrageous!"

"I agree."

"What are you going to do about it?"

"Arrest you for obstructing justice unless you get out of the way." Kennaway took two steps back and Rawls went past him and into the headmaster's office. Kennaway stared after him, then sat down and grabbed for a telephone.

Jay was already behind the headmaster's desk in the large office, Jack Dane staring over her shoulder at a computer screen. The office was a trophy room of photographs—Blackwood headmasters and students gone on to greater things. Behind the desk there was a large wooden plaque containing the Blackwood crest and motto.

"You've probably got five minutes before the shit hits the fan," said Rawls, his voice even. "Our academic friend out there is raising hell just as fast as he can."

"It won't take that long," Jay answered, her eyes on the screen and her fingers working the keyboard.

Rawls watched her working. "He doesn't have a password?"

"Sure." Jay nodded without looking up. "That's the easy part." She smiled and tapped the Enter key. "That's it."

"You got it?" Rawls asked, surprised.

"Most people have really dumb passwords. Same for their bank card PIN numbers. Date of birth, that kind of thing. Takes a little while but you can usually get it eventually."

"How'd you figure it out?" he asked.

"I didn't," Jay said. "The programming was set up by somebody here at the school. There's a back door into the data." She shrugged. "Looks like magic but it's pretty easy when you know how."

Billy could get into this as easy as pie, even from the loony bin in Spring Grove.

The screen in front of her cleared, then filled with long strings of file data. Less than a minute later she had what she was looking for. "Here it is. Four names." She read them off. "Alexandra and Michaela Byrne, boarding with Mrs. Isabel Croft; Derek Lancaster, boarding with Dr. and Mrs. Eberling; and Brittany Shields, boarding for the summer with the headmaster himself."

"Rule out the sisters and the boy," said Jack Dane. "It's gotta be this Brittany Shields kid. A girl, alone. Connelly's niece."

Rawls turned on his heel and left the room. Jay and Dane went after him. In the front office, Kennaway the English Master was speaking urgently into the telephone. Rawls grabbed the receiver from the man's hand and hung up. "Brittany Shields. Know her?"

"She's one of my students. Exceptional reading skills . . ."

"Her uncle is a man named Hunter Connelly?" Jay asked.

"I wouldn't know," Kennaway answered.

Rawls took over again. "What does she look like?"

"Plain in a pretty sort of way. Red hair and freckles."

"How old?"

"Seventeen."

"Where does the headmaster live?"

"On the far side of the common."

Rawls gripped the younger man by the elbow and pulled him to his feet. "Show us."

"You can't just come in here and . . ."

Rawls pinched the tender joining of nerve and muscle at the other man's elbow and Kennaway buckled, sweat popping out on his forehead.

"Yes I can," Rawls murmured quietly into the younger man's ear. "Now take us to the headmaster's house."

Rawls led Kennaway out of the office and out into the sunlight, fingers still gripping the teacher's elbow. "This guy kind of grows on you after a while," said Jack Dane as Kennaway pointed to a large white house a couple of hundred feet away. Rawls marched Kennaway across the common, and Jay and the marshal followed.

"I just hope we're not too late," said Jay.

They reached the small front porch of the house and Rawls banged the wrought-iron ball-and-hand knocker several times. There was no answer. He tried the door handle.

"Locked."

"I'll try the side," said Jack Dane, and before Rawls could stop him the marshal was jogging across the lawn. Jay saw the English teacher pale as Dane reached under his jacket and pulled out the big Colt automatic. Rawls didn't look too pleased either. A long moment passed, and then Jay heard footsteps inside the house. There was a heavy thump as a bolt was drawn and then the click of a latch being thrown. As the door opened Jay noticed that Rawls's free hand had slipped under his own jacket, chest high.

"Empty," said Jack Dane, holding open the door and standing aside to let them enter.

It took them another five minutes to check every room completely. There was no sign of anyone. Two beds had been slept in, a queen-size in the master bedroom and a four-poster twin in what looked like the guest room, both on the second floor. The dishwasher in the kitchen was loaded with a few pots and pans.

"Where's the headmaster and his wife?" Rawls asked Kennaway as they all stood in the kitchen.

"They went to Boston for the weekend." The teacher was still rubbing his elbow, scowling at the Blackwood detective. "I'm the only House Master on campus, which means I'm in charge."

"Of what?" Jack Dane grunted.

Rawls spoke again. "Anyone else in the house?"

"They have a housekeeper; she doesn't live in."

"Would the headmaster have taken the girl to Boston?"

"I don't think so. Mr. and Mrs. Littlehall like to get away on their own sometimes." Kennaway cleared his throat. "Romantic weekends, that kind of thing."

"Anywhere else the kid could be?" Jack Dane asked.

Kennaway rubbed his elbow and shook his head. "She could be anywhere." He shrugged his shoulders. "There's a bus into Blackwood."

"She didn't take the bus," said Jay, looking over Kennaway's shoulder. "Look." She pointed to a blackboard on the wall beside the large refrigerator. There was a neatly chalked note on it:

> Brittany—
> Sat. 11:00 A.M. Mrs. Graihle-Baker.
> Don't forget!!

"Who's this Mrs. Graihle-Baker?" Jay asked Kennaway.

"She's a piano teacher."

"Where does she live?"

"The old Zummer house. At least that's where she lived when I took lessons from her. She's been in Blackwood forever."

"Take us there," said Rawls.

Jay looked at her watch. It was 11:15. Absurdly, she found herself thinking about Alice in Wonderland.

She's late, she's late, for a very important date.

Located at the south end of the village, the Zummer house was a small, one-story late 1700s Cape Cod, the shingles on the roof and walls so old they had long since turned the color of tar. The house sat on a small lot that faced an open farmer's field on one side and the Blackwood Academy athletic field on the other. There were flower boxes on the windowsills and a rainbow-colored whirligig on the little front lawn, paddle arms twirling slowly in the light breeze.

Kennaway sat slumped and sulking in the back seat of the cruiser as they stopped in front of the cottage-sized house. Somehow the Motley Crue T-shirt looked absurd on him now, almost an affectation.

"This the place?" Rawls asked.

"Yes." Kennaway nodded.

"Stay in the car," Rawls ordered. The others climbed out, leaving the English teacher behind. Jay took the video camera.

The Blackwood cop stepped up to the front door of the house and knocked firmly, but there was no reply. He put his ear to the door. "I can hear something."

"What?" said Dane.

"Crying, moaning, something like that." Rawls took out his weapon and so did Dane. Jay stood back, feeling ridiculous with a camera in her hand instead of a gun. She pushed back a flood of memories including the ghostly sensation of the Beretta 9mm snug in the small of her back.

You hated it. You hated being a cop.

Liar. You loved it all, even this.

"Try the door," said Dane.

Rawls thumbed the old-fashioned latch. The door opened into the short, narrow hall, and they saw the girl. She was sitting on the blood-slick floor, backed up against a floor-to-ceiling bookcase, eyes wide and staring, seeing nothing, great ropes of blood thick in her hair, more blood on her face and chest and soaked into the fabric of her blue jogging shorts. The floor of the hall was highly polished, pegged oak but most of the planks had vanished under the spreading pool, almost as though someone had taken a bucket and slopped gore toward the front door the house. The girl on the floor was in her socks, the white cotton turned crimson.

"Jesus," whispered Rawls as the rich, sweet, and sour smell filled their nostrils. Jay stared at the girl and saw that the eyes had teared, leaving tracks through the red that stained her cheeks. As Jay watched a bubble of spit formed on the girl's lips and they heard the little moaning sound again.

"She's alive," Jay said. She moved forward but Rawls put an arm up, stopping her.

"Don't touch a thing. I'm calling for an ambulance." He turned and ran back to the cruiser. Jay knelt down beside the girl. She was terrified, in shock, but she didn't seem to be hurt.

This isn't right.

Billy doesn't make mistakes.

He never misses.

The girl spoke then, her voice coming in little jerks and sobs. "He had a knife. . . . He made me watch. . . . Cut her and the blood . . . all the blood . . . her head . . . whispered a name to her when he . . . when he . . . her head . . . he CUT OFF HER HEAD!" The last was a rising scream. Jay yearned to reach out and bring the terrified girl into her arms, tell her it was going to be all right, but she stopped herself and stood up, backing away, turning to Dane.

"She's okay. The blood isn't hers."

"Back door," Dane said urgently. "We may not get another chance."

They went back out and sprinted around to the rear of the house. There was a tiny fenced garden and a one-step brick stoop. The door was hanging open.

"Look," said Jay, pointing. A pair of unlaced Nikes stood on the bricks beside the door, the soles clotted with dark earth. "This is the way she came in."

Jack Dane nodded and lifted his weapon. "Stay behind me." He went up the single brick step and into the house, easing himself forward, a tense muscle twitching along his jawline. Jay went in after him, knowing that Billy was long gone, keeping out of the sweep of his handgun, her eyes quickly scanning the territory in front of them.

It was a kitchen. Not as old as the house, but old. The cabinets above the white enameled sink were thick with paint, and the plain white refrigerator and stove had the plump, aerodynamic shape of a 1940s Ford. A doorway on the right opened onto a narrow, well-stocked pantry, and straight ahead a zinc-topped food preparation table stood below the black, wrought-iron door of a dutch oven set into a massive chimney stack. The floors were pale yellow linoleum. Four plain chairs stood around a maplewood kitchen table in the middle of the room, and a glass bowl of fruit was centered on the table. There was no sign of blood.

There were two exits from the room, a door to the left and an open archway to the right. Dane moved toward the archway and Jay followed. Neither of them spoke. They stepped into the living room of the little house. Out in the hallway they could hear the girl moaning softly. "A name. He whispered a name. Jay, he whispered, Jay."

A black baby grand facing them under the far window took up a third of the little room. There was a braided rag rug on the wide-planked floor, three cozy-looking upholstered chairs arranged around an open-hearth fireplace that shared the chimney stack in the kitchen, and more bookshelves. There was a painting over the fireplace mantle and half a dozen framed photographs on the mantle itself. Outside Jay could hear Rawls yelling something. She lifted the camera and began taping.

"Christ," Dane muttered, staring across the room. He lowered his weapon and Jay followed his look with the camera. The old woman's body filled the viewfinder. She was lying on her stomach beside the piano, just out of sight of the front door. The shapeless dress she wore had once been a pale yellow like the linoleum in the kitchen, but now it was dark with blood. The fabric had pulled up almost to her waist, revealing rolled down nylons and heavy, blue-veined thighs. Her arms were at her side, palms up. She'd been wearing thin slippers but one of them was missing. Jay zoomed in.

"Where's her head?" she whispered, horrified, dropping the camera from her eye. Above the scalloped neck of the dress there was only a stump of ragged open flesh, source of the bloody river that was flowing toward the front door. Dane followed a dripping trail over to the window then turned and looked down at the piano.

"Here." Dane pointed with his gun hand. Jay crossed to him. The head sat in the center of the keyboard, tilted back slightly on the knobbed white knuckle of a spinal vertebra. The long, iron-gray hair of Mrs. Graihle-Baker's usually tidy bun spread out around her face and over the keyboard like a nun's cowl. Like Connelly, bright butterflies were pinned across her eyes like a mask at a fancy dress ball. All the blood had drained away from her face and the flesh was as pale and translucent as candle wax. Brain matter oozed out over the keys and dripped down onto the floor. In the distance Jay could hear the sound of approaching sirens. Hands shaking, she lifted the camera again and began to shoot the scene before her.

The girl saw him whisper into her ear. She heard my name. The last thing the old woman heard was Billy whispering my name.

You bastard, you made her watch.

And then she understood.

It was never the girl. It was the piano teacher. The old lady was the target.

Brittany, still in deep shock, had been whisked off to Franklin Hospital and was under observation. Mrs. Graihle-Baker, her head in a separate bag, had been initially taken to the same hospital, but her remains had later been shipped off to the Chief Medical Examiner's office on Albany Street in Boston.

Overwhelmed by the situation, Rawls had almost immediately asked for help from the State Police, and they in turn had called in the Medical Examiner's Mobile Forensics Laboratory. By late afternoon the little cottage was swarming with police and technicians, and it seemed as though Jay Fletcher and Jack Dane had been forgotten, at least for the moment. At the first opportunity they'd hitched a ride back to Blackwood police headquarters with one of the local cops, retrieved the marshal's cruiser, and headed back to the outsized motel not far from the interstate. Jay set up her laptop and camera in one room, while Jack Dane started making calls in the other. An hour later Dane called room service for coffee and joined Jay in her room.

"Karlson wants us out of here as fast as possible," the marshal said, dropping into a tub chair across from Jay. Her equipment was spread out on the coffee table between them.

Jay lit a cigarette, took a slurp of coffee, and sagged back against the couch.

"Rawls giving him heat?"

"Not yet, but Karlson's expecting it. The whole thing is blowing up in our faces. Connelly was pretty much of a big wheel, and it turns out the kid is even more important. Vanderbilt style. The girl wasn't born with a silver spoon in her mouth, it was twenty-four carat gold."

"In other words, there's going to be media."

"CNN's on the way and all the tabloid shows smell blood already. By tomorrow morning this place is going to be a zoo."

"You think someone might recognize me?"

"I don't think we should stick around to find out. You said Rawls may have recognized you, even with the different hair and everything. Somebody else might do the same."

"So what do we do, drive aimlessly around waiting for Billy to send us a message?"

"No luck with the tape you shot?"

"Not really."

"From the looks of it, we didn't miss Billy by very much. He wouldn't have had a lot of time to set up anything very elaborate."

"That's what I thought." Jay shrugged. "But unless I've gone blind there isn't much of anything to see except for the head on the piano and the butterflies."

"Let me give it a shot," Dane answered. He came around the table and sat down beside Jay. The camera was still linked to the laptop. The screen was divided into four separate windows, each window showing a different still shot of the front room of the Zummer house. "How does this thing work?" the marshal asked.

"Tape is downloaded into the hard drive and stored digitally. You can access it as close to real-time video or you can look at it frame by frame, like a photograph. You can use the touchpad to zoom in on any image as close as you want. Eventually, the pixels break down but it's pretty good really." She demonstrated, coming close in on a shot of the piano

keyboard taken after the head had been bagged and removed.
She brought it up tight and the name "Steinway & Sons"
could be read clearly. She zoomed out again.

"Did you do all the rooms?" Dane asked.

Jay nodded. "I managed to get 360s of everything. One
bedroom, the parlor, living room, kitchen, and bathroom. Not
much to see. Not anything obvious anyway."

"Like you said, he didn't have much time," Dane agreed.
"Start with the kitchen and run through the rooms for me,
one by one." The marshal watched silently as the images
clicked by until they reached a shot of the old lady's bedroom.
"Stop," he said. "Zoom in on the wall there."

"What do you see?" asked Jay. She tapped the keypad until
the section of wall he wanted filled the screen. There was a
painting on the wall. A heavily varnished portrait of a figure
in a frock coat seated at a table, smoking a pipe. He was
wearing some kind of outlandish military uniform topped by
a bizarre, bright red Turkish fez.

"A Zouave," Dane commented.

"A what?"

"A Zouave. I think the regiment was from New York.
Fought in the Civil War."

"You think that's a clue?"

Dane shrugged. "It seems like a funny kind of painting for
an old lady to hang in her bedroom, that's all."

"Maybe it's an ancestor," Jay suggested.

"That's the point, you don't hang paintings of your ancestors in the bedroom, do you?"

"I don't have any," Jay answered. "Not that anybody
painted, anyway."

"But if you did?"

"I'd hang them over the mantelpiece," said Jay softly, seeing where Dane was heading. She clicked rapidly through the
images until she reached the panorama of the living room.
She let the images run as video until the shot moved across
the mantle; then she changed to single frames, clicking them
past one by one until she had a wide shot of the fireplace,
the mantle, and the painting above it. She zoomed in.

"Seven silver framed pictures on the mantle itself," said Dane, counting. "A graduation shot, a bunch of kids, and one newborn in a pink blanket."

Jay zoomed in on the picture over the mantle. "Look."

"It's a drawing." Dane shrugged, peering down at the image. "Charcoal maybe. The courtyard of a house."

"Forget the picture," Jay instructed. "Look outside the frame." Zoomed in that closely, the image was perfectly clear. There was a six- or seven-inch border of lighter brick around the drawing. Something larger had been hanging there in the not too distant past.

"He moved it," said Dane. "He switched the painting of the Zouave with the drawing." The marshal frowned. "Why the hell would he want to do that?"

"So we'd notice," Jay answered.

"What kind of stupid clue is a painting of a Civil War soldier?"

"I don't think that's the one we're supposed to worry about," Jay answered. "He killed that woman in the living room, caught her running to the door and pulled her hair back and slit her throat." She stared down at the screen. "That's his killing zone, that's the place that's important to him."

"So what's important about the drawing?"

Jay zoomed in even more tightly. The drawing showed an arched opening with a stone-paved courtyard beyond, the left side containing a two-story galleria and at the far end, a pair of heavy double doors topped by a fan-shaped window. "It's signed," said Jay. She pushed the contrast. "G. F. Castleden, 1928." She zoomed a little closer. "And there's an inscription. Looks like it was done in pencil. It's faded a lot."

"Can you get in tighter?"

"Maybe." Jay worked the touchpad. The inscription came into focus and Jay read it out loud. "Old Graihle House, 621 Royal Street, New Orleans." Jay leaned back against the couch. "That's what he wanted us to see."

"You sound pretty sure of yourself."

Jay sighed. "Are you really that obtuse or are you just trying to piss me off?"

"I'm trying to get you to defend your statement," said Dane. "We're dealing with a fucking psycho here. Maybe he moved the pictures to screw us up."

"Why would he want to do that?"

"Why does he go around cutting the heads off music teachers?" He shook his head. "I still don't get it. What does this have to do with Connelly or the girl?"

"Nothing. Not directly. I think it's called six degrees of separation."

"What the hell is that?"

"The theory is, there are only six degrees of separation between you and everyone else in the world. Beads on a string. Let's say the Bannerman woman in D.C. turns out to be Connelly's sister, the girl is their niece. For Billy, that's the end of that line, so he deviates slightly. The girl and the piano teacher are connected by happenstance."

"Deviates is right." Dane snorted. "But what exactly is he trying to do?"

"He's telling us where he's going."

Dane frowned uneasily. "It's too easy. Not devious enough. There's no . . . mystery to it."

"This isn't an Agatha Christie whodunit," Jay answered. "This is like a shiny lure on the end of a fishing line. It has to be obvious or it doesn't catch the fish."

"Which makes us the guppies?"

"Something like that." Jay nodded. She glanced at her watch. "Shit. Billy's probably coming online again."

She plugged the laptop into the phone line and booted up. Once again she found Billy in the chatroom. Dane stood behind her, reading over her shoulder.

—**I've been waiting.**
—I've been busy.
—**The old lady hit high C on the way out.**
—Why not Brittany as well? Getting sentimental in your old age, Billy?

"Jesus! What are you trying to do?" said Dane angrily, standing behind her. "Get him pissed off?"

"If he gets pissed off maybe he'll make a mistake."

"Or start killing faster."

—I left her for you as a gift.

Jay sat back in her chair, staring at the screen. "Gifting" was a common trait in psychotics, like Van Gogh's ear sliced off as an offering for the woman he loved. But serial killers were totem takers, not gift givers. Billy was playing games again. Or maybe trying to believe that he was something other than just a simple killer.

Get his goat. Hit him where it hurts.
Ego bust him.
She sat forward and worked the keyboard.

—The gift wasn't for me, was it?

"What the hell are you talking about?" Dane said. Jay ignored him.

—What do you mean?
—Ricky.

"Stiles?" said Dane. "The guy you whacked in Vegas?"

—What about him?
—You left Brittany alive as a gift for Ricky. A memorial. A love offering.
· · · · · · ·
—It's because the two of you never actually met, isn't it? Because of the fantasies you had.
—I make my fantasies come true. I live them.
—Not the fantasies you had about Ricky.

She was winging it now, playing to his responses, wondering where it was leading her, and Billy.

—What fantasies?
—The two of you. Together. Killing. Teacher and student.

—We were equals.

—Not even close, Billy boy.

—**You should have seen the fear in the old woman's eyes when I cut her. When I whispered your name.**

—Ricky was a genius. An artist. You're nothing but a wannabee.

—**Then why can't you catch me?**

—I did once, I'll do it again. I'll take you down just like I took down Ricky.

—**Fuck you, bitch.**

—In your dreams, Billy boy.

. . . .

"He's gone." Jay sat back in her chair again and let out a long, ragged breath.

"Maybe you struck a nerve," Dane said quietly.

"Let's just hope it was the right one."

THIRTEEN

They managed to slip away from Rawls and the growing investigation of the old woman's murder, completely avoiding the media blitz that had begun to swirl around Brittany Shields. Reaching Boston late in the afternoon, they caught the first flight out, then spent half the night sleeping in airport lounges as they hopscotched their way across the continent and down to New Orleans. They arrived just after dawn, staggered off the plane, then followed the signs to the taxi stands on the lower level and headed for the exit.

Stepping through the automatic doors and out of the air-conditioned airport, they felt the heat like something alive and breathing: a great, fat, smothering blanket wrapped sopping wet and thick around them, wanting to choke them or drown them, but just not able to make up its mind and so was intent on doing both at once. This was swamp heat, yellow fever heat, mosquito heat, the kind of terrible hot that suffocated old men and women in their sleep and killed dogs in the back seats of locked cars.

"Jesus," groaned Jack Dane, peering out at the steaming curtain of rain. "It's like the goddamned Amazon!"

Jay nodded, looked left and right, then spotted the waiting shuttle bus for the Hilton. She and Dane stitched their way along the sidewalk through the crowds waiting under the canopy and climbed aboard, sighing gratefully as the cold, blasting air roared over them.

Dane slumped into the window seat. "Sorry I'm not a better flier."

"You're a great flier." Jay grinned, sitting down beside

him. "You held the plane up all the way down here, all by yourself. Impressive."

"It doesn't bother you?" he asked.

"Not in the slightest." Jay shrugged. "I just take it for granted."

"Amazing."

"They say people who can't fly are afraid to give up control."

"Is this going to be one of those New Age sensitivity lectures?"

Jay held her hand up, palm out. "An idle comment."

"Getting into an airplane and flying all over the world at forty thousand feet isn't natural," said Dane. "The physics is all wrong and besides, they say that people with heart conditions are at risk from breathing all that recycled air—oxygen starvation."

"You have a heart condition?"

"Not that I know of."

Jay laughed. "Why is it that people who are afraid to fly know so much about airplanes and what's wrong with them?"

"Same reason cops drive Crown Vics," he answered.

"You really are a very stubborn person, aren't you, Dane?"

"Back at you," muttered the marshal. He yawned widely. "Now what?"

"Suite at the Airport Hilton and a rental car," said Jay. She adjusted her watch to local time. "We'll go take a look at this address later. Dinnertime maybe."

"What about you?"

"I'll figure out something to do." She patted the laptop case slung over her shoulder. "Maybe surf the Net and see if Billy's left us any more clues."

"No going off on your own?" Half a question, half an order.

Jay smiled and shook her head. "Don't worry," she lied. This was the opportunity she'd been waiting for since being dragged into the whole sorry mess. By the time the shuttle reached the hotel Dane was snoring noisily.

The Airport Hilton was just like every other airport hotel

Jay had ever stayed in; the only thing that varied was the
color of the walls—in this case pale gold, the furniture in the
lobby cream-colored. The suite was a slight variation, with
beige walls instead of gold. Dane didn't even make it under
the covers. He cracked a miniature Jack Daniels from the
minibar and fell asleep with the glass on the bedside table
and a cigarette smoldering in the ashtray. Jay picked up the
cigarette, left the drink where it was, then tiptoed out of the
room, flipping off the lights and closing the door. She spent
five minutes in the bathroom repairing as much of the overnight damage as she could, then let herself out of the suite.

She thought about renting a car, but a short conversation
with the concierge convinced her otherwise; too little parking,
especially where she was going, and too much chance of a
carjacking if she got lost and found herself somewhere wrong.
According to the concierge, there were a lot more wrong
places nowadays in New Orleans than there were right ones;
cocaine was king in the Big Easy now, not crayfish.

The doorman whistled up a White Line cab, handed her a
complimentary Hilton umbrella, and a few minutes later Jay
was swishing down the Airline Highway, wind and rushing
curtains of rain sweeping over everything, pushed up from
the Gulf of Mexico on her right. She sat back in the rear seat
and closed her eyes, glad that the driver was silent and that
his air conditioning worked.

She listened to the sound of her heart and tried to slow the
too-fast hammer in her chest. It was too much like being
aboard a ship just casting off or a jet leaping from the ground;
she had no idea where it was all taking her.

The worst of it was her sure knowledge that she was right
about Billy Bones. For Karlson and Dane, this was business
as usual with a bigger than average public relations downside
if they blew it. To Karlson and Jack Dane, William Paris
Bonisteel was just another fugitive, and to the Bureau Billy
was nothing but one more serial killer out to make his reputation like a wild west gunfighter.

To the FBI and most other law enforcement agencies, not
to mention a pantheon of true-crime writers and a horde of

media "experts," there were two basic subgroups to the Serial
Species: the Sex Killers who used murder as an aphrodisiac,
like Dahmer and Gacy, and the Truly Loonies like Berkowitz,
the Son of Sam. There were some who said there was a third
group, the Predators, which included soulless horrors like Ted
Bundy and Ricky Stiles, her final kill. But Jay knew better,
she knew there was another kind of killer out there, perhaps
the most dangerous of all.

Billy's kind.

Jay stared out the streaked window and watched the rain
falling as the gray-brown city climbed up around her. She
shivered. It felt as though she was riding down into a mouth
of rotting teeth. She knew it was her imagination, but she
thought she could smell the swamps and bayous all around
her, feel the quick snake-slither of Billy's presence not too
far away. And that was what Jack Dane and the others didn't
understand. They had no sense of the man they were after,
no feel for the terrible game they played with him.

Billy was no sexual psychopath, no morbid masturbator.
Neither did he kill for some mad religious urge, nor because
his predatory nature demanded it, reaching murderously up
from some black hole of an unconscious.

After she had killed the murderer Ricky Stiles, Jay had
spent a little more than half an hour alone in the computer
freak's dark Las Vegas lair. That was where she'd had her
first meeting with Billy Bones, the Net-name Stiles himself
had given his young friend and colleague. Billy's file on
Ricky's computer had been prefaced with a quote of his own
choosing from Herman Melville's classic novel *Billy Budd*,
and it was still burned into her memory, a perfect description
of the man she and Jack Dane were now facing:

His evil nature was not engendered by vicious training or
corrupting books or licentious living, but was born within
him and innate. Toward the accomplishment of an aim,
which in wantonness would seem to partake of the insane,
he will direct a cool judgment, sagacious and sound. These
men are madmen, and of the most dangerous sort.

Some killed for sex, some killed to still their demons, and some killed like predatory throwbacks to a distant, savage age, but Billy killed for none of those reasons. Billy killed for sport. Like a deer hunter in the forest, he loved the choosing of his victim, the stalking, at one with the universe around him, and finally the moment of truth as blood flowed, breath faltered, eyes dimmed, and the heart stilled at last. Standing above his dead prize Billy was the great white hunter, the Beatles' Bungalow Bill (what did you kill?), the Ubermensch, superior man, Darwin's theory born out, Homo sapiens fully realized.

No wonder he became an anthropologist.

The museum would have been a hunter's paradise, right down to the tigers that Teddy Roosevelt had shot. Elephant-foot umbrella stands, whales hung on hooks above the crowds, and dinosaurs. A million butterflies pinned to cards. Surrounded by trophies. Surrounded by death at every turn. Everything Billy had ever dreamed of.

Until I ruined everything.

No wonder he hates me.

Looking out through the rain-streaked window, she found herself thinking about George Gaddis, the Star Trek freak whom the Albuquerque cops had named Hand Job for the particular mutilation he employed on his victims. It was the first time anyone had died at her hands, the boundary crossed, the turn taken, setting her irrevocably on her path.

Irrevocable.

Such a frightening, final word.

No going back.

Like the *Star Trek* episode where the two men, their skin in harlequin black and white, doomed by each one's prejudices against the other, fought through the ages, endlessly.

Me and Billy, till death do us part.

The taxi cruised through the rain across the Ponchartrain Expressway overpass and on the other side dropped down into the old city along Tulane Avenue, finally reaching Royal Street at the edge of the French Quarter. With the rain there wasn't much action on the narrow street, but even through the streaked and foggy window Jay could see small hints of movement behind high, wrought-iron gates, and higher on the gallery balconies of the crowded old buildings. The steaming rain was everywhere, flattening shadows to nothing. Thin, cloud-sifted light turned the air to beaten brass and sulfur, picking up even the slightest hint of color and turning it shockingly bright.

Just a little look, then I go back to the hotel.

Nothing stupid.

Jay's taxi stopped and she stared out through the glass. The drawing in the old lady's living room was out of date. The gateway was still there and even with the rain she could see into the courtyard beyond, but at the far end of the court the fan of glass had been replaced by a glowing neon sign, red and green and yellow advertising something called Abita Turbo Dog, whatever that was. Another sign declared this was Ti-Jean's Place.

"You sure this is it?" Jay asked the driver. He didn't even turn around in his seat to look at her, just leaned forward and tapped a button on the meter, freezing the tab.

"Eighteen dollars."

"You're sure this is it?"

The driver finally turned. He had a narrow face that might have been Irish or French or both, and sunken cheeks over bad dentures. His skin was pocked and his hair was too black to be real. He let out a sigh that filled the cool air between them with garlic and tobacco. "You say you want six hundred twenty-one Royal, that's what I give you." He nodded toward the archway across the street. "621 Royal."

"It looks like a bar, not a house."

"You got that right, madame. Make you anything you wan', get you anything you wan', even do anything you wan', for sure." Jay nodded and gave the man a twenty and a five and didn't ask for change. She popped the door and got her finger ready on the button of the umbrella.

"Thanks for the ride," Jay said and opened the door. The man's voice stopped her and she turned, half in and half out of the car.

"Ti-Jean's not so hot a place for a woman all alone. Not for tourist ladies if you know what I'm saying."

"I thought this was the French Quarter. Tourist central."

"Not this time of year, madame, not with all this rain, dis heat. Only people come here this time are crazy, yes sir."

"I can take care of myself."

"Sure you can, uh-huh, but I can wait, just in case you change your mind."

"No thanks."

"Up to you, but me, I don't think I'd do her on my own if I was you, no sir."

"I'll be all right."

"Sure you will, madame." He coughed out a short laugh. "An N'Orleans is all modern now you know, we got 911 just like everywhere else, okay?"

"Okay."

"One more thing."

"Yes?"

The taxi driver showed off his gray teeth. "Everyone in the Quarter bound to lie to you at least one time and mostly all the time, and that's a true thing, believe it."

"Thanks for the advice." Jay nodded stepped out of the car, got the umbrella up as fast as she could, then slammed the door. The driver put the car in drive and headed away down Royale Street until its taillights vanished in the foggy dripping rain. Jay crossed the street, stepped over the swirling trash-water in the gutter, and stood on the sidewalk, staring into the misted window of a narrow store called the Old Praline and Novelty Shop.

The shop was dark and there was a hand-printed sign on the inside of the glass door that said "Fermé." Through the gates and down the courtyard the Abita sign flashed on and off in no sequence she could see, like something out of an old *Twilight Zone* or a Stephen King story where it turns out the sign is sending out a secret message in Morse code to warn off strangers.

With the rain tapping hard on the umbrella, Jay pushed open the iron gate and went into the courtyard, the hidden cobbled square filled with the perfume of magnolia and hibiscus, rich with a sweet-rot scent like old honey. She crossed the court and looking up she saw the windows above her on the gallery, shuttered and dark, the snake-twisted old iron of the decorative railings thick with dripping vine. Once this had been home to the dead piano teacher's ancestors and somehow Jay knew that they wouldn't have been surprised at the way of her death. Murder was no stranger here.

You're crossing the line now, kiddo. No backup, no nothing. Bad procedure.

Breaking all the rules.

What I do best.

She reached the doors, pushed the umbrella closed, and ducked into Ti-Jean's Place. It took a few seconds for her eyes to adjust to the light and then she saw that there were only a dozen or so people in the large, long room. Some of them were eating from large bowls at small tables set against one of the long walls while the rest were seated at the bar across from the tables. Big wooden fans ticked lazily overhead, and at the far end of the place Jay could see a small stage and speakers. No one was playing now, but there was music, the volume set just high enough to hear. Marianne Faithfull's grained and broken voice backed by thin, distressing music.

The man behind the bar was a black version of the cab driver, thin as a nail, the faint stubble on his chin and cheeks rough gray against his dark skin. There was an embroidered name on the pocket of his pale green bowling shirt: Eli. He watched her come to the bar and he wasn't happy having her there. No one moved or spoke or looked at her, but walking over to the bar Jay found herself wishing that she had a gun. The cab driver had given her sound advice; this was no safe, Sunday-evening Disney dream of Cajun-town, this was just straight-out big-time bad with a capital B.

B for Billy. Just his kind of place. Retired junkie's voice on the stereo and a bartender who looks like he swats flies with his bare hands.

"You want something or you just going to stand there?" the bartender said.

Jay sat down. "Turbo Dog," she answered quickly, hoping she wouldn't regret the order. It turned out to be a tall-necked local beer, dark with a back taste like butterscotch and chocolate. The bottle was sweating. Ti-Jean's wasn't air conditioned except for the twitching fans above Jay's head.

She stared at the bartender and he stared back. Jay took another sip of her beer and pretended she did have her gun hard in its holster at the base of her spine, pretended that she was still a cop and still had a cop's power and invulnerability. Show a badge right now and the place would empty out in a second, leaving her and the badass bartender to go at it, cold and mean. She'd bark, he'd cringe and she'd find out what she needed to know. Something must have changed in her eyes because the bartender suddenly looked a little uneasy and moved away, fiddling with something under the bar a few feet away.

Okay, let's put this together.

The basic pattern on Billy's game board was emerging. She had no confirmation yet, but she was willing to bet that there would be some connection between the Bannermans in Washington and Hunter Connelly in New York, something Billy had picked up on in the Watergate. Connelly was Brittany Shields's uncle and she in turn was Mrs. Graihle-Baker's piano student. From the little house in Blackwood, the picture above the mantelpiece had taken them here.

But Billy was working on the fly. He knew he didn't have much time in the old lady's house and the picture offered a simple solution, complete with an address. Maybe he assumed that 621 Royal Street was still a private residence, or maybe he didn't care. He'd push a square peg into a round hole if need be, which meant that one way or the other, Ti-Jean's Place was part of the game. But what part.

Only way to find out is ask Mr. Eli Badass here.

"Nice place," she said. There was no art on the walls and nothing but bottles and glasses behind the bar. Mr. Badass looked up from whatever it was he was doing under the bar and then shifted even farther along.

"Ti-Jean around anywhere?" Jay asked, casting her line into the water. Mr. Badass looked up again and stared.

"Ti-Jean dead," he said. Ten feet down the bar on Jay's side of it a man in a wrinkled seersucker suit and thin carroty hair broke wind noisily and sipped from a shot glass.

"I'm sorry to hear that," Jay said, wondering if the bartender or anyone else would get the joke.

"Ti-Jean dead about fifteen year now."

"He was a friend of yours?"

"Ti-Jean was a dog," said Mr. Badass. "Toll Dog, that's what someone call him. You know what a Toll Dog is?"

"No," Jay said, shaking her head. She took another hit of the sweet dark beer.

"Me neither," said Mr. Badass. "Never found out." He shrugged. "Had that dog all of three days, then he hit by a truck and put his insides all over the street."

"But you named the bar after him."

"Couldn't think of nothing else." He shrugged again, then gave Jay a long look, scratching the gray stubble on his chin. He moved back in her direction. The carrot-headed man broke wind again and added a long sigh of satisfaction. "Pig," said Mr. Badass quietly. Marianne had switched to a long, monotone dirge documenting the life and death of a married couple.

"You a little bird?" Mr. Badass said. He took the five dollar bill from in front of her bottle of beer and offered no change. He swabbed the spot where the money had been with a damp rag.

"Why?" Jay asked, and felt her heart beating harder again, smelling Billy here, not so long ago, maybe even sitting on this same stool.

"If you a bird, what kind of bird you are?"

"I'm a Jay," she said slowly and Mr. Badass gave her what had to be his secret smile, the expression so rare the stiff muscles of his face weren't quite sure how to handle it.

"That's the one." He nodded.

"Why'd you ask?"

"Man paid me a hundred dollars so I would."

"What did he look like?"

"Paid me another hundred not to tell you." The secret smile again. One of the lies the taxi driver had mentioned. Billy wouldn't have wasted his money and he was like a chameleon anyway; by now he would have changed and changed again.

"When was he here?" Jay asked. Mr. Badass seemed disappointed that she hadn't risen to his bait about Billy's description. He shrugged and wiped the bar.

"Not so long ago. Just after opening. Six A.M. around."

Jay nodded to herself. He'd caught a red-eye and come here straight from the airport, quick to check the location out for a new victim, knowing she and Jack Dane wouldn't be far behind. She checked her watch. Just after one; only seven hours lead time. "He say anything else?"

"Only that you'd be coming. Maybe you and someone else. A man."

"He leave a message?"

"Uh-huh."

"What message?"

"Cost a hundred."

"Used to be twenty to buy bar bullshit."

"Inflation, *cher,* and this no bar bullshit, this a fact you need to know."

Jay pulled out her wallet and counted out four twenties and two tens. It left her just enough cash to get back to the hotel. She laid the money on the table but kept her hand covering it.

"What's the fact I need to know?"

Mr. Badass nodded toward the back of the room. Jay could see the little stage, an exit sign, and a pay phone on the wall next to the bathroom door. "He going to call you here tonight at midnight, but he's only going to let it ring twice so you'd better be standing right there, that's what he said."

Jay kept her hand on the money. "Anything else?"

Mr. Badass looked down at her hand over the money then back into her eyes. The message was pretty clear: anything he told her was a gift because he could just as easily take the money from her and throw her out into the rain, or worse. No Disney dream for sure.

Jay took her hand off the money and wrapped it around the sweating bottle. Mr. Badass swept the cash under his once-white apron and came up with a slip of folded paper. He put it down on the bar and Jay picked it up, unfolding it:

122910

"He tell you what it means?"

"He tell me nothing," Mr. Badass answered. "And I don't ask."

He looked as though he was going to say something else, but his small mouth closed up and his face blanked.

"You look . . . upset," Jay said, trying to find the right word for the man's suddenly changed demeanor. Marianne Faithfull was gone now, leaving nothing but the thump-and-rattle rhythm of the rain outside. The carrot-haired man tapped the bar with a quarter a few times and Mr. Badass took him another drink. After a minute he came back to Jay.

"I don't like him."

"The man who gave you the hundred?"

The bartender nodded. "He said to call him Billy but I couldn't do that. Kept calling him sir." He plucked at the pocket of his shirt. "He called me Eli and laughed like it was some kind of joke." He shook his head. I didn't like him at all."

"Why?"

"Ti-Jean's not a place for everybody." Mr. Badass spread his arms. "I got nothing except what these people want. My people. People who stay in the Quarter their whole lives, never go into the big world out there."

"I understand."

"Woman come here alone, she's a woman sell herself, you know?"

"Yes." Jay nodded.

"But he different," said the bartender, shaking his head.

"How?"

Mr. Badass flipped his cloth over his shoulder and leaned back against the counter behind him, his thin arms crossed over the chest of his apron. The veins and tendons on his arms were like old tarred rope. "I tell you a little story, *cher*, so maybe you know what I mean."

"All right."

"Long time ago, right here on Royal, there was a jeweler called Tabouis, and he had a daughter called Euphrasine."

"Pretty name," said Jay.

The bartender nodded. "Pretty girl too, from what I hear people who knew her say. Went to school with the Ursiline Sisters over to Chartres Street. Married too young, fifteen I think, something arrange by her daddy and she had no love for the man at all, no." The bartender paused and for a moment Jay thought his story was over, but it wasn't and he spoke again, his voice a little slower now and a little colder.

"She get bored with her husband real quick, this girl Euphrasine, and she decides she want excitement more. One night she sneak from the house and go with her friends out to Bayou St. John where she was going to *fait voudou*, you understand what I'm saying, *cher*?"

"I think I do." Jay nodded. A young girl in a bad marriage doing something to change her life even if the something was frightening and maybe dangerous. But normal really, just as it had been for Jay and every other girl she knew growing up in Tomahawk, Wisconsin. Saturday night backroad drag racing doing a hundred miles an hour in somebody's too-fast car and drinking from a paper-bag bottle. Jay nodded again and wondered where Badass was going with his story.

"So off she go to Bayou St. John wit her white friends and what they see? They see some woman in the clearing by the swamp and she wearing a *tignon* and callin' the rhythm for about twenty dancing black men, sweat on their naked bodies like oil, moanin' and just carrying on and then . . ." The bartender stretched it out.

"What?"

"Well, the story go she saw *Voudou, le Gran' Zombi* himself, old Doctor John and the woman in the middle was the Widow Paris too, but really, yes it was a man name Prince Basile. She never saw no man like that before, Euphrasine. Quadroon black like *café au lait* to her pure white, not so tall but with perfect muscles, legs like a dancer, wearing nothing but a red strip across himself and on one ankle a ring of little bells that made a little bit music when he walked. All her friends said he looked like the devil himself and they ran off home and maybe they were right, because Prince Basile took that little girl back into the bayou and that was the last anyone ever saw of her and people thought Prince Basile had done her back there in the swamp and disappeared himself." The bartender paused and rubbed his chin, and for the first time Jay had an idea of just how really old the man was—seventy-five, maybe even more.

"There was an old hag showed up here on Royal, came in here once, for sure, and said that she was Euphrasine, and told about Prince Basile and what he could do with a woman, *voudou* things turn her into a snake, make her kill for a man, but no one believed her, really, maybe just an old whore with a filthy mouth, and she went away again."

He shook his head, remembering. "Back there on Bayou St. John they say you can take a pirogue out into the swamp and if you listen hard you can still hear those little bells, and know Prince Basile is coming and if you a pretty girl that means get out *à tout pied, cher*, because he coming for you, that's for true, yes sir."

He pushed himself away from the back counter and took the rag down from his shoulder, twisting it in his hands. He took a step toward Jay and looked at her hard. "When your friend Billy come in here all dark and too pretty and he smile to light up a dark night, I swear I hear those little bells, me hear them tinkling somewhere, like a warning."

"You think this man is Prince Basile come back to life?" said Jay.

Jesus! You sound like you believe it could be true!

"No, *cher*," the bartender said soft enough so that only she could hear. "I think Prince Basile he never died at all. I think I saw him here this morning, six A.M."

FOURTEEN

"You lied to me," said Jack Dane, pacing back and forth across the living room of the suite at the Hilton. He'd only been awake for twenty minutes and he still had a sleeper's slack-faced look. Jay sat on the couch smoking and drinking room-service coffee, watching him pace.

"I didn't lie. I said I'd find something to do and I did." She took a sip of coffee and glanced out the window. The rain was still coming down steadily. According to the weather channel, there was a chance there'd be a hurricane. "We've been through this before, Jack. You're not my baby-sitter and you're not my boss, either. I was brought in on this to help and that's what I'm trying to do."

"You could have been killed. It could have been a trap for Christ's sake!" He ran a hand through his hair, still pacing. He stopped in front of the big picture window and looked out. "Goddamn it! You should have known better than to go in to a place like that without backup! You were a cop!"

He's right. I should have known better.

Apologize now and he'll never let you forget it.

"I wanted to check the place out, that's all." Jay stubbed out her cigarette. "If it had looked dangerous I wouldn't have gone in."

Dane stared at her, his jaw set. "I thought you were a wild card right from the start. I told Karlson you were trouble." He paused. "Do anything like that again, anything even *close* to that, and I'll take you back to Arlington with cuffs on."

You would too, wouldn't you?

"We're wasting time with all of this." She ticked her finger against the coffeepot standing on the low table in front of the couch. "Sit down and have some coffee."

The marshal turned, scowled, then moved away from the window and sat down across from her. He poured coffee, lit a cigarette for himself, then leaned back in the upholstered tub chair, groaning. "I feel like shit on a stick."

"I'm not going to comment on that," said Jay. "How about giving Billy's secret message a try?"

"I hate that kind of thing," Dane answered. He leaned forward, picked up the scrap of paper she'd brought back from Ti-Jean's Place, and glared at the numbers as though trying to make them coherent through strength of will alone. "Six digits. Means it's not a telephone number."

"Unless he left off the first number or the last," Jay suggested. "Just to make us dial up all the combinations."

"Does that sound like something he'd do?" Dane asked.

Jay thought for a moment and shook her head. "No. He'd be more direct."

"Make us think, in other words. Actually work for it."

Jay nodded. "Something like that."

Dane got to his feet, went to the veneered desk on the other side of the room, and pulled out a fake leather folder full of hotel material. He slipped out several sheets of writing paper, took the ball-point out of its holder, and came back to the coffee table. He wrote out the numbers, large, stroking through them.

"Maybe it's a date?" He said, turning the sheet around for Jay to inspect.

12/29/10

"December twenty-ninth, 1910? What the hell is that?"

"Doesn't ring any historical bells?"

"History was never my thing."

"You and me both," said Dane.

Jay sighed. "Forget it then. We're back to Billy being obscure." Jay lit another cigarette and stood up. Now it was her turn to pace. "This is all improvisation on Billy's part," she said slowly. "He's making it up as he goes along. He's got, oh, let's say an hour or so alone with the piano teacher. Winging it, looking for something to focus on, something he could leave behind to give us a clue, keep us coming. He switches the pictures and gets out of there. Comes to New Orleans, goes to the address on the drawing . . ."

"And finds out it's now a bar."

"As much a surprise to him as it was to us." Jay nodded. "Maybe that's part of his fun—dealing with the unexpected. The randomness of it all. That's been the key to this thing right from the start."

"How does that help us with the message?"

"Picture it," said Jay, stopping in the middle of the room, turning to face the marshal. "It's six or seven in the morning. Billy suddenly finds out there's no house on Royal Street, no obvious victim, so instead, he decides to leave us a message. I don't think he had time to make anything up."

"I don't get you."

"He's not playing by the rules," Jay said carefully. "It looks like it's all impromptu and improvised, but he's got his own agenda here, his own direction. I remember thinking about that back at Ti-Jean's. Square pegs and round holes."

"He already had the message made up?"

"I think so." Jay nodded. "It's the only thing that fits." She dragged on her cigarette and went back to pacing. Then she stopped again. "He's skipping one victim."

"The hypothetical one he might have found at the address on the picture."

"Right."

"So the message relates to the one after that—already planned."

"I think so." Jay started to pace again, window to door, door to window.

"Even if we're right, it doesn't get us any closer to an answer," said Dane. "Every code needs a key, and we don't have it."

"Key," said Jay, the word stopping her in mid-stride. "There was this really awful thing I saw on TV, years and years ago. World War II spy story, set in Egypt. There was a code in it . . ."

"*The Key to Rebecca*," Dane said.

"The key was a book, right? Both the bad guys had the same book."

"That's right." Dane nodded. "Daphne DuMaurier. *Rebecca*." Then he saw where she was going. "We're looking for a book?"

"I think so."

Dane frowned. "Telephone book? He'd know we'd have one here."

Not enough meat on the bone.

"Not his style," said Jay. "It has to be something simple, obvious."

"A book with numbers?"

"Or a magazine. Like *National Geographic*. They run the page numbers consecutively for a whole year." Jay shrugged. "He worked for a museum. It *could* fit."

Dane shook his head. "Too obscure." He frowned. "Something like a catalogue?"

"A book that uses numbers," said Jay, and then the light went on. "Of course!" She crossed to the coffee table, kneeled down and stroked out the numbers Dane had written, adding her own configuration beneath.

1/22/9/10

"Numbers. Acts. Deuteronomy! We're not looking for a book," Jay said. She went over to the desk and pulled open the drawer. "We're looking for *The* book." She turned, holding up a gold covered Gideon Bible. "The book Billy knew we'd have access to no matter where we were." She brought the book back to the couch. "Genesis is the first book in the Bible, so that would make it Chapter 22, verses 9 and 10." She found the page, ran her finger down the columns, then stopped. "Oh no," she whispered.

"What?"

She handed Dane the book. He read the verses aloud. "And

then they came to the place which God had told him of and
Abraham built an altar there and laid the wood in order and
bound Isaac his son and laid him on the altar upon the wood.
And Abraham stretched forth his hand and took the knife to
slay his son."

"A child." Jay felt sick at the thought. "He's going to murder a child this time."

Once upon a time, perhaps as long ago as when the jeweler
called Tabouis and his daughter, Euphrasine, were still alive,
some wealthy plantation owner might have used this house
as a summer place. It sat alone, miles from any other, and to
bring the wood and other material deep into the swamp by
small boat would have been fiercely expensive.

Originally, it had been two full stories high, with a galler-
ied *garçonnière* above with rooms for kitchens and servants
down below, all of it held up by pillars of strong thick cypress
pounded deep down into the muddy little island far out in the
bayou that the locals called Lachine. Changing levels of the
Mississippi and changing policies of the Army Corps of En-
gineers had raised the water in Bayou Lachine at first by
inches, then by feet. Somewhere along the way the house on
the island had been abandoned, and the island itself had disappeared under the water. The steps that had once led from
the lower gallery to the upper were used to dock the native
pirogues and rented flat-bottoms of fishermen and hunters
who sometimes used the old place for shelter.

Naked, slick with sweat, Billy Bones lay stretched out on
the sleeping bag he'd spread on the dark wood planks of the
upper gallery, listening to the crack and rattle of the rain on
the old, rusted tin roof above his head. He liked being naked,
always had liked it, right down to nothing at all—even the
Rolex taken from the doctor's dead wrist was in the room
behind him with his other things.

From what he'd read, most of the psychiatric community
as well as the operators of the majority of penal institutions
thought nakedness was cause for humiliation and embarrassment, but as a scientist Dr. William Paris Bonisteel was well

aware that clothing-for-modesty was a fairly recent concept in human history. In fact, if anything, nakedness was power; the power, for instance, of a man demonstrating physical strength and virility, or the power of a woman to display her attractiveness and nurturing capabilities. Strength, sex, fecundity all springing from the single naked source, hence, topless and nude beaches, athletes competing in as little clothing as possible, boxers wearing nothing but trunks and gloves. Not to mention narcissism and vanity if you had what it took. Billy sat up, smiling.

Know thyself, Doctor B.

He stood up and padded to the gallery railing, feeling the wet wood, slick on the soles of his feet. He leaned down, bracing his elbows on the balustrade, fingers laced together, hands and arms out in the warm rain as he looked out over the backwater swamp. Listening, he breathed in the night air, parsing and cataloging all the sounds and scents assailing him. The rain, like stones on the roof above him, like satin shivering down on the waters of the bayou; the wind in rising, soft little screams and wails through the cypress stumps and clumps of swamp grass on scattered hummocks and rises of mud within the marsh.

Wild rose and jasmine, the wet rot reek of hibiscus and water lily, to cover the thick flesh of dark peat mud which, left alone for a million years, would become the coal and oil that lay a thousand feet below it now. Life and death all wound up in a single breath, so rich it was almost overwhelming. In some other life, this might have been his landscape, a place to have as a home, a place to live and even die if it was necessary.

But that wasn't the way it was going to be, and that of course was the fault of his nemesis, the devious Fletcher, architect of all his woes. He'd had a near perfect life before she entered it, and had she not done so there was no telling how far he might have gone. No one in a thousand years would have or could have suspected him of any wrongdoing at all, let alone murder, and what they did know was only the half of it of course.

Three expeditions to the museum's site in Mexico, two trips to the Alberta Badlands, and half a dozen private holidays had netted him more specimens than the Fletcher bitch could even imagine, but that life was over now, destroyed by her, murdered by her. And for what? A few useless lives that no one would ever miss? Lives taken to hone a young man's skills and mind, the manner of their deaths more meaningful than their continued life could ever be.

God only knew, though, you couldn't really place the blame on her shoulders; she was merely the instrument of the theory he embraced and used to rule his life. But she was an instrument like a craven cancer, and as such she had to be removed, excised, sliced out like any other tumorous tissue.

And then? What then?

He'd thought about that part of it, long and hard. In Ricky's terms, this would be the end game, the last moves made to see who would prevail. Fletcher would see it as a tournament between good and evil, while he saw it as a simple scientific fact: The strong survived and the only thing inherited by the meek was the first clump of dirt thrown down to fill their dead mouths. Billy gazed out across the misted swamp and shook his head. Fletcher didn't really have a chance when you got right down to it.

Not only was she a woman, but now she was encumbered by that blond refugee from *Endless Summer* she seemed to be towing around, almost certainly a caretaker from the U.S. Marshal's Office. Foolishly, Billy had stayed in the area after killing the old woman, trolling once up the long Blackwood street and catching a lucky glimpse. Fletcher looked strong and a lot fitter than she'd been at his trial, almost as though she'd been working out in preparation for their contest. The man with her looked like a middle-aged Luke Skywalker with thinning hair.

Help or hindrance? Almost certainly the latter. Everything he'd read or heard about the Ladykiller painted her as a loner. Blond Luke would be about as bright as a block of wood with an imagination to match. A law-abiding, by-the-book man, a slow-and-steady-we-always-get-our-man guy. A Boy Scout.

A ball and chain, slowing her down, which suited Billy just fine.

You still haven't answered the question: What happens when all this is over?

Over the sound of the wind and the rain he heard two small noises. One was soft, a kitten mewling from somewhere below him; the other was the peeper-frog chirping of the little travel alarm clock he'd picked up at the airport. No time to answer foolish questions that he didn't want to think about just yet. It was time to make the call.

The bitch.

The sleepy little three-piece band was doing a weak version of Hugh Smith's "High Blood Pressure" when the pay phone at the back of Ti-Jean's Place rang sharply. Jay let it ring a second time, then picked up the receiver. Jack Dane was standing close beside her, holding a Radio Shack microcassette recorder close to her ear. The band finished up with the Hugh Smith song, and for a few moments there was nothing but small background noises from the bar and the tables.

"Yes?"

"Ms. Fletcher, I presume. So much better to speak to you in person instead of those silly little chatrooms." The voice was upbeat, pleasant, maybe on the edge of manic. Definitely Billy. Jay cleared her throat.

"What do you want, Billy?"

"Your blond friend with you?"

"Yes."

He knows about Dane. He's seen him.

Trying to spook me.

"A marshal?"

"Yes."

"What's his name?"

"You don't need to know that."

"I don't need anything, Ms. Fletcher. On the other hand, perhaps telling me his name would make me more . . . compassionate in the future."

Beside her, Dane nodded silently. Jay nodded back, then answered Billy. "His name is Jack Dane."

"Very bold." In the background Jay could hear the sound of rain on metal. A tin roof? Billy kept talking, his tone almost wistful. "He looks like a wrinkled version of the blond cop on a show I watched when I was a kid." He thought for a moment. *Chips*, he said finally. "All about the California Highway Patrol. Lots of action." He paused. "You remember?"

"Sure," said Jay. "I remember."

"You seem to be following my clues," Billy said.

"They're not that difficult once you get the hang of it."

"Time to change the rules." Billy's tone darkened. "Time to raise the stakes."

"What does that mean?"

"You figure it out," Billy answered.

Jay knew she was losing him. "No more clues?"

"Just one," said Billy. There was a long pause and Jay could hear the faint tin-roof sound again, and something else behind it. Wind? Trees?

Too clear to be an analog line. Digital. A cell phone.

"Well?" Jay prodded.

"Prenez un beau regard dans la Chine," said Billy, then laughed long and hard. There was an electronic popping sound and the line went dead. Jay hung up the phone.

"You get all that?" Jay asked. Dane rewound the tape then played a little back. He nodded.

"Was that last thing in French?"

"Take a good look in China." Jay translated, frowning. "My high school French is a little rusty but I think that's it. But what the hell does it mean?"

"I don't think the Gideons are going to be any help this time," Dane responded. "Doesn't sound too biblical."

The little band was tuning up again. More sleepy instrumental jazz. Jay and the marshal went back to the front of the room and sat down at the bar. It was a little busier than it had been earlier in the day, but not by much. Mr. Badass was still swabbing the bar with his wet rag and putting beer down in front of slope-shouldered drinkers. Jay gave him a raised hand, and he wandered over toward them.

"You get your phone call?" he asked. His eyes slid across Jack Dane, and Jay knew the old man had instantly read her companion as a cop.

"He called." Jay nodded.

"You hear what you want?"

"Not really."

"Too bad." Mr. Badass pushed his rag around. "He not coming back this way, I hope."

"I don't think so."

"A good thing, *cher*. He's *méchant* that one, for sure."

Cher. Méchant. French.

She took the little tape recorder from Jack and fast-forwarded to the end. She put the recorder down on the bar in front of the old black man and let it play.

"Prenez un beau regard dans la Chine."

"That mean anything to you?"

Mr. Badass thought for a long moment, then nodded slowly. "Beauregard's a little town I been to, up where Highway 10 cross the Atchafalaya."

"What's the Atchafalaya?" asked Jack Dane.

"Swamp," answered Mr. Badass. "Big swamp."

"And 'la Chine'?" Jay pressed. "Is that a place, too?"

Mr. Badass nodded. " 'Cept no one call it that in a long time I don't think."

"No one called it what?" Asked Dane.

"Lachine," the old man answered. "Little south of Beauregard. Used to be a big place for oil, years ago. They call it China Bayou now."

FIFTEEN

They were on the road with the wet, breaking dawn, turning their backs on New Orleans as they headed around the lower edge of Lake Ponchartrain up to Baton Rouge. Then they turned due west and crossed the Mississippi, finally reaching the little town of Webre and the approach to the eighteen-mile-long Interstate 10 bridge that spanned the entire Atchafalaya floodway.

Webre was barely a town at all, just half a dozen streets within sight of the highway and a few stores. There was one truck-stop restaurant, the Tiger. Dane pulled the rental up to the pumps and filled the tank while Jay went off and retrieved a pair of fried-egg sandwiches and coffee.

Jay spelled Dane behind the wheel, eating as she drove, alternating bites of the dripping sandwich with sips of aromatic coffee. Two miles down the road they reached the low-span bridge. In front of them and on either side, there was nothing but a misted ocean of deep green and bark brown stretching as far as the eye could see, all of it blurred by the iron gray of the steady rain.

Here and there Jay saw wider stretches of water through the mist, like dozens of silver chains cutting randomly through the rich green. The gray appeared to be long beards of Spanish moss hanging in the branches of the trees, and every now and again she caught flashes of white as flights of long-legged egrets took to the air.

"Looks pretty from up here," Dane commented. "Not the same when you're down in it, I guess."

"No," she agreed, and both of them knew that was exactly where they were going.

"What's he up to, do you think?" Dane asked. It was the first time they'd talked about Billy since leaving New Orleans almost three hours ago.

"I'm not sure." Jay took a drag on her cigarette. "He's letting us get closer every time. I think he was watching us back in Blackwood. He knows what you look like."

Dane turned up his lip. "A wrinkled California Highway Patrol officer."

"He was close enough to pick off the color of your hair."

"You think he's getting himself off that way or something? Tempting fate."

"More like getting to know his enemy," Jay replied. "Figuring out where you fit into his crazy equation."

Stalking. A predator and his prey.

"On the tape he says the rules have changed. Any idea what he means?"

"There never were any rules. Like I said before, he's making this up as he goes along. He's just giving us what he considers fair warning."

"You really know this guy, don't you?" said Dane.

From the look on his face Jay couldn't tell if Dane was impressed or disturbed at the thought. "I spent four months tracking him down and eight hours a day for six weeks of the trial watching him on a closed-circuit monitor," she said. "He almost cost me my sanity." She let out a long breath. "Yeah, I guess I know him."

They reached the end of the bridge and turned off the interstate, driving through the village of Henderson, then south along the Old Coffee Road, a slippery washboard track that ran along the edge of the Atchafalaya, with stands of ancient, dripping trees marching along on either side. The heavy, death-smell of rotting vegetation was everywhere when they cracked the window.

"About another mile," said Dane, consulting the map on his lap. "The road isn't marked but the town is. Just a little dot on the edge of a big green blob."

Jay nodded, saying nothing. Once again she could feel Billy's presence closing in on her and she could hear his voice, clean and clear over the phone. *"Time to change the rules. Time to raise the stakes."*

"Are we going to talk to the locals?" she said finally.

"No other choice," Dane responded. "It's the only way we're going to find out anything."

"We could ask around."

"I think we'd need an interpreter."

"I think I'm going to need a gun," Jay said bluntly.

Dane looked across the seat. "No gun. Not part of the deal," he said flatly, shaking his head.

"Billy said it," said Jay. "He's changing the rules, raising the stakes."

"I put a gun in your hand, I might as well hand in mine. Along with my badge." He shook his head. "You're a civilian."

"I'm a cop."

"Not anymore."

"Then why am I here?"

"To offer your assistance. Your expert opinion. That's all."

"And if Billy's armed?"

"I'll deal with him."

"What if you can't?" said Jay bluntly. "What if you're dead?"

"Then you'd better run, sweetheart."

They passed a portable signboard on a trailer beside the narrow road. It read "Welcome to Cajun Country. Crayfish Shack 1 Mile Live Bait Best Boudin Po Boys a specialty," all run together. The rain had put the water level in the ditch up above the trailer wheels.

"This isn't like before," Jay said quietly, forcing down the hot flush of her anger. "This isn't hit and run with us always two steps behind. Billy's reeling us in like fish on a line. He's telling us he's going to kill a sacrificial child, and he knows we're going to respond to that." She tightened her grip on the wheel of the rental. "He's depending on that, Jack, he's assuming the predictable course of action."

"So what are you saying?" the marshal answered. "We turn around and drive back to New Orleans and pretend that crazy son of a bitch isn't going to hack off some kid's head like he did to that old lady in Massachusetts?"

"No, I'm saying there's no way I'm going into a situation like this without a weapon."

Dane reached under his jacket and pulled the big Colt out of its holster. "You want me to give you mine?"

Jay rolled down the side window an inch and flipped her cigarette butt out into the rain. "No. I want you to give me the backup piece you keep in that ankle holster." Dane opened his mouth to speak, then thought better of it. "I saw it when you were sacked out on the couch last night," Jay added.

The marshal gave her a long, cool look, then holstered the Colt, reached down to his right ankle, and pulled up his jeans. The pistol was a short-barreled Glock 19, weighing in at just over a pound. He pulled out the weapon and put it on the seat between them. Jay picked it up and slipped it into the pocket of her jacket.

Dane turned away and stared out through the side window, silently watching the dripping scenery. Finally, he turned back to Jay. "Maybe it's time to call in the cavalry," he said. "The Marshals Special Operations Group is based not far from here. An hour and we could have everything from tracking dogs to helicopter gunships on hand."

"And CNN not far behind," Jay answered. She shook her head. "Karlson would have your ass in a sling for going public."

"Screw that," said the marshal. "The object is to get this maniac back in custody before he kills anyone else." He paused, frowning. "This isn't some kind of contest. We've got the resources, maybe we should start using them." He waved vaguely out the window. "Special Operations Group operates out of a National Guard camp about a hundred miles from here. Choppers, special weapons, assault teams, the whole nine yards." He shook his head angrily and scrabbled around on the dashboard looking for his cigarettes.

"You don't play hide-and-seek with this crazy fucker, you track him down with as many people as you can find and then you blow the cocksucker's head off like the mad dog he is."

He found his cigarettes and lit one, slowly calming down. "I'm tired of games and clues and fucking computers."

Jay had been feeling Dane's frustration from their first meeting. He'd spent his whole career with the visible power of the U.S. Marshals Service to back him up wherever and whenever he needed it. Now he was outside the loop with none of that to call on, and it was getting to him.

"We're not going to take Billy down with a SWAT team," Jay said finally. "He works his own turf and you can bet he's got a dozen escape routes already planned. We can't overpower him, so we have to outthink him." She paused for a moment, realizing that she was skirting the issue. Finally she went on. "Not to mention the fact that Karlson and my old boss are pretty gun-shy about the media on this. Bad enough Billy escapes, but bringing me in on it would just make things worse if and when it leaks."

Dane snorted. "It'll leak. You said it yourself. That cop in Blackwood was itching to go on *Hard Copy*. It's only a matter of time. It'll leak and we still won't have the bastard!" He banged his palm against the dashboard, open-handed. "We should have been up-front right from the start. Screw all this cloak-and-dagger bullshit."

And then you wouldn't have had to deal with me, that's what you really mean.

The terrain suddenly opened up, the trees on both sides thinning, then fading away to wet-looking fields, planted with something that looked like wild rice. To the right, the swamp had become a wide band of open water. In the distance, on the far side of the river, Jay could see cows huddled together against the rain. Straight ahead the stark shapes of a trailer park appeared. Passing it, they saw a sign in squared-off oriental characters. Beyond the trailer park, a hundred yards down the road, there was a large, squat, tin-roofed building with a name neatly printed in black above a pair of rusty-looking barn-sized doors: Atchafalaya Fisheries Inc.

Next door to the fish factory there was a run-down Texaco station with its pumps removed and its windows white-washed. There was a big, crudely painted sign nailed up over the garage doors of the station, names and words getting smaller and smaller as space ran out: "T. K. Lepine Campaign Headquarters. Re-elect Mayor Pete LaFramboise, Elect Pete LaFramboise Police Chief, Baxter & Pellegrino Alderman." Under the old pump pull-in was another mobile sign like the one they'd seen a few miles back down the road: "Jean Dupuis, you're a triple-faced liar."

"Looks like they take their politics seriously around here," Dane commented as they drove slowly past the Texaco.

"Wecome to Beauregard, Louisiana," said Jay. "Crawfish and name-calling a specialty."

"Doesn't look much like Billy's kind of place."

"Billy's just as much a prisoner of his rules as we are. He's going where those degrees of separation take him."

The main street was three blocks long with residential side streets angling off on the right. Most of the buildings looked old and worn, stained with rain, their tin roofs spotty with rust and green with moss. The asphalt on the road was cracked, potholed, and patched, the sidewalks crumbling. The operative word for Beauregard seemed to be "tired."

In the middle of town Jay spotted a low, flat-roofed stucco building that said Beauregard Police Department over the door. There was a ten-year-old light blue Ford pickup in front of the building with the same words on the door panels and a battered-looking aluminum boat in the back. Jay parked the rental beside the pickup.

"How much do we tell them?" Jay asked.

"Everything," Dane answered, cracking open the door. "We don't have time to be coy."

The Beauregard Police Department headquarters was one big room, half a dozen metal desks, and a wall full of filing cabinets. Above the filing cabinets was a huge map of the town with an advertisement for T. K. Lepine Real Estate and Insurance in one corner. There were two people in the big room: a frighteningly thin woman in a flower-print dress eating a strange-looking doughnut covered with powdered sugar while she manned a CB radio, and a short, bald man in uniform reading a copy of *Field and Stream*. From the look of the art on the cover of the magazine, it was at least twenty years old.

The beanpole woman at the radio looked up as Jay and Jack Dane came through the front door. Seeing them, her face lit up and she graced them with a broad smile that was too friendly to be anything else but genuine. "Help you?" she asked. She picked up a paper napkin from her desk, dabbing at the powdered sugar caked on her lips. Rain tapped and rattled on the roof overhead. It was exactly the sound Jay had heard when she talked to Billy.

Dane spoke. "We'd like to see the chief."

The bald man spoke up without lowering the magazine in his hands. "Not here."

The woman scowled at him and turned her smile back on for Jack Dane. "He's over at Mama Boudin's."

"Restaurant down the street," said the man behind the magazine.

"Thanks," said Jack. They turned to leave.

"This about the Chink kid?" The bald man put down his magazine. His face was perfectly round with hot, red cheeks and watery blue eyes.

"It's not Chink," the thin woman snapped. "It's *Veet-na-messe*."

"Who the fuck can tell the difference?" said the bald man. He shook his head wearily. He winked at Jay. "All she knows is fucking *beignets* and Mr. Donut." The bald man had a protruding belly like a bowling ball.

"Doesn't seem to be doing her waistline any harm," said Dane. He winked at the woman, who turned to the man and gave him the finger.

"What about this Vietnamese kid?" asked Jay.

The man pursed his lips into a fleshy little O. "Thought you might be here for that. Media or something. Kid got himself lost yesterday comin' home from school." He shook his head again. "Don't know what all the fuss is about. One Chink more or less isn't going to matter much. It's not like we got a lot of perverts here, stealin' little *Veet-na-meese* babies." He lifted the magazine again, then spoke around it.

"Gator prob'ly got him." He laughed. "Gator like Chink food, I guess."

The woman made a face. "I don't hear you practicin' your shitty mouth when Tran around."

"Tran can kiss my ass," said the man.

"More like kick it," snorted the woman. She took another bite from the pastry she was holding delicately between her fingers.

"Thanks again," said Jack Dane, speaking to the woman. She nodded around the piece of sugary confection in her mouth. They left the office and went out into the rain again.

"Deliverance country," Jay muttered. "Any minute now Burt Reynolds is going to show up wearing a rubber suit and carrying a bow and arrow."

Mama Boudin's was half a block down on the other side of the street, wedged in between Suzy & Ruby's Beauty Bar and Babineaux Hardware. The storefront windows were steamed up and there were half a dozen vintage trucks angle-parked out front. Jay Fletcher and Jack Dane ran the fifty yards from the police station, but they were both soaked by the time they pushed in through the front door of Mama Boudin's.

The restaurant was an old-fashioned greasy spoon, booths running down one wall, grill and Formica bar running down the other. It was a chrome and vinyl version of Ti-Jean's Place in the French Quarter, except at Mama Boudin's the music was delivered up from miniature quarter-fed juke boxes in each booth and spaced along the bar. A lanky man in a chef's hat was smoking a cigarette and churning scrambled eggs on one of the griddles, while a plump, white-haired woman was sitting on a high stool behind the cash register reading a thin romance novel with a badly rendered white rose on the cover. Travis Tritt leaked out of the tinny jukebox speakers.

Jack Dane spoke to the woman behind the cash register. "We're looking for the police chief."

She used her book to point down the room. "Last booth." Of the eight booths against the wall, four were occupied and their occupants stopped eating as Jay and Jack Dane passed. The men were all eating breakfasts of one kind or another, the portions enormous. Most of the men were dressed in T-shirts, blue jeans, and red-stripe rubber boots that came up almost to their knees. There were no women.

Jay and Dane reached the last booth. It was occupied by two men. One, broad-shouldered, heavyset and white, was mopping gravy up off his plate with a biscuit. The other, seated across from him, was almost as big, pock-faced and Vietnamese. The only thing in front of him was an empty coffee cup. They were both wearing the same uniform as the bald man back at the police station. Two yellow slickers hung from a row of hooks on the wall leading to the toilets. The white man looked up as Jack Dane paused in front of the booth. Jay sat herself down on one of the stools at the bar, her eyes on the Vietnamese.

"Chief LaFramboise?" Dane asked.

The big man smiled. "You're not a voter so you can call me Pete."

Jack Dane pulled out his USMS ID folder and showed it to LaFramboise. He glanced at it, then handed it back. LaFramboise didn't ask about Jay's status, presumably assuming that she was a marshal as well.

The police chief looked across the table at the silent Vietnamese man. "These people are federal law enforcement officers, Tran. What do you think of that?" He turned to look at Dane and Jay Fletcher. "This is my deputy, Tran Van Dang."

The Vietnamese man nodded his head a fraction of an inch, but his expression didn't change at all. Jay was staring at his thick, short neck. A long ropy scar tracked down from the black bristled hairline at the back of his head and around his neck to the base of his throat. It looked as though someone had tried to hack off his head with a machete and come close to succeeding.

"What can we do for you on this rainy day?" the chief asked. "U.S. Marshals all the way out here, likely means you lost someone, am I right?"

"A killer." Dane nodded.

"Bad one?"

"The worst."

"What makes you think he's in these parts?"

"He told us he'd be here," said Jay, speaking up for the first time.

"Told you?"

"Called us on the telephone," said Jay. "Gave us a little riddle. It brought us here."

"Sounds like a crazy man," said LaFramboise.

"He is." Dane nodded. He slid into the booth beside the Vietnamese deputy.

The chief popped the last piece of biscuit into his mouth, wiped his hands on a napkin, then took a crushed package of Camels out of the breast pocket of his uniform shirt. He lit the cigarette from a book of matches, tossing the spent one into the congealing gravy on his plate. "You hear about our problem?"

"The child?"

"Uh-huh." The chief drew on his cigarette. "Been almost twenty-four hours. Much longer and I'm going to have to call in some help. FBI, I guess." He squinted through the smoke. "Not the Marshals." He took another drag on the Camel. "You think my problem could be the same as your problem?"

"Yes." Jay nodded. "He said he was going to sacrifice a child."

"Sacrifice?"

"It was a quotation from the Bible."

"We need to act as quickly as we can," said Dane. He glanced at the Vietnamese man across from the chief. "If our boy has the child, it may already be too late."

"Anything you can tell me, might make it easier to find this crazy person?"

"We think he might be somewhere called China Bayou," Jay said.

"Now that's nowhere good, for sure," said the policeman. "One time Bayou Lachine was pretty good for fishing, hunting but all these new levees ruin it. Pretty bad in there."

"Bad?" Jay repeated. "What kind of bad?"

"Every kind, *cher*. Crawfish and catfish taste like oil from old leaky rigs they capped off years ago, air pollution all the way from Big Easy killing the moss. Half the time it's wet, half the time dry as old bones." He grinned. "And all the time in China you find every kind of poison snake you ever want to see."

Jay grimaced. "Sounds like a real tourist mecca."

Dane spoke. "If our boy's in there, he'd need a boat, right?"

"He ain't walking, no."

"Which means he'd have to rent one or steal one."

"True."

"Any strangers in the last day or so?"

"Not so you'd notice," said LaFramboise. "And believe me, a town this size you *do* notice."

Jay frowned, working it out. "He must have passed through."

"Beauregard's what they call an end-of-the-line community," said the chief. "Road goes on maybe half a mile to the dump, then that's it. Swamp behind and nothing else all the way down to Morgan City." He shook his head. "Till you came along we thought maybe he just wandered off. This makes it different."

"I saw a trailer park coming into town," Dane said. "That where the kid lives?"

LaFramboise looked across the table then back at Dane. "That's where all the Vietnamese people in Beauregard live." He dragged on the cigarette. "Pretty much keep themselves to themselves. Work the boats, peel crawfish in the factory. A few on the rigs but not many. Too small for oil work."

Jay smiled thinly. "How many Vietnamese live here?"

" 'Bout four hundred," LaFramboise answered. He smiled. "And I know just where you're going with that question, *cher*. Town of fifteen hundred, that means they're just short of a third of the population. Most of them American citizens now, not like before when they was just refugees getting money from the government."

"Lot of people," said Jay. She glanced at the Vietnamese man across from the police chief. The last surge of refugees had been in the early eighties; most of the Vietnamese in Beauregard would be eligible to vote. She remembered LaFramboise's name from the sign on the Texaco station, on the same ticket as T. K. Lepine, the mayor, the same Lepine with the real-estate and insurance company on the map in LaFramboise's office. Not only did the people of Beauregard take their politics seriously, they kept it up close and personal.

"You think I've got a Vietnamese deputy for votes?" LaFramboise said, laughing. Across from him, Tran, the deputy in question, smiled briefly. "They'd vote for me anyway because I've spent the last fifteen years making sure some of the good old boys out here don't cause these hard-working people trouble, and I've got Tran for a deputy because he was a good cop back in Saigon and he's a good cop here."

"You were one of the White Mice?" Dane asked.

The Vietnamese man nodded. "Fifth District. Cholon. You?"

"M.P." The marshal answered. "Spent a lot of time on Tu Do Street."

"They call it something else now," said Tran Van Dang. "*Dong Khoi*. Street of the General Uprising, as you would say it." His English was precise and almost without accent.

"Tran spent two years in Sham Shui Po Detention Center in Hong Kong before he came here," said LaFramboise, pronouncing the words carefully, by rote, smiling as though it was a badge of honor. "His wife and daughter died there." The Vietnamese deputy touched the long, thick scar on his neck. Jay turned to him.

"What do you think happened to the child?" she asked.

"The boy's father ran away two years ago," Tran answered. "At first we thought it was him." He looked Jay directly in the eye. "Now I am not so sure."

"What's the boy's name?"

"Vin Hoa. Everyone calls him Vinnie. His mother is my cousin."

Jay nodded. "How old is he?"

"Eleven."

"And he was walking home from school?"

"Yes. For his lunch."

"He made his own lunch?"

"No," replied the deputy. "His mother works for Atchafalaya Fisheries. She would take her own meal break to prepare it for him. The factory is close to the trailer park."

"We saw that coming in." Dane nodded. "What about the school? How far is it from the boy's home?"

"The school is on Dauterive Street," said LaFramboise. "Two blocks south of here, toward the dump. About a mile from there to the trailer park. We already talked to his friends. They didn't see anything."

"Vietnamese friends?" Jay asked.

LaFramboise glanced at his deputy again. "Like I said, these people keep to themselves. There's two, three other Vietnamese kids in the boy's class."

"And they didn't see anything at all?"

"They bring their lunches to school. The boy's the only one who goes home."

"He have any particular way he goes?" Dane asked, aiming the question at Dang.

"I asked his mother. She says he walks down Dauterive to Main Street, then follows Main Street along to the trailer park."

"And no one saw him?"

"Nobody we asked."

"He would have walked right past the police station," said Dane.

"I suppose that's true." LaFramboise nodded. He took a last drag on his cigarette, then butted it into the skinned-over gravy on his plate. He picked a tobacco crumb off his lip and looked at Dane. "Your boy crazy like a mad dog's crazy, or is he the subtle type?"

"The subtle type," Dane answered.

"And smart," Jay added.

LaFramboise took a deep breath and let it out, almost as though he expected to see a cloud of smoke rise up into the air. "Stranger gets noticed quick in a town like this. He's not going to snatch a little boy off the main street, and he's not going to be caught hanging around no schoolyard fence."

"What are you saying?" Jay asked.

"Mile's a long way for a little kid to walk. Maybe he took a shortcut. Got picked up where he shouldn'ta been, where nobody'd know to look."

Dane shrugged his shoulders. "Your town, Chief."

Pete LaFramboise nodded and smiled broadly. "That's right, Mr. Marshal. That's exactly what it is. My town." Territorial imperative in place, he slid out of the booth and put on the stained old Stetson he'd kept on the seat beside him. "Come on. You can follow me and Tran."

The police chief and his deputy went back to the police station. Tran got behind the wheel and LaFramboise stepped into the office. Jay and Jack Dane climbed into the rental, Dane on the driver's side this time. Jay rummaged around in her pockets and handed him the keys.

"What are the 'White Mice'?" she asked.

"Slang for a Saigon cop. They had these white helmets and white gloves with buttons, like Mickey Mouse."

"What's Cholon?"

"Hell," said Dane. "A couple of million people living in one-room shacks, ten, maybe a dozen people in each one. No running water, no toilets. Rats the size of rabbits. Not the kind of thing you saw on the evening news back then." He glanced out the rain-streaked window at the profile of the man in the truck beside them. "That was his beat. Probably where he lived, too. The Mice didn't get much in the way of high pay."

"Sounds like hell."

"You got that right," Dane answered. "You had to be there."

LaFramboise came out of the office and got into the truck. Deputy Tran headed up Main Street, then turned up a side street. Dane went after them. They passed a boat repair store and a couple of small warehouses. After that there was a sprinkling of fifties-style bungalows on both sides of the

street. No sidewalks. There were trucks and boats on trailers
parked in most of the yards. Jay spotted clusters of chickens
under trees, keeping out of the rain.

The road ran out at a gated fence around an empty field
that looked too wet to grow anything. Beyond that was a line
of scrubby trees. The land seemed to slope downward. The
truck turned down an almost invisible track running along
beside the fence and Dane followed, the rental sluicing back
and forth through the mud. Ahead of them the truck had
slowed almost to a walk.

"The Vietnamese guy's looking for a sign," Dane said.
Ahead of them the truck stopped. Dane pulled up behind it
as Tran Van Dang climbed out of the cab and slogged through
the mud until he reached the fence, his slicker bright against
the green and the gray. He squatted down, digging around
with his hands in the muck. A moment later he stood, carrying
two objects in his hands. He went to the back of the truck
and laid them on the open tailgate. Jack Dane and Jay Fletcher
got out of the rental and LaFramboise stepped down from the
cab of the truck.

The police chief stared at the pair of muddy artifacts; a
child-size running shoe and a small, pale green umbrella,
vanes snapped and crushed. He picked up the shoe and peeled
back the high top. "Vinnie Hoa," he said, reading the name
inscribed with a black marker.

"So this is where he was snatched?" Jay said.

"Appears to be." LaFramboise nodded, rainwater sluicing
down from his hat. Tran Van Dang turned away and moved
up the pathway away from the truck. The police chief looked
around. The empty field still stood on their left, the back of
a run-down house and a fenced yard fifty feet away on their
right. "We already canvassed the neighborhood. Nobody
around here saw any strangers." He picked up the umbrella
and tried to work the mechanism. "Maybe it wasn't your boy
at all," he said. "Maybe it was someone from around here."
He didn't like the idea very much. Jay shivered; the rain was
soaking through her clothes and she was getting cold.

The Vietnamese deputy came back to where they were

standing, his jet black hair plastered down over his forehead. "Truck," the man said. "Old. Narrow tires. Turned around up there." He pointed. In the distance, Jay could see a vacant lot and then the side of the fish factory.

"He almost made it," she said.

"Your boy have a truck like that?" LaFramboise asked.

"Not that we know of," said Dane.

"Shit. It really is starting to sound like someone local."

"No," Jay said. "It's our Billy."

"How can you be so sure?"

"Because he said he was going to do it, because it fits." She chewed on her lip, then glanced at Jack Dane. "Because we made a mistake."

"What mistake?" the marshal asked.

"Not here," Jay answered, shivering. "I stay out in this much longer and I'm going to catch pneumonia."

"I'll second that." Dane nodded bleakly.

"We can get you into some dry clothes back at the office," LaFramboise offered. "We got hot coffee, too."

"We've got our own stuff in the car," Jay said. "But I'll take the coffee and a place to change."

Back at the police station Jay went into the bathroom, changed into fresh jeans and a T-shirt, then pulled on a sweater borrowed from Antoinette Peychaud, the skinny woman at the radio. The sweater was dark green covered with blue and yellow tulips and obviously handmade; wearing it, Jay was instantly warm again. Louis, the bald man with the magazine, had discovered he had errands to run a few seconds after Tran came through the door. Pulling the sweater down over the bulk of the Glock tucked into her jeans, Jay went back out into the main office. LaFramboise handed her a mug of coffee and pointed to a battered chair beside one of the empty desks. Jack Dane sat a few feet away. Tran Van Dang was nowhere to be seen.

Jay pushed up the sleeves on the sweater. It smelled as though it had been soaked in White Shoulders perfume for a week. She sipped from her mug of coffee and sat back in the squeaky wooden office chair she'd been offered. Antoinette

Peychaud sat at her place behind the radio, eating from a Mr. Donut box, watching Jay like a fan watching her favorite soap opera star.

"So what mistake did we make?" Dane asked, angry that she hadn't said anything to him privately in the car.

"We missed a step," said Jay. "We forgot the pattern."

"What pattern we talking about here?" LaFramboise asked. Jay ignored him.

"Billy goes from Blackwood, Massachusetts, to New Orleans because of that painting on the wall, but what takes him from New Orleans to here? What's the connection between Billy and this China Bayou?"

Dane turned to LaFramboise. "What's out there, exactly?" he asked.

"Lotta swamp."

"Place has got a name," Dane insisted. "There's got to be more to it than that."

"One time maybe. Back before the big flood in 1927 maybe. Three, four streets, maybe a store, a fish factory. Nothing there now, though. Drowned. Flooded out from the levee."

"No one goes there?"

"Just for the crawfish. Oil rigs down that way all gone now."

"That's not the point," said Jay. "Billy doesn't know any more about China Bayou than we do."

"Shit," Dane muttered, seeing it. "Someone told him."

"Who we talking about here?" said LaFramboise, frustrated at his fiefdom being undermined by strangers.

Jay turned to him. "Our man Billy must have run into someone from Beauregard while he was in New Orleans. Someone who knew something about China Bayou. Maybe even about the boy."

"I still don't understand," said LaFramboise. He lit a Camel, puffing hard.

"I do," said Tran, coming into the office and shutting the door behind him, his slicker dripping onto the linoleum floor. "I went to speak with my cousin. Her half-brother, Nguyen, has not come home. He has a truck like the one we are seeking. Old, with narrow tires."

"Was he going to New Orleans?"

The deputy's expression hardened. "Nguyen is *Con Lai*, a half-breed, what you call an Amerasian. He shares the same mother as my cousin. His father was an American soldier. He is not very accepted among the Vietnamese people here." Tran cleared his throat. "He is also known to be . . ." He made a limp-wristed movement.

"Gay?" Jay suggested.

"Yes." Tran nodded. "Not so easy to be here either, Vietnamese or not." He looked at LaFramboise, but the police chief showed nothing on his face. "He has done this before. He lives alone, saves up, spends his money on clothes. After a good catch he will sometimes leave town for several days. My cousin thinks he goes to a place called Rawhide and another called Lafitte's." Tran paused. "She says she knows this because her brother Nguyen is very proud of his collection of matchbooks from these places."

Jay nodded to herself, trying it on for size. "Billy picks up Nguyen in a gay bar and they come back here." She paused. "Or Billy comes back here by himself."

"This Nguyen guy," said Dane. "He has a trailer?"

"Yes." Tran nodded.

"Then maybe we should take a look," said LaFramboise.

The trailer belonging to Nguyen Vinh Duong was a 1953 Tour-a-Home in two-tone cream and pale green, its tires long rotted into the spongy ground, the chrome strip running along its mid-section and the aluminum frames of the windows pitted brown with rust. Somewhere along the way a plastic awning had been added over the concrete-block steps leading up to the front door, but the plastic was cracked, the metal poles supporting it sagging drunkenly. There was a new-looking satellite dish perched on the roof. All the curtains over the windows were closed.

Nguyen's home was set at the far end of the trailer park, hidden by a screen of low, scrubby trees. Its closest neighbor was fifty feet away. The shortcut that the boy had followed went almost directly in front of it. Off to one side, half hidden under a blue plastic drop sheet, was a lean-to covering a set of empty boat cradles. As Jay and Jack Dane pulled up behind Chief LaFramboise's truck, the rain began to ease and the clouds overhead were blown away in ragged strips. They got out of the rental car and joined the police chief and his deputy.

"What kind of boat did he have?" Dane asked. "One of those little dugout things?"

"A pirogue you mean?" said LaFramboise.

Tran shook his head. "He didn't like them for round-net fishing. He had a Crawdad."

"What's that?" Dane asked.

"Flatboat made out of plastic," explained LaFramboise. "Coleman made them ten years ago." He looked across at the trailer. "They don't rust, at least."

"He had an outboard?"

"Yamaha 50." Tran nodded. "They are both gone."

"Kinda thing you don't need a trailer for," said LaFramboise. "Just dump it in back of the truck and go."

"Let's take a look in the trailer," Jay suggested.

The police chief used a screwdriver from his truck to pop the lock on the front door of the trailer. One by one they stepped up on the concrete blocks and went through the doorway into the kitchen. It smelled faintly of sesame oil, but other than that it was clean and tidy. Next to it the living room was just as well kept.

There was a small couch done in a yellow-and-black tartan, a matching tilt chair, and a massive television under the window. On top of the set there was a new-looking VCR and on top of that, sitting on a protective cloth, there were several brightly colored votive candles, a plastic-framed picture of a pain-wracked Jesus, another Jesus, this one nailed to a plaster cross, and two statuettes of the Virgin, one with child, one without. Jay stepped forward and popped a tape out of the VCR. It was something called *The Boys of Cellblock Q*. On a coffee table in front of the couch there was a fishbowl half-

filled with matchbooks. Jay picked out a handful. They were
from gay bars all over Mississippi, Louisiana, and Texas. She
showed them to Dane.

"He gets around."

Adjoining the living room was a small bedroom which
Nguyen was obviously using as a storage area. There were
two curved wooden hooks screwed into the wall about two
feet apart, one lower than the other. Dane pushed several
boxes aside and went to the wall. He reached up and ran his
finger around the inside of one of the pegs.

"Oil," he said, rubbing his fingers together. He sniffed
them, then turned to Tran. "Gun oil. He hunt?"

Tran nodded. "Nutria sometime. Sold the skins."

"Lotta people do it," said LaFramboise, almost defen-
sively.

"What kind of rifle?"

"Army surplus," Tran answered. "Bought it in Lafayette a
long time ago. M1, I think."

"Thirty ought six," LaFramboise grunted. "Right cartridge,
put a two-bit hole right through you."

Dane squeezed through the doorway and they continued to
search the trailer. Beyond the storage area was the bathroom,
and at the end of the trailer there was a master bedroom. It
was as neat as every other room in the house, bed made and
closet doors neatly shut. Jay opened them. Of the four closets
in the room, three were filled with dress clothing and one
with work clothes. The young man had two dozen pairs of
shoes and at least fifty ties.

They all went back to the living room. "Doesn't look as
though he ever came back here," said LaFramboise. The police chief frowned, then looked across the room at Jack and
Jay. "You think maybe he went off with this Billy character
of yours?"

"Unlikely," said Jay. "Too big a risk."

"Then he has probably been killed." Tran nodded.

"Probably," Jay agreed.

They left the trailer, climbing down the concrete blocks to
the muddy ground. The rain had stopped completely. Tran

stood for a moment, his nose lifted slightly. "There is an odor."

LaFramboise inhaled. "That would be the smell of shit, Tran. Your cousin's brother probably needs to clean out his septic." Jay sniffed. The police chief was right, the smell of human excrement was very strong beside the trailer.

"No," the Vietnamese man said slowly. "It is more than just shit, I think." He crouched down, moving along the length of the trailer, breathing in the wet, warm air. With the end of the rain, the heat was growing and Jay was suddenly aware of the hot weight of the sweater she'd borrowed.

Tran stopped at the far end of the trailer and moved aside a stack of plastic-webbed lawn chairs. The chairs had masked a deep drawer set under the trailer just past the rear axle. Presumably, the drawer had originally been designed to hold extra gear on the road—like the lawn chairs. The Vietnamese police deputy reached down and pulled the drawer open. He stared down into it. He looked up, his expression blank, and motioned the others forward.

The mutilated corpse of Nguyen Vinh Duong lay spread-eagled in the drawer as though he'd been laid across some latter day Procrustean bed, his head, forearms, and lower legs hacked off to make him fit, the spare parts tossed in after him like leftover vegetables in a refrigerator crisper. There was a leak somewhere and rainwater had seeped in, mixing with the blood and feces to form an odious red-brown soup in the bottom of the drawer. The man's head lay face up in a corner of the drawer. The bright yellow handle of a screwdriver jutted from between the dead man's lips. Almost certainly the killing blow. With the end of the rain, flies had begun to settle, crawling across the pieces of flesh in flashes of iridescent green. A butterfly had been pinned into each eye, exactly like Connelly.

Jay bit her lip and looked away, but despite herself she could picture the events in her mind's eye. It wouldn't have been hard for Billy to have learned about China Bayou from his new friend, Nguyen, and somewhere along the way, details about the boy would have been discovered, including his secret shortcut home. From the look of the work clothes she'd seen in his closet, Billy and Nguyen were just about the same size; dressed in coveralls, a cap pulled low over his eyes, Billy would have looked enough like his uncle for Vinnie to have clambered into the truck, grateful to get out of the rain.

After that it would've been too late.

Jay felt her gorge rising in the back of her throat, and the feel of the Glock tucked into her waistband was a burn. Had Billy killed Nguyen before kidnapping the boy, or after? What had the child seen or been forced to witness, what terror was he feeling now, or had he already been slaughtered like his uncle?

LaFramboise had taken two steps back from the drawer. He turned away completely and quickly lit a cigarette. The big man looked as though he'd suddenly deflated, all his power suddenly dissipated like helium released from a balloon. His face had turned the color of cheese and he was breathing rapidly through his half-open mouth. "I can't deal with this," he said, blinking at Jay. "We don't have things like this here." He shook his head rapidly, his accent thickening with each word. "No, I mean that for sure, me. This thing is too much." He turned to Jack Dane, standing beside him now. "You people, you handle this, I give it you, okay? We call in your people, the Staties maybe, yes? FBI maybe, okay?"

Jay opened her mouth to speak, but Dane beat her to it. "No," he said flatly. "We don't have time. Get your shit together, man, and get us to this China Bayou place of yours."

Behind them, Tran Van Dang pushed the drawer shut. He stepped forward, touching the marshal lightly at the elbow. "I will take you there," he said.

SIXTEEN

The Vietnamese deputy sat in the stern of the flat-bottomed aluminum boat, the thick fingers of one hand holding the tiller of the fifty-horse Evinrude, guiding them through the endless carpet of small-leafed, bright green duckweed. Jack Dane sat in the middle seat, facing forward. Propped against the seat beside him were a pair of army surplus M16's from the Vietnam era and an even older wooden stock Ruger varmint rifle—the Beauregard Police Department's version of SWAT.

Jay Fletcher sat forward on the narrow bow seat, looking ahead, watching the hot mist rise from the water and hang vaporously in the cypress trees, caught by the hanging skeins of Spanish moss and by the bony, wet fingers of overhanging limbs. She'd taken off the borrowed sweater, but even so the T-shirt she wore beneath it was dark with sweat.

This was the green hell they'd seen from the long span of the Atchafalaya Bridge, and down here within it the view was much more unsettling than it had been from above. The end of the rain had brought out every animal and insect the great swamp had to offer. Huge, ratlike nutria were gathered in squirming, tail-twisted fists on every stump and floating log; fat, spade-headed water moccasins glided everywhere, cutting narrow paths through the duckweed. More than once since they'd taken to the water, Jay had seen the twin, woody knuckles marking the raised eye sockets of a waiting alligator.

Squadrons of damsel flies droned inches above the weeds, and clouds of mosquitoes circled the small boat, attracted by the scent of human sweat, put off for now by the lemon-oil perfume of the homemade repellant that LaFramboise had insisted they use before heading out onto the water. All of this and the rich, seasonal reek of ceaseless rot and death that was too close to the smell issuing from the storage drawer of the trailer back in Beauregard.

"How much farther?" Dane asked, lifting his voice over the hum and whine of the outboard.

"Two, three mile yet," said Tran. "I will give you warning."

They'd struck a reasonable agreement with LaFramboise. The piecemeal corpse of Nguyen Vinh Duong had put the small-town policeman on the edge of bureaucratic panic. Without any investigative resources, he would eventually have to call in the services of the State Police Crime Lab in Baton Rouge, and that in turn would cascade into a law-enforcement and media feeding frenzy once the word got out. Both Jack Dane and Jay insisted that any kind of mainstream operation, probably using helicopters, would seriously prejudice any chance of returning Vinnie Hoa alive. Whatever efforts were made had to be done on a small scale, and quickly.

In the end, LaFramboise agreed to delay bringing in the state police until Dane and Jay completed a reconnaissance of the old Bayou Lachine site with Deputy Tran in command of the operation. If they found evidence that Billy or the boy was there, they were to withdraw and report back to LaFramboise immediately, using Tran's belt radio. The police chief was giving them until dusk.

"You come out here a lot?" Dane asked.

Tran lifted his shoulders and adjusted their course around a set of looming cypress knees jutting out of the duckweed sludge. "Sometimes."

"To fish?"

"No. Not much," the Vietnamese cop answered. "I just come to . . . be here." At the bow, Jay turned, hearing something familiar in the man's voice. Not nostalgia, but something close to it. A place to come for peace, to forget that there had ever been any other world, a place to lose himself for a little while. A place she hadn't really known since she was a child, out fishing with her dad on a still morning river in Wisconsin so long ago.

Five-pound trout on a three-pound line.
I miss you, daddy. I miss you every day.

"This China Bayou," said Dane. "What are we going to find there?"

"Chief Pete says it used to be a good place to fish a long time ago. Sac-a-Lait, crappie, bass, I think. Some people used to build places on the *cheniers* around, but that's all over now. Everything is abandoned."

"What's a *chenier*?" asked Jay.

"Little island, three, four feet up above the swamp. Not big."

Jay swallowed and cleared her throat. "What happened? Why were the fishing places abandoned?"

"Big oil rig come and make the water close by very polluted." The deputy used his free hand to make a choking motion at his throat. "No oxygen, I think. Chief Pete says the well was capped off after a big fire, years back, but oil still leaks into the water. No fish, so no people."

"China Bayou was a town?" asked Dane.

"Not since I have lived here. It was for the oil people. When the oil went, so did the town. It was left to be flooded. All underwater now." He smiled. "Alligators use the old buildings to take their food and hide it away."

"What about roads?" Dane asked, and Jay knew why; the truck was Billy's only means of escape. He would have left it only a short boat ride from where he was hiding the boy.

"A few roads, I think. There is still a big gas field at Butte LaRose, and there are country roads around Bay A'Bot."

None of it meant anything to Jay except for the knowledge that Billy's understanding of the Atchafalaya wasn't much better than their own. Not only would the truck be close, it would be easy to reach without any complicated maneuvering and navigation in a small boat.

He's going to kill the boy and it's going to be awful. It's going to be the worst yet. I have to know. I have to.

She turned to the bow again, swallowing a sudden surge of nauseating mental vertigo as though the mist and the sick heat and the smells and sounds had combined to create some potent psychedelic miasma forcing her in and out of her body and time. Why did she have to know what Billy was going to do to the boy? The child wasn't her responsibility any more than the deaths that had preceded his kidnapping.

Billy's my responsibility, though.

Why? Why yours?

But she knew the answer, felt it now in the sour taste at the back of her throat. She'd killed four men but she hadn't killed enough. She would have tracked down Billy eventually, and if she had, and if she'd killed him then just as she'd killed his mentor, Ricky Stiles, then none of those other people would be dead now and there'd be no terrified little boy lost with Billy in this mad place.

She swallowed hard and lit a cigarette, cupping her hand around the match and staring down the narrow winding trail of black water oozing between the dark, overhanging trees. There was no sense of distance or perspective here; everything was flat and every sound was swallowed whole, dulled and echoless. She tried not to think about what lay under the boat, or what watched and waited, hidden in the trees. Smoking, she concentrated on keeping herself mentally intact, remembering how close she'd come to utter madness not so long ago.

All four of me.

Jay before: the victim, able at will even now to feel the weight of her adolescent rapist pressing down onto her breasts, stealing the breath from her lungs even as he crushed her innocence beneath him without a thought. The scent of fresh cut grass could still make her chest pound with fear.

Jay, trying to forget: being the best goddamned FBI agent that ever lived, piling up one degree after another to prove that she really was accomplishing something, making something out of a life that she secretly thought wasn't worth anything at all, and cracking under the weight of all the time and energy it took to keep the façade intact.

Jay, over the edge and on her own: For a moment, a force for something neither good nor evil, only necessary. Telling herself that it was common cause, that she was nothing more than the expression of people's real feelings about Billy Bones and all his brethren, not a judge or a jury, only an executioner.

And then Jay healing: coming to terms with what she'd done and had almost become, trying to build something new from all of it, to be at peace with the past at last. Fooling herself into believing that such things could be buried once and for all, secretly knowing that they were sure to rise again and that she would rise with them, and in the end, rise eagerly.

Almost over, Billy. For one of us.

Not yet, shitfucker!

Oh God, he's in my head!

No! Shitfucker was Ricky! Shitfucker was Ricky Stiles!

"We are here," said Tran quietly, killing the outboard.

The boat slid forward another twenty or thirty feet, then slowed to a stop, trapped by the whisper hold of the duckweed and its long, dangling roots. The banks of the stream were massed with coffee weed and Virginia creeper, fighting with the even denser growth of low palmetto, leaves shaped like fans, and sprays of resurrection fern stealing any last vestige of the filtered sun.

Ahead of them, just at the edge of shadow, a pair of huge, arthritic cypress leaned across the narrow weed-choked stream, one on each side, arched into a cathedral entrance that looked out across China Bayou. The shallow lake was no more than three or four hundred yards across, the farther side a solid carpet of bilious green that marked an encroaching slab of water hyacinth, stealing whatever food and other nutrients were left in the water.

In the middle of the green, the skeleton of the dead oil rig loomed, leaning to one side, eighty feet high, a monstrous crippled water bug, half covered now with vines and creepers and shadowy patches of mold and moss. Her four tall spindly legs were iron, but the platform was wood and a hundred storms and the passage of time had rotted out the center, collapsing it down in a tangle of old beams and cable into the black water below.

To the right of the abandoned rig, shape and color almost lost against the background of the thicket bank, was a tumbledown summer place, the low *chenier* forming its foundation flooded out so that the ground floor of the little house was partially under water. A sagging set of steps led to an upper gallery, shading dark windows without glass that stared back across the bayou like dead, blind eyes. A camouflage green flatboat was tied up to the base of the steps. Nguyen's Coleman Crawdad.

"Can he see us?" Jay whispered.

Tran answered quietly. "No, we are in the shadows here. He sees nothing."

Jay sensed movement out of the corner of her eye and looked down into the water at the bow. A cottonmouth slid by, four feet long and wrist-thick, its spade head slightly lifted, a dozen olive green stripes running along its back. Jay almost screamed at the sight but caught herself and bit it back, covering her mouth with one hand. She watched as the snake reached the far side of the stream, then glided up and into the undergrowth on the far side.

"What's wrong?" Dane asked urgently.

She turned in her seat and shook her head. "Nothing. Snake."

"There are many snakes in this place," Tran offered. "Some kinds are poisonous, others are not."

"How do you tell the difference?" asked Dane.

Tran allowed himself a momentary smile. "When a poisonous snake bites, you die."

All three of them stared out across the water. Tran dug into his overnight bag and took out a pair of military-style binoculars. He lifted them to his eyes for a moment, then lowered them. "It is Nguyen's boat." He handed the binoculars to Dane, and after a quick look, the marshal passed them forward to Jay.

The mist hung in rags above the slick water, motionless in the still, overheated air. It obscured the details of what she was seeing, but the boat tied up at the bottom of the steps was clearly visible. It was empty, engine tilted up, a long pole tucked into simple clamps along the gunwale. Jay eased the binoculars up, following the steps up to the gallery. No sign of movement, no sense of waiting eyes.

Give me a sign, Billy. Anything.

But there was nothing. Jay tracked the glasses along the length of the gallery, straining to pull some image from the dark squares of the empty windows and the blank rectangle of the single doorway. If the boat was there, then Billy was there, too. She tilted down, checking the main floor. Two windows and a door, one of the windows shuttered, the door gone like a missing tooth, the pickets of the porch rotted away to brown stumps poking a few inches up from the water.

"Sleeping?" said Jay, handing the binoculars back.

Dane checked the building again, then shrugged. "Maybe." He turned to Tran. "You ever do any river work, Tran?"

The Vietnamese nodded and Jay saw his hand come up to gently touch the rope of scar tissue at his neck. "Rung Rat Special Zone. Six months, out of Cao Di."

"What doing?" Dane asked.

"Collecting intelligence for your Seal Team One." He paused and offered up the faint smile that was becoming familiar. "You too, I think."

It was Dane's turn to nod. "Perfume River."

"Hue," said Tran, and the smile was gone. "Very bad."

"Yes. Very Bad." Dane gave the binoculars back to the Vietnamese deputy. He put them back into his bag and looked out over the water.

"How do we do this?" asked Jack Dane.

"From behind," said Tran. "If we keep close to the shore, in the shadows he may not see us until we have him."

"What about LaFramboise?" Jay said, even though she knew the answer.

"By dusk it will be too late," said Tran. "After that it will not matter. We will have succeeded or failed." He paused. "If we wait, the boy will surely die." He paused again. "La-Framboise knows. He expects us to do this."

"Lock and load now," said Dane. "Let's not give ourselves away up close." He reached down, picked up one of the

M16's and handed it back to Tran. In turn, the deputy reached into his bag and pulled out two double-clip magazines, bound together with electrical tape, a few inches offset so the empty clip could be reversed quickly and the full clip inserted.

"That's sixty rounds apiece," said Dane. "One hundred twenty in all. If we can't nail him with that maybe we should shoot ourselves." He pulled back the cocking lever, snapped the taped clip into place, and slid the lever forward again, locking the clip into place. Tran repeated the process with his own weapon.

"You're running true to form," Jay said dryly. She duck-walked two steps toward the center of the boat and grabbed the gopher gun, taking it back to her seat in the bow. She pressed the magazine floor-plate release on the trigger guard, snapped back the bolt, and checked down the barrel. She lowered the rifle and stared at Dane. "Presumably you have ammunition for this thing."

"Presumably you know how to use it," he answered.

"In the middle of winter I used to cull timber wolves on my Uncle Max's place in Bad River, up by Lake Superior." Jay smiled. "What were you doing when you were thirteen?"

Silently, Tran reached into his flight bag and pulled out a handful of five-round clips for the Ruger. He gave them to Dane, who passed them forward. Jay snapped one into the floor plate in front of the trigger and stuffed the others into the front pockets of her jeans.

Dane looked out over the water. "Let me have the glasses, would you?" Tran handed them over. The U.S. Marshal lifted them to his eyes again and scanned the old fishing camp. "How deep do you think the water is around the shack?"

The Vietnamese man squinted out across the motionless lake and made his assessment. "Foot, maybe more, but not too much. Just the rain. A day or two and it will drain away."

"How big do you think that *chenier* thing is?"

"Twenty, maybe twenty five feet bigger than the building, all around."

"So we could walk on it?"

"Yes. Old shells and sediment beneath the water, but good enough footing if you move carefully."

"All right," said Dane. "We stick close to the shoreline to the right. The sun will be in his eyes if he comes out onto that porch thing after his nap."

"And if he does?"

"Then I'll blow him away. No lineups, no waiting," said Dane. "I'm going to be keeping that doorway in my sights while Tran poles us around to the back."

"Then what?" Jay asked.

"We drop you off at the near end of the *chenier*. Tran and I will go around to the far end."

"We flank him."

"That's the idea. See if you can get around to the foot of the stairs and cover us. If he's still not up and around, I go up first and Tran follows me." Dane looked at her squarely. "And you stay put, no matter what."

"Afraid I'll take him out before you do?"

He closed his eyes briefly, shaking his head. "Don't be an idiot. If he gets past me and Tran then you'll be the only one left to make sure the bastard gets what he deserves." He sighed. "Not to mention the fact that you're still a civilian."

"I'll stay put."

But not for long.

Tran loaded his own weapon, then stowed his bag under the transom seat.

"Ready?" Dane asked.

Tran nodded. He carefully tilted up the Evinrude on the transom and reached down for the long wooden pole lying in the bottom of the boat. Standing in a half crouch, he dug the pole into the muck and eased the boat forward, keeping close to the gently rising bank on their right. Jay kept the Ruger loosely in her lap, squinting out across the water, her eyes on the swaybacked little building on the island. Still nothing moved.

Dane was right. It was well past noon now, the sun lowering in the steadily clearing overcast left over from the rain. If Billy came out onto the gallery and looked their way, he'd be half blinded by the sun, and the hot mist was still heavy enough to camouflage them as well.

She held her breath, heart pounding again as a flight of ducks clattered into the air from the marshy area in the middle of the lake. She tensed, waiting for Billy to come out through the doorway, aroused by the frantic splash and squawk of the rising flight of birds. Calmer now, the ducks jigged and skittered into formation, then winged away, flying directly over the little island. Jay tracked their flight then looked back at the doorway, now half as close as it had been in the shadows of the creek mouth. Still nothing. Tran kept poling.

She let her eyes move across the length of the still lake. The mangroves and cypress, dressed in mourning skeins of gray-green Spanish moss, the broken, sun-shot sky, the black water, and the crippled hulk of the old rig had become something else now. She had a passing image of her shelf of treasured children's books back in Mendocino and she knew why they'd suddenly come into her mind. This place wasn't true; this was the Archenland of C. S. Lewis, Tolkien's evil Mordor. There were Gollums here and trees that walked.

Wake up now, Billy. We're all having the same nightmare.

Jay blinked a trickle of salt sweat from her eyes and tried to hypnotize herself into an artificial state of calm. Billy was asleep in his rotting lair, dreaming his frightful dreams, and they were here, his appointed executioners, preparing to do their ritual business.

Just like the wolves at Uncle Max's place. "Just a job that needs doin' darlin'," wasn't that what he used to say?

Tran edged closer, pushing up bubbles of foul-smelling gas as he pulled the pole out of the sucking ooze below the water. The heat was exhausting and the sweat was washing away the lemon oil. Mosquitoes found the boat, rising in clouds around the boat, settling on any area of exposed flesh.

Trying to ignore the biting insects, Jay looked down for an instant and watched as the prow of the little boat sliced through a migrating sheet of fire ants, their bodies so light they were actually walking on the water, pushed by invisible currents and the slightest breeze. Some of their company were holding up glistening white pupae, safe from the water as they migrated blindly in their thousands to some new world.

Between the boat and the shore, another snake slithered through the duckweed, this one bright green and twice the length of the one she'd seen before. A banjo frog poised at the base of a sodden, jutting cypress knee, crushed a dragonfly between its small green jaws, and only a second later leapt away too late as the green snake struck. Death in China Bayou was just another kind of recycling; in a million years or so a body buried here would turn to coal, and finally, long after that, to oil.

Still no sign of Billy, and then Tran was moving them farther out, the windowless side of the fish camp building shielding them from view for the moment. In front of her, no more than fifty feet away now, Jay could see the narrow patch of water hyacinth that marked the near side of the sickle-shaped island. She looked down at her feet. Keds. Not the greatest thing for wading around in snake-infested swamps.

There was a faint scraping sound and, looking directly over the bow of the boat, Jay could see that they'd gone aground, the water here only inches deep. Dane gave her a nod and she slipped out of the boat and onto the *chenier* as quietly as she could. She felt something like loose, broken gravel through the thin soles of the deck shoes, and then something oozing up and into them.

For a panic-stricken instant she thought about quicksand, but then the sinking stopped. She lifted one foot and checked the mark on her light colored sock. It looked as though she'd gone down into the muck about three inches. She gave Dane a little wave with one hand, then watched as Tran poled them off the *chenier* and back into the open water. Cradling the Ruger in her arms for balance, Jay moved higher up the submerged island, trying to ignore the pull and suck of the muck, her eyes fixed on the gallery and the stairs that seemed to run right down into the water.

Less than a hundred feet separated her from the ruined house now; she was close enough to notice every detail. The house itself was made from broad, thick cypress planks, so old they'd cured to black, iron-hard beneath the shoddy, peeling coat of white paint that had gone moldy green and gray in patches and streaks. Too many years had bowed and rusted the tin roof badly, and the rising water had rotted out the original support beams and posts, letting the entire structure fall into a drunken, dangerous tilt. A serious storm would be enough to topple it.

The boat was tied up to the bottom post of the stairway, the motor tilted up and out of the way, the only thing out of place being a long rope painter trailing back into the water. Jay frowned, wondering why a painter was needed at all, considering the simple, single-line mooring, but then her attention shifted back to the stairs and the gallery. There must have been a rise in the earth beneath her because the footing was suddenly much better. She shifted the varmint rifle to port arms in case Billy appeared before Dane and Tran Van Dang got into position. It had been a long time since she'd fired a rifle, but at this close range she knew it would be hard to miss.

Hit or miss, you have to fire and I don't know if I can do that any more.

Something had broken in her that day in the Baltimore psychiatrist's office and she still didn't know if she wanted it fixed. At first she thought it was only fear brought on by the close call, but passing time hadn't given her back the confidence she'd once felt about herself, the sure knowledge that what she was doing was fundamentally right. It was the same confusion that kept her from closing the circle of her relationship with Robin back in Mendocino and the same overall unease that sometimes made her feel as though she wanted nothing more than to be alone with her house by the sea. But like it or not, she knew that Billy was bringing her back to the world.

Murder as a make-up test.

She almost laughed but stopped herself, choking off the sound halfway up her throat. She stopped thirty feet from the base of the steps, then ducked down, looking under the risers to see if Jack and Tran were in place. She saw them pull the boat up and climb overboard, Tran easing a small rope and stone anchor onto the *chenier* to keep the boat from drifting off. They started to move forward, Tran leading, Jack behind but off to one side, the M16 high in his hands, his index finger already wrapped around the trigger. Both men were focusing all their attention on the upper gallery, and neither of them noticed the swift stab of fractured light winking from the abandoned oil rig.

Sunlight reflecting off a telescopic sight. Oh Jesus, he's not in the house at all!

Trap!

"Down!"

Too late.

The bullet had crossed the two hundred yards of open water before the warning shout was out of her mouth, and a quarter of a second later the harsh crack of the shot snapped into the air.

Jay was on the ground, water up to her chin, arms out, keeping the rifle just above the surface, waiting for the second shot. It didn't come. She stared across the shallow lake, trying to see through the reeds and tall grass in the marshy area between the *chenier* and the old drilling platform, but it was impossible to see anything this low down. She turned her head slightly, her line of sight running under the stairs and across to the other end of the *chenier*. From somewhere she heard a low groan. Both Jack Dane and Tran were down, pressed into the wet muck, but there was no way to tell which one of them had been hit.

After the quick thunder of the single shot, the silence was perfect for a few long seconds, and then the wetland sounds began again. Digging in with her elbows and her toes, Jay began to pull herself forward and to one side, reasonably sure that if she couldn't see the drilling platform from where she was, Billy probably couldn't see her. She kept edging to the side until she had the side of the plastic flatboat between her and the open water. Screened by the narrow boat, she lifted herself up a little and began to move faster, finally reaching the little craft.

Head down, she reached up and undid the mooring line, expecting the shattering pain of a bullet in her exposed hand at any second. Still no second shot from Billy. She tossed her rifle into the boat, then gripping the gunwale with one hand, she pushed off from the bottom of the steps, using the boat as a shield and guiding it blindly, half swimming and half crawling to the far end of the submerged island. The water in her mouth and nose was rank, sediment fouling her nostrils cloyingly, gritty and evil-tasting on her teeth and tongue.

It took her almost five minutes to move to the far end of the *chenier*, and by the time she reached Dane and Tran Van Dang, she was exhausted, every muscle in her body rigidly tense with the expectation of another shot. Ten feet from the two men she saw Dane raise his head slightly.

"You okay?"

"Yes. Tran's hit." Dane's voice was coming in small, panting gasps.

"Badly?"

The marshal reached back and touched the sodden sleeve of Tran's shirt. At first Jane thought the stain was just water, but then she realized it was blood. "Hard to say. He's unconscious. I've been keeping his mouth out of the water so he can breathe."

Jay maneuvered the flatboat directly in front of the two men, screening them from Billy's line of fire.

"He's on the drilling platform. He's been there all the time."

"Waiting for us."

"But the boat was tied up . . ."

"He must have had another one," Dane said. "One we didn't know about." The rain was starting up again, tapping on the plastic boat and puncturing the black water all around them.

"The boy?" Jay said urgently.

"Maybe in the fishing shack," said Dane. "But I doubt it. Either he's with Billy or . . ."

Jay let out a short breath, nodding. Brittany Shields had

been a tease; she knew Billy wouldn't let the little boy live. "Let's get Tran to the shack."

"How?"

"Same way I got here. Use the boat for cover."

There was a faint, growling noise in the distance, coming from the far side of the lake.

"Motor."

"Shit!" said Dane. "He's coming to finish us off." Beside them the Vietnamese deputy groaned.

"No! Listen!" Jay insisted. Above the spitting patter of the rain the outboard engine sound was fading. A few seconds later it died out altogether. "He's leaving!" Another thirty seconds passed, quiet except for the sound of the rain and the rough breathing of the wounded man a few feet away. In the distance Jay heard the sound of another engine, much larger than the outboard, followed by the honking of a horn.

"The son of a bitch is saying goodbye!" Dane concluded furiously.

"No time for being angry," Jay answered. "We've got to get Tran to the fishing shack and call for some help before he bleeds to death."

"The boy," Tran muttered. "Vinnie."

Dane shook his head. "Either he's with Billy or he's dead. One way or the other there's nothing we can do for him now. We take care of you first."

"How do you feel?" asked Jay.

The Vietnamese man groaned. "Not so bad," he said, dragging himself up out of the water, rolling into a crouch, knees in the water. The front of his shirt was soaked with blood and there was a darker spot where the bullet had entered. Jay could see white bone; from the looks of it, the rifle shot had torn through the deltoid and broken the collarbone before exiting. A lot worse than a flesh wound, but survivable, even out here.

"Can you stand?"

"I think so."

Dane picked up Tran's weapon and handed it to Jay. He helped the Vietnamese man to his feet, then into the boat.

"I'll take him in this boat, you get ours and bring it around to the stairs."

Jay nodded, then turned and made her way back across the widest part of the *chenier* to the place where Dane had anchored the aluminum boat given to them by LaFramboise. She climbed in, dropped the M16 onto the floorboards, then tipped the engine back into the water. She hit the starter, and with the engine at half throttle guided the boat back the way the two men had come, arriving at the foot of the stairs in time to help Dane take Tran up to the gallery. The rain was back in full force now, hammering insistently on the old tin roof.

There were three rooms on the gallery level, but two of them had bad leaks and neither one of them looked as though it had been recently occupied. The third room had been fitted out with an air mattress, a new-looking hand-pumped pressure lamp, and a cooler. Inside the cooler there were two thawed-out cold packs, a partially filled carton of orange juice, and a half-empty bucket of Kentucky Fried Chicken. The gnawed bones of the already eaten chicken had been tucked neatly away in a paper bag. The only other thing in the room was an old copy of *Boat Trader* beside the makeshift bed. There was no sign of the little boy.

Jay and Dane helped Tran to the air mattress and eased him down onto it. Jay managed to unclip the radio on his belt, but it was clogged with mud and shorted out. "No way this is going to work," she said.

"Cell phone?"

"My battery's low, but it's worth a shot." She went down to the boat, retrieved the phone from her jacket, and came back up to the room. "What's the number?" she asked Tran.

"Let me call," he said, holding out his hand. "You and Marshal Dane should go out to the rig." He paused, wincing, then pulled himself together. "There may still be some chance for Vinnie."

"All right," said Dane.

Jay handed Tran the phone. "Med-Evac but nothing more, no circus out here, make sure the chief knows that. If the kid is still alive we don't want Billy getting spooked."

Tran nodded. "Agreed." He paused and tried to smile. "I heard you yell and I turned to find out where you were calling from," he said quietly. "If I had not done so, the hit would have taken me here." He reached up with his good hand and put two fingers at the base of his throat. "I would be dead now. You saved my life."

"You're welcome," she said. "You sure you're going to be okay?"

"I will be fine."

"Let's go," said Dane urgently. He headed for the door and went through it to the gallery. Jay followed him and a moment later they were on the lake in the new rain, heading for the drilling rig. This time Jay handled the throttle while Dane sat in the middle seat, the M16 across his lap.

"You're the expert," Dane said, keeping his eyes forward. "You think Billy took the kid with him?"

"No," Jay answered flatly. "Vinnie was bait to bring us here. He's no use to Billy now."

"He must have seen us coming from the time we came out of the creek. Why didn't he shoot then?"

"I think he wanted us separated," Jay answered, thinking out loud. "There's nothing in his file about being an expert shot; he was never in the service or anything. Maybe he didn't want to hit the wrong person."

"You think he shot Tran on purpose?" said Dane. "Why?"

"Because Tran's not part of the game. He's an extra piece on the board. We broke the rules by bringing him along."

"This whole thing is insane!" said Dane, despair heavy in his voice, and exhaustion.

"I know," Jay answered.

They reached the tangled mass of old timber and girders, then eased the boat through the skeleton of the disemboweled rig, killing the engine and using the pole. "There," said Dane, pointing up into the soft rain. "Some kind of platform." Jay poled forward to a ladder of wreckage, wrapping the mooring rope around one of the inner steel support beams and holding the boat still as the marshal clambered out and began to climb.

She waited there, blinking, staring up into the rain, waiting and trying not to think about what Dane might find.

"I've found a couple of shell casings!" he called down finally.

Fuck the shell casings, what about Vinnie?

"Any sign of the boy?" she called. For a moment there was no answer and Jay was sure he'd found something terrible up there.

"No. Nothing but a rope that goes down to the water. Probably used it to climb down to his boat. You see it?"

Jay peered into the wreckage of the old oil rig, blinking the rain out of her eyes. Then she spotted the rope, thin and pale and taut, twenty feet in. Beyond it there was a clear path back to the far shore. "I see it," she called up. "I can get to it from here."

"Wait," said Dane. "I'm coming down." He appeared a few moments later, the empty shell casings cupped in his hand. "Tran was right," he said, stepping into the boat. "Looks like he got a hold of Nguyen's M1." He tossed the casings on the floor of the boat. "Probably got a new sight for it, too. A blind man could have taken out anybody with one of those things."

"But he didn't."

"No." Dane looked at her. "He wanted us here, right? He shot Tran to take him out of play, but he knew we'd wind up coming here, didn't he?"

"Yes."

To find what he left us.

She poled the boat through the fallen debris from the upper levels of the half-collapsed rig, heading for the taut line of the rope. Ten feet away, even through the slanting rain she could see the glistening spot of color marking the place Billy had pinned the butterfly, its wings broken and torn by the raindrops. For the first time she could see that the nylon rope had been knotted at intervals of about a foot.

I don't want to see this.

Abraham's Isaac.

She pushed the long pole into the water and they slid forward through the dark wreckage, the smell of the rain and the hibiscus sweet as death in her nose. The bow of the boat touched the rope and tipped away. Dane grabbed the line, holding them in place, then looked down into the water.

The marshal slowly shook his head, then brought up his free hand and wiped the rain away from his eyes. "Aw jeez," he whispered. He took a long breath, then let it out again, shivering with the release. He leaned out and reached down into the water with both hands, the muscles of his jaw tightening with barely controlled emotion. Jay desperately wanted to look away but couldn't, her eyes on the water as Dane lifted the small, naked form up and out of the lake, bringing it into the boat, cradling it on his lap while he undid the loops of rope around the little boy's armpits, trying to pull away the duct tape that bound the thin wrists together behind his back, and failing. The ankles had also been taped together, and there was tape over the mouth as well, but the eyes had been left free, the sockets empty, already fed upon by small foraging creatures in the lake.

"Bastard," said Dane, almost choking on the word. "You bastard."

There were no obvious wounds on the body. Billy had bound the child, then lowered him into the water to drown, watching the brief hopeless struggle as the small pale form went into the dark, suffocating water.

"No butterflies," said Dane.

The water would have ruined them.

Gently, Jay peeled the tape off the little boy's mouth, knowing what she would find. She eased her index finger between the small jaws, then hooked out a folded butterfly. A wad of soggy paper had been wedged between its wings. She flattened the paper on her knee and read the message written in neat, schoolboy script, each letter carefully formed. Vinnie had taken school seriously.

> *Lady, he says he is going to hurt me and that you could have saved me.*

Why didn't you stop him, Lady? Why did you let this happen?
Signed,
Vinnie Hoa, 11 years old.

No mercy now, Billy.
I'm going to find you and kill you, just like Ricky.

SEVENTEEN

The helicopter from Baton Rouge Air Med picked up Tran and the others less than an hour after Pete LaFramboise placed the call. All of them, including the small corpse of Vinnie Hoa, were taken to Our Lady of the Lake Regional Medical Center in Baton Rouge, and after two hours of being treated for various cuts and bruises, Jay Fletcher and Jack Dane were released. According to the doctors, Tran's injuries were serious but not life-threatening. LaFramboise and Antoinette Peychaud had driven from Beauregard to the hospital in Baton Rouge and were waiting for them outside the emergency room. LaFramboise had taken care of the paperwork, and as far as Jay and Jack Dane could see, no other law-enforcement agency appeared to be involved. LaFramboise came quickly to the point. When he spoke, his voice was tight with anger and more than a little tension.

"Y'all got my best man shot up and you didn't even catch the fellow who did it. Pretty fucking sloppy police work, Mr. And Mrs. fucking U.S. goddamned Marshal." He paused, breathing hard through his nostrils. "On top of that, I got a little boy horrible dead and his mother distraught and no answers for her, none at all, no sir."

"He was dead by the time we got there," said Dane, his voice flat and tired. "Long dead."

"I told you to go and *look*, federal boy. Look, not go in there playing fucking Roy Rogers and Dale fucking Evans for the love of Christ!"

"We never fired a shot," said Jay.

"You walk into a trap like you on day one of your goddamned big-shot police academy. Jesus!"

"Are you going anywhere with this?" Dane asked.

"I'm going to hell with this, that's where I'm going *bon 'homme*. You think this is going to lie down and die? You bring in a little boy bound up with tape and drowned, his eyes chewed out by the crab and the gar, you think that just going to go away?" He shook his head. "Questions going to be asked, friend, and it's me who going to have to come up with the fancy answers."

Jay sighed. "We didn't bring this to you, Chief La-Framboise." She paused. "We tried to stop it."

"Tell that to the mother of Vinnie Hoa," said the police chief. "But it's going to make her feel all good and warm inside, sure it will. I want you gone. I want you good and gone from this place, *cher*, and I don't ever want to see you back again." LaFramboise stared at her coldly. "This man you chasing, the one kill Vinnie, he's bad, but so are you. You bring this evil with you, I think."

No, it comes to me, I don't have to chase it.

Quit it, Jay, you're just rationalizing.

"Our rental's back in Beauregard," she said.

LaFramboise shook his head. "No it's not. That's why Toinette is here; I got her to drive it behind me." He reached into his pocket, took out the keys, and gave them to Jay. "Go away. Anyone comes to ask me questions, I just tell them what you told me about this man, this Billy." He turned away from her then, his shoulders stiffening. Jay turned her back as well and followed Jack Dane out of the hospital. They found the rental and drove out of Baton Rouge, heading back to New Orleans, Jay behind the wheel, Dane slumped beside her, staring out the windshield at the lowering sun. It was almost night.

"Now what?" Jay asked. She steered the car up the Julia Street ramp and put them on Interstate 10 heading back to New Orleans.

"We hang up our spurs," said Dane. "We go back to D.C. and tell them we blew it."

"That's not acceptable," Jay answered. "We can't give up."

She turned briefly and looked at the man on the seat beside her. "Not after what he did to that little kid."

"Don't tell me how we're going to proceed," Dane said. "We stepped into an ambush in the middle of a swamp, almost get ourselves killed, and our man gets away clean as a whistle with two more victims racked up on the scoreboard. That's five to zip for Billy, and this time he didn't leave us any clues unless there's something on your computer back at the hotel."

"What about this?" Jay took one hand off the wheel and dug into the back pocket of her jeans. She pulled out the rolled-up copy of the pulp paper magazine she'd taken from beside the air mattress in the fishing shack. Dane picked it up and flipped through the papers."

"*Boat Trader*?" asked the marshal skeptically. "You think this is a clue?"

"It has to be. It's the only thing he left behind except for the bucket of chicken."

"Why not toss the goddamned bones and see if we can't get a reading? 'Hey Julie, don't go to the Senate today, Brutus is looking for you and, boy, is he pissed.' "

"Billy wouldn't have left it behind unless it was important," insisted Jay. "That's why he didn't kill us when he had the chance. He wants to keep playing the game."

"And I want to sleep," Dane answered. "Tomorrow we go back to Washington. Period, stop, end of story, okay? It's finished." He tossed the magazine down onto the seat between them, tilted his seat back, and closed his eyes. He didn't open them again until they reached the Airport Hilton.

Back in their suite Jay booted herself onto the Net and found Billy waiting in the chatroom, right on schedule.

—**Interesting chain of events, don't you think?**
—You didn't have to do that, Billy. Not a child.
—**Got your attention though, didn't it?**
—How many more?
—**As many as it takes. Like I said, a chain of events.**
—I won't let this go, Billy, I can't.

—I don't expect you to. Like the President said, stay
the course. Full speed ahead.
—You're going to die.
—We all die.
—I'm going to kill you, Billy. Any last words?

A clue, goddamn it, giving me something to work with!
Give me something to kill you with.

—Really, when you get right down to it, it's all a matter
of sensitive dependence on initial conditions: nails and
shoes and horses.
   "My eyes are cameras; I have the world and the uni-
verse as my own. At my will I walk your streets and am
right out there among you."
—What's that supposed to mean?
—How about,
"This royal throne of kings, this sceptered isle,
This other Eden, demi-paradise."

Jay logged a <?> query into the chatroom but there was
no answer. Billy was gone. She came off the Net but left the
back-and-forth conversation on the screen.

"Boasting," said Dane. "More of his obscure clues." He
shook his head. "Like I said, I've had enough. I'll leave a
message with Karlson's office, tell him we're leaving here on
the first flight out in the morning."

Jay kept her face blank. She shrugged. "Your call."

"I'm going to bed. You want the bedroom?"

"No," Jay answered. "I'm fine out here."

"You should get some sleep."

"I will." He gave her a long last look then turned away,
went into the bedroom, and closed the door behind him.

Night.

Jay lit a cigarette, sipped her coffee, and stared at the
screen. There were two things she was reasonably sure of:
the copy of *Boat Trader* and the note on her screen contained
the information she needed to plot Billy's next course, and

possibly his next victim. Using pen and paper, she began to parse the note like a child analyzing a sentence on the blackboard for the teacher.

"Sensitive dependence on initial conditions: nails and shoes and horses." Nails and shoes and horses appeared to be a reference to the old nursery rhyme:

> For want of a nail the shoe was lost;
> For want of a shoe the horse was lost;
> For want of a horse the rider was lost;
> For want of a rider the battle was lost;
> For want of a battle the kingdom was lost.

In other words, one thing leads to another, or shit happens. A pretty fair description of Billy's apparently random actions since his escape.

But nothing he does is ever random. It all has meaning, kiddo, don't let him fool you.

But what the hell was "a sensitive dependence on initial conditions"? Once again she circled the phrase on her notes and moved on. "*My eyes are cameras; I have the world and the universe as my own. At my will I walk your streets and am right out there among you.*"

The quotation was familiar and Jay was fairly sure where she'd heard it before. On a hunch she dumped out of her e-mail program, went all the way back to the C prompt, and spent the next twenty minutes hacking her way into the FBI mainframe in Washington, using the old "back door" she had coded in back when she worked for Charlie Langford in the Computer division. From there, it was a short digital hop to the Main Justice offices at 950 Pennsylvania Avenue and an even easier hack into the unclassified Files Division.

She cruised the file index until she found the transcripts of Billy's Trial: *United States of America v. William Paris Bonisteel.* She seemed to remember the words from Billy's own impromptu postverdict statement. She scrolled quickly through the transcript to the end and there it was in black and white. Jay poured herself another cup of coffee, trying to make sense of it all; even in context the phrases didn't sound like Billy. He was quoting someone else, but who?

Jay backed out of the Main Justice computer, went back to the Net, and used the Yahoo! search engine to look up the phrase "Sensitive dependence on initial conditions." Her first search came up empty: There were no matches for the complete phrase. She tried again, cutting it back to "sensitive dependence." It took a few seconds for the search engine to come back with its hits. Jay sat back, stunned as she saw the first listing; it was, bizarrely, from the "Prayer and Share" column of the Heathmont Baptist Church weekly newsletter in Heathmont, Australia, and was entitled "Sensitive Dependence—The Butterfly Effect."

"Jesus," Jay whispered. She clicked on the title and watched as the whole text came up. According to the article, the term *butterfly effect* was coined to illustrate the sensitivity of complex systems on minutely small variations in initial conditions or perturbations: potentially, the flapping wings of a butterfly in one part of the world could eventually result in a hurricane in some other place at a later time. This butterfly effect was the root of what has now come to be known as chaos theory. She went back to the list and scanned several more entries.

She'd heard about chaos theory before—usually related to computer-generated "fractals" and "Mandelbrot sets," but until now it had never really interested her. Reading through the entries on the Internet she quickly got a rough idea of what the theory suggested.

Essentially, regardless of how "random" or "chaotic" events appeared, there was always a more complex, deeper rationality to it all; in other words, chaos was simply another form of order, but unless you looked at it the right way that order was invisible. "Sensitive dependence on initial conditions" was really just a fancy, updated version of the nail, shoe, horse rhyme. One thing led to another, each "thing" depending on the conditions around it to choose the next "thing" on the list.

It took Jay another five minutes to get back into the FBI

computer in Washington. This time she made her way through
the system to the inventory taken from William Bonisteel's
apartment in New York after his arrest. She found the entry
for Books and scrolled through the titles. Very little fiction,
a dozen volumes about Charles Manson and the Tate-
LaBianca killings, several hundred anthropology and archae-
ology titles, and at the end, a list of a dozen or so books on
chaos theory, one of them entitled simply *The Butterfly Effect.*

That explains the butterflies.

Each of Billy's victims was "chaotically" responsible for
the choosing of the next. Mrs. Bannerman was cotrustee with
Hunter Connelly, the murdered man in New York, which in
turn led to Mrs. Graihle-Baker, the piano teacher in Blackwood, which led to the bar in New Orleans. . . . Nails, shoes,
and horses, not random at all if you factored in butterflies and
chaos.

She looked back at the screen, read through the familiar
lines from Shakespeare. Thrones, Islands, Paradise. It was like
the first poetic squib about waiting for sparks to fall from
heaven. More chaos?

An interesting chain of events, don't you think?

Something is missing.

A bucket of KFC and a copy of *Boat Trader.* You might
make some kind of connection between the chicken bones
and Billy, but that was too much of a stretch even for him.
No. It was the magazine.

It has to be. There's nothing else.

She picked up the magazine and flipped through it. Page
after page filled with small, usually poor quality photographs
of boats. Everything from outsized rowboats to huge yachts
with helicopter landing pads. There didn't seem to be any
order to the pulp paper production except that the first two-
thirds of the magazine were for powerboats and the last third
was for sailboats. The magazine was published by something
called YachtSell International with a post office box number
in Norfolk, Virginia. No clue there.

Something missing.

If it's missing, how am I supposed to know it's gone?

Because it's not really missing, stupid.

Jay let out a long, frustrated breath, tossed the magazine aside, and lit another cigarette. She turned and glanced back at the closed door leading into the bedroom, wondering if it was worth waking Dane to see if they could brainstorm an answer together. She decided against it; relations between the two of them were strained enough as it was. She took a long drag on the cigarette and picked up the magazine again, letting it fall open in her hands, the page choosing itself randomly, chaotically.

Is this how Billy did it?

No, because Billy was telling her that there was method to his madness and order to his chaos; the magazine held the answer, she just wasn't seeing it.

Why not? Why don't I see it?

Because it's missing.

And that gave it to her. She went through the pages, front to back, checking the page numbers in the lower right-hand corner as she went. She stopped at 144. The next page in the magazine was 147. Something was missing. She pulled the magazine fully open and saw that the page had been neatly sliced out with a blade of some kind. Jay looked at her watch. Where the hell did you pick up a copy of *Boat Trader* magazine at 4:00 A.M. in New Orleans?

Then she noticed that there was a World Wide Web address on every page of the magazine, right between the page number and the issue number: http//www.boatsell.com. She booted the laptop up again, got on the Web, and surfed to the appropriate address.

Boatsell.com was as slick as it came, complete with an online version of the magazine. She checked to make sure she had the right issue, then clicked her way through the magazine. The missing page came up clear as a bell.

There were ten boats on the first missing page, four with 954 area code phone numbers, two with 405, three with 815, and one with a 305 number. Knowing she was close, she leapt off the couch, grabbed the phone book out of the desk drawer, and went to the area code listings in the front. Area code 954 turned out to be Fort Lauderdale; 405 was Oklahoma City; 815 was Rockford, Illinois; 305 was either Miami or Key West.

Of the ten boats, the 305 area code picture was the only singleton. Playing with the program, she enlarged the advertisement until it filled the screen. What she got was a large, grainy picture of something called a Grand Banks 46 which was being offered as a "must sell." As she worked the commands to enhance the picture, a vague, slippery shard of memory floated to the surface of her mind, something about Key West.

She concentrated, then remembered: It was back at FDR High in Tomahawk, Wisconsin, and Wanda Kilsabian was actually doing a "What I Did on My Summer Vacation" public speaking thing in front of the class. According to prim and proper Wanda, plain daughter of an accountant who would die shoveling his front walk a few years later, you were mistaken if you thought that Key West was named Key West because it was the westernmost key. The real reason was that it was from the Spanish, *Cayo Hueso*, which meant Island of Bones.

"Son of a bitch," Jay whispered. She didn't have to look any further. The side of the boat filled the screen, and she could read the name without difficulty: Charming Billy.

Billy Bones.

She turned and stared at the closed door to the bedroom. Even if Dane agreed with her interpretation, he wouldn't follow through. He'd take it back to Karlson and forget about it. Forget about her. Forget about Billy.

Something she couldn't do. Screw Dane. Screw Karlson, screw them all. It wasn't over for her, not yet.

Not by a long shot.

EIGHTEEN

Acting on the logical assumption that Jack Dane would report her sudden defection to Norman Karlson at the U.S. Marshals, Jay Fletcher did as much as she could to predict their actions and thought patterns. Instead of driving out of New Orleans and heading for the Keys, she left the rental at the long-term parking lot at New Orleans International, took the shuttle to the main terminal, then found an ATM machine and maxed out the Kelly Morgan Visa card. If they tracked the card, it would show a cash withdrawal at New Orleans International, which was just fine, since she had no intention of flying from there. Instead, she found a taxi and took it back into New Orleans and the old Lakefront Airport.

The restored Art Deco terminal on Lake Ponchartrain dated back to the thirties and had long ago stopped being the city's main airport, but it still handled a good cross section of local airlines, including Gulf Charter and Air Florida. The Gulf Charter flight left at 7:30, half an hour later than the Air Florida flight, but Gulf Charter bypassed Miami International and landed at Marathon Airport in the middle of the Keys, saving her at least an hour or two drive time from Miami, not to mention the horrors of the huge, notoriously inefficient and overcrowded airport. She booked onto the Gulf Charter flight, paying cash, picked up a copy of the *Times Picayune*, and ate a McDonald's breakfast while she waited for her flight to be called.

Jay knew from her own experience at the Bureau that even when someone used cash instead of credit, a money trail was left. In the case of airplane tickets, the selling agent was required to put an asterisk by every cash-paying entry on a flight manifest, but this only applied to the main scheduled airlines, not charters.

Dane and Karlson would assume that she was paying cash, but her trail of breadcrumbs pointed to New Orleans International, not Lakefront, and using Gulf Charter she knew there would be no specific record of her paying cash. The best case scenario would be Jack Dane and the others not finding the rental car for at least a day or two, and the worst case was a dead end at Lakefront Airport. Either way, she had at least a day's grace to do what she had to, and by her calculations Billy was no more than twelve hours ahead of her now. If she was lucky there was still time to stop him.

Dead.

Jay trashed the last half of her breakfast, broke a ten dollar bill into quarters, and called the number listed in *Boat Trader* for *Charming Billy*. All she got was a generic message for something called Harry's Key West Charters and an invitation to leave a message so that Harry could return the call as soon as possible. She would have preferred a human being on the other end of the line, but at least she'd narrowed the 305 area code down to a specific location.

She scooped up the rest of the quarters, then went outside to smoke a last cigarette before getting on her flight. She sat down on one of the concrete benches outside the terminal and lit up. A few days ago—a million years ago, she was making a new life for herself in California and there was even the possibility of romance on the not too distant horizon. All that was gone now, or at least it was on hold for the time being.

Stop kidding yourself. You really were born for this.

And she knew it was true. For almost as long as she could remember life had been a question of white hats and black hats. Stories of knights and knaves, sheriffs and outlaws, heroes and villains had been her intellectual bread and butter, even when the heroes were flawed or mad, or both, like Captain Ahab in *Moby Dick*. It had been clear to her long before her rape; good didn't triumph over evil without assistance, you had to work at it.

So she became a cop, with a badge and a gun and a purpose. She wasn't just stopping criminals, she was doing her own small bit to make life better for the good guys. But with time and circumstance, the innocent philosophy changed in a slow metamorphosis that eventually came full circle, all shades of gray forming back into cops and robbers' black and white, taking her heart and soul to a terrible place and time where there was only one law, the law of kill or be killed, of eye for an eye, of do as you have been done by.

Oh dear me, Janet Louise Fletcher, you really are a supremely arrogant piece of work. Who died and made you the arbiter of truth and justice?

Vinnie Hoa died, that's who, and with my name in his mouth, screaming all the way to wherever little kids go when they die.

She thought of Robin, her friend and almost lover back in Mendocino. Berkeley, beads, and be-ins with a degree in political science that had been martyred on the cross of political activism somewhere along the way. That in turn had taken him through the ritual gauntlet of sex and drugs and angst, leading him inevitably to the sanctuary of his art and craft in a Mendocino hot glass shop. Every synapse in his liberal Democrat mind would fuse and short-circuit if he knew who and what she really was. And thinking of him, she finally admitted to herself what the trouble was between them: She just didn't care enough. If there'd been a chance for her to be an ordinary person, it had now slipped away.

I crossed the line.

And knew she could never go back. She took a last drag on her cigarette as her flight was called. No wonder she'd loved reading *Interview with a Vampire*. She hadn't known it then, but she was on the same path as Lestat. Once bitten, not shy at all, but even so she could mourn for the loneliness of her life, now and in whatever future lay in front of her, even as she felt the fierce joy of what she knew she'd now fully become.

None of it matters.

She stubbed out the cigarette, went back into the terminal, and checked onto her flight. The 737 filled up quickly with passengers, almost all of them Brits with a variety of Manchester and Birmingham accents, wearing Hawaiian shirts and straw hats, part of some package junket intent on taking them to every theme park in America. As the jet jolted down the runway and out over Lake Ponchartrain, the only words Jay could decipher were "Disneyland," "Knotts Berry," and "Seven Flags." Next on the itinerary was a bus trip down to Key West for the Hemingway Days Festival, then back up to Orlando for Disney World and Universal Studios.

The Fasten Your Seatbelts sign went off as the jet angled out over the Gulf of Mexico and headed southeast. A very large woman in skintight white shorts and a label on her parrot-covered shirt that said "Daphne" was staring hard out the window, using one hand to shade her eyes. The rattling of the approaching liquor cart distracted her for a moment and she turned to Jay, her broad face smiling.

"Fancy we'll see Cuba then?" Daphne asked. Jay forced herself to keep the smile off her face. The voice fit the name perfectly—she sounded exactly like the Daphne character on *Frasier*.

"Maybe."

"Think we might get hijacked?" Daphne gave her a slow wink. "Always liked men with beards."

"I think Fidel might be a little old for you."

"It's not how old it is, love, it's how hard." Daphne hooted with laughter, and Jay realized that the woman was drunk out of her mind at eight o'clock in the morning. The drink cart stopped, Daphne ordered a vodka and tomato juice and Jay passed altogether, remembering the Egg McMuffin and sludgy coffee she'd eaten in the airport. Daphne sipped her drink from its plastic glass, her finger extended like a debutante, the plump fingers of her other hand holding a napkin under the glass to catch any drips that might mar her shorts.

"So then," the woman said. "You're on vacation are you?"

"Just getting away for a bit," Jay answered.

"You don't sound like you're from New Orleans."

"No," Jay answered.

"I'm from Manchester," Daphne answered, sipping. She

licked her lips. Jay noticed her wedding ring. Her fingers were so fat you could barely see the gold band. "Well, I tell a lie. Not really Manchester." She sipped again. "Glossop actually." With another sip the drink was gone. "Can't really tell the difference anymore really, Glossop's been swallowed up."

"Too bad," said Jay.

Daphne shrugged her large shoulders. Parrots swayed back and forth on her shirt. "Oh, I don't know," she said philosophically. "Some things are better."

This is the Twilight Zone.

Daphne beamed at a passing stewardess and waggled her empty plastic glass at the woman. Then she turned back to Jay. "You never did say where you were from."

"A little place called Tomahawk, Wisconsin."

"Sounds interesting." Daphne's next drink arrived and she began sipping again.

"It wasn't," Jay answered.

"Nice?"

"Used to be," Jay said. "It hasn't been the same since the rape, though."

Daphne went goggle-eyed and took another sip. "Rape?"

"Mine."

Welcome to America, Glossop Girl.

"Oh," said Daphne. She didn't say another word for the rest of the ninety-minute flight.

The 737 landed at Marathon Airport right on schedule, and after picking up the overnight bag containing her laptop and Jack Dane's Glock 19, Jay walked down the long, terra-cotta-tiled concourse of the small terminal and out into the baking sunlight. She'd already ruled out renting a car since that would require a credit card, which left her with the shuttle bus or a taxi. Spotting the parrot-shirted Daphne and the rest of her sozzled tour climbing onto the shuttle, Jay opted for a taxi, even though the hour-long trip was going to cost her the better part of a hundred dollars.

They turned onto the highway, crossed the Vaca Cut Waterway, and headed south on the Overseas Highway. Jay settled back in the seat and tried to relax, glad that the driver was content to commune with his own thoughts rather than try to engage her in conversation. She adjusted her watch for the change in time zone. Eleven o'clock here, ten in New Orleans. Jack would be waking up just about now which meant she still had time before the shit really started hitting the fan.

She spent the next half hour staring out the window of the air-conditioned cab, taking in the astounding view. The water on either side of the long, snaking highway came in every shade of blue and green. The Keys themselves were a strange assortment of desert islands, coral outcroppings, and lush, marshy atolls capped with dark green pine and gigantic date palms. Every mile or so she saw what looked like giant birds' nests topping the telephone poles on the left side of the highway, and once she spotted a large bird resembling a hawk, with a fish hanging heavily from its talons, as it returned to one of the huge, bowl-like assemblages of twigs. She mentioned it to the driver, whose name was Tony Hand, according to the ID taped to the back of the front seat.

"Osprey," he answered. "Mate for life. Nest for life, too."

"Oh?"

"Yeah. Nest gets bigger every year. Bigger the nest, longer they've been together."

"Monogamous birds," said Jay.

Tony shook his head and laughed, looking back at her in the rearview mirror. "Nah. They screw around whenever they get the chance, but they always come back to each other."

"Sounds pretty human."

"Yeah. Like me and my wife." He laughed again.

"Can I ask you a couple of questions?"

"Sure. Long as it's not about me and my wife."

"I saw an ad for a boat, but I don't know where it's parked."

Tony laughed again. "You don't park a boat, you dock it."

"So how do I find out where it's docked?"

"No phone number?"

"Just an answering machine."

"You know the name of the boat?"

"Charming Billy," said Jay.

"Never heard of it." Tony shrugged. "But call the Key West Harbormaster's office. They'll know if Key West's the home port."

"What about a hotel?"

"Expensive or cheap or in between?"

"In between."

"Belle's."

It was Jay's turn to laugh. "Sounds like a whorehouse."

"Probably was, back in the old days." Tony grinned. "Most places were. Pretty rowdy place once upon a time."

"Now?"

"Belle's or Key West?"

"Both."

"Belle's is a really nice place. Big old Victorian. Pool in the back. Smells like a perfume factory with the frangipani and the jacaranda and all. Nice prices too, especially in the summer. That's off-season for the Keys, you know."

"And Key West? Still rowdy?"

"Not so much," said Tony. "Pretty down in the mouth until the druggies came in and spent a lot of money. Then that died out and the gays came in and cleaned everything up. Pretty tame really unless you're Jerry Falwell, but I don't think he gets down to the Keys very much."

"One more question."

"Shoot."

"Where can I get a battery for my cell phone?"

"Radio Shack," said Tony. "Where else?"

They found the Radio Shack in a small plaza on the western outskirts of the small city, and Tony waited while Jay went in and bought two batteries for the out-of-service telephone. From there he took her along Roosevelt Boulevard into Key West proper, giving her a tour of the thousand and one tacky T-shirt and souvenir stores on Duval Street before swinging back into a pleasant, reasonably upscale neighborhood full of tree-lined streets and large homes in various states of repair

and renovation. The dominant color seemed to be yellow with
white trim. Half of them had B&B signs by the front gate.

Belle's was an exception. The house was white as a wedding cake and just as trimmed. There was gingerbread everywhere. The fence around the lush garden was scrolled out in
hearts, diamonds, clubs, and spades; the baluster around the
main-floor porch was pineapples; the second-floor porch was
fleurs-de-lis, and the upper windows and the eaves were done
in actual gingerbread men, dancing their way around the
house.

Jay paid Tony, adding a hefty tip, toted her single bag onto
the porch of the old mansion, and rang the buzzer. A few
seconds later a tall, full-breasted woman in shorts and a halter
top opened the door. She had orange hair piled up on her
head tied off with a pink ribbon, floppy blue mules on her
feet, too much makeup, an Adam's apple, and just the tiniest
bit of five o'clock shadow. She was also smoking an unfiltered Camel cigarette in a faux tortoiseshell holder. She was
dressed thirty and looked well west of sixty-five.

"Looking for a room, are we?" She gave an orange-topped
nod to the flight bag in Jay's hand.

"That's right," Jay said, trying not to stare too hard. "Tony
Hand recommended you."

"Tony's a dear." The woman smiled. Jay watched the coral
pink lip gloss crack at the corners of her wide mouth. She
extended her hand. The nails were two inches long and as
blue as the mules on her tendon-knotted feet. "I'm Belle."

Jay shook the offered hand. "I'm Carrie Stone." She'd
been using the name for almost two years now, and it came
off her tongue more naturally than Kelly Morgan.

"Well, do come in." Jay stepped into the coolness of the
foyer, then followed Belle up a long, carpeted stairway. There
were framed photographs inscribed to Belle on the wall all
the way up. There was even one of Bess Truman, standing
in bright sunlight, the nose of a DC3 behind her with the
name "Sacred Cow."

Belle noticed Jay's interest. " 'Sacred Cow' was the first
Air Force One. When Harry went on his all-day fishing trips,

Bess would come over and we'd play cribbage. A truly great lady."

"No kidding," said Jay. Not only was Belle older than she looked, but she was better connected. Next to Bess Truman was Frank Sinatra and the one up from that was Lucky Luciano. Belle apparently knew everyone of consequence who'd ever set foot in Key West since the late forties.

They reached the second-floor landing, and Belle ushered Jay into a large, sun-drenched room that overlooked the backyard. The yard was mostly taken up by a full-size swimming pool surrounded by an astounding array of flowering trees.

"It's beautiful," said Jay, looking out the window.

"Just like me." Belle beamed. "Iced tea?"

They sat by the pool in pink split-cane chairs and watched the water in the pool, the surface broken and creased in the sunlight like transparent tinfoil. Jay had asked for her iced tea unsweetened, but the murky brown brew in Belle's hand was obviously laced with something much more potent than sugar.

"Glassblowing?" said Belle, eyes wide. She sucked up an ounce or two of her tea through a clear plastic straw. "Now isn't that interesting. You've been doing it for a while, I suppose."

"A while," Jay agreed.

"Fun?"

"Lots." She nodded. "You can't really think about much else when you've got a blob of molten glass on the end of your pipe; takes you out of yourself, everything's in real time." She smiled at the transvestite, amazed at how easy it was for her to think of Belle as a woman. Jay broadened her smile. "I guess you'd call it an existential moment."

"Well dear, I don't know much about existential moments, but I do know about real time." She touched her throat in a long, stroking motion and then let out a bellowing laugh that a stevedore would have been proud of. "Real-time wrinkles!" she snorted. She took another long sip of iced tea, then fitted a cigarette into her holder and lit it. "Not a lot of glassblowing in Key West, dear. Far too hot for that sort of thing."

"I'm not here to blow," Jay answered.

Belle laughed again. "Then you're just about the only one

who isn't, sweetie. Everyone blows everyone else in this town, that's part of its charm."

"Glass." Jay grinned.

"I knew that, dear; just testing the waters, seeing which way the wind blows." She giggled. "There I go again."

"I'm looking for places that might sell some of my work," said Jay.

"Lots of galleries," Belle offered. "Gingerbread Square is the one that's been around the longest."

"I'm also looking for someone."

"Oh," said Belle. The twinkle went out of her eye and Jay could see her taking two steps back.

"For a friend."

"Really."

"Not someone actually. More like something."

"Such as?"

"A boat."

"Lots of boats in Key West." No "dear" or "sweetie" now. Jay tried the straight-ahead approach. "I'm looking to buy it," said Jay. "I saw it advertised in *Boat Trader* magazine. I was coming down here anyway, so I thought I'd check it out."

"Glassblowing and boatbuying. Odd combination." Belle scratched the powdered stubble just under her chin with one long blue nail. "Does this boat have a name?"

"*Charming Billy*," Jay responded. "I don't suppose you know it. Like you said, lots of boats in Key West." Jay waited, banking on Belle's ego to come charging forward.

"I know everything about this place," Belle said. "Including *Charming Billy*." She shook her head. "Not the kind of boat I'd want, mind you." She grinned.

"Why's that?"

"The owner. Harry's had her up for sale for as long as I can remember."

"Harry?"

"Maxwell. Used to be a shrimper, runs it as a charter every once in a while. Preys on innocent Japanese tourists mostly. Anyone fool enough to pay him for a ride in that old tub." Her reluctance was gone and so was her suspicion. By the sound of her voice she was fond of this Harry, whoever he was.

"Where can I find him?" Jay asked.

"Not far," Belle answered. "After dark he polishes a stool down at Schooner Wharf."

NINETEEN

"When I woke up she was gone. So was the rental car."

Norman Karlson leaned back in his chair, pinched the bridge of his nose with two fingers, and let out a long-suffering sigh. "Goddamn," he said quietly.

"Yes sir," agreed Jack Dane. He lit a cigarette and waited for his boss to gather his thoughts. The deputy marshal looked out the window behind Karlson and watched the lights of a jet dip down through the night sky toward the airport a few miles away.

Eight hours ago he'd awakened in the empty suite at the Airport Hilton in New Orleans. He knew his only option was to report personally to Karlson, which meant flying again, and that was the real focus of his anger at Jay Fletcher, not just her sudden disappearance. With the flight behind him, the anger was fading and he was actually feeling quite proud of himself; two airplane rides in the last forty-eight hours, not to mention surviving an ambush in the Louisiana bayous, and he was still breathing.

"Why did she sneak off?" Karlson asked finally, sitting forward in the big leather chair.

"Because I told her we were coming back here."

"Giving up?"

"That's not quite how I put it," said Dane. "But yeah. She was pretty upset by the little boy." He paused. "So was I. Still am."

"Do you have any idea where she went?"

"No." Dane shook his head. "She thought there might be something in the copy of the magazine Billy left behind. I disagreed. I still do. It's a red herring."

"Where's the magazine now?"

"Evidence Analysis Unit. I dropped it off before I came up here."

"The car?"

"Unless she turns it in or gets stopped for a ticket it's going to be hard to track." He paused. "We could put her on the hit list."

"No," Karlson said emphatically. "Logging her as a wanted fugitive is almost as bad as telling the *Washington Post* and *Hard Copy* that we lost Billy." There was a brief silence. Karlson stared across the desk at Dane. "You're not telling me something."

Jack Dane took a deep breath. This was the moment he'd been dreading. "She's got a gun," he said, pushing the air out of his lungs.

Karlson groaned. "You've got to be kidding."

"When we went after Billy in China Bayou, she insisted. I gave her my backup piece." He shrugged. "She was right."

"Screw right!" Karlson snorted. "You're telling me that Jay Fletcher is on the loose with a gun given to her by a U.S. Marshal and that she's up to her old tricks again." He groaned. "If she winds up bagging Billy or getting whacked herself we're both out of a job, Jack, I hope you realize that." He shook his head. "*Sixty Minutes*, made-for-TV movies, *Time* covers. A goddamned nightmare!"

"It gets worse."

"How?" Karlson groaned.

"The last time she talked to him with the computer, she told him she was going to kill him."

"Threatened him?"

"Told him."

"Shit." Karlson repeated. "Is there any record of this chatroom conversation?"

"On her computer."

"Goddamn her!"

"Billy half blackmailed her into helping us and you went along with it. Now you're giving her shit for doing exactly what you wanted in the first place."

"You're defending her?" Karlson asked, surprised.

"No, but I understand her." He frowned. "Better than I thought I would."

"Understand her?" Karlson made a small moaning noise. "Please tell me you weren't sleeping with her."

"I wasn't," Dane answered, trying not to lose his temper. "I said I understood her, that's all. She wants this guy. Bad." The deputy marshal leaned forward and stubbed out his cigarette in Karlson's heavy glass ashtray. "So do I."

"Find her first," said Karlson. "I'm revoking her WitSec status. Take her into custody."

"On what charge?" Dane asked. "She hasn't done anything illegal."

"To hell with charges, Jack! You've been chasing people all your professional life. You know how to do this shit better than anyone in the service. We'll call her a material witness in the deaths of Connelly and the piano teacher, how's that? Just get the woman, and do it quick!"

"Any hints on how I should do that, Norm?"

"Get one of the tech types downstairs to track her through the computer. You think I sent her off without some salt on her tail?" Karlson unlocked one of his desk drawers, took out a thick black address book, and jotted down a series of numbers on one of his own business cards.

"What's this?" Dane asked.

"Her computer address and password. You can read anything she's received or sent. I can also get you the LUDs on her cell phone if you want them."

"You really are an evil shit, aren't you?"

Karlson smiled for the first time since Dane had walked into the office. "Part of the job description." The meeting was over. Dane stood up and walked to the door. He paused and turned back to Karlson.

"What if she doesn't want to come? What if she refuses?"

"As of this minute she's a fugitive, just like William Paris Bonisteel. What would you do if Billy Bones resisted arrest?"

Jay sat on her stool at the Schooner Wharf Bar, nursing a beer and trying not to eat too many of the nuts in the freebie bowl in front of her. It was full dark now, but the ebb and flow of people walking up and down the wooden Harbor Walk pier was still constant. There was no back wall to the bar, and Jay could see across the boardwalk to the crowded mooring. The boats bobbing up and down in the marina were as diverse as the bar's clientele.

There was everything at anchor from sleek corporate yachts flying Power Squadron pennants to plump little day cruisers with canvas tops and names like *Tinkerbelle* and *Ruff Knight*. The place seemed utterly democratic, sixty-footers cheek by jowl with runabouts, battered live-aboard sailboats sharing dock cleats with low-slung Cigarettes that looked like ads for *Miami Vice* reruns.

Over the last two hours Jay had seen just about every possible type come into the Schooner Wharf, from hard construction workers to old men in tennis shoes and yachting caps. So far she'd seen two men dressed up as pirates, right down to the eyepatch, and a long-haired fellow whose chest and arms were tattooed with scores of brilliantly colored parrots. In the garden area behind her a jazz band was playing softly while dinner patrons chewed their way through an endless supply of conch fritters, buffalo wings, bluepoints, all kinds of shrimp, and even the occasional Philly cheese steak.

But so far no Harry Maxwell. According to Belle, Jay would know him when she saw him. As far as she was concerned, Harry was God's gift to women, a frighteningly handsome blend of Gregory Peck as Atticus Finch in *To Kill a Mockingbird* and Anthony Quinn as Gauguin in *Lust for Life*. A heady combination that had apparently served as a potent aphrodisiac for half the good-looking women in Key West, unmarried or otherwise.

"What about the other half?" Jay had asked.

"Hasn't got around to them yet," Belle had answered.

Jay sipped her beer and let her eyes rove over the people around her. So far no one even close to Belle's description had come into the bar, and it was now getting on towards midnight. Harry the Stud was either drinking in some other bar, cavorting with one of the other half he hadn't got around to, or Billy had beaten her to the punch and added another body to his box score.

Come on, come on. . . . I don't have time for aging boat bums. Billy's out there killing and I'm sitting in a goddamned bar!

She set down her beer bottle, put a foot on the floor, and half turned on her stool, preparing to make her way back to Belle's, only two or three blocks back up William Street. She felt a hand on her shoulder and caught a whiff of Lagerfeld.

"Belle said you were looking for me."

Jay turned fully in her seat and found herself staring into exactly the man Belle had described. He was painfully handsome, and Jay felt a sudden surge of utterly pure lust rush through her entire body and an attendant guilt for the rawness of her feelings. He was every mother's worst fear, and every wife's best fantasy. A brief image of Robin back in Mendocino flickered in her mind, then vanished like a snuffed candle.

"You must be Harry," Jay managed. Mid-forties, perfect shape, tight black jeans, and a T-shirt that said "End Discrimination: Hate Everybody." He lifted his hand off her shoulder and she started breathing again.

Oh God, can he tell?

Of course he can tell, you idiot. You think he doesn't know the effect he has on women?

Billy, concentrate on Billy.

"And you're Carrie, right?" His voice wasn't Gregory Peck's, but it was a nice, even baritone.

"Right."

She realized she was still frozen in a half turn on the stool, but she didn't know which way to move. He helped her decide, seating himself on the stool beside her, his hip brushing against her knee as he did so. He had a folded newspaper in his free hand that he put down on the bar in front of him.

Relax.

Oh, sure.

Think of something to say. Fast.

"Why do you call your boat *Charming Billy*?"

He shrugged. "I like cherry pie."

"I don't get it."

"Can she bake a cherry pie, charming Billy? The kids song, remember?" He smiled and she melted a little more. "You know, the young girl who couldn't leave her mother?" He ordered a Canadian beer from the bartender. "Anyway, she already had the name when I bought her. Supposed to be bad luck to change the name so I left it." The bartender put the Molson's Black Label down in front of him and he took a short swallow. "So why did you want to see me?"

Right now I want to . . .

Oh for Christ's sake! Get a hold of yourself before you do something really stupid.

I'm running out of time.

She took a deep breath, let it out slowly, and placed her palms flat on the bar. Out in the marina the boats squeaked and moaned at their moorings. People were laughing and joking and talking all round her and she really didn't know how to proceed. The only thing she knew for sure was that she'd beat Billy to the punch. This time she'd be the one to set the ambush.

"I'm interested in buying your boat." She smiled, trying to look him right in the eye. "I saw your ad."

"In *Boat Trader?*"

"Yes."

He doesn't believe you.

"Then maybe you should take a look at it," said Harry. He stood up, put some bills on the bar to cover the beer, and put his hand behind her elbow. "Come on."

Is he coming on to me?

No, he doesn't believe you about the boat. He's putting you on the spot.

"Okay." She smiled as brightly as she could and dropped off her stool, letting him steer her out onto the harbor walk. "Where is it?"

"Over there." He pointed vaguely with the folded newspaper. "Other side of the marina."

He walked her along the boardwalk, steering her closer to

the moored boats than the busier landward side. The marina
was a maze of narrow docks and walkways, and within a
minute they were well out of the noisy, brightly lit crowds.
Harry slowed his steps then, and his hand dropped away from
her arm.

It was dark, and the creaking, moaning screen of boats was
suddenly a sinister foreground to deep night. For a single,
numbing instant Jay found herself considering the possibility
that the man beside her was somehow mixed up with Billy,
and the whole thing had been a setup from the beginning.

*Don't be stupid. This is a seduction and you're going right
along with it.*

"It's dark," she said.

"Usually is at night." He laughed. "Don't worry, almost
there."

Jay felt the floating walkway wobble slightly under her
feet and reached out, grabbing the man's upper arm. The bi-
cep felt like a piece of stone under her hand.

He could snap you like a twig. Get the hell out of here.

"There it is." He nodded toward a chubby looking Grand
Banks trawler backed into its slip a few yards away. Jay could
easily make out the name on the transom: *Charming Billy*. In
the darkness it was hard to tell her color but Jay thought it
was a medium gray. She caught a faint hint of something in
the shadows under the cabin well and paused.

"There's someone on board," she said.

"Relax," Harry answered. He took her arm again and
guided her toward the boat. Looking hard, Jay was positive
now. She threw off the man's hand, reached around to the
small of her back and hauled out Jack Dane's Glock. Someone was sitting in the shadows, a shotgun lying across his
lap.

"Stay back," she said and then she heard the man behind
her laughing quietly. The figure on the boat remained motionless.

"It's just Manny."

"Who?" Jay paused, uncertain and looked back at Harry
Maxwell for an instant.

"I'll show you," he said. Brushing past her, Harry climbed onto the boat and waved her forward. Keeping the gun in her hand, she followed him onto *Charming Billy*. He stood beside a folding deck chair, his hand resting casually on the shoulder of the figure sitting in it. A blowup sex-store mannequin wearing shorts, a Hawaiian shirt, and a straw hat. The shotgun in its lap was real, a short barreled Remington pump action with a chain running through the trigger and down into a cleat buried in the deck.

"Manny's harmless," said Harry. "But he serves his purpose. An inflatable guard dog. I think in another life he was a Basset. Scared off more than one boat-jacker in his time." He gestured at the gun in Jay's hand. "I think you can put that away now."

Jay pushed the Glock into the back of her jeans. "Sorry."

"You always buy boats with a gun in your pants, Ms. Fletcher?"

She felt the same surge of sudden terror that ripped through her when she saw that first message from Billy on the screen of her computer in Mendocino. Trapped like a bug in a spiderweb.

Butterfly pinned to a card.

Run.

"You know who I am."

He flipped open the newspaper in his hand and showed her the front page. It was the late edition of the *Miami Herald*. There were two photographs above the fold, a recent one of her and a mug shot of William Paris Bonisteel. "Hot off the press. The Ladykiller is back and so is Billy Bones."

"Shit," Jay muttered. She sank back against the gunwale of the boat.

"Come on inside," said Harry. "I'll make us some coffee and we can talk." He gave Manny a pat on the head, then turned and went down through a narrow doorway into the cabin below. Jay went after him, pausing for a second to stare down at the shotgun in the mannequin's lap. The stock was old and worn but the barrel was clean with a soft skin of oil. Harry, whoever the hell he was, took care of business.

And so should you.

She took out the Glock again, holding it loosely in her hand, then followed Harry through the narrow door. She went down three steps into a low-ceilinged, cozy dining area with a long drop-leaf table, two chairs, and a bench. Harry had dropped the newspaper onto the tabletop. Beyond it was a low counter separating the dining area from the galley. Everything was done in pale woods of various kinds except for the floor, which was dark blue battleship linoleum.

Harry stood on the galley side of the counter, working a shiny Italian coffee machine. He smiled, noticed the gun in her hand, and shook his head. "You really don't need it, believe me."

"We'll see." She slid in around the table and sat down on the bench seat, her back to the cabin bulkhead. She looked around. Everything in the cabin had a pleasant, well-worn look. This was a home. The coffee maker hissed and steamed, and a moment later Harry stepped back into the dining area, two small cups in his hand. He put one down in front of Jay then sat in one of the chairs directly across from her. He spun the newspaper around looked down at it.

"What a mess."

"I wouldn't know." Jay kept her gun hand down on the leather-covered bench. "What does it say?"

"It says that this William Bonisteel character escaped from a Washington psychiatric hospital and that you were trying to help get him back for the feds."

"Who blew the whistle?"

"Some cop in Massachusetts. CNN got hold of it."

Rawls, back in Blackwood. I guess someone finally offered him enough money.

"Shit."

Harry laughed. "So you said."

"What else do they have?"

"The story hooks you up with a murder in New York as well as this one in Massachusetts. There's also some rumors about New Orleans. You're getting a lot of play."

"How did you know it was me?"

"That was Belle." He took a sip of his coffee and leaned back in his chair. "Miss True Crime; give Anne Rule a run for her money anyday. That Olsen guy, too. She reads it all."

"She recognized me?" Jay was surprised; she thought she'd changed enough to avoid being picked off that easily.

"She watched the Billy Bones trial on court TV," explained Harry. "Belle recognized your voice from the testimony. She's really something." He took another sip of coffee and let out a small, satisfied sigh of approval. "She had it all on tape. Checked it this afternoon just to make sure."

"And told you?"

He shrugged. "Belle's an old friend. Sometimes she runs interference. She wondered why someone like you'd be asking questions about me. I'm wondering the same thing."

Tell him the truth.

"I'm pretty sure you're his next victim."

Harry nodded. "I thought it might be something like that."

"You don't seem too surprised."

"I've seen too much shit go down over the years to be surprised by anything any more. As far as I can tell, this Billy Bones character kills randomly, so why me?"

"It's not random," said Jay.

Harry laughed again. "What? I did something to upset this guy in a previous life?"

"He's after me. Revenge. You're just bait." She shook her head. "This whole news thing just makes it all more complicated."

"The newspaper is making it sound like some kind of one-on-one vendetta."

"What does the FBI say?"

"That you were brought in to consult and now you've slipped the leash. Gone rogue." He cleared his throat uneasily. "Just like before."

Jay nodded stiffly. "I see."

You're the Judas goat. Karlson's worst nightmare, but it might just work for him in the end, take the heat off the Marshals.

"Belle says CNN and everyone else is playing their old

tapes. They've got some old boyfriend of yours coming on Larry King tomorrow night." This time his smile was a grin. "Face it, you're a folk hero."

"Shit."

"That's three times now," Harry said. "You want more coffee?"

Jay nodded. "And a cigarette if you've got one."

Harry gathered up the cups and went back to the coffee machine again. He started it hissing and steaming, then rummaged through drawers in the galley until he came up with a very old package of Camels and a package of matches. He brought fresh coffee, the cigarettes, and an ashtray around to the dining area and sat down. Jay shook out a Camel and half the tobacco drifted out onto the table.

"I quit six months ago. Probably a little stale."

"I'll live." Jay lit one of the old cigarettes and sucked down a lungful of smoke. "Woof," she said, exhaling. "So, you going to turn me in or call up the local TV station?"

"If I was going to do either I wouldn't be sitting here now."

"So why are you?"

"Belle figured you were going to need some help."

"That's Belle, what about you?"

He laughed. "I thought maybe you could bring some excitement into my otherwise dull life."

Jay looked across the table at him. She let the gun stay where it was and brought her hand up to lift the coffee cup. "Somehow I don't think you lead a dull life." She glanced around the room. "If you ever did."

"You'd be surprised." He paused, his expression becoming more serious. "Now tell me why you think I'm on Billy's hit list."

"He left a copy of *Boat Trader* at the last . . . crime scene. The page with your boat on it had been sliced out. The name of the boat was the giveaway."

"*Charming Billy.*"

"Yes."

"He left you the clue?"

"He didn't leave anything else." She paused. "How long have you had the ad running?"

Harry hooked his thumb toward a pile of magazines lying on the counter a few feet away. "The last four issues," he answered. "Too many boats for sale, though." He grinned. "You were my first nibble."

"Sorry."

"You mean you don't want to buy her?" he asked, eyes wide with mock astonishment, one hand coming up to his cheek.

"I wish I could. I'd pack my bags and sail away forever."

"That's what I thought when I bought her. Didn't work out that way." Jay watched as he bit the corner of his lip, thinking. "If this Billy Bones character was out to kill me, why aren't I dead?" he said finally.

Just what I was thinking.

"I don't know," she answered honestly. "Doesn't fit the pattern."

"So what are we going to do about it?"

"I don't know that either."

Harry climbed to his feet. "Well, I'm not going to hang around and wait for him." He smiled down at her. "Want to go for a ride?"

"Where to?"

"Anywhere but here. The paper puts you in New Orleans. Tony the taxi driver picked you up at the Marathon Airport and he's got a mouth like running water. It won't take long to put you in Key West."

"Who the hell are you? The Good Samaritan?"

"Nope," Harry answered. "I'm the friend you never thought you had."

"I've got my stuff at Belle's. I need it."

"Already on board," said Harry. "Belle likes to think ahead." He gave her another smile, then turned and went back out onto the deck. He cast off the lines warping *Charming Billy* into her berth, then went up to the flying bridge and started up the twin Cummins diesels.

A few minutes later they were heading out of the marina

and rounding the light marker at the entrance to the bight. Harry spun the wheel lightly, lining the bow up with a second light that stood dead ahead in front of Wisteria Island. He waited for a count of twenty, then spun the wheel again, this time to starboard, taking them up beside the old Naval Air Station on Fleming Key, then finally out into the safe darkness of the Gulf of Mexico.

TWENTY

Jay climbed up to the flying bridge, taking deep breaths of the salt air. She turned and looked back the way they'd come. The lights of Key West were fading into the distance. A billion stars streaked and danced above them in the black silk sky. She stood and watched Harry Maxwell at the wheel of the boat, his face lit softly by the pale lights from the instrument panel in front of him. For the moment she'd decided to follow her feelings instead of logic. Dangerous ground, perhaps even fatal, since she didn't really know this Harry Maxwell from Adam, but for some unfathomable reason she felt perfectly safe with him and perhaps even a little happy.

Maybe a little caution is in order here, Jay.

Screw caution.

"So where exactly are we going, Mr. Maxwell?"

He glanced in her direction. "Everglades City."

"Never heard of it."

"Neither has anyone else, which is one reason we're going there."

"Pretty sure of yourself, aren't you?" she asked.

"What's that supposed to mean?"

"Having my stuff put on board the boat."

"Just call it enlightened self-interest." He grinned.

"Now you're the one who's being obscure."

He glanced down at the instrument panel and adjusted the wheel slightly. Ahead there was nothing but blackness. The sea was ripple-smooth and the only sound was the muted vibrating purr of the engines and the white hiss of the wake streaming out behind them like a phosphorescent comet's tail.

Harry finally spoke up. "I was being selfish. I didn't want to get involved with your . . . situation."

That's why he got you out of the bar so fast.

"You've got a funny way of not getting involved."

He shrugged, hands still on the wheel. "If the *Miami Herald* has a line on you, the whole world has a line on you. Tony the taxi driver would have led them to Belle's and that would have been that. Your interest in this boat would have become public knowledge."

"And you'd have your fifteen minutes of fame."

"That's exactly what I *don't* want."

"Why?"

"Because I value my privacy." He paused. "A lot."

"I still don't get it," said Jay. "This is a charter boat, isn't it? Fishing trips à la Hemingway?"

Uh-oh. Something else is going on here, isn't it?

"That's right."

"So it would be great publicity."

He sighed. "I don't want publicity."

Why not?

Because he's got something to hide.

The light bulb clicked on. "Oh shit. You're a drug smuggler."

He shook his head emphatically. "No drugs."

"Then what?"

He offered her that wonderful smile, then turned back to his instruments, tapped several keys on a small, computer-like console, and stepped away from the wheel.

"I'll show you."

Leaving the flying bridge he went back down to the cabin, Jay following right behind him. She sat down at the table again while Harry rummaged around in one of the cupboards above the sink.

"This thing drives itself?" she asked. Beneath her feet the vibration of the two big Cummins engines was still smooth as silk.

"It's got an autopilot, just like an airplane." Harry was still rooting around in the cupboards. "Set the controls and she goes that way until you tell her to stop. I won't have to make another correction until we get to Snipe Key."

He found what he was looking for and pulled down a big vacuum-packed tin of Planters cashews. He brought them to the table and popped off the yellow plastic top, then pulled up on the ring set into the metal top beneath the plastic cover.

"You smuggle cashew nuts?"

"Nope. I smuggle these."

The can's contents scattered across the table like a spray of scintillating ice chips, each one the rich, cool green of a south seas lagoon or the forest cover of a South American jungle. There were dozens of them, from tiny specks of glowing stone to rocks the size of walnuts.

"Are they real?" asked Jay.

"Colombian green beryl. The finest emeralds money can buy. Most of it from the Muzo mines in Colombia, some the Santa Teresinha mine in Brazil. The best the Green Mafia and the *guaqueros* had to offer."

"Guaqueros?"

"Treasure hunters. Bandits."

Jay reached out and picked up one of the larger emeralds. She held it up so it caught some of the light from the overhead. "It's beautiful," she whispered. She put it back on the pile.

"Here's where I'm supposed to say something like, 'for you, senorita, a gift!' Except I can't. That particular stone will probably wind up retailing for somewhere around a quarter of a million dollars." He spread his hand out across the spray of stones on the table. "This whole shipment will come in around three or four million eventually."

"Not as bulky as cocaine, that's for sure."

"And a lot safer." He smiled. "They don't have dogs that can smell emeralds yet."

"You . . . own these?"

He laughed. "Sadly, no. Just the man in the middle." He lifted his shoulders. "I get my piece of the action, nothing to complain about." He began sweeping the gemstones back into the can. Jay watched as his fingers curled into the stones, fascinated by the richness of the color and the quick fire of their reflected light. "So now I guess you can see why I didn't want any publicity." He popped the yellow plastic lid back onto the can. "The people I deal with value their privacy even more than I value mine."

"Gee, and I thought you were trying to hustle me a little."

"That's not entirely out of the question."

There was a long pause. They sat across from each other, staring. Jay felt as though something was going to break, but she wasn't quite sure what. It was all getting out of hand, and certainly out of her control.

"What about Billy?"

"I've got a delivery to make," he said. "We can figure out the rest of it after that."

"Okay." Jay nodded. She wanted to reach out and run her fingers over the back of his hand, which was now covering the closed lid of the Planters can. She stopped herself.

"How does it work?" she asked.

He grinned. "I'm supposed to give a cop trade secrets?"

Jay reached for the old package of Camels and lit up again, coughing hard. "I'm not a cop anymore."

"Maybe not. But that's what you are, down deep."

"You see down deep?" She tried to make it light.

"Sometimes I do. Like now." He smiled. "But I'll tell you my secrets anyway." He took his hand off the can and waved away the cloud of smoke that hovered over the table. "I was going to retire soon."

"That why you had the boat for sale?"

"And other things." He shrugged again. "Time for a change." He came around to Jay's side of the table, leaning over her. The Lagerfeld was still there, but it was mixed with something a little more human and elemental. Jay was suddenly glad that she was sitting down. Harry pulled back the window catch to let in some air, then sat down again.

"You were going to tell me how it works."

"Emeralds come from a lot of places, even the States, but the best of them are from Colombia and about 80 percent of them are illegal. Colombia has a tax on them so most are smuggled out."

"By people like you?"

"Not a chance. Too many guns." Harry paused. "No, they come out all sorts of ways, a lot of them fronted by the big Japanese dealers who control most of the market. That's where I come in."

"How?"

"Cruise ships. I've got contacts with all the major ones. The stones get taken onto the ships as kitchen inventory; cashew nuts for the bars and lounges on board. No one gives them a second look. The nuts get dropped off at one of the Caribbean ports of call and I take it from there.

"Big business?"

"Big enough. They figure $850 million a year worth of stones on the black market." He grinned. "I do my part."

"Victimless crime."

"I like to think so. There are some who would disagree, of course."

"You're awfully free with your trade secrets."

"I don't think you're going to turn me in, Miss Fletcher." He grinned. "Sort of like the pot calling the kettle black really."

She smiled back. "Call me Jay."

"Besides, like I told you, I'm getting out of the business." He tapped the plastic lid of the nut tin in a little drumbeat trill. "This is my last shipment."

"Because of me?"

"No." His expression turned serious. "It's just time, that's all."

"You sound like you're going to miss it."

"I've missed a lot of things over the years." He stared at her thoughtfully. "Like you."

"Like everyone on the planet," Jay answered.

"Some of us are different. We get off on the wrong foot, turn left when everyone else turns right."

Blowing away a serial killer or two, does that count?

"Is that how you got into the smuggling business?"

His expression went from serious to hard. "No. I got into the smuggling business because they changed the divorce laws."

"You're being obscure again."

"Not really. My father was a divorce lawyer. Back in the days when adultery was the only grounds. There were a lot of staged proceedings back then—photographers bursting into motel rooms, that kind of thing. Then they changed the laws. They used him as a precedent and accused him of collusion. He was disbarred and put in jail. He lasted about a year and then he died of a heart attack. I was eighteen. In college."

"I'm sorry."

"That's not the end of it." His jaw tightened. "My old man's ashes were barely cold when the IRS came down on my mother like a ton of bricks. They took her money, my father's life insurance, the car, her house, all of it. She lasted for about six months after that and then she took pills."

He gave the plastic lid of the nut tin a single hard tap with one knuckle. "They changed the rules and never even thought about the human consequences. I figured, okay, if you change the rules, then all bets are off. You choose your own values and moral order because what you were brought up to believe in turns out to be a crock of shit."

He shook his head. "Truth, justice, and the pursuit of happiness. I don't see much of any of it these days." He offered her his smile again and she could feel the depth of his sadness behind it. "But I guess you know what I mean."

"Yes."

There are no rules anymore, nothing to believe in except yourself.

Harry looked at his watch and stood up. "Oh well, two sides to every story, I suppose, and everybody's got one to tell." He pointed upward. "We should be coming up on Snipe Point. I have to make that course correction."

Jay nodded absently, something bothering her, nibbling at the edge of consciousness like a wary fish darting for the hook then backing off. Harry went out through the doorway leading to the aft section of the boat and she heard his footsteps on the outer companionway as he climbed up to the flying bridge.

What did he say?

Five-pound trout on a three-pound line.

No, that was dad.

Harry.

Two sides to every story.

She frowned, staring at the idiotic image on the side of the Planters can. Mr. Peanut wearing a top hat, carrying a cane, and wearing spats. Even funnier knowing that the can was filled with three million dollars' worth of smuggled emeralds.

Two sides to every story.

What's wrong with that?

"Oh shit," she whispered. She scuttled along the bench, leaned over and grabbed the stack of *Boat Trader* magazines off the counter. She riffled through them, finding the same edition as the one Billy had left behind at China Bayou.

Two sides to every story.

"Two sides to every page." She fanned through the magazine until she found the page advertising Harry's boat. Page 144. She flipped it over. Page 145.

You were so fucking sure of yourself, weren't you, Janet Louise? You never even bothered to look at what was on the other side.

There were six small ads in the bottom half of the page, but her eye was drawn to the half-page advertisement that ran across the top. The picture was clean and crisp, clearly taken by a professional, showing off the neat practical lines of a modernized West Coast halibut trawler. The boxy little pilot-house was set well aft, with a dinghy-sized Zodiac inflatable lashed to the roof.

According to the text, she was thirty-six feet long, only ten years old, and offered for sale at the Bainbridge Island Yacht Club in Seattle, Washington. The owner must have been a Beatles fan. The name on the transom jumped up from the page, screaming:

Helter Skelter

Another name for chaos. Charlie Manson's theme song. *Like father, like son.*

Thinking about his mother, Billy Bones drove the Porsche down the winding ramps of the Seattle-Tacoma Airport, the dead owner of the vehicle, a TV executive named Gahagen, folded up securely in the trunk. Five minutes after maneuvering through the complex of cloverleafs around the airport Billy slotted the high-powered automobile onto the 15 and headed north.

In mid-December 1970 and nine months pregnant, Mary Jane Shorter, aka Mary Jane Shenker, aka Mary Jane Haggar, skipped bail in Los Angeles and fled to Lynden, Washington, not far from the Canadian border. At the time, Shorter was under indictment for her involvement in the Tate-LaBianca murders masterminded by Charles Manson.

It was decided not to go after her, even though it was known that she was living in Lynden. There were more than enough witnesses to try the case; Shorter had already proved to be decidedly unhelpful; and evidence tying her directly to the killings was nonexistent. Even though there was a bench warrant for her arrest, Mary Jane Shorter, known to the Manson Family as Starr, got away scot-free. Ironically, up until the time her baby was born, Mary Jane was living in a crash pad less than a block away from the Lynden Police Department.

For Billy, finding out this much information had been remarkably simple. Taking it beyond that hadn't been very difficult either, even though the events had happened so many years ago.

Checking birth records at the Lynden District Hospital showed a male child born out of wedlock to a woman named Mary Jane Haggar on December 22, 1970. There was no record of the child having been put up for adoption, but a computer-hacked attack on the Vital Statistics Bureau in Seattle showed that one Mary Jane Haggar, using a social security number matching the one on file in the L.A. District Attorney's Office for Mary Jane Shorter, had married someone named Victor Nathan Jaworksi in July 1972 at City Hall in Lynden.

By hacking into the Lynden computers, Billy found out that Victor Nathan Jaworksi had drowned in his own swimming pool in 1975. There was no sign of foul play, but the police report stated that a large amount of LSD had been found among Jaworski's effects. His wife denied any knowledge that her husband used drugs. A further search of the local records listed a house sale and deed transfer in the name of Mary Jane Jaworski four months after the death of her husband.

The price paid for the house was $165,000, not an inconsequential amount in the mid-seventies. Using the powerful computers at the Museum of Natural History, Billy also managed to piggyback himself into the mainframes used cooperatively by the half-dozen largest insurance companies in Hartford, Connecticut, and discovered that Jaworski had also taken out a $200,000 joint full-life insurance policy shortly after he and Mary Jane had married. Since there was no question of foul play in the death of Jaworski, the company paid out. After that, and with $365,000 in her purse, Mary Jane Jaworski dropped out of sight, at least in Washington.

Billy's search for his mother slowed at this point, but he continued looking in his spare time. With the advent of CD-ROM telephone directories in the mid-nineties, the job became much easier. Using "Shorter," "Haggar," and "Jaworski," as baselines, he narrowed the field considerably, even though he knew there was a good chance she'd remarried and changed her name yet again. In the end he came up with thirty-two possible matches. He ruled out fifteen of those by pretending to be a pollster from Gallup doing a survey; the last seventeen he checked out one by one over the space of eighteen months, using sick days and holiday time to crisscross the country, searching for his mother.

He found her at last in a tiny place called Trumansburg, ten miles north of Ithaca, New York, a few miles west of Cayuga Lake. Trumansburg was a town of less than five thousand people, most of them living in immaculate gingerbread

Victorian houses. It was the kind of place Walt Disney would have approved of, complete with a town square and streets with names like Juniper, Washington, Elm, Pine, and Congress.

Once he found her, Billy stalked his mother for the next six months, mostly on weekends, renting cars, driving up from New York City, staying at a variety of Ithaca motels. She lived in a deconsecrated church on Seneca Street on the outskirts of the little town. The barn-sized building was made out of brick and had stained-glass windows and a pale yellow clapboard steeple. Someone had planted a heavily overgrown vegetable garden, and when Billy first saw the place, the garden had been filled with giant-leaf rhubarb plants and huge, drooping sunflowers. There were two vehicles parked in the shady driveway at the back of the church; an old, sky blue Toyota Corolla up on blocks and a bright yellow corrugated sheet metal Volkswagen "Thing."

Just like the dune buggies Charlie used to love. Even after all the years, it looked to Billy like you could take the girl out of the Family, but you couldn't take the Family out of the girl. Over the next weeks he took hundreds of photographs of her, taking the film back to New York, processing it in the museum labs, poring over the images of the woman he was now positive was the mother who'd borne him, the mother who'd lain with Charlie, taken the sacred madman into her, passed on the legacy until it finally came full circle.

Even in her late forties Mary Jane Shorter/Jaworski was a beautiful woman. The soft, oval face with the big dark eyes and the sensuous mouth was a little harder now, the high cheekbones more prominent, small crow's-feet appearing around the eyes, deeper caliper lines framing the lips. There was no sign at all of the X she'd carved lightly into her forehead as a protest at Charlie's trial, and the dark hair, still worn to her shoulders, was heavily streaked with gray.

Over time Billy learned a great deal about her, discovering that she lived with a man in his mid-sixties with the unlikely name of Steven Free and had a twelve-year-old daughter by him named Breath. The family had an old black dog named

Kicker who slept in the Toyota and was stone-deaf.

Steven Free worked at the Greenstar Co-operative Market in Ithaca, and Mary Jane was a weaver and fabric artist who sold her work in several Ithaca galleries as well as as a part-time waitress at the Rongovian Embassy, a down and dirty bar on Main Street, Trumansburg, that hosted most of the musical talent in the area. From what Billy could find out, Free was a graduate of one of the local communes, which was presumably where he'd met Mary Jane, sometime in the late seventies.

None of which Billy cared about very much at all. Eventually, the fury in his soul having risen as high as it could go without overflowing and jeopardizing everything he'd worked for, Billy made his move, waiting until the twelve-year-old was alone in the converted church. Using a chloroform-soaked sanitary napkin, he easily overpowered the child, then stripped her naked, duct-taped her mouth shut, and bound her spread-eagled on her parents' iron bed.

Several hours later the parents returned to the church, and with a knife to the little girl's throat, he forced Steven Free to use the duct tape and bind Mary Jane to a chair close to the bed. That done, Billy slit Free's throat with one quick slash and cast him aside. Then he turned his attention to Mary Jane, asking her the question he knew she couldn't answer.

"Why did you leave me? Why did you abandon me?"

Couldn't answer because he'd already cut out her tongue, blood pouring down from her mouth like a shining, crimson apron.

"How could you do that to a little baby?"

Like Charlie, his father, abandoned by his whore mother and sent to a boy's school when he was twelve.

"How could you let this happen?"

"I have to right the wrong."

"Someone has to pay the price."

While his mother watched, Billy raped the little girl again and again until the bedspread under her was soaked with blood, and then he killed her while his mother watched and then he killed his mother, stabbing out her eyes and then her heart, using her own blood to put the X back on her forehead where it belonged, a reference to the Manson murders which was understandably overlooked by the local Trumansburg Police Department.

In the end he killed them all, even Kicker the dog, who never even heard his killer coming. Then, the deed done, the fantasy come true, the circle closed, Billy's anger subsided.

For a little while.

TWENTY-ONE

"Helter Skelter," said Jay, standing beside Harry on the flying bridge. "The whole thing was a wild goose chase. Billy was on the other side of the continent all along." Harry had insisted that she catch a few hours' sleep, making up a bunk for her in the forward cabin, and now dawn was breaking on their starboard side. The sea was still calm, and ahead of them Jay could see the humped shapes of small islands forming out of the dark water ahead.

Waking, Jay had figured out the coffee machine and had made a mug for herself and Harry, bringing them up to the bridge.

"Did he know what he was doing?" Harry asked, sipping from his steaming mug. The only effect of his all-nighter was the salt-and-pepper stubble around his mouth and chin.

Jay nodded. "Sure. It's just like him." She lit the last of the ancient Camels, ducking down behind the protection of the forward windscreen. "You said it yourself. Turn left, turn right, two sides to every story."

"And two sides to every page." Harry nodded.

"Exactly. It's the whole random game." She shook her head wearily. "He must have laughed himself sick when he saw the two ads. Either one would have fit the bill. He offered me a choice, except I didn't even see it."

"I'm glad you didn't," said Harry.

"Quit being so charming and help me figure this out."

"That depends," said Harry, "On the direction you choose. The smart thing to do is drop out of sight until all of this blows over." He looked away from the horizon and into her eyes. "You can stay here if you want."

She stared back at him, touched his arm gently. "Thanks for the offer, but I can't go that way. Not yet anyway."

"Why not?"

"Billy was pretty clear about that. If I'm not on the case he steps up the killing."

"Damned if you do and damned if you don't."

"Something like that." Jay dragged on the cigarette, watching the smoke tear away into the turbulent air of their passage. "If I go after him I'm some kind of crazed FBI Ladykiller. If I drop out of the picture there will be another half-dozen corpses before somebody catches him by accident." She shook her head. "I can't have that on my conscience."

"Then there's no choice," said Harry. "You have to go after him."

"How?" she asked bleakly. "My face is on the front page of the *Miami Herald*. Old boyfriends on *Larry King Live*." She dropped the butt of her cigarette into the dregs of her coffee mug. "Ain't easy being a folk hero," she snorted.

Harry edged the throttle open a little wider, and Jay felt the kick of the heavy engines as the bow rose a little higher out of the water. The sky had gone from black to purple on the left, and to the right there was a perceptible line of brightness as the sun fought its way over the eastern horizon. Directly in front of them, the islands Jay had seen the night before had become more detailed. Beyond them, in the far distance, she could see a faint, dark line running from side to side. The Everglades. Night was ending.

"Well," said Harry, "If your face is the problem, then we'll just have to change it."

"How?"

"You'll see."

Everglades City is an oxymoron; it's not actually in the Everglades at all, and with a resident population of four hundred, it hardly rates as a city. It is close to the Everglades, however, hanging onto the northwestern edge of that great swamp, and it is the only real town for thirty miles in any direction. Once upon a time it was a busy commercial fishing village with generation after generation harvesting rich stocks of mullet and pompano, stone crabs and oysters. All of that came to an end in 1985 when the National Parks people banned commercial fishing within the boundaries of Everglades National Park, including Cape Sable and all of the Ten Thousand Islands.

The fishermen didn't give in that easily, and with an ever-increasing demand for mullet roe for use as ersatz caviar, the financial opportunities drove a lot of them to a "criminal" life, complete with fast boat chases, surveillance of the Gulf Coast Ranger station at the southern edge of town, and a sharp increase in the sale of cellular phones and police band scanners. On a good day a boat was capable of bringing in a five-thousand-dollar catch.

Not that crime was particularly unusual in the area. For a brief period in the late seventies and early eighties, Everglades City was knee-deep in Lincolns, gold chains, and people paying for coffee at the Circle K convenience store on Camellia Street with hundred-dollar bills.

According to the locals, there was local precedent for this going back to the time of Prohibition, but the DEA thought otherwise and instituted Operation Everglades. When the smoke cleared, 20 percent of the population of Everglades City had been put in jail. Since then, tourism had replaced smuggling as the town's main source of revenue, complete with "Authentic Seminoles," a professional golf course, two RV parks, and the Barron River Marina. Other than that, the town's only recent claim to fame was being used as the main location for a Sean Connery–Laurence Fishburne movie called *Just Cause*. A sleepy, humid town in a sleepy, humid backwater with very little to say for itself. There were, however, a few holdouts from the good old days.

Charming Billy reached the Barron River Marina just after seven-thirty in the morning, and Harry Maxwell eased her expertly into an empty berth close to the marina office. Standing on deck, Jay could see across Riverside Drive to the broad, unpaved streets beyond. Lots of tall shade trees and a litter of tired-looking one-story clapboards that looked as though they dated back to the forties. Somewhere in the distance she heard the familiar slap of a screen door closing and then children calling to each other and laughing. Life was going on but she was removed from it, occupying space in another, more dangerous reality.

The screen door slapped again and the sound took her back two thousand miles and thirty years. Summer holidays and dust motes dancing lightly in a bar of sunlight; the cold, sensuous bite of lake water as you eased yourself in up to the waist for the first time. Watching boys in bathing suits, wondering if they were watching you. Jay grit her teeth and went back in to the cabin, fighting back tears and the tight, gentle twist of pain that lay just below her heart.

What was it Poe's Raven said?
Nevermore.

Harry made them coffee and fried-egg sandwiches, and when they were done with breakfast he dropped the Planters can into a paper bag and prepared to leave. "I'll be a few hours," he said. "Stay on the boat. Everglades City isn't the news capital of the world, but they do get the *Herald* and the Rod and Gun Club Lodge just got a satellite dish." He put a hand on her shoulder and squeezed gently. "When I come back we'll get you set up, okay?"

"Okay." She gestured at the bag in his other hand. "Be careful."

"Always." He smiled, and then he was gone.

Jay went and fetched her luggage from the forward locker between the shower and the lavatory, or "head," as Harry called it. She linked up the cell phone to her laptop and checked her mail, but there were no messages from Billy or anyone else. She packed up, checked a narrow shelf of books in the tiny forward cabin, and chose an old Michael Connelly paperback. Taking both the book and the overnight bag back to the dining area, she made more coffee, then settled down on the bench to read and wait for Harry's return.

He was back just before noon, pulling into the marina's gravel parking lot driving a mid-seventies Honda Civic, its chocolate brown paint faded to something not quite as palatable. He climbed out of the car carrying several grocery bags and came down to the boat.

"Sorry I took so long." He stepped down into the cabin. One of the bags he was carrying gave off an incredible combination of junk food aromas. He emptied the food bag first, setting out a selection of dripping hamburgers, fried shrimp, and french fries. Last out of the bag were two tall milkshake cups. "One's strawberry, the other's chocolate. I thought you might be hungry."

"You're a genius," said Jay. "I'll take the strawberry."

They ate in silence, using the food wrappers as placemats, and when they were done, Harry stuffed the garbage into the empty bag. Jay leaned back against the back of the bench in the dining area, sucking up the last dregs of the milkshake. Harry peered into one of the other bags on the counter and pulled out a fresh package of Marlboros. He tossed them across the table to Jay.

"My old brand." She smiled. "You're corrupting me."

"My criminal influence." He smiled back.

"Business done?" she asked.

He nodded. "All done. Now we can deal with your problems."

Jay stripped open the Marlboro package and lit up. "I think I should just get out of here. Take my chances without getting you involved any more than you already are." She frowned. "There are some U.S. attorneys out there who could make a fair case against you for being an accessory."

"To what?" Harry asked. "You haven't committed any crime."

"Not yet."

There was a short silence. Harry brought the other bags back to the table. "Not a lot of choice at the Right Choice and the Drug Mart," he said, digging into the bags. "Hair coloring, really ugly glasses, bad lipstick, nail polish, and a baseball cap." He hauled out a fistful of clothes as well: a black-and-red Miami Heat basketball shirt with matching shorts and a pair of bright pink sandals.

"What the hell is this?" asked Jay, trying not to laugh.

"Your disguise." He shrugged. "Best I could do on short notice."

She picked up the hair coloring. "Sunset Orange? You've got to be kidding."

Harry dug a pair of brand-new hair cutting scissors out of the bag and snipped them in the air. "Not kidding at all." He answered. "The best disguise is an ugly disguise, believe me." He gestured toward the hair coloring on the table. "You rinse it right in, no need for peroxide."

"You've done this kind of thing before?"

"Once or twice," he admitted.

Jay shook her head. "Nice try, but looking like Phyllis Diller isn't going to do me much good if I can't get on an airplane." She took a drag of the cigarette. "They ask for ID, and any credit card I have is going to ring all sorts of bells."

"Been taken care of," Harry replied. He reached into the next bag and brought out a tartan fanny pack. Unzipping it, he took out two laminated driver's licenses, a Visa, a MasterCard, and an American Express Card. Stunned, Jay picked up the licenses. One was a pale State of Florida issue, plastic laminated with a fuzzy-looking picture of her on the left side of the license. The other was a much simpler Washington State license with the same picture on the right. On both licenses and all the credit cards her name was Letitia Fairbanks.

"Letitia Fairbanks?"

"Sorry." Harry smiled. "Best I could do on short notice."

"The only Letitia I ever heard of was in a book called *Swallows and Amazons*," said Jay.

"Titty." Harry nodded. "She was the youngest."

Jay stared at him, not quite believing it. "You read *Swallows and Amazons*?"

"I read all of them. *Peter Duck, Swallowdale, Winter Holiday, We Didn't Mean to Go to Sea.* I was raised on Arthur Ransome and E. Nesbit; my mother was a war bride from England. Before the war she was a librarian."

He's perfect.

Forget it, kiddo, you've got other fish to fry right now.

"How did you get all these?" Jay asked, gesturing at the spread of cards on the table in front of her. "Not to mention that car you drove up in."

"Friends in low places. I borrowed that U.S. Marshals temporary ID in your purse for the license pictures. They're only laminated color photocopies, but they're good enough for airport use. I've got the car on loan for a few days. It isn't hot."

"The credit cards?"

"They're real."

"You mean Letitia Fairbanks actually exists?"

Harry nodded. "Right about now old Letitia should be going through the Panama Canal on her way to Honolulu."

"How does that work?"

"Ever been on a cruise?" asked Harry.

Jay shook her head. "Never high on my list."

"The cruise lines make a big chunk of money off the 'extras' they sell you on board," explained Harry. "Everything from perfume to fur coats and diamond bracelets. The last thing they want you doing is hauling out your credit cards all the time, so usually you register one card with the purser when you get on, then just show your room key from that point on. You don't even think about your credit cards after that."

"Somebody snatches them?"

"Right," said Harry. "First port of call, the steward who pinched the cards Fed-Ex's them back to Orlando or Fort Lauderdale, the two big home ports. The cards get used for the length of the cruise and then they're thrown away so the thief doesn't get nabbed."

"The cruise lines don't get suspicious?"

"The card thieves are pretty smart," Harry answered. "They only hit one or two people on each ship for each cruise, and they try to slick the cards from old people . . . They've got high credit limits and they usually think the mistake was theirs. Most of the time they don't even report the cards as being stolen." He picked up the Gold Visa. "Letitia's on a twenty-one-day Lauderdale to Honolulu run. First port of call was Key West. You've got almost a three-week window with these."

"I'm not sure I like the idea of beating a little old lady out of her life savings."

"She'll be able to prove that she wasn't liable," Harry said. "The credit card company will eat it."

"Another victimless crime?"

"No such thing." Harry smiled again. "But some victims get what they deserve." He reached into one of the bags and came up with half a dozen bundles of shrink-wrapped currency. He slit one of them open and peeled off a half-inch stack of bills. They were all hundreds. "If you have some moral qualms about using Letitia's Visa, then use this instead." He put the money into the fanny pack and slid it across the table to her.

"Your smuggling fee?" He nodded. She shook her head and pushed the fanny pack back across the table. "I can't take money from you."

"Why? Because it's profit from a criminal act?"

"No," Jay answered. "Because you've done too much for me already. Because I can't pay you back."

"That's not what friends are for."

"Is that what we are? Friends?"

Let it be more than that.

Not now. There's no time for this.

"Kindred spirits? Like minds? Ships passing in the night? Who knows." Harry paused, then pushed the fanny pack back toward her. "Belle said she saw it in you and so did I. You're a good person in a bad spot, out there in the ozone by yourself. I know what that's like and so does Belle and so do a few other people I know. People who jumped the fence somewhere along the way."

"Turned left instead of right."

He nodded. "Us left-turners have to stick together, Jay Fletcher, because that's all we've got."

Jay looked down at the fanny pack for a moment, then nodded silently and stuffed the credit cards and the two licenses into it. "Now what?" she said after a long moment.

"Take the Civic out there to Fort Meyers up the Gulf Coast and leave it in the long-term lot. Somebody will pick it up there in the next couple of days. There's one of those little magnetic box things under the left front bumper. Leave the key in it."

"Why Fort Meyers?"

"Smugglers' choice." Harry smiled. "It has direct flights to most places you'd want to go and the security is nothing like it is at Miami International. You've got the whole world looking for you, Jay. Try to avoid the hubs no matter what."

"All right."

They sat together silently for a few moments, not looking at each other and not looking away either. She knew he was offering her a stay-or-go choice, a way out, a place to fall.

Why this? Why now?

You know you don't have that choice anymore. Maybe you never did.

"I guess I should take a shower, rinse in the color," Jay said finally.

"Okay." Harry held up the scissors. "Then I'll cut it."

"Okay."

Touch me.

Jay swept the clothes back into the bag, picked up the box of hair color, and stood up. She eased herself out around the table, stopping as Harry put out his hand and gently laid it flat against the upper curve of her hip.

"It's going to work out."

"I hope."

Tell me I don't have to do this. Tell me to stay.

He won't. He knows I have to do this and knows I'd hate him forever if he stopped me.

His voice was as gentle as the touch of his hand.

Too late. Too late to stop now.

"When you find him, what will you do?"

He knows. He wants me to say it to make sure that it's what I want.

She didn't hesitate for a second. "Kill him."

*   *   *

With all his credentials, clearances, and authorizations in order, Jack Dane signed out a car from the Headquarters Motor Pool, pushed his way through the heavy mid-morning traffic, and finally managed to exit the sweltering city, the air conditioning full-on as he fled down Interstate 95. He had plenty of time to think on his way south, and most of what he was thinking, he didn't like. For all of his adult life he'd been a straightforward, black-and-white guy. Bad guys break laws, good guys uphold them. Bad guy breaks a law, he goes to jail, he escapes jail, you go after him. It wasn't a complicated philosophy, and over the years it had never led him down the path it was taking him now.

"Shit, piss, and corruption," he said, banging his palm on the wheel of the car as he drove on, dredging up the curse from his youth, a curse learned literally at his grandfather's knee and treasured ever since. Once upon a time Jay Fletcher had been a cop, but then she'd gone wrong, killed, broken any number of laws. She'd also flushed out a whole stinking online congregation of murderers and managed to do away with their leader and a few acolytes as well. Later she'd tracked down Billy Bones and was largely responsible for gathering the evidence that finally put him out of commission. Saint or sinner, crook or cop, white or black?

According to the popular press and literally hundreds of victims' relatives, she was definitely on the side of the angels, but from day one Jack Dane's root intuition told him that there was more going on in that woman's heart than a simple search for justice. If ever there was a woman running with the wolves, it was Janet Louise Fletcher. He'd seen her eyes after the killing of little Vinnie Hoa on China Bayou, and all he'd seen there was cold death. One way or the other, he knew that William Paris Bonisteel would never come to trial for what he had done these past few days.

The marshal turned off the Interstate at the 143 Exit, drove through the little town of Garrisonville, and entered the huge Federal Reservation that included the Quantico Marine Base and the FBI Academy. He drove down the narrow, tree-lined road, turned off at the entrance to the campus, and checked in at the Y intersection a hundred yards farther along. He took the right arm of the Y, turning away from the cluster of buildings spread out above the reservoir, following J. Edgar Hoover Road to Garand, then Browning, both of the latter named after Hoover's favorite weapons for dueling with the bad guys. He was here by Karlson's order, delivering the laptop to a man named Clay Waterman deep in the bowels of the building. With Waterman's help he would supposedly get in a line on Fletcher, and possibly her whereabouts.

Sitting there in the parking lot, engine running, fanned by the air conditioning, Jack Dane wasn't sure he wanted to know where Jay was now, or what she was doing. According to Karlson, she was a fugitive in flight, material witness to Billy's crimes, and thus fell under the Marshals Service mandate. A week or so ago Dane wouldn't have hesitated for a minute, but now he wasn't so sure. Maybe all the people out there who read the tabloids and watched Sally Jesse and all the others were right. Just with the world going to hell around their ears, they needed a new hero, an avenging angel to cut through the crap and bullshit that put convicted murderers on the street and gave civil rights to monsters.

Snapping off the ignition, he picked up the laptop from the seat beside him and climbed out of the car. For now he was going to do what Karlson asked him to, but soon he knew he'd have to take a side.

TWENTY-TWO

The house at the end of Wing Point Road had been the centerpiece of Michael Deaver's world, an eighty-foot-long homage to the Prairie School of architecture in pale green and slate. It followed the hooking arc of a beachfront lot that looked west across Eagle Harbor to the small town of Winslow on Bainbridge Island in Washington State.

The east-facing windows on the second floor of the house looked back across Puget Sound to the Seattle skyline, a thirty-minute ferry ride away. It was the last residence on Wing Point, screened from its nearest neighbor to the north by a rocky outcropping and a scattering of Madrona, fir, and alder. The southern portion of the land was open to the Sound.

In contrast to the sleek, modern exterior with its plain, angular lines, the interior was a slightly lunatic assortment of styles and tastes from Biedermeier secretaries to Toby Jugs, and from a fourteenth-century full-size Lombard white marble Virgin and Child standing in an equally life-size twelfth-century stone doorway to a huge, Mondrian-like Ole Baertling canvas from the sixties.

There was Rodin's *Bust of a Laughing Boy* in the downstairs powder room, a straw-colored Tang Horse in the front hall, and on the living-room wall, bracketing the fireplace, two paintings, both expensively framed, one an anonymous and very bad black velvet portrait of two weeping clowns from a garage sale in Tacoma, the other a magnificent Renoir, *Girl with a Rose in Her Hair,* which had once belonged to the San Francisco Museum of Art. The house, custom-built five years ago, had cost slightly less than a million dollars. The contents were valued at four times that amount.

Michael Deaver had been fond of telling the story of the velvet painting. According to him, he and his wife, Karen, had been newlyweds without a pot to piss in and the five-dollar painting had been all they could afford in the way of art for their tiny apartment. The crying clowns, Deaver declared, reminded him of his humble roots, the Renoir of how far he'd come.

In fact, there was nothing particularly humble about Michael Deaver's roots. His father had taught political science at the University of Washington, and his mother was an editor for a Seattle publishing company. Michael went to Nathan Hale High School, not too far from the campus, played half-decent basketball and was given a secondhand Karman Ghia when he graduated. Using his "faculty preferred" status, he enrolled at U of W in what was then their fledgling Computer Sciences program.

Halfway through his second year, realizing that he knew more about the subject than the people teaching him, he went to work with Bill Gates and half a dozen other "computer nerds," creating what would eventually be known as Microsoft. He was married at twenty-three, a millionaire at thirty, retired at forty. Three years after that, he was diagnosed with inoperable liver cancer and a year after that he was dead.

Sitting on the rocky outcropping that separated her property from the one next to it, Karen Deaver thought about her husband, the house, and the rest of her life. She rested her chin on her updrawn knees and looked out over Eagle Harbor. The lunchtime ferry was going out, doing the little zigzag the big boats always made to get around the invisible shoal that jutted out just below the surface at the entrance to the bay.

Half the vehicles on the shuttle would be either Land Rovers or BMW's off to an afternoon of upscale shopping before the evening rush. A lot of wealthy women on the island, most of them bored, some of them devoted to causes they volunteered for, others taking tennis or golf or yacht club lovers to oil their ennui.

It had never been like that for her and Michael. During their time together they'd been constant friends, constant

companions, and constant lovers, each devoted to the other.
They'd met at college, but while he dropped out, she continued on, eventually getting a master's degree in art history
followed by a year away at New York University's Conservation Center of the Institute of Fine Arts. This had led to an
impressive and fulfilling career as an internationally known
conservation and preservation expert.

During her time away in New York, she'd been unfaithful
twice, but Michael had never asked her about it, and she had
never told him. She assumed, although never confirmed, that
Michael hadn't been celibate for that year any more than she
had. Not that it seemed to matter. Right up until the time his
illness really took hold, they'd had an active sex life together,
and while she'd had the occasional yearning and more than
occasional fantasies, there had been no real temptation to step
over the traces again.

For twenty years their marriage had flourished and their
love for each other had only grown deeper. The money and
the perquisites that came with being the wife of a leading
Microsoft executive were nice enough, but they both knew
the glue that held their relationship together had nothing to
do with finance.

But all of that was over now, and that was what Karen
Deaver was finding difficult to accept. For half of the years
she'd been on the planet, Michael had been there with her;
living without him now was unfamiliar, uncharted territory.
Even after a year she could hear him faintly calling from
another room, sometimes see him, a blurred face above his
battered leather bomber jacket, standing on the dock, waiting
for her to walk off the ferry so he could drive her home, taste
his tongue and the salt lick of the sweat that glistened in the
hollow of his throat.

She stood up and walked across to the low sandy slope
that led down to the beach, listening to the dry hiss of the
dune grass as it brushed against the fabric of her jeans, hot
sand pushing between the toes of her sandals. The tide was
ebbing and the strong scent of seaweed and kelp was heavy
in the air. That smell was Michael as well, on the walks

they'd taken together, sundown walks where they talked and planned, discussing a future that was never going to be. Michael. It was all Michael, all the time, and she cursed him for it. He'd given her a perfect life, then left her with it.

"Why did I have to love you so much?" she said out loud, trying to break the spell of her thoughts. It didn't help. She turned away from the view, turned her back on the falling tide, and went back up to the house. She was forty-one years old, her body tight and fit and pretty because she worked at it hard, her dark brown hair, rough cut to her shoulders, only just now showing small streaks of gray. She could wear tight jeans and a bikini and still get away with it, but what did that matter any more? Sex and lust and that kind of sensuousness had all been Michael too, and so she saw the remainder of her life in terms of emptiness and loneliness, forever.

"Oh, quit feeling sorry for yourself." She reached the huge deck that ran almost the entire length of the ocean side of the house, pulled open the sliding glass doors, and went into the living room. She crossed it, trying to turn a blind eye to the furniture and the paintings that were so much "theirs" or "his" instead of her own, trying not to think about the irony of a near perfect love turned to almost suicidal widowhood. This was one thing *Martha Stewart Living* couldn't help you with, that was for sure.

She went up the curving stairs to the upper level, ignoring the big master bedroom and the bathroom with its tempting array of therapeutically prescribed drugs designed to ease her through and cope with her "time of transition." Instead she turned into the large, airy, east-facing studio, the only space within the house that she'd ever been able to say was truly hers.

The room was high-ceilinged and rectangular, painted white, larger windows facing east, the west wall blank and fitted with a gallery rail close to the ceiling for hanging paintings. One short wall was taken up by a long bench for mixing paints and solvents, the other by a sink and storage cupboards. In the center of the room was a massive easel, capable of carrying paintings six or seven feet on a side. In the ceiling there were two large skylights, the glass lightly sandblasted to diffuse the sun.

On the easel now was her current project, a Gauguin, approximately three feet by two, titled *Piti Tiena*, which translated roughly as Two Sisters. The painting was a portrait of two Tahitian girls of twelve or thirteen, both wearing red dresses and standing against a background of brilliant, hot orange and green, with big, vaguely shaped white blossoms blooming around their heads like halos. The painting was stunningly beautiful, the two girls radiantly and mysteriously on the edge of womanhood, their large, thoughtful eyes much older and wiser than their apparent age.

The painting, taken from Germany as war booty in 1945 and never returned, was seriously damaged, having spent the last fifty-odd years stacked in a too humid basement of the Hermitage in Leningrad, now St. Petersburg again. The painting was badly cracked, and humidity was also lifting large chips of color up from the already rotting canvas. Piotrovsky, the director of the Hermitage, had offered the Gauguin to Karen for restoration just after Michael died, and she'd been working on it ever since. It was almost finished now, but she was superstitiously wary of the project coming to an end and kept on finding excuses to delay longer. Somehow she saw the canvas as a last link to her husband and and felt as if completing it would break the final connection with him forever.

"You have to get on with your life." How many friends and therapists had told her that over the last twelve months? Easy to say, harder to do, impossible to think about. Karen heard the faint sound of the doorbell and, glad for the distraction, turned away from the painting and went back to the main floor. Opening the door, she saw an extremely good looking, well-dressed man standing on the front step. Behind him, parked in the driveway was a brand-new, burnished silver Porsche Boxter. Definitely not a Jehovah's Witness passing out tracts about the end of the world.

"Can I help you?"

"Mrs. Deaver?" The handsome man smiled and the smile

turned him from handsome to almost angelic. There was beauty in his face like the beauty of the girls in the Gauguin painting upstairs. Danger too, and some deep, strong passion that Karen found almost hypnotic.

Maybe this stranger is just what I need. A spellbreaker.

"Yes?" said Karen.

"I've come about the boat," replied Billy Bones.

Jay Fletcher made the two-hundred-mile drive from Everglades City to Fort Meyers in slightly less than four hours, arriving just before the five o'clock rush hour. She parked as Harry had instructed, then went into the small, almost cozy terminal and looked for a flight. At that hour the main concourse was busy enough, but it was nothing close to the nightmare of a main airport like Miami, LAX, or worst of all, O'Hare.

Ten points, Harry.

She found a Delta flight to Las Vegas with only a one-hour wait for an Alaska Airlines flight to Seattle, arriving at ten-thirty, Pacific time. At the Delta desk she held her breath for the ninety seconds it took to process Letitia Fairbanks's Gold Visa card.

The girl behind the desk gave the phony State of Florida driver's license a cursory glance, and then the ordeal was over. Jay headed for the ladies' room just outside the security gate, locked herself into a stall, and stripped off the redneck disguise that had taken her this far. She lost the hat, the shorts, the pink sandals, and the basketball shirt, replacing them with a plain T-shirt, her jeans, and her sneakers. The only thing left were the glasses and the boy-cut, tinted hair.

She stuffed the redneck clothes back into her bag, took out the Glock, and tapped out the magazine. She emptied the clip, opened up the back of the toilet tank, and tossed them in. The Glock was made of graphite and other nonferrous compounds, but the cartridges would ring bells at any airport metal detector. It was a lesson more than one television-educated bad guy had learned the hard way.

She put the Glock back into the overnight bag, peeked out

of the stall, then spent two minutes with her hair, using her fingers to rake some tiny shred of femininity into Harry's quick and dirty styling. Checking her watch, she saw that she was running out of time. She left the ladies' room, crossed the last hurdle at the security barrier, and headed down the long, low-ceilinged corridor to her gate. Fifteen minutes later she was in the air, drinking a well-earned Scotch and wishing for a cigarette. She glanced up at the overhead luggage compartment, thinking about the laptop. When she was born they didn't exist and now they were as ubiquitous as telephones, with as much potential for evil as they had for good.

Computers don't kill people, they just make it easier for some people.

Like Billy.

She closed her eyes and leaned back in her seat, letting reality fall away for now, retreating into kinder dreams. She slept until the announcement of their landing at McCarran Airport in Las Vegas, smoked up a storm for her hour layover, then slept again all the way to Seattle.

Landing at SeaTac she was wide-awake, even though by her biological clock it was two o'clock in the morning; the only thing she was missing was shells for the Glock. She rented a car using Letitia's card, silently vowing to pay her back when all was said and done, bought a road map and a package of cigarettes from the smoke shop, then headed north into the city.

She arrived at the waterfront at the foot of Columbia Street just in time to drive aboard the 11:15 to Bainbridge Island. According to the schedule posted in the upper lounge, the last ferry returned to Seattle at 1:30 in the morning; it didn't give her much time, and if she suddenly found herself backed into a corner, being on an island didn't seem like the best idea, especially with an empty gun.

Forty minutes later Jay was among the first to drive off the ferry and up the steep hill into the little town of Winslow. She stopped at an illuminated phone booth tacked onto the side wall of a Seven-Eleven and called the number listed in

Boat Trader magazine. It rang four times and then clicked onto a message machine.

"Hi, this is Karen Deaver. I can't take your call right now but if you'll leave a name and . . ."

What kind of people named a boat Helter Skelter?

Beatles freaks who never read the Bugliosi book, or didn't care.

Jay hung up and dialed again, just to make sure she'd had the right number. She did. She hung up the phone and checked for Deaver in the local phone book. There were two of them, a Charles Deaver on Shepherd Way and an M. J. Deaver on Wing Point Road. The Wing Point number matched the one in the magazine.

Jay went into the convenience store, bought a map of the town that showed her destination, and headed off. Ten minutes and two wrong turns around a dark, empty golf course later, she reached the end of Wing Point Road and pulled in to the semicircular drive in front of a large, low slung house. M. J. Deaver and his lovely wife, Karen, were rich by the looks of it.

Let's hope they're not dead; Billy's got a forty-eight-hour head start.

Her lights swung over the shape of what looked like a brand-new Porsche as well as a clutter of garden tools against the back wall of an empty garage. She switched off the car and the lights, then rolled down her window, listening, peering out into the darkness: insect sounds and the nearby hiss and whisper of waves hitting a beach, the breeze making little ghost sounds in the trees. Nothing from the house and no lights either.

Jay unzipped the flight bag on the seat beside her, found the Glock and stepped out of the car, easing the door closed and listening again. Still nothing. She moved toward the front door, listening to her sneakers crunch over the gravel on the driveway, eyes scanning the darkness in front of her.

Think. Be ready.

It was a two-car garage, which meant that even if the Porsche belonged to the house, there was another car missing.

Somebody in Seattle, not back from town? It was a possibility. Jay reached the Porsche and stopped. The license-plate holder was stamped with the name of an exotic car rental company in Seattle. A visitor.

Billy?

Just like him to arrive in style, leaving the Porsche to taunt Jay and to advertise his own superiority. Two scenarios from that little fact. Either no one was home when Billy arrived and he was in there waiting right now, or Billy had gone off with the Deavers' vehicle.

And maybe the Deavers.

Jay slipped toward the door, pausing every few seconds to listen. Nothing. Intuitively, she knew that Billy had been and gone and she felt her heart sink, realizing that there was no real need for stealth anymore. She topped the steps and saw that the front door was standing slightly ajar. Billy. She spread the fingers of her free hand against the door and pushed, bringing the Glock to bear even though it was nothing more than a two-pound prop in her hand. She might just as well have reversed it in her grip and used it as a club.

She stepped into the foyer and paused. From where she stood there was a clear view across the foyer, through the living room and out onto the wide rear deck through a pair of sliding glass doors. Beyond the deck she could see a faint line of high grass, a beach, and then the blackness of the bay beyond.

Jay froze where she stood and swallowed. A darker shadow was humped on the edge of the deck. Every few seconds she saw the rise and fall of a small glowing light, streaking red in the darkness. A cigarette moving in a person's hand.

Oh shit, now what? Arrest him with an empty gun?

She took two slow steps into the living room and spotted the huge fireplace off to the right. There was a stand loaded with andirons, including a brass-knobbed poker, but it was a good twenty feet away and another twenty back to the sliding glass doors. Any sign of movement out of the corner of his eye and she'd either be dead or he'd be gone. Instead, Jay kept directly behind the figure and walked quickly toward the sliding doors. She cast quickly to left and right. No sign of the bodies, no telltale burn of copper blood or voided bowels and bladders. This was no killing ground.

So where the hell are they?

She didn't hesitate. Reaching the doors she slid the left one open with a bang and stepped out onto the deck, the Glock extended. The figure on the edge of the deck barely reacted. The red glow of the cigarette butt arced into the air, throwing off sparks, then dying in the darkness. The figure rose and turned, the heavy shape of a large, nickel-chrome-plated handgun clearly visible.

"Put the stupid thing down, Jay, we both know your gun is empty," said Jack Dane. "And mine's not."

TWENTY-THREE

They went into the living room of the Deaver house and Jack Dane switched on the lights. Jay dropped down onto a chrome-and-leather chair, watching as Dane meandered over to the fireplace. There was an array of silver-framed photographs on the marble mantelpiece.

"So," she said wearily. "Now what, Jack?"

"That's up to you."

She smiled. "We're going to play the hard way–easy way game?"

"You're now officially a material witness as far as Karlson is concerned. There's a warrant out on you."

"Which makes me a fugitive in flight, correct?"

"Right."

"He wants me in custody?"

"He wants you in custody real bad. The newspapers are having a field day with this. You're back in prime time as the Ladykiller. Give it another day or so and they'll be giving odds in Vegas on whether you whack Billy or he gets you first."

"What's the alternative?" Jay said quietly.

"There isn't one," the marshal answered.

"You know what I mean."

"Karlson isn't particularly interested in your health, let's put it that way."

I'm a loose end and Karlson doesn't care how I get tidied up.

"I'm not going back."

"I know that. I knew that when I woke up in New Orleans and found you gone." He sighed. "It's gone all personal now, hasn't it? The Vietnamese kid, the old lady, Connelly, all of them. It's just you and Billy, right?"

"It's what I do, Marshal Dane." She leaned back in the chair, so tired of it all. "I've been thinking about that a lot. Who I am, and what I am. I'm not fighting that any more. Until Billy goes down I won't know, don't you understand that? He's unfinished business."

"Yes, I understand," said Dane.

Jay shook her head. "No, I don't think you could. You're not that kind of person; to you law and justice and right and wrong are absolutes."

"Maybe there's still a new trick or two in the old dog yet." Dane grinned. "I've been doing a lot of thinking, too."

"Which brings us back to Karlson and just what you're going to do with me now that you've got me."

There was a long pause. When Dane spoke, his tone was as weary as Jay's had been. "Karlson doesn't even know I've gone. He thinks I'm still trying to locate you."

"I thought you were the ideal by-the-book U.S. Marshal."

"So did I." Dane lifted his shoulders. "Sometimes you have to close the book and just wing it." The marshal glanced down at the gun in his hand, then slid it back into its holster.

He's not doing this for me, he's doing it for himself. He wants Billy as much as I do.

A convert.

"Okay," said Jay. "Given that you've just joined my little Hole in the Wall gang, what do you think we should do next? Go after Billy in that Porsche of yours?"

The marshal made a snorting sound. "I wish." He shook his head. "It's Billy's. Rented under the name of Thomas Jacobs. Keys are in it. I left my rental down the road, parked in the trees. Didn't want to spook you."

"You were that sure I'd come?" Jay said.

Dane nodded. "I was that sure."

"How did you track me down so fast?"

"It wasn't all that difficult." Dane shrugged. His clothes were wrinkled, he had five o'clock shadow, and he looked as jet-lagged as Jay felt. "Karlson had your laptop tagged right from the start and your cell phone, too." He blew out a long breath. "Your guys out at Quantico have all sorts of toys. You left a trail on the Net, and they followed it right to the *online Boat Trader*. We figured out the missing page of the magazine, picked up on the boat in Key West and the one here. After that it was simple." He smiled. "*Charming Billy* and *Helter Skelter*. We had two choices, I came here."

"You sent someone to Key West?"

Dane nodded. "They talked to your friend, the one with the boat." Dane paused, his expression changing slightly. "Seems he was a little worried about you."

"You leaving him alone?"

"So far." Dane frowned. "Why? He done something wrong we should know about?"

"No, nothing you should know about."

But we won't say anything about what Customs should know about.

"What about the Deavers?" Jay asked. "Any sign of them?"

"I did a little research before the flight out. Michael Deaver was a big shot at Microsoft in the early days. Millionaire and more. He died a year ago, cancer; there's only the wife, Karen."

"The voice on the answering machine."

Dane nodded. "The phone rang about fifteen minutes ago. That was you?"

"Yes."

"Figured," said Dane. "You can see the ferries docking from out on the deck. The call came just after one came in."

"What about the boat—*Helter Skelter*?"

Dane sighed. "I got here around four o'clock this afternoon. The man who runs the marina said the boat went out around two."

"Did he see Karen Deaver?"

"Yes. Our boy was with her. According to the guy who saw them go, there was nothing out of the ordinary. She's taken two or three prospective buyers out for a spin."

"And they never came back?"

"No." Dane pulled his cell phone out of his jacket pocket. "I told him to call if the boat came back in." He rubbed a tired hand across his forehead. "He hasn't called. I don't think *Helter Skelter*'s coming back." He turned, picked up a photograph from the mantel, and brought it over to where Jay was sitting. The picture showed a handsome couple posed partway along a narrow dock. Steps led up a low, solid-stone rise to a large log cabin–style vacation home above. "Turn it over," said Dane. Jay did so. There was an inscription on the back: *Michael and Karen/Sparks Island, San Juans/August 1996.*

"Shit," said Jay. All the pieces were coming together.

He knew. Billy knew right from the beginning of all this.

"Yeah," said Dane. "It took me a little while, but I got it too. Sceptered Isles, Sparks falling from heaven. Cute." The marshal pointed across the room. "Michael Deaver had a den on the other side of the house. I went through his filing cabinet. There's a deed to the whole island. I also found a chart book. Sparks Island is in the northern San Juans, right up by the International Boundary. He even has aerial photographs. Big spread."

"You think Billy's making a run for it? Going into Canada?"

"Eventually," said Dane. "But right now he's taken Karen Deaver to that island knowing that you'll try to rescue her."

Jay thought about it and nodded. "He kills me, he kills her, and then he takes the boat north and vanishes."

"Something like that."

Jay checked her watch. It was one o'clock in the morning. Billy and Karen had been gone for nine hours. "Big head start."

"Not so big," said Dane. "It's at least a hundred and twenty miles, and half of that at night. I checked the charts; it's not easy navigating either. Tricky water. They won't be there yet."

"So what are we going to do about it? Call in the troops? Navy Seals, SWAT, the boys from Waco and Ruby Ridge?" Jay paused. "Even if it winds up getting Karen Deaver killed."

She stared at Dane. "That's what your boss would do."

"I'm not Karlson and what makes you think she's still alive?"

"Because there's nothing in William Bonisteel's file that says anything about knowing how to navigate a halibut schooner through your so-called tricky waters in the middle of the night. The closest he ever came to that was a scuba course he took at the Y in high school." She paused. "Billy needs her, but he'll kill her if he has to. The first sign of any gung-ho types dropping out of the skies and he'll slit her throat just like he did to Connelly in New York."

"You're right about Billy," Dane agreed. "If he gets even the slightest whiff of some kind of major operation, he'll kill the woman. We have to get to him first."

"How?"

"I checked the map. There's a town called Bellingham about a hundred miles north, close to the U.S.–Canada border. There's a Coast Guard station there and a bunch of marinas. We could be there in a couple of hours."

"Very spooky," said Jay. "Bellingham is where Ricky Stiles came from. A Catholic orphanage."

"Billy's friend? The one you fried in Vegas? You think there's some kind of connection?"

"In Billy's mind, everything is connected. In real life it's probably just a coincidence, but to Billy it's some kind of chaotic omen, believe me."

"On the map it looks as though Sparks Island is only about fifteen miles or so off the coast. Less than an hour in a fast boat."

"What if no one wants to charter us a boat in Bellingham?" Dane smiled. "We steal one."

Jay got to her feet. "The last ferry leaves for Seattle in less than twenty minutes. We'd better hurry. Whose car do we take, yours or mine?"

"Billy's," Dane answered.

"You know what I think?" Billy Bones asked.

"What?" Karen Deaver answered. She stood handcuffed to

the wheel on the bridge of *Helter Skelter*, keeping on course
in the pitch darkness using the glow of the Si-Tec radar screen
and the Pinpoint Systems plotter. The console in front of her
also held a Raytheon Thermal Imager, and she used it to make
small corrections every few minutes, steering to port or starboard of buoys and markers.

Billy smiled, sitting in the mate's seat beside her. "I think
the term *serial killer* has become a little passé." Karen didn't
answer and Billy kept on talking. "It's like the word *abuse*;
it just doesn't mean anything anymore." Billy sat with his
hands loosely together in his lap, looking out into the darkness.

"The term was invented by some FBI agent not all that
long ago," he went on. "It's not even accurate. Serial doesn't
mean one after another, it means one *because* of another.
Each event or item adding to the next. Like an artist putting
daubs of paint on a canvas until it's done."

She ignored him and used her free hand to ease off slightly
on the throttle. "Why are you doing that?" he asked.

She could hear the slight catch in his voice. "The weather's
getting worse. She'll break her scantlings if we go too fast."
He nodded, clearly nervous now, and Karen Deaver allowed
herself to believe that maybe there was a way out of this after
all.

Just after sunset it had begun to rain, and the farther north
they went, the worse it was getting. An hour later Karen suggested that he deploy the boomlike port and starboard para-
vanes to stop the steadily increasing roll of the boat. He had
done so, following her instructions, and they no longer wal-
lowed so heavily through the steadily rising seas. Even so,
the seas were getting rougher and *Helter Skelter* was barely
making ten knots headway. On the other hand, the scantlings—the short, strong beams forming the side and ribs of
the boat—were massive and well beyond the design specifi-
cations for a boat the size of *Helter Skelter*.

"All right," said Billy. "Just don't do anything silly."

"Whatever you say."

Billy's initial charm had vanished abruptly, ten minutes after leaving the marina and rounding the port side of Eagle Harbor. That's when he'd shown her the knife, taken the handcuffs out of the big, heavy canvas bag he'd brought on board, and shackled her to the wheel.

"It's almost as though people don't want to admit the truth," continued Billy.

Karen couldn't stop herself. "What truth is that?"

"That people like me are a different species entirely." He smiled, looking at her fondly. "We're the aliens doing all the abducting, not those fey little androgynes Whitley Strieber writes all those books about."

"I don't know what you're talking about."

"Predators," Billy explained. "Creatures who kill organisms to sustain life. From the Latin, to plunder."

"Fascinating," Karen said flatly.

"It is actually," said Billy. "Although I don't really expect you to be interested in my little theories. Predators are necessary in any ecological infrastructure, including human civilization. When a herd of deer becomes too large, the local ecological balance becomes upset, threatening the entire system. Mother Nature steps in with a pack of wolves to balance things out. Serial killers, for want of a better definition, are merely an expression of Nature's attempt to cull the herd, so to speak."

"You really believe that?" Karen said. In front of her the rain was ticking and spattering across the windscreen, obscuring the night.

"Of course not." Billy laughed. He reached over and slid one hand between her thighs, two fingers expertly stroking up along the crotch of her thin cotton shorts. She froze, repulsed by the firm insistent touch. She knew that any chance she'd had of talking him out of this was gone in that moment. She wasn't human to him; she was flesh, meat, nothing more.

"I kill people because it gives me a rush," Billy said softly, head bent close to her ear, the fingers working her expertly. "Because fear is just one big turn-on." And then the hand was gone and Billy was sitting as he was before, hands together in his lap.

Karen felt her breath coming in little short gasps. Her heart began to slow, but then the anger began welling up, catching in her throat as judgment and logic took hold again. She knew all he was looking for was an excuse, and she refused to give it to him.

She kept her eyes forward, staring blankly out into the darkness, letting her hands on the wheel feel the rhythmic pounding as the bow of the big boat rose and fell on the face of the incoming chop. According to the Plotter, they were at the top of Rosario Strait, just past Peapod Rocks on the eastern side of Orcas, one of the largest of the San Juan Islands. Once they reached Lawrence Point they would be out of the island's protection. To reach Sparks she'd have to change course and turn almost directly into the teeth of the storm.

"Let's play Twenty Questions," said Billy.

"Whatever you say."

"That's right. Whatever I say." Billy paused. "Ready?"

"Sure."

"Don't lie."

"I won't."

"You'll be punished if you do, remember that."

"I told you I wouldn't lie."

"Good. Here goes." Billy took a deep breath, the let it out. The boat corkscrewed into another wave and it felt as though the side of the hull had been smacked with a massive club. Billy didn't show any concern. "How old were you when you lost your virginity?"

"Sixteen."

"How was it?"

"Terrible."

"Why?"

"He was a virgin, too. There was a lot of fumbling."

"I was almost seventeen the first time I tried sex," said Billy. "She was a little bit older, a high school senior. Her name was Jeanette, I think. She seduced me more or less, with her mother and father snoring just down the hall." He paused and smiled, but there was no humor in the expression. He looked cold as sharp steel. "I couldn't perform," he continued. "The more I tried the worse it got. She started making fun of me and then she told me to leave."

"Not very nice of her," Karen offered.

"No. It wasn't. Two weeks later her drama class went on a field trip to some drama festival in Seattle. Jeanette sent me a postcard. That wasn't very nice either. Do you know what it said?"

"No." She played along. "What did it say?"

"Nothing." Billy answered. "The message part was blank, but the picture was a low-level photograph of the Space Needle. I got the point." He paused again. "Do you know what I did?" he said, his voice soft.

"No."

"I waited until she got back from the field trip and then I cut out her tongue and nailed her to a tree in Little Tujunga Forest. I never told the police about that one. Too embarrassing. She was found three weeks later by a group of Boy Scouts on a camp-out." He smiled, reached out again, and stroked her cheek. "That's how I lost *my* virginity."

TWENTY-FOUR

It had begun to rain even before the ferry reached the dock in Seattle, and the Porsche didn't make nearly as good time as Jack Dane and Jay had expected. By the time they hit the I-5 North and reached the suburbs, they were driving through a full-fledged downpour with winds that buffeted the little car all over the road and rain that sheeted heavily on the windshield, dropping visibility down to only a few car lengths.

It was five-thirty in the morning before they reached Bellingham, slipping gratefully off the Interstate at the 253 Exit. The Porsche rumbled through the sleeping downtown, navigating the wet, empty streets until they found a way down to the waterfront and a straight road that followed a set of railroad tracks.

"There it is," said Jay, pointing. A sign loomed out of the rain advertising the Squalicum Harbor Marina. "It looks like a shopping mall."

Dane nodded and pulled into the parking lot. She was right; the complex looked like a folksy, one-story shopping mall crisply painted in marine gray, which was fitting, considering the weather. Even blocked by the bulk of the connected group of buildings that made up the harbor complex, the wind blowing off the water was gale force, blowing the rain sideways in blurring gusts.

They ducked out of the Porsche and ran under the broad, overhanging eaves of the building complex and huddled on the wooden boardwalk. Neither one of them was dressed for a gale and Jay was shivering.

"We've got to get out of this," said Dane, raising his voice over the gusting wind.

"It's six o'clock in the morning. Who's going to be up at this hour?"

Her name was Happy Lowell and she weighed at least 350 pounds. She wore her long gray hair in a bun, smoked idiotically thin Virginia Slims, and had Tensor bandages on both knees. She was the owner/operator of Happy's Dinette and Mobile Marine Services, located at the far end of the marina. It was the only thing open at that time of the morning.

The dinette was tiny, with only four tables and half a dozen stools at the counter. The décor was made up entirely of framed group photographs of National Hockey League team photographs advertising a brand of Canadian cigarettes. The teams were at least thirty years out of date and didn't include a single expansion team. There was a huge television on a swivel bracket close to the ceiling tuned to CNN but muted.

There were two large windows in the dinette, one facing down the pier, the other looking out over the marina and the breakwater beyond. Even if it hadn't been raining, the view through the windows would have been obscured by the grease and condensation on the inside of the glass.

"It smells like heaven," said Jay as they came through the door, dripping wet.

"It smells like fifty years of hashbrowns and bacon grease," Dane retorted.

"Like I said, heaven." Jay sat down at the counter. In front of her, Happy was scraping the grill down with a spatula. On one side of the grill there was a stainless-steel bowl full of eggs and half a dozen loaves of white bread and a plastic container of bacon strips on the other. Beside the bacon strips there was a ten-gallon pail of half-cooked hashbrowns.

"You're Happy?" Jay asked the huge, floral-print-covered backside of the woman waving in her face.

"Sometimes," she answered, looking back over her shoulder, still scraping the grill with the spatula. "Mostly I'd just describe myself as reasonably content."

Jack Dane sat down beside Jay and pulled a napkin out of

its chrome holder and tried to wipe some of the rain off his face. "Funny," he muttered.

Happy shrugged her massive shoulders and expertly flicked ash into a slop bucket under the counter. "Hey, come on. It's the only joke I've got." She took a huge drag on the cigarette and turned to face her customers. "Breakfast for you two?"

"Absolutely," Jay answered with enthusiasm. Dane didn't look quite so sure.

"Your friend appears to have doubts."

"He's from D.C.," Jay explained. "But we are in kind of a hurry."

"You have orange juice?" Dane asked.

"Just High-C."

"Jesus."

Happy gave Jay a warning look. "He's not going to ask me for Eggs Benedict, is he? Because we don't do Eggs Benedict, or Florentine, or anything but fried and scrambled. Are you having coffee?"

"Yes, please." Jay nodded.

Happy brought two heavy mugs up from under the counter, filled then from the Silex, and pointed to a saucer full of cream containers and a sugar shaker on the counter. "Don't ask for sweetener or honey or brown sugar because we don't have it." She crossed her arms and stared at them from the other side of the counter. "What brings you to beautiful Bellingham this god-awful hour of the day?"

"We're looking to charter a boat."

"In this weather?"

Jay nodded. "Yes."

"You're crazy," said Happy. "What's the story?"

"We're looking for someone." Jay said.

"Uh-huh."

"His daughter." Jay nodded toward Dane.

"Uh-huh."

"She's run away with her boyfriend."

"Umm."

She's buying it . . . sort of.

"We think they're heading for a place called Sparks Island."

"That's private," said Happy. "Some rich people from Seattle."

Jay nodded. "That's the boyfriend she's run off with."

"They're out in this?" asked Happy, gesturing toward the greasy window with her spatula.

"We think they're already there."

"So they're eloping," Happy said, pursing her lips. She poked the Virginia Slim into the middle of the little cupid's bow, sucked in, and then blew out. "What's the problem?"

It looked as though Jack Dane was going to say something but Jay beat him to the punch again. "She forgot her medicine."

"Medicine?"

"Insulin," Jay patted the pocket of her jacket. The only thing she could feel was the weight of the Glock. "She's diabetic. Ran off without it in all the excitement."

Happy made a little snorting noise and sucked on the cigarette again. She flipped more ash into the slop bucket. "Pretty stupid of her."

"She was only diagnosed a year ago." Dane added his two cents' worth to the lie. "She's still not used to it."

And I'm not used to winging it like this.

"Uh-huh." Happy flipped the butt of her cigarette into the slop bucket.

"So," said Jay. "Know anyone with a boat? It's sort of life and death."

"Life and death is the Coast Guard's business," Happy replied. She looked carefully at Jay, then turned her attention to Jack Dane. "Tell your story to them." She hooked a finger over her shoulder. "The base is right next door to the marina." She made the piggish little noise again, the small mouth turning up at the corners. "But don't tell them Happy Lowell sent you."

"Why's that?" Dane asked.

"We're not on the best terms."

Jay decided to leave that one alone. "We were hoping to do this . . . unofficially," she said.

Happy gave her a long, skeptical look. "Uh-huh." The huge woman bent down, fetched a mug from under the counter, and poured herself some coffee. She wiped her face with a tea-towel hanging from a hook above the counter, took a delicate sip of her coffee, and lit another Virginia Slim. "Either one of you got any experience with boats of any size?"

"I do," said Dane, giving her his most sincere smile.

She frowned. "Such as?"

"Swift Boats in the Perfume River."

"Huh," said Happy. "PCF's—Patrol Craft Fast." Her eyes actually twinkled. "Remember a little metal identification patch riveted to the bridge console?"

Dane thought for a moment and then smiled broadly. "I'll be damned. I do remember—Bellingham Boat Company."

"A lot of the PCF's were made right here." Happy nodded, obviously proud. "Kept the town afloat so to speak. Worked for them myself. So did my husband, Walter, bless his dead and gone heart." She waved the spatula around. "Bought all this with the proceeds of his insurance."

"We still need a boat," Jay prompted. Even in the bad weather Billy would have reached Sparks Island by now. If there was any chance at all of saving Karen Deaver, they'd have to move quickly.

"Well, now that you mention it, I might be able to do something for you."

"You know someone?" Dane asked.

"I am someone. I bought a couple of surplus boats when the company shut down. I've got one for myself, gave the other one to my kid." She shook her head. "I can't let you have mine, but I could rent you Tommy's for a price." She paused, the cupid lips twisting unpleasantly. "He's away right now."

"Away?" Dane asked.

"Walla Walla Penitentiary. Caught him smuggling bud. Marijuana from British Columbia." She shook her head.

"Used to be wetbacks coming up from Mexico. Now it's those foreign devils from Canada." She frowned and looked at Jack Dane. "Why is it this country always seems to need some kind of enemy?"

"They didn't seize the boat?" the marshal asked.

"It was in my name. Had to put up a fight to keep it, though. Tommy had it all tricked out as a dive boat. He was doing a pretty good business that way. At least he'll have work when they let him out."

"How much?" Dane asked.

"Five years. Three if he doesn't do something stupid in the meantime."

"I meant for the boat," said the Marshal.

"A grand," Happy answered. "No ifs, ands, or buts."

They checked their wallets and between them came up with the cash. Dane put it down on the counter in a neat pile. Happy Lowell looked down at the money and took another pull on her cigarette.

"Truth time," she said quietly.

"What?" said Dane.

She bent down, reached under the counter, and came up with an ancient Dakin side-by-side 10-gauge double-barreled shotgun. The stock had a crack in it bound up with black electrician's tape, and the barrels had been cut down to about ten inches.

Happy put the shotgun down beside the money, reached down again, and this time came up with a box of shotgun shells. "I don't know who your friend is, honey," she said to Jay. "But you're going to have to do better than a bad haircut and a red rinse."

She half-turned and picked a folded newspaper off a shelf to the left of the grill. She opened it in front of Jay. Her face and Billy's were just below the fold. From the header it looked as though the *Bellingham Herald* was using Ricky Stiles's connection to Bellingham as their bridge to the Return of the Ladykiller story. The first line described her as a "Hard-line feminist's Joan of Arc."

"I'm beginning to really hate this folk-hero crap."

Happy laughed. "Good thing it's not three hours from now or you'd have everyone in the place staring at you." She glanced at Dane. "You think this crazy guy is around here somewhere?"

The marshal nodded. "Sparks Island, just like we said."

"Why not bring in the cops? We got anything you need— State boys, Local PD, Coast Guard, Border Patrol."

"He's got a hostage," said Jay.

"Well shit," said Happy. "Too many cooks, that sort of thing?"

"Exactly." Jay nodded grimly.

Happy scooped up the money and shoved it into the pocket of her dress. She gestured to the shotgun. "Take that. If it doesn't blow up in your hands it'll take the crazy bastard's head right off."

Jack Dane picked up the shotgun and shoved the box of shells into his jacket. "How far are we from Sparks Island?" he asked.

"Twelve, fifteen miles," said Happy. "Stay on the lee side of Lummi Island just outside the bay. Reach the tip of the island, you bear northwest." She found a big, silver-sided Thermos on the same shelf as the newspaper and began filling it with coffee from the Silex. "Straight out of the box a Swift does around twenty-eight knots, but Tommy goosed the engines a little. In a pinch you can get forty knots out of her, but not in a sea like this. Twenty if you're lucky and your teeth are in tight. About an hour's run." Jay checked her watch. It would be daylight then, even with the storm.

"Charts?" Dane asked.

Happy nodded. "All in the boat. Everything's pretty up-to-date. Radar, GPS, the works." She smiled wistfully. "Tommy liked to be able to see them coming."

"Radio?"

"CB, VHF, and shortwave." She gestured down the diner. "Base station is in the back room."

Dane looked at his watch. "I'll check in every fifteen minutes," he said. "Quarter, half, and on the hour. I miss two consecutive checks and you call in the cavalry, tell them what's going on and who we're after."

Happy screwed the top on the Thermos and handed it to Jay. "Give me a minute to get some slickers for us and I'll take you to the boat."

She came out from behind the counter and steam-rollered toward a door at the back of the diner. Jay turned to Jack Dane. "I thought you were an MP in Vietnam?" she whispered urgently.

"I was." He shrugged. "Like I told that Tran guy in Louisiana, I did some work with the Black Berets on the Perfume River." He frowned. "Third Marine Amphibious to be exact."

"Work?" Jay asked. "Driving one of those Swift boat things?"

"Not exactly."

"What exactly?"

"Prisoner transport from Hue back to MACV."

"Did you *ever* drive one?"

"Sure, lots of times they'd let me sit at the wheel."

"Lots of times," Jay muttered.

We're screwed.

Happy came waddling up from the back room, several yellow slickers draped over one massive arm.

"Don't worry," said Dane. "We'll figure it out."

Happy reached them and started handing out the slickers, putting one on herself, doing up the front clips and pulling the hood up, cinching it tightly around her face. "Ready?" she said.

"As we'll ever be," Jay answered.

"Follow me then," said Happy, and they trooped out into the lashing rain.

TWENTY-FIVE

"Comfy?" Billy asked, winding on a last layer of duct tape around Karen Deaver's wrists.

"Peachy," she answered coldly, trying to keep the fear out of her voice. He'd taped her hands behind her back and her ankles to the two front legs of the antique kitchen chair. So far he hadn't put any tape over her mouth; not that screaming for help was going to do her any good. For some reason he'd brought a high stool out of the kitchen and placed it directly in front of her.

Rain was slashing hard against the big front windows of the log home and she could see the sky getting appreciably lighter. Morning. With the downpour she could only see halfway along Siren Bay; beyond that there was nothing but a gray blur that hid the small outlying islets and shoals.

The fact that she'd managed to bring *Helter Skelter* home without any damage was mostly pure dumb luck; coming into the shoal-strewn bay, they had almost gone hard aground twice and even reaching the dock she'd almost broached onto the rocks because she hadn't throttled back quickly enough. In the end, though, she'd managed to dock without incident, tying up snugly and putting out anchors fore and aft just in case.

Billy examined his handiwork and rose to his feet, joints cracking. He yawned and stretched. He smiled down at her. "No rest for the wicked." He picked up the big canvas bag he'd carried onto the boat and disappeared into the ground-floor bathroom. He came out a few minutes later dressed in bulky, waterproof, RealTree camouflage gear and L. L. Bean Gore-Tex trail boots.

"How do I look?" He smiled, dropping the canvas bag and doing a little pirouette in front of Karen's chair.

"How do you want to look?" she said out loud.

"Invisible." He smiled again, then picked up the bag, stepped forward, and kissed her lightly on the cheek. "I've got to go and wait for my friends, but when I come back we'll do something fun together." He reached down into the bag again and came up with a small, decorative box. Opening it, he set the box on the stool, tilting it up on the lid so she could see what it contained. Inside, pinned through its fragile thorax, was a large butterfly, orange and black and iridescent blue. "*Heliconius cydno*, otherwise known as the Passion Vine butterfly. When their surroundings change they are able to acquire a whole new set of markings to ensure their survival. A little something for the eye," Billy whispered. "A little something for you to consider while I'm gone."

Oh dear Jesus God.

Billy gave her a smile and a wave, then went to the front door, still toting the canvas bag. He stepped out into the storm and disappeared.

Karen gave herself five minutes to cry out the tension that had been winding her up like a spring since Billy had come knocking on her door less than twenty-four hours ago. Like Michael's death; life changed in the blink of an eye without rhyme or reason. She twisted around in the chair, fighting the duct tape bonds, taking stock of her surroundings, trying hard to blink the tears out of her eyes. Sometime soon he was going to come back and the two of them were going to do something fun together and it wasn't going to be fun at all. She felt it all starting to slip away and forced herself to focus and calm down.

Billy had put the old chair dead center in the middle of the living room in the big log building. They'd hired an architect friend of Michael's to design the place in a way that would take advantage of the stunning views down the bay to the open sea. Directly ahead of her was a two-story wall of glass with two offset French doors leading out to the deck for a main entrance.

To her left was the big fireplace made from native sandstone and to the right was the dining room. Behind her right shoulder was the kitchen; behind her left, the staircase leading up to the second floor. On the other side of the fireplace was the master bedroom, and on the other side of the dining room was a powder room, pantry, laundry room, and side door leading to the woods behind the house.

As her breathing and heartbeat eased back to normal, Karen tried to think it through, one step at a time. She tested the duct tape again. He'd wound it at least three times around her hands and twice around the ankles. There was some give, but she wasn't going to be able to twist herself out of her predicament. She tried to move her feet, but with her ankles so firmly bound, she couldn't get any purchase; she wasn't going to be able to move the chair that way.

Which left the possibility of rocking the chair backwards. If she could get to the kitchen she might be able to get to a knife and somehow cut through the tape. It wasn't much of a plan, but it was the best she could come up with. She started to rock the chair, shifting her hips and buttocks with each movement. She was moving in tiny increments, but at least she was moving. If given the time she knew she could reach the kitchen, but how much time did she have?

Geologically and geographically, Sparks Island was a 319-acre island formed from folded layers of sandstone combined with interwoven strata of glacial sedimentation and the fossilized remains of millions of clams, snails, and other sea creatures embedded sixty-five million years ago.

The island was technically an archipelago made up of Sparks Island, Little Sparks, the two Winter Islands, North and South, Dog Island to the northeast, and the elongated finger of Skibereen Head and Wicklow Point. The main island looked like an elongated C, forming Siren Bay, with the majority of the other, much smaller islands lying within it. Seen from the air, the overall shape was roughly that of a jellyfish with drifting tentacles. For the most part, the main island was heavily forested with tall, old-growth cedar interspersed with low-lying marshy areas and much higher sandstone outcroppings.

Aside from Siren Bay, there were only three other safe anchorages: Jericho Bay between Skibereen Head and Wicklow Point; Fox Cove on the west side of the island, its entrance all but hidden by the button shape of Little Sparks Island; and Rathnew Bay, farther north, just before the higher ground of the Tatlow Bluffs, a series of forty- to sixty-foot-high sheer cliffs which formed the rugged "back" of the main island and which faced the open sea of the Strait of Georgia. There was only one small, uninhabited island between those bluffs and the invisible line of the International Border.

Historically, the isolated bays and coves of Sparks Island had once served as seal-hunting grounds for the nearby Lummi Indians. In the 1840s it had briefly seen prosperity when a Protestant Irishman named Eamon Sparks established a paving-stone quarry there, which accounted for the Irish nomenclature throughout the island. When Seattle belatedly decided that sandstone from Sparks Island was too soft for paving bricks, Eamon Sparks shut down his business and became a prospector in the Klondike. Following the collapse of the quarry, the island was worked by a fur farmer named Tatlow who raised fox and mink, but like the quarry before it, the fur business failed as well.

For the next hundred years no one seemed interested in establishing another legitimate business concern on Sparks Island, but it continued to thrive as a haven for smugglers. In the late 1800s it was used as a hiding place for everything from illegal Chinese immigrants to untaxed wool and even opium. Still later, the island was used by rum runners from Canada who slipped into the United States through the Prohibition blockades.

By the end of the Depression, however, Sparks Island was once again deserted, occasionally visited by a few nautically minded vacationers from both sides of the border as well as the occasional sport fisherman and the odd Lummi Indian hunting seal from time to time, just to keep in touch with the old traditions.

Eventually the tree growth on the island attracted the attention of a large forestry company that wanted to clear-cut the old growth. The property had long since reverted to the state for taxes, and rather than let the island become a bleak, denuded eyesore, the state rejected the forestry company's bid for the land in favor of Michael Deaver's offer on condition that the Washington State Parks Board be given right of first refusal should the Deavers ever decide to sell. The Deavers agreed to the conditions and were given a single-use building permit. The result was the cathedral-ceilinged, two-winged, four-thousand-square-foot log home at the far end of Siren Bay which had now become Karen Deaver's prison.

There were several hills on Sparks Island, the highest rising almost two hundred feet above Fox Cove. On old charts of the island it was called Friar's Hill. From a tiny meadow on the slanted, rocky summit you could see the length and breadth of Siren Bay, with Fox Cove directly below to the west and Rathnew Bay to the north. If a smuggler's lookout had ever been posted on Sparks Island, it would have been here, and it was in that place Billy Bones established his command post.

Reaching it an hour or so after leaving the log house, he opened up the big canvas bag and brought out a much smaller nylon bundle. Like his clothing, the bundle was done in RealTree camouflage. Undoing the tapes, he rolled the bundle out onto the patch of grass, snapped together the telescoping, color-coded aluminum poles, and erected the little one-man tent. Like the rest of his gear, the tent had been purchased at a large sporting-goods outlet in a mall on the outskirts of Seattle. Digging into the bag, Billy next took out a big, battery-powered Grundig marine scanner, switched it on, and set it down inside the tent, turning up the volume until he could hear the back chatter clearly, even standing outside the tent. That done, he took out his brand-new pair of Canon Image Stabilizer binoculars and did a slow 360-degree turn. No matter which direction they came from, he would see them first. He put down the binoculars and smiled. The stage was set, the curtain was going up again. The last act of the play was about to begin.

The heaving bow of the Swift Boat rose up on the wave and then crashed down again, several tons of freezing cold Pacific Ocean racing down the narrow gunwales of the shallow-draft craft, breaking around the little forward cabin in a frothing explosion of spray that brought forward visibility down to nothing. It was a sequence of events that had been repeating itself with nauseating regularity ever since they'd left the protection of the lee side of Lummi Island and set their course northwest into the teeth of the storm.

Jay Fletcher, still wrapped in her yellow slicker, was standing in a half crouch in the forward cabin, back braced against the portside bulkhead as they were tossed up and down on the waves. Beneath her feet she could feel the deep rumble of the twin diesels, the only constant in her life at the moment. "Do you have any idea where you're going?!" Jay yelled above the roaring thunder of the wind.

"Out of my fucking mind," snarled Jack Dane, struggling to keep a two-handed grip on the big wheel. Ever since coming around the tip of Lummi Island he'd had to fight to maintain their course, both wind and water conspiring to push him southeast and back down into Puget Sound. Somehow, though, at least according to the glowing screen of the GPS navigator, they were actually making progress, with only three miles to go until Sparks Island. If the boat held together for another twenty minutes, they'd be able to find safe harbor somewhere out of the furious storm.

The PCF Swift Boat used in Vietnam was based on a commercial design for a sturdy, mid-range shuttle boat used to service offshore drilling platforms in the Gulf of Mexico. The broad-beamed, snub-nosed craft was fifty feet long, displaced nineteen tons, and was made of continuous-weld aluminum alloy. The pilothouse was close to the bow and attached to a lower cabin that comfortably held eight to ten men. The original boat was powered by a pair of heavyweight diesel engines to turn the vessel's twin props. The military version had twin .50 caliber machine guns in a tub on the pilothouse and another two .50 caliber guns on the fantail as well as an 81 mm mortar.

On Tommy's boat, named the *Real McCoy* after the famous East Coast rum runner, the gun emplacement on the fantail had been replaced by a diving locker, and the tub on the roof of the pilothouse now held the boat's radar mast. There were sleeping accommodations for four in the after cabin as well as a retrofitted galley and head.

Tommy had also added extra large gas tanks and replaced the original diesels with a pair of Volvo Penta engines capable of outrunning the V8-powered utility boats used by the Bellingham Coast Guard. On Tommy's last run down from the border with ten plastic-wrapped bales of British Columbia's best in the diving locker he'd easily managed to elude his pursuers until he threw a screw in Rosario Strait and abruptly ended his smuggling career.

The *Real McCoy* slammed down into another trough between rolling waves, and Jay smashed her head against the overhead for the tenth time in the past hour. The wind seemed to be dropping a little as the sky lightened, but the terrible pounding seas continued unabated.

Jay's initial seasickness had vanished after the first twenty minutes, replaced by a single-minded fear so focused that it only stretched from the crest of one wave to the trough of the next. Every thought was dedicated to keeping the small vessel afloat on seas she was sure would have scared the hell out of Noah himself. Now she knew how Dane felt when he was forced to fly.

"Get me the charts!" the marshal bellowed. "We've got to find some place to make a landfall."

Jay nodded and unhinged her white-knuckled grip on the steering console. She staggered back toward the small hatch leading back to the after cabin and half-tripped down the short flight of steps. The cabin was a mess; the Coast Guard had turned the whole boat on its ear after Tommy Lowell's arrest and his mother hadn't done much to clean up after them in the meantime.

There was diving gear all over the place, including a rack of tanks, assorted hoses, and a portable compressor. Jay found the clear plastic slipcase of charts for the San Juans on the bolted-down table where Happy Lowell had left them along with the shotgun and the shells. Picking up the charts, she turned and navigated her way back to the pilothouse and Jack Dane.

"Now what?" she asked.

"Find the chart for Sparks Island and spread it out on the console!" He banged the flat of his hand on the ledge in front of the wheel. Jay went through the pack of plasticized maps and found the one he wanted. An errant wave came sweeping in off the port quarter, sending the boat into a twisting cork-screw and Jay slid across the pilothouse, crashing into Dane. For a split second he lost his hold on the wheel, then pushed her roughly aside and grabbed at it again. Grunting loudly, he dragged the big wheel around, putting them roughly back on course.

"According to those aerial photographs I saw back on Bainbridge Island, they built their house right at the end of the main inlet," said Dane.

Jay leaned over the chart, squinting in the weak light from the red safety lamp in the ceiling. "Siren Bay." She nodded. "It's got little speckles all over it and things that look like lights."

"Reefs and beacons. We can't land there," said Dane. "He'd see us coming up the inlet anyway. We need surprise. We have to find somewhere else."

Jay pored over the chart, trying to keep her eyes focused on the map and not the sickening rise and fall of the gray horizon dead ahead. It was hard to believe that there was any safe haven out there; the sea seemed like an endless watery hell. Trying to ignore it, she traced her forefinger around the island's shape, looking for some place to land the boat that would be reasonably close to the location of the house. "Am I looking for anything in particular?"

"Something shallow," said Dane, still struggling with the

wheel. "Low numbers on the chart. A bay, a cove, anything like that."

"Here," said Jay, jabbing her finger down on the map. "Rathnew Bay. According to this it's on the west side of the island about halfway up."

"What are the numbers?"

"Where?"

"Going in for a start."

"Five on the left, ten on the right, and sixteen down the middle."

"Perfect!" Dane crowed. Another huge wave broke over the bow of the boat and Jay held her breath as the water broke over the pilothouse, the aluminum seals on the windows screeching with the force of the onslaught. They rolled up another, even larger wave, then twisted down into yet another trough. "What are the numbers inside the bay?!"

Swallowing her fear, Jay concentrated on the chart again. "Three and four in the center of the bay dropping down to one, and then zero with some smaller numbers beside the zero."

Dane nodded. "The big numbers are fathoms, the little ones are feet. That means the bay is three to four fathoms in the middle, one fathom down to three feet close in, and the soundings probably mean low tide."

"You really do know this stuff," said Jay, impressed.

"Just barely," Dane answered.

"How deep is a fathom?"

"Six feet."

"Is that enough?"

"Plenty." The wheel spun in his hands as they smashed through a wave and corkscrewed again. He regained control and glanced at Jay. "I'm going to need a heading," he said.

"What's that?"

"There's a diagram like a protractor at the top of the chart. Numbers all the way around, 0 to 360 degrees. North, south, east, and west marked on it."

"Got it."

They slid and twisted down into another trough, and Dane

risked taking one hand off the wheel to pull open a narrow drawer on the left of the console. He fumbled around inside, found a plastic ruler and flipped it toward Jay just as the bow hammered into the face of the next wave. Once again a wall of water caromed down the shuddering hull of the Swift Boat, and once again they survived the hammer blow of water.

"Put the ruler down on the circle and move it around until you've got a straight edge that gets you closest to Rathnew Bay. Read off the number on the outer ring of the circle. That will give us a rough course to plot." Dane instructed.

"You learned all this in Vietnam?"

"No. Give me the number."

"Where?"

"Where what?"

"Where did you learn how to do all this?"

"Just give the goddamned number!" Dane fumed.

"Tell me."

"Don't laugh."

"I won't."

"I was in Sea Scouts."

Jay laughed, despite her promise. The sight of Jack Dane in little shorts and a sailor hat was just too much. "I thought you said you grew up in Kansas or something."

"Missouri."

"Not a lot of ocean in Missouri."

"A lot of it was hypothetical. Now give me the goddamned number!"

Jay checked again. "Two hundred eighty degrees."

The marshal waited until they were sliding down the back of the next wave, then reached out and tapped the numbers into the keyboard of the navigating computer. The glowing image of Sparks Island hiccuped slightly to the left and a thin red line appeared, lining them up with the saddle-shaped bay.

"How far?" Jay asked.

"About two miles now. Winds falling off. Shouldn't take long."

"Then what?"

"We go and get the son of a bitch."

"You have some kind of plan," Jay asked, "or do you intend to just wing it?"

A gust of wind slammed into the boat and she heeled over sharply. Dane lost the wheel, and following the wind, the *Real McCoy* turned almost sideways to the oncoming wave. The water dropped massively down onto the boat in a full broadside that almost turned her turtle.

Thankfully the doors on both sides of the pilothouse were hinged outward to withstand just such an occurrence, but the two windows on Jay's side had long ago lost their temper and shattered under the full weight of the breaking wave. Several hundred gallons of water hammered into the tiny enclosure with the force of a battering ram.

There was a tremendous crash from the cabin behind them as the boat began to roll hard. Jay lost her footing and slid wildly across the pilothouse again. This time Dane managed to catch her with one arm and simultaneously hold onto the wheel. As the boat came back onto an even keel, the water began to sluice back and forth at their feet, then ran back through the hatchway down into the rear cabin. Jay gripped Dane's supporting arm, levering herself off his chest, and felt the hard strength of the man's muscles and the bristle of his beard against her cheek.

She flushed hard, grabbing the console for support. "Sorry."

"No problem," Dane answered. Rain was pouring in through the broken windows now, adding insult to injury. Even in her slicker Jay was soaked. She tried not to look at the marshal. She could feel the heat rising in her cheeks and wondered if he'd noticed.

Not now, for Christ sake!

"See if you can find something in the cabin to put over the windows," Dane suggested. Jay nodded silently, glad to be gone from the tiny pilothouse. She knew danger was supposed to make you horny but this was ridiculous. Celibate for the better part of two years and now it seemed as though she was surrounded by opportunity.

First Robin, then Harry Maxwell, and now Jack Dane.

She pushed the three men out of her thoughts and clambered back into the rear cabin. Most of the water that had come onto the boat had wound up here, and the near overturn had made the mess in the rear cabin even worse. The rack of scuba tanks had come loose from its supporting bracket and the tanks were spread all over the floor of the cabin, rolling around in six inches of water. Most of the crockery and cookware had come down from the cupboards in the little galley alcove, and from the slightly sour smell in the air, something had gone wrong in the head as well.

The shotgun had fallen into the water on the floor and the box of shells had slid off the table as well. The box had come open and the red and green shells were soaked. She picked up half a dozen, opened her slicker and used the damp fabric of her shirt to dry them off as best she could. Then she stuffed them into her pockets and picked the shotgun up out of the water. Jay rooted around, found a roll of plastic wrap in a galley drawer and some duct tape in another.

Turning away from the mess, she went back up into the pilothouse and started working on the windows, tearing off multiple layers of plastic then taping it down. By the time she had the window opening covered, they'd come in sight of Sparks Island, the tip of Skibereen Head standing like a great stone knife blade on their starboard side. The rain was still coming down, but the wind had definitely abated and even inside the pilothouse Jay could hear the sound of the surf thundering onto the rocks.

"Almost there!" said Dane. He was dividing his concentration now between the blurred view out the front windscreen and the electronic screen in front of him, making adjustments with the wheel to keep the boat on course.

"A plan, remember?" Jay asked, finishing up the second window. The plastic flapped and fluttered noisily but at least it was keeping the rain out.

"I've been thinking. When was the last time you looked for e-mail on your laptop?"

"Yesterday," Jay answered, barely able to believe that so little time had passed. "I checked at the airport in Seattle."

"Nothing?"

"Not a word."

"Before that?"

"There hasn't been anything since New York."

"I thought his whole MO revolved around computers? Why isn't he using them, teasing you?"

"I've thought about that, too."

"Figure anything out?"

"A couple of theories. In the first place, I think he's going through some kind of transformation process. That might be another reason for the butterflies."

"I didn't know you'd come up with a first reason."

"A pun. I did a little end run into the inventory files at Main Justice, the ones for Billy's apartment. Looks like he was heavily into chaos theory."

Dane scowled. "Lorentz's butterfly effect. Shit! I should have been able to figure that out, too."

"You know about the butterfly effect?"

The marshal nodded. "A butterfly flaps its wings in one place and a hurricane starts ten thousand miles away a week later. One thing leads to another. Yeah, I know about it."

"Very erudite," said Jay, arching her eyebrows.

"I told you before, even us good old boys read a book now and again." He edged the wheel around slightly and Jay noticed a small shift in the feel of the boat as it turned a little more into the waves. "What's the other theory?" asked Dane.

"Billy's smart, but he knows he's not as smart as the collective brains in my old bunch at the Bureau and your technical guys. He's probably assuming we put a cookie on his transmissions, so he's not taking any chances on being traced."

"Okay, assume you're right. He sets us up with the magazine. That means he's been out of the loop for . . . how long?"

"Three days. The last time we had direct contact was in China Bayou."

"Christ!" Dane breathed. "It feels like a month."

"Three days," Jay repeated.

"So what's he done in that time?"

"A day traveling."

The marshal nodded thoughtfully. "A day to set up the snatch." He frowned. "That leaves an extra day. What was he doing, sightseeing?"

"Strange," agreed Jay. "Like I said before, he's pretty meticulous . . . focused. I can't see him taking a day's worth of R&R."

"Okay, forget that for a minute. What about weapons?"

"Tran said the Nguyen character we found chopped up in the drawer had an M1. The way he was shooting in the swamp, it probably had a scope as well."

"He'd risk taking that onto a plane?" asked Dane.

Jay shrugged. "Why not? People do it all the time. He gets the right tag at the airport, shows the security people he's not carrying any ammunition, it wouldn't be a problem. He was long gone from New Orleans by the time the story broke in the papers."

Dane nodded again. "And he could ammo up once he got to Seattle. You don't need to have a permit to buy shells for an M1. All you have to do is show some ID and sign the book."

"So he's armed and dangerous, what else is new?" said Jay. "Chances are good he'll have the woman trussed up like a turkey in that cabin of theirs, just waiting for us to play dragonslayer." She reached into the pocket of her slicker and pulled out a soggy pack of Marlboro's. She dug around for matches, but the only ones she could find were soaked and useless. "Shit," she muttered.

"You say that a lot." Dane grinned.

"So I've been told," she answered. "I just think better when I smoke." She stared out the front windscreen. They were passing Little Sparks Island now, the impossibly narrow passage between it and Fox Cove a lashing cauldron of waves breaking and smashing on hidden rocks. Dane was keeping well off but even so it seemed as though they were coming dangerously close to the land.

"Relax." He pointed to a small screen beside the glowing

GPS indicator. "I've got the depth sounder on. We've got twenty fathoms under us."

More than enough to drown in.

Dane guided them out even farther, giving the broken shoals at the upper end of Little Sparks a wide berth. Then he turned north and east again, moving steadily up the ragged coastline of the main island. Three hundred yards ahead Jay could see the dark, forested promontory that marked the lower arm of the entrance to Rathnew Bay. Waves were breaking against the base of the low cliffs, shattering wildly in all directions and sending great plumes of foam twenty feet into the air. They came up on the promontory and Dane first turned the *Real McCoy* out into the waves, taking them head on as he piloted the boat out in a wide, yawning turn to avoid a shoal-like scattering of light gleaming on the depth sounder.

Ducking down, Jay looked across and out through the foam-streaked windows on the starboard side of the pilot-house, and for a few seconds she got a side-on view of the shore lying at the inner edge of the bay. There were no visible rocks, just a shelving, pebbled beach leading gently up to the edge of a line of looming trees.

A hundred yards out from the entrance Jack Dane took a deep breath and held it as he spun the wheel hard right, swinging the stern of the Swift Boat directly into the oncoming waves, pointing the leaping bow as close to the midpoint of the bay as he could.

"Here we go!"

They caught a wave and Jay felt it push the back end of the boat high into the air, the force cascading all the junk in the rear cabin against the pilothouse bulkhead with a clattering roar. The hatchway leading back into the cabin burst open and the water trapped in the rear cabin poured forward, throwing the cabin's litter furiously into the pilothouse. A steel scuba tank careened through the open hatch and smashed into the back of Jack Dane's leg. The impact was so hard she actually heard the bones in the marshal's ankle snap as the tank struck him.

Dane screamed, his hands flying off the wheel as he

dropped to the floor and clutched at the ruined ankle. Jay stood frozen for an instant, staring at the blood pouring from the spot where the shattered bone had sliced through flesh. Coming out of her brief daze, she could feel the rear of the boat rise at an almost impossible angle as they were thrown forward into Rathnew Bay.

"Grab the fucking wheel!" Dane bellowed. Jay tore her glance away from his leg and threw herself across the wheel-house, grabbing the spinning wheel. Dead ahead the bow of the *Real McCoy* was sliding to the left as the stern rose even higher and the entire boat began to list dangerously, putting her shoulder into the killing wave that was pushing her into the bay. Even to Jay it was obvious that she was going to roll.

"What do I do!"

"Straighten out!" Dane yelled. He tried to drag himself upright but he slipped, his weight coming down fully on the ankle. He moaned in agony and slid back onto the floor of the pilothouse, his face gray with the pain.

Jay swung the wheel to the right, a flash of memory taking her back to those stupid safety tips they used to put on TV in the winter—*"When you feel yourself begin to skid, steer in the direction of the skid."*

And just as stupidly it had worked, taking her out of a few dangerous situations on frozen backwoods Wisconsin roads. Putting all of her strength into it, Jay kept pulling hard right on the wheel and finally felt the bow begin to slew around. The trees ahead seemed dangerously close, but the sense that they were about to roll began to ease.

"What now!?" Jay yelled. She chanced a fast look at Jack Dane, but he'd passed out with the pain, his head lolling back against the steel plate of the steering console. Another, tougher wave smacked into the stern and Jay had to fight for control of the wheel, but the wave passed under them with a whispering howl against the aluminum hull and Jay watched, horrified, as it smashed itself to pieces on the shore barely fifty yards ahead.

The only controls she could figure out were the two ball-

ended throttle levers on the left of the console, but she knew
that slowing down now would only put the boat completely
at the mercy of the waves that continued to push it forward.
Not that slowing would have made much difference because
the stone beach was coming up too fast anyway. She gripped
the wheel hard, gritted her teeth, and held on for dear life.

At the first sound of the hull grinding into the bottom she
dropped down, braced herself over Jack Dane's body to prevent even more injury, then closed her eyes and prayed. A
split second later the *Real McCoy* struck bottom for real, surg-
ing forward and up onto the beach, engines howling as the
last wave caught the stern and brought the props up out of
the water. The back end of the old boat came fully around,
tearing a huge gouging trench into the pebbled foreshore and
then piled up on its side, solidly aground. In the wheelhouse
Jay's head smacked against the steering console and then the
lights went out.

TWENTY-SIX

Karen Deaver lay on the cool tile floor of the kitchen, blood still flowing from her mouth and nose following the fall she'd had halfway through her desperate journey from the living room. Her head was ringing and somehow she couldn't get her eyes to focus, but even tipped over she continued to struggle forward, pushing the bound toes of her running shoes against the tile and inching herself along. All through the ordeal she'd known that her life was being counted off in minutes and seconds until the madman returned, and with every push of her toes she whispered the name of her dead husband like a mantra, chanting through her bruised and bloody lips.

Soon the bastard would be back and then he'd kill her, slowly, painfully, and with as much humiliation as he could bring to bear. The look on his face as he'd set up the butterfly in front of her told it all. It was a look she'd seen on a few men over the years, going back as far as kids she'd known in school, the kind no one would talk to, the kind with the dark, cold eyes that were always staring at you, not so much sexually, but more like a pathologist standing over a corpse, choosing the point for his first incision. The kind who liked to see small animals in pain.

Had it been this way for his other victims? A terrible time when there was hope and then, when the hope was gone, only the prayer for the end to come quickly. Each time Karen paused for breath, the same thoughts rose up in her, beating like the banging of her own heart, like the rasp of her breathing and the heaving of her chest.

Inch by inch she kept on moving, resting, pausing to listen

for each sound, each crack of wind, each slash and rattle of rain on the big windows behind her, sometimes so frightened that he was standing on the deck, watching her agony, waiting, one hand on the door handle, making it last as long as he could before he came back in and ended all the fun once and for all.

"No!" she yelled, and kept on pushing with her toes and then her head slammed hard against something and she stopped. She blinked. She could feel the blood still bubbling out of her nose and she tried to blow out, clearing an airway, but it was impossible. She sucked in air through her mouth, trying not to think of the pain there and the sharp edges of a broken tooth against her tongue. She concentrated on her head, pushed a little with her toes, knowing that her only salvation lay in reaching the island, a maple and marble L shape in the center of the kitchen. A sink set into it for washing vegetables. The big butcher block cutting board.

The knife block.

Half a dozen matched red-handled Victorinox blades from paring knife up to a broad-bladed butcher. She visualized them, handles poking out of the unvarnished wedge of hardwood. The sink was offset towards the far end of the island, the butcher block cutting board was next to it, and snuggled up to the cutting board were the knives. They were almost directly above where she was lying, but it might as well have been a million miles because there was no way in hell she was going to get at them.

She felt a sudden terrible muscle spasm curl up her spine, and she screamed again as it coursed through her, writhing against her bonds. She heard a faint popping sound and as the spasm faded she realized that something had happened to the chair. She tried to move her right leg and she heard the popping sound again. The chair was an old arrowback, one of a set of six they had scattered around the big living room, more for accent and color than for seating. They were more than a hundred years old, and like any good antiques, they had been left untouched in their flaking original paint, but once upon a time there'd been a plan to reglue them.

It had been one of the projects on Michael's list just before the diagnosis, something he'd just never gotten around to. Experimenting, Karen tried to wiggle her leg against the duct tape and was rewarded with the popping noise again. She knew the chair leg must have come partway out of its socket in the seat when she fell over. She wiggled harder and then it came out entirely and her leg was free.

She bent her knee and the chair leg came up into the air, still connected to her ankle by the tape. With the knee flexed she could push herself along easily and she laughed out loud. She could shunt herself to the inside of the island's L then brace her back against it and either stand up or get enough swinging movement going to smash the chair completely. She started to move, blinking tears away and grinning through the blood that was smeared on her face.

"Here I come, asshole."

Billy had kept watch on Friar's Hill for a little more than an hour before he spotted the gray fifty-footer pounding up the sound, each duck of her bows sending up huge feathering arcs of spray. The radio was silent except for some general chitchat between base stations; no one was stupid enough to come out into foul weather like this, and the Coast Guard station was silent except for brief weather advisories every fifteen minutes. Billy had no doubt that Jay Fletcher and her friend were in the oncoming boat, and he was equally sure they'd come alone.

He watched through the binoculars as they turned west around the headland, then beat their way up the shoreline, rolling and corkscrewing as they rode the endless series of waves pushed inland by the storm. As they rounded Little Sparks Island, Billy put down the binoculars, ducked into the tent, and rummaged through the canvas bag again. He pulled out the old WW2 rifle that had belonged to the late Nguyen Vinh Duong.

It was a classic M1, a mass-produced, general-use weapon with an effective range of one thousand yards. It was mounted with a modern Burris telescopic sight, and somewhere along the line, one of the rifle's owners had seen fit to bed the barrel with a layer of fiberglass for increased accuracy. It even had a bipod attachment, which he had used to take the shot in China Bayou. If he wanted to risk giving himself away he knew he could stay right where he was and potshot the boat as it came into Rathnew Bay. But that, of course, wasn't the point of the exercise.

He fed a clip of ammunition into the base of the stock, put two more into the upper pocket of his cammo jacket, and went back into the rain. From the looks of things, it would take the boat another ten minutes or so to reach the bay and Billy wanted to be there when they arrived. Toting the gun easily in his right hand, he put his face into the misting rain and began heading down the steep hill, moving toward the screening trees below.

Jay came to and tasted blood. Groaning, she pushed herself off the still-unconscious figure of Jack Dane and rolled to the left beside him, her back against the starboard doorway leading to the outside. The whole pilothouse was canted over on its side and Jay could hear the sound of surf running up the beach.

Every few seconds one of the waves slammed into the hull with an explosive, shuddering impact, but the *Real McCoy* seemed solidly ashore. The electronic gear from the console was hanging from its wires and dangling over the wheel, and above her head the radio had ripped out of its brackets and smashed all over the deck around her.

Dane's eyelids fluttered and he let out a long moan. Struggling, Jay scuttled up the angled decking and checked his ankle. The shattered end of the bone was sticking up out of the puckered, soaked flesh of his ankle, but most of the bleeding had stopped. She winced; it had to hurt like hell and there wasn't much she could do for the man out here. The only good thing was his unconscious state, and from the looks of it that wasn't going to last much longer. She took a deep breath, let it out slowly, then grabbed the big wheel with one hand and levered herself into a standing position. From there she crabwalked back to the rear cabin door and ducked through it.

Amazingly, she found a big first-aid kit still clipped to the bulkhead just inside the door as well as a couple of hard plastic snorkels. She took the first-aid kit and the snorkels back into the pilothouse and got to work on Dane, trying to get his ankle taken care of before he woke up.

She used the snorkels to splint the ankle, wrapping them with the same duct tape she'd used to fix the windows, then took a little tin of sulfa powder out of the first-aid kit and sprinkled all of it onto the exposed bone and the puncture wound surrounding it. When that was done, she used gauze bandage and adhesive tape to bind it all together. Not perfect but it would do until they could get him to a hospital.

Dane's eyelids fluttered again and this time his eyes opened fully. The blood drained from his face as the pain hit home, but he clamped down with his jaw and rode it out, his eyes closing for a few seconds, then opening again. "Jesus," he whispered.

"I splinted you up. Don't move and it'll be okay."

He blinked. Moved his head a little from side to side. "We're not moving."

"I got us up on shore."

"You should have been the Sea Scout," Dane said. Another bolt of pain shot through him and he stiffened. The pain slipped away and he sighed. "What about Billy?"

"I'm going after him now. The radio's out."

Dane shifted himself back against the bulkhead, obviously trying to ignore another savage bolt of pain. With his back raised, he reached under his slicker and came up with the outsized Colt. "Take this."

"You keep it in case Billy decides to come here first."

"Don't be an idiot, Fletcher. You're the bait, remember? It's you Billy wants, not me. Take the fucking pistol and leave me the shotgun. Besides, it's my turn to have a shot at being the hero."

He's right.

She nodded took the heavy pistol and shoved it into the

pocket of her slicker. She picked up the shotgun out of the corner where it had fallen, broke it open, and fed in two of the questionable shells she'd picked up out of the water. She laid the shotgun across his thighs.

He'll be okay.

If the shells aren't waterlogged.

If Billy doesn't find him first.

She gave him her best smile, then clawed herself upright again. "I won't be too long." She paused. "I hope. If I'm not. . . ." She let it hang and Dane finished it for her.

"If you're not back by dark we're both dead."

"If we're not back by dark Happy's going to call in the cavalry, remember?"

"You know as well as I do that'll be too late. Not to mention the fact that you couldn't lift a chopper in this weather and certainly not at night." He gave her a pained excuse for a smile. "Just go and kill the bastard, Jay. Do the world a favor."

She nodded silently, then turned away, clawing her way up the sloping deck to the portside doorway. She found the chart showing Sparks Island, folded it, and jammed it into the other pocket of her slicker. She turned to the door again and twisted the handle. She threw back the door, then climbed out onto the deck and disappeared from sight. Biting down hard to fight the pain, Jack Dane put his head back against the bulkhead, closed his eyes, and waited, listening to the steady roar of the waves thundering onto the shore, wondering how it was all going to turn out.

Set a thief to catch a thief.

Mark Antony was right, the cagey son of a bitch:

"Cry Havoc," whispered Jack Dane. "And let slip the dogs of war."

Karen Dane stood, back hunched, and twisted as hard as she could, smashing the back of the chair against the edge of the kitchen island's granite top. There was a cracking sound, but her hands were still tight against the wood. Panting, she kept her eyes fixed on the prize ten feet away at the other end of the counter—the knife block and its contents. She twisted again, even harder this time, and the chair back finally splintered. Laughing out loud, tears streaming down her face, she straightened, then backed up hard, snapping off the last pieces of wood.

She slid down onto the floor, put her knees together, and after a brief struggle, managed to get her bound hands underneath herself, then brought her legs up even higher. She pushed her arms forward and suddenly her taped hands were in front of her. After that it was almost easy. Half rolling, she staggered to her feet then edged down the counter to the knife block. She pulled out the big butcher knife using both hands, twisted it backwards and began to saw at the duct tape.

The knife sliced easily through the tape, and a few seconds later Karen was free. She bent down and used the knife on the tape around her ankles, throwing the last pieces of chair leg furiously across the room. Logic told her that the smart thing to do was get to the boat as fast as she could, but logic had deserted her, replaced by simple fury. The man had invaded her home and her body, left her nothing but terror and now he would pay. Dropping the big knife onto the tiled floor, she turned and raced out of the kitchen, still aware that he could step back into the cabin at any moment.

She took the steps up to the second floor two at a time, pelted across the open area at the head of the stairs, and ran into the master bedroom. She turned into the big walk-in closet beside the bathroom door, pulled out the little step stool, and reached up to the shelf above the linen section. Her fingers closed on the cardboard shoe box she knew was there, and she pulled it down, dropping down onto the stool and ripping off the rubber bands that kept the lid on.

She tore the top off the box and pulled out the heavy Sig-Sauer automatic pistol. Michael hadn't been any kind of gun freak, but he liked the comfort of knowing that Karen could protect herself if she was by herself on the island, and the heavy-duty pistol had seemed like a good idea at the time.

After buying the gun and getting the permit, both of them had taken a small-arms course at a local Seattle shooting club.

Even with frightened fingers, Karen had no difficulty loading the big shells into the magazine, then sliding the magazine into the butt of the pistol. She cranked back the slide to pop a round into the chamber, made sure the decocking lever was thumbed down, and went down the stairs to the main floor again.

She stopped at the doors leading outside and put her free hand over her chest, feeling the hard banging of her heart. From where she stood she could see down to the dock. She blinked, wondering why she hardly recognized her own boat. She squeezed her eyes closed for a moment, then opened them again. The adrenaline that had driven her forward across the floor was draining away, leaving exhaustion in its place. She reached up and touched her fingers to the caked blood around her nose and mouth, feeling a bite of pain cut through the numbness. Not all reason had fled. The radio in the boat still worked, and that had to be her first objective.

She nodded to herself, jammed the gun into the waistband of her shorts, and took a dark green Hood River nylon jacket down from the peg beside the door. She slipped it on, took the gun out again, and pulled open the door. First the radio and an emergency call to the Coast Guard and anyone else who was listening, *then* she'd go and blow the shithole's brains out.

She stepped outside and onto the deck. The rain had almost stopped and the wind was falling. Above her head the clouds were tearing apart like old rags and there was even a little blue sky breaking through. Karen looked around carefully, then headed down toward the boat.

Stumbling away from the half-turned hull of the *Real McCoy*, Jay found her way up the beach and reached the line of trees. She turned once and saw that the bay behind her was torn with waves, so many of them and so erratic that they were breaking over one another in their haste to reach the shore. She realized then just how lucky they had been to make a landing without being killed.

Jay pulled the chart out of her pocket, unfolded it, and

managed to find Rathnew Bay. The chart didn't give much detail about the island itself, but she could see several lines linked together that looked like trails through the woods. From the looks of it, two trails met a little to her right, one going south, the other north.

The northern one split further on, one branch turning almost due east across the neck of the island to the bottom of Siren Bay, the other branch following the line of the bluffs that made up the northern side of the island. The trail following the bluffs looked as though it led to some kind of lighthouse or beacon, but the shorter route was the most obvious way to reach the place where the Deavers had built their cabin.

Still feeling the effects of her harsh landfall and almost twenty-four hours without sleep, Jay pushed through the trees until she reached the junction of the two paths. She turned left and began walking quickly. The land slanted gently upwards as she made her way along the trail. Above her she could see the overcast begin to break up, and she felt her senses suddenly sharpen, taking in the salt air, the dark scent of the cedars all around her, and the wet earth under her feet.

He's here. I can feel him.

Like a ghost.

She kept walking but more slowly now, picking her way carefully, making sure she made as little noise as possible, stopping every few feet to listen. Nothing but the wind shuddering through the trees and somewhere in the distance the Doppler sound of the waves and the irritated, angry cry of a crowd of gulls. It occurred to her that this might well be the last time she saw or heard or smelled any of this, but she forced the thought away and concentrated hard on what lay ahead.

He'd have her staked out like some sacrificial goat, most likely in the house but possibly outside. Like his mentor Ricky Stiles, Billy Bones liked things up close and personal; every victim he'd taken in the course of his career had died on the blade of one of Billy's knives. If she was being led

into a trap, the action was going to come at close hand and
there would be almost no warning at all.

Jay reached the second split in the trail and paused again.
She pulled Dane's fat, gleaming Colt out of the pocket of her
slicker, clicked off the safety, and curled her finger under the
trigger guard. Half a second saved, and half a second could
easily be the difference between staying alive and having
Billy open up her throat from ear to ear. She stopped and
listened again, hearing nothing and not expecting to. A thousand thoughts raged in her head, and she fought hard to keep
them all at bay. No time for thought, or fear, or anger; there
was only time for instinct now.

The first bullet slashed a three-inch white wound into the
trunk of a cedar less that a foot from her shoulder, the bark
and flesh of the tree flying up like something alive a split
second before the huge sound of the rifle reached Jay's ears.
The old training took hold, and instead of stopping and turning toward the sound, she threw herself forward, running
headlong down the path that led toward the bluffs. She heard
a second shot coming from behind her and poured on the
steam, reaching deep within herself for whatever reserves she
still had, adrenaline pumping into her system and jackham-
mering her heart.

He never uses guns.

Never say never.

She kept on running, trying to put distance between herself
and his position. He had to be higher because she could see
both ways along the path and there was no high ground. On
the other hand, he hadn't fired again which meant that he
probably couldn't see her anymore.

He never uses guns.

This is wrong.

Like the scissors and the watch.

Oh God, it's happening again.

The path kept climbing and she followed it. She tried to
remember the chart and the way the trails worked, but as far
as she could remember there was no other way to the cabin
except the trail behind her. All there was ahead was the bluff

and the object on the chart. If it was a real lighthouse, she could use it for cover; if it was just a beacon, she was shit out of luck. It sounded as though she'd been right and Billy was still using the Vietnamese man's army rifle which had an effective range ten times that of the Colt. If there was no cover, he'd be able to pick her off at his leisure.

She kept on running and the trees began to thin out on either side and the sound of the surf was a lot louder. Suddenly the trees vanished entirely and the path was now out in the open, the rising bluffs only a few feet away on her left. She risked a look behind but there was still no sign of Billy.

What's he doing?

She stopped, almost out of breath, and let her hands drop down to her knees as she filled her lungs again and again. None of this made any sense, this wasn't Billy's way. The Billy she knew, the Billy who fancied himself a scientist, would never do anything so crude as run his victim into the ground or give chase like some kind of hound.

It's not classy enough for Billy.

It's not his style.

And for a horrible second the thought rose in her exhausted mind that maybe none of this was Billy Bones at all, that maybe they'd all been led astray by some bizarre doppelgänger impostor. The thought evaporated and she stood up. Ten feet ahead of her, standing on the path, was Billy. A black, terrible calm suddenly enveloped her, and she felt strangely comforted, knowing that one way or the other their entwined lives were about to be severed at last.

Let's end this thing.

"It had to come to this," Billy said brightly. "It's really quite elementary, my dear."

He had the rifle aimed directly at her chest. Oddly, she noticed that the bolt was open and drawn back. Her eyes flickered left. She was standing no more than three feet from the unprotected cliff edge. The drop wasn't too bad, no more than twenty or thirty feet, but swimming in that water would be suicide even if she survived the fall.

No Butch and Sundance, thank you very much.

She started to lift the Colt.

With a quick hand Billy slapped the bolt handle and chambered a round. "This is exactly the way I always imagined it," said Billy, smiling wistfully. "You and me alone together on a deserted island, just the two of us."

"Three, you sick fuck." Karen Deaver stepped out of the trees a few feet farther back from the bluffs, the Sig-Sauer gripped in her hands, rock steady.

Both Jay and Billy turned at the sound of the voice, Jay startled by the pretty woman's bloody face, the hardness in her eyes, and the heavy automatic in her hand.

"You don't have any part to play in this," said Billy. There was anxiety in his tone.

He wasn't counting on her showing up.

Wild card.

Jay edged away from the cliff, tensing as she saw Billy's finger squeeze on the trigger, taking up the slack. The Deaver woman let out a long racking cough, doubling over, but before Billy could make a move in her direction she recovered and raised the automatic. "Don't you dare! Don't you fucking dare!" She coughed again, but she was back in control. "What do I do now?" she asked, her eyes flickering in Jay's direction.

"Keep the weapon on him," Jay answered. She moved another foot or so away from the cliff. Billy moved in concert, his eyes never leaving hers. He seemed to be ignoring the other woman and the second gun.

"We can't stand out in the rain like this all day, ladies," said Billy.

"One of us should go for help," said the Deaver woman.

"And leave me alone with the one remaining?" Billy shook his head. "Not a good idea."

"Is there a radio on your boat?" said Jay.

"Yes," said Karen Deaver.

"Smashed," Billy declared calmly. "To smithereens."

"Phone?" asked Jay.

"No," said Deaver, shaking her head. Jay saw the pistol in

her hand wavering. The woman looked as though she was
going into shock. Any advantage of having Billy's attention
split was fading fast. Jay had to do something, and do it now.

"He who hesitates is lost," said Billy, and he smiled. Then
everything happened together as he raised the rifle and the
two women fired almost simultaneously, sharing the same
thought and fear, then exorcising it.

Both shots took him hard in the chest, blowing him back
off the cliff as though he'd been pulled by secret strings, the
rifle flying out of his hands as he went over the edge. The
sound of the two explosions held in the air for a final moment,
then whipped away with the breeze. Faintly, in the far distance Jay thought she could hear the sound of a helicopter.
Jay went to the edge of the cliff and looked down. There was
no sign of the body.

Gone. Simple as that.

Quick as a wink. Now you see him, now you don't.

"We got him, didn't we?" said Karen Deaver, shaking hard
now, the gun falling from her hands. Jay turned at the sound.

"Yeah." Jay nodded. "We got him."

She spent a week at Marshals' headquarters in Arlington being debriefed by Karlson and his people, spending whatever
free time she had visiting Jack Dane at the Medical Center in
Bethesda. On her last day Karlson had a final, brief meeting
with her.

"If I had my way I'd have Jack tossed out on his ass,"
said the older man, handing Jay a cup of coffee.

"What are you going to do with him?" Jay asked.

Karlson let out a long-suffering sigh and leaned back in
his chair. "He's getting early retirement and a bonus disability
clause in his pension."

"I hear he's turning down book deals." Jay grinned.

"What about you?" Karlson asked. "I had a long conversation with Charlie Langford at the Bureau yesterday. He
thinks maybe you should come in out of the cold." Karlson
shrugged. "He'd hire you back in a minute."

"I don't know," said Jay. She took a sip of her coffee, then put the mug down on the edge of Karlson's desk. "Right now I just want to be left alone for a while."

"Back to Mendocino?"

She nodded. "For a little while."

Karlson stood up. The meeting was over. He extended his hand across the desk and Jay took it. "Keep in touch," said the marshal. "Maybe we can use you sometime. A consultant." He cleared his throat self-consciously. "For the really bad ones." He paused. "We just got a call from the Czech cops; some crazy man in Prague is making like Jekyll and Hyde. They asked for our help."

Jay nodded. "I'll think about it."

No I won't.

TWENTY-SEVEN

Janet Louise Fletcher sat on the porch of her house at the end of Lake Street in Mendocino, smoking a cigarette in the night-time dark, watching ragged clouds slide across the searchlight glow of a full moon. Out there, invisible beyond the head-lands, the Pacific was rolling in with the regularity of a heart-beat. She dragged in a lungful of smoke, feeling only the slightest twinge of guilt. She hadn't really thought about quit-ting since coming back here, and as far as she was concerned, she deserved another couple of weeks with her Marlboros before she seriously got down on herself.

All wrapped up with a ribbon and a bow.
Billy's dead and I'm out of a job.

When it became clear that she wasn't going to do any Larry King or Letterman, the networks and the tabloids turned their attention to Karen Deaver, the new avenging angel, a somewhat younger, prettier one, too.

Old folk heroes never die, they simply get replaced.
Thank God for small mercies.

There was talk of a feature, negotiations for a miniseries, and three different publishers had suggested a duet book au-thored by Jay and Karen Deaver as comrades-in-arms. Which was ludicrous, of course: Jay had spent a tense sixty seconds with the bloody faced woman on Tatlow Bluff and they'd shared a helicopter ride to a trauma center in Seattle, but that was just about the extent of their relationship even though the entire world was making them out to be kind of some Rambo-esque sister act.

Coming back to Mendocino with her cover blown had been easier than she'd imagined. There'd been a little flurry of interest, but by and large she'd been given her privacy. Robin hadn't taken it too well, though; they'd talked about it, but there was a distance between them that she was reasonably sure would never be bridged. He hadn't said anything definite but she could feel the underlying currents—for him her identity as Carrie Stone had been a lie, and her previous incarnations as an FBI agent and the Ladykiller were anathema to his own philosophies. He was an honest, peace-loving, honorable man; he could afford to be. She knew that, in his mind, she had betrayed him. Worst of all, he looked at her and saw a killer.

She sighed and stubbed out her cigarette into the little tin ashtray on the porch rail, listening to the sound of the distant surf. At least she didn't have to confront that part of it immediately; yesterday Robin had filled his van and was on his twice-a-year trek to the California craft fairs all up and down the coast and wouldn't be back in Mendocino for at least a month.

Time enough for her to figure out what to do with the rest of her life. She knew now that all the demons she'd fought so hard to quell for the last few years hadn't been defeated at all. It was all very nice to pretend that she could live a life like Robin's, a carefully constructed routine and a way of thinking that was almost perfectly passive, making no mark on the world except to create small, pretty things to sit on shelves and mantels, to be collected like baseball cards. No passion, just quiet craft, and no matter how hard she tried, Jay Fletcher just didn't fit that mold.

Something to do, something so I don't have to think.

She took a deep breath of the cooling air and felt the warm, twisting sensation in the pit of her stomach that meant her thoughts were turning toward Harry. She stood up, forcing herself to ignore the feeling.

I want Harry. I want to be on Harry's boat, on Harry's bed, with Harry inside me, rocking on the deep green waters of the Gulf of Mexico. Emerald green.

I don't want to hide who I am anymore.

Too soon, not yet, I've got to think.

She pulled open the screen, stepped into the house, and let the door slap shut behind her. Bed with a book or do the dishes now? Neither apparently, since she could hear the insistent voice of her computer coming from her den at the back of the house.

The synthetic voice was cold and toneless. "You have mail. You have mail." She sidestepped the stairs, went down the hall, then froze in the doorway to her study, listening to the voice again, feeling here throat clutch closed with fear.

The voice came again. "You have mail. You have mail."

Maybe she had mail but one thing she didn't have was a voice messager that told her so. Her computer didn't even have a sound card.

"You have mail. You have mail."

She stepped into the room, eyes fixed on the starfield screensaver.

"You have mail, you have mail."

Still staring at the screen she eased down into her chair and tapped a random key. The screen cleared to the standard blue-sky Windows 98 desktop. The mail icon was blinking in the lower right-hand corner.

"You have mail you have . . ."

She clicked the icon and the voice stopped. The blue-sky screen slid away, replaced by her e-mail program. There was a single message with no senders name and nothing in the little "subject" box. Jay clicked open the message. There was only a single word.

Duck.

"What the hell?" she stared at the message, its irrelevancy almost making her forget the question of the voice in her machine. "Duck?"

Then the computer exploded and she screamed. She got her arm up across her face in time to save herself from being blinded by flying shards of glass and plastic, instinctively throwing herself to one side and behind the questionable protection of her desk. She peeked up and caught a glimpse of the shattered, uncurtained window on the far side of the little room.

Gun.

With a silencer. Someone out there in the darkness was shooting at her. Absurdly, her first thought was that it was Robin, taking revenge for her breach of faith, but that was ridiculous. More likely some lunatic Billy fan who'd found out where she lived and had decided it was payback time. There were more than a dozen Billy Bones Web sites on the Net now, and more were coming every day, patterned after the first Charles Manson sites that had been on the Net since day one.

A second shot came, blasting the splintered remains of the computer chassis. The concussion of both shots had been enormous, which meant either a large-caliber weapon or explosive bullets of some kind. Jay assumed that it was the latter since big caliber silencers were notoriously ineffective. Not that it really mattered; she was under siege and her nearest neighbor was a quarter mile away across the western meadow section of the Mendocino Headlands State Park. She quickly glanced at her watch. Already past one o'clock. The bars were closed and the town was asleep. She was trapped.

Phone.

Even as the thought formed in her mind, the phone suddenly rang. Staying low, she reached up blindly, scrabbling through the blasted debris from her computer until her fingers found the telephone. She grabbed and pulled it off the desk, pressing the receiver to her ear.

"I'm under fire. Someone's trying to kill me. I'm at . . ." There was a clicking sound in her ear and then she heard a scratchy, distant voice.

"Oh Christ! He's got me and he's going to kill me unless you do exactly as he says!"

"Robin?" The hand holding the telephone was suddenly slick with sweat and she almost dropped it.

"Help me! Please help me!"

Her mouth went dry. There was no doubt. It was Robin. *My fault, my fault.*

"Where are you?"

There was another click and then the phone went dead in her hands. No static, no echo on the line, no dial tone. The wires had been cut. Her heart was beating so fast she could barely breath. She got to her knees and peeked up over the edge of her desk. A split second later a huge splintered hole appeared in the doorframe three feet behind her.

He can see me.

Night-vision goggles.

She dropped down to the floor again and did a knee-and-elbow crawl out through the doorway and into the hall. She closed her eyes, willing herself not to think about Robin and what was happening to him, desperately concentrating on the situation at hand. Staying on the floor, back pressed to the wall, she tried to think it through. Kitchen across the hall, back door locked. Two windows, one above the sink facing north, the other facing east, looking out across the meadow. Dining room, two windows facing south, living room, two windows west. Porch, front door.

Open. Nothing but the screen.

She heard its rusty squeak and then the wickering crack as it slapped closed.

Jesus. He's in the house.

Who! Who! Who!

It doesn't matter, never mind.

She heard the sound of heavy boots on the wide-plank floorboards in the foyer and then a duller tread. The rugs in the living room. Ten steps would take her to the back door, twenty seconds to pull back the bolt, open it, and run. She tried to slow her breathing. He'd hear. From the living room to the kitchen would take fifteen seconds and then there'd be a single shot to the back of her head, or blowing out her spine.

No. Think.

Five feet away behind louvered doors like the ones upstairs there was a walk-in linen closet. A trapdoor in the floor, covered by a rug, leading down into a service crawl space so the plumbers and electricians could get at the guts of the little house. She held her breath, toed off her sneakers, and pushed

herself standing, listening. The footsteps had stopped. The
only way from the front of the house to the rear was down
the hall; if she didn't move now he'd find her. She let out
her ragged breath, took in another, then slid two steps across
the hall, pulled open the doors praying that they wouldn't
squeak, and stepped into the darkness. She froze then, listening hard.

Which way?

Three squeaks, one, two, three, and a pause, then three
more.

He's going up the stairs.

Jay dropped to the floor, scrabbled back the rug, and found
the trapdoor. She hooked her index finger into the recessed
ring and pulled. The trap came up easily and without a sound,
suddenly filling the small space with the dark, rich scent of
cold earth and basement mustiness.

Gacy buried his victims in the crawl space of his house.

Stop it!

Without another thought, she eased herself into the crawl
space, carefully pulling the door shut above her head. She
could hear small scratching sounds, and the damp earth under
her hands seemed to be alive. Her hands sank deeply and she
had to bite her lip to stop herself from screaming, telling
herself there were no skeletal fingers down there, waiting to
pull her down.

She closed her eyes, trying not to breathe. She'd gone
through the trapdoor facing south, which meant a half-turn
would set her east, facing the meadow common at the far
edge of town. Two hundred yards, a couple of football fields,
and she'd be on Kelly Street. Laura Monkman's place, the
woman who ran the flower shop on Main Street, facing the
mouth of the Big River. No NRA bumper stickers on her
Volvo, but she'd have a telephone.

Hunkering down, she turned and began to crawl toward
the edge of the house, edging around a twisted intersection
of pipes, eventually reaching the flimsy latticework that dis-
guised the open concrete-block foundation. She stopped then
and listened. Only three rooms upstairs to check, her bed-

room, the guest room, and the bathroom. How long had she been in the crawl space? Too long. She reached out, gripped the latticework in clawed hands, and pulled, wincing as the narrow slats snapped loudly under her fingers. When she'd torn open a big enough space, she wiggled herself through and out from under the house. She stood and began to run, counting off the seconds in her head, knowing it would take her at least a minute to make the two hundred yards; time enough for any number of shots. Easily time enough to die.

Shut up! Shut up!

She kept on running but there was no shot, only the wet grass soaking through her short sweatsocks, a stumble in a small chuckhole, and thank god for the full moon so she could see where she was going, see the black, familiar shape that was the shadow of Laura Monkman's house. Idiotically, she wished she'd bought more flowers in the woman's store or had been a better neighbor, because she was about to become a nightmare visitor from hell.

Don't look back!

She didn't, and ran for the small light that was the square of glass in Laura Monkman's kitchen door. Lungs burning, she reached the woman's backyard, jumped the low picket fence, and tore her way through several flower beds before she reached the porch. She finally risked a look back over her shoulder but there was nothing to see.

Panting, her heart slamming up into her throat, she pounded on the door and it opened under her hand. She found herself in Laura's kitchen, with Laura in bra and panties sitting against the cabinets, blindly staring at the dried flower arrangement on her old pine table, hands pressed against the broad vertical slash that had gutted her, trying to pull the wound together while she bled out through the second slash that had opened her throat from side to side like the laughing, ghastly smile of some Stephen King clown. To finish things off, there was a hole the size of a silver dollar where her right eye should have been, blood and brain matter leaking down across her cheek like rose-colored porridge. A bloody tack hammer lay on the tile floor to one side, a gore-covered butcher knife gleamed wetly on the tile between her outspread legs.

"Oh God no!" Jay whispered, feeling the first sting of tears welling in her eyes.

My fault. My fault.

There was a pale blue wall phone beside a bulletin board in the breakfast nook to her right. It rang and Jay knew it was for her. Eyes still on Laura's corpse, she stumbled across the room and pulled the telephone down from the wall.

"You bastard!" she screamed, but all there was on the other end of the line was a hiss and then a click.

"Help me! Help me!"

Robin again, and frightened. It was a recording and somehow then, she knew.

"Billy," she whispered. Back from the dead, risen from the grave like the last few seconds of a horror movie when all's well that ends well suddenly becomes a nightmare once again. "Billy, you son of a bitch." She slammed the phone back into its cradle, then picked it up again, but it wouldn't disconnect; somehow he'd tied up the line. She tried again, but now there was nothing at all except a dark hole in the ozone. Dead, just like Robin would be if she didn't hurry up.

What was it he'd said up there on the cliff? "Elementary, my dear . . ." Elementary, my dear Watson. Holmes and Moriarty at Reichenbach Falls. The end of the serial in the *Strand* magazine. Not the end for Holmes, and not the end for Billy, either. The end but not the end, and his huge ego and his vanity forced him to give her the message, even if she hadn't been smart enough to pick up on it at the time.

"Elementary that you die, shitfucker."

Ricky's word.

She turned from the phone, scooped up the bloody knife from between Laura's legs, and ran from the house and into the yard again. Down the road, where Kelly Street met Ukiah, she could see the barnlike bulk of the hot shop. She stopped in the middle of the gravel street, clutching the knife, catching her breath. The nearest police were in Fort Bragg, the nearest help one of the houses on the other side of Main Street, but none of that meant anything. Billy was close and he was watching and if she took one wrong step Robin would die, just like Laura Monkman.

Like Hunter Connelly.

The piano teacher.

Nguyen Vinh Duong, Vinnie's uncle.

Vinnie, the little boy, his pale dead flesh like wax, so cold against her hand when she touched him.

My fault. My fault.

"No more," she said, and headed for the distant shop at the end of the road. "No more."

She reached the end of the street and went down the little alley that came out into the yard of Robin's shop. She paused, gripped the knife harder, and looked around carefully, eyeing the battleground Billy had chosen for them. As usual the gravel-strewn court was littered with cars in various states of disrepair, half of them taxicabs, all of them ghostly in the bright moonlight, like sleeping monsters. A line of wood-frame and sheet-metal U-rent garage cubicles ran along one side of the yard, and Robin's shop flanked them on the other side. Robin's big, dark blue van was back in its usual spot close to the loading bay. Somehow Billy had managed to get him back, or maybe even kidnapped him somewhere down the road.

My fault. My fault.

I brought Billy here; he's my disease but you caught it.

The yellow plank-on-frame building had undergone a number of transformations over the years. Once it had been an electrical manufacturing plant where they wound motors, then a welding shop, and finally a metal sculptor's studio. Each tenant had left his mark, adding and subtracting, including Robin.

The last incarnation included an outsized garage door cut into the back, a big wooden-plank corral for glass tailings and the installation of a furnace, glory holes, benches, and annealers to replace the forges and kilns left behind by the sculptor, a man named T. C. Robertson who had simply

packed his bags and left one day, never to be heard from
again.

The sculptor had already roughed in a small apartment on
the right side of the main studio area, and Robin finished it
off, adding a bathroom, small office, sinks, and new wiring.
He also built a room for doing cold work on the glass, fitting
it out with grinding wheels and a sandblasting booth for frost-
ing some of the pieces he produced. A lot of the equipment
was old and jury-rigged, but the place had a nice rough-and-
tumble feel that most people found relaxing.

Not tonight.

Mendocino being the kind of place it was, there was no
lock on the big door. Jay climbed up onto the loading bay
platform. She grabbed the handle and pulled, the door rum-
bling upwards on its counterweights. She pushed the door up
halfway, found the wooden wedge Robin used, and jammed
it in the runner to keep the door from coming down again.
Door open, she picked up a clipboard from its nail just inside
the door and began going through Robin's neatly printed list
of instructions. She was cold as ice now and infinitely calm,
heart slowed, and palms dry.

"Come on out, Billy, I know you're in here."

She waited, listening as all the pieces fell into place. The
shots fired to get her attention, maybe even some kind of
listening device to tell him where she was within the house,
along with the added voice card in her computer. She'd been
absent from the house for almost two weeks between Billy's
"death" and this night. Plenty of time.

Holding the knife in a fighter's stance, she edged to the
side of the doorway and felt for the light switch. She flipped
it on and the big overheads flickered, then came alive. She
let her eyes scan the interior of the shop. The fans were on
and everything looked "hot," as though Robin was in the middle of a production run. Eyes roving across the shop, she put
the knife down on the powder box, picked up a pipe, and
opened the furnace. She drove the pipe deep into the molten
ball of glass, taking up a gather. Five pounds of white-hot

dripping glass on the end of a five-foot pipe was a better weapon than a butcher knife.

"Come on, Billy, let's get this done."

Out of the corner of her eye Jay saw movement. She half turned and then a shadow passed in front of the open garage doors that led out to the yard. The door rumbled down and the dark figure behind her tossed the wooden restraining wedge down at her feet.

She pulled the pipe up out of the furnace, the tip loaded with a glowing gather of semiliquid glass. She stood, turning the pipe to keep gravity from pulling the glass off the end, and stepped back from the furnace. The figure moved out of the shadows behind the bench, but she didn't need the light to know who it was.

"Hey, Billy."

"Hey yourself, Ms. Fletcher." Billy Bones stood there, dressed in sneakers and jeans and a black Grateful Dead T-shirt with a big smiling Jerry Bear on the chest. He'd dyed his hair white blond.

Handsome as hell.

He had a Vietnam-era sniper rifle in his hand, fitted with a powerful scope. "You don't seem too surprised to see me." He took a step, unscrewing the modern suppressor from the end of the weapon and slipping it into his pocket.

"It was too good to be true." She stared at him. "As though we were all actors in your play. I thought something was wrong almost from the start." She kept the pipe moving, the cooling glass turning. He walked past her and pulled open the door to the apartment. Robin was sitting in a wooden kitchen chair, bound with duct tape, a strip of it over his mouth. His eyes were wide open and he was looking directly at her. The only feeling from the look was fury.

"Smart girl." Billy grinned and took one step toward her.

Jay took a step back, feeling the blasting heat of the furnace on her shoulders. "Everyone wanted to believe it, so they did," said Jay. "I guess I wanted to believe it, too." She shook her head. "I fell for it all."

"All?" Billy said and took another step. Jay raised the

loaded pipe and he backed away. She took the moment, turned, and sank the pipe into the furnace again, leaving it there this time, but still holding the pipe, feeling the heat slowly begin to rise.

"The whole charade." Jay nodded. "It was all calculated right from the start, wasn't it? A grand plan and we fell for it, even the chaos bullshit and the butterflies. Playing the perfect madman." She turned slightly, still keeping her eyes on him, and pushed the blowpipe deeper into the furnace, turning it, gathering more glass. "None of it was crazy at all, just smart. All those people had to die so you could put on your show and have your big death scene in the end."

"Pretty much," Billy agreed. "Connelly was easy, I just browsed some of the newspaper-clipping databases and found everything I wanted. His interest in art, he and his sister as guardians for the girl. Her piano lessons were on her schedule in the school computer. All simple enough."

"How did you know about the drawing in the piano teacher's house?"

"I didn't." He shrugged and smiled and stepped a little closer. "I knew there'd be something I could use and it didn't really matter what happened next, because it was all a sideshow anyway. The picture could have just as easily been a postcard on a bulletin board, like the one in the apartment at the Watergate."

"So you could have a cover story. A way out."

Keep him talking, he loves to talk.

"Hole in one, Ms. Fletcher."

Goddamn it, you should have figured it out before this!

Maybe you didn't want to. Maybe you wanted to believe it was over at last.

If she didn't do something soon it wasn't going to happen. "The Deaver woman. The island. That was the beginning, wasn't it, not the end?" Everything suddenly fell into place.

He used us. This wasn't about revenge.

Run and he'd run forever. Dying was the perfect escape and we were the perfect witnesses.

"Deaver was a big contributor to the museum." Billy nodded. "I even met him once or twice, her too. Years ago. She was the easiest, the best."

"And if I screwed up, Karen Deaver would have been the perfect witness. A fallback in case I didn't show up." It all made perfect sense. Karen Deaver had never been a hostage at all, she'd been Jay's understudy. "How did you know she'd come after you? Wouldn't run?"

"Everything I read about her told me she was a fighter. And I knew about the gun. Karen Deaver was meticulous about keeping good computer records. The permit was only good for the place on Sparks Island, so I knew it would be there." He laughed. "Besides, I ripped the distributor leads off the engine after I tied her up. She wasn't going anywhere." Billy took one more step. He was close now.

Too close. Do something.

"I had to die," he said quietly, his voice barely audible above the roaring fan. "I knew that from the start. Your friend the marshal and his pals would have made my life a living hell. Dead, I could reinvent myself."

"That was the extra day."

Gearing up, buying everything necessary for the illusion.

"Almost two," said Billy, clearly pleased with himself. "Plenty of time to set the stage."

"You went to the island." It was all coming together now, the wispy threads of thought that had been nagging her, twisting now into a thickening skein. She could feel the conducted heat from the pipe begin to burn into her hands.

Not much time left.

"Of course." He nodded. "Found the gun in Karen's closet and loaded it with blanks. Found a little hidey-hole at the foot of the cliffs."

That's how he knew so much.

"A Kevlar vest under the cammo jacket?"

"Second Chance, just in case." He nodded. "A set of scuba tanks buried under some rocks at low tide at the foot of the bluffs just in case I had to play dead underwater. The inflatable from the top of the cabin on the Deaver woman's boat." His smile broadened. "That's what gave me the idea in the first place, you know. The inflatable. I saw the *Boat Trader* advertisement in a copy they had in the hospital library. That was the only chance event in all of it, and if it hadn't been that it would have been something else. Opportunity always knocks for people like you and me, Janet."

Backwards. Mirror image. Start at the end and end at the start.

Chaos.

"They found a body in the Straits just across the border on the Canadian side. Wearing your clothes. Not much left of him to identify."

Billy nodded pleasantly. "The guy I took the Porsche from at the airport in Seattle. Chloroform and then I drowned him in a garbage bag full of sea water I had in the trunk of my rental. Worked like a charm."

"Pretty smart," said Jay. Another thirty seconds and the flesh of her palms would start to burn. She willed herself to keep holding the pipe. "Too bad you made some mistakes. Let your ego get in the way."

"What mistakes?" He smile wavered and became a pout.

Jay smiled, trying to ignore the searing pain in her hands. *Got you, didn't I?*

"Something Karen Deaver told me. Something that you said."

"What?" Another step. Less than ten feet between them now. Barely enough room.

"About the butterflies: 'When their surroundings change they are able to acquire a whole new set of markings to ensure their survival.' No reason to say something like that unless you were telegraphing some kind of message. Telling her you were switching identities." Jay paused, gripped the end of the blowpipe tightly, kept turning it as she talked, distracting him. "The rifle was a bit much too, out of character. Looking back, we also should have smelled a rat with her escaping that way. None of your other victims ever got off that easy."

"Very Freudian."

"How are you going to explain all this?" Jay asked. "The

gunfire, Laura Monkman. Me." She nodded toward the open door to the apartment. "Robin."

"Easy." He hefted the rifle in his hands. "Did you know this belonged to your hippy-dippy boyfriend?"

"Bullshit," said Jay, but her eyes flickered to Robin's bound figure and she saw the fear. Billy'd already talked to him, worked it out for him. He knew how it was going to play, knew that Billy was going to get away with it.

"Never told you about his other life, did he?" Billy went on. "How he graduated from Third Marine Division Sniper School at Xa Truong and went on to be top dog? Khe San, An Hoa, all sorts of other places? Scored an even 100 kills, almost as good as the best in the business, some guy named Mawhinny with 103 confirmed. Lots better at it than me, or you for that matter."

She stared at Robin, saw that it was true, saw the hate.

All the secrets, all the lies.

Both of us were killers after all.

"The cops will figure it like this: Your boyfriend goes crazy when he finds out who you really are, that you're just like him. Somewhere along the line poor old Laura gets in the way, so he takes her out. Maybe he was screwing her and maybe not, it doesn't matter much. It all comes together back here. First he shoots you, then himself, and then the fire starts and it all goes up in smoke." He looked around. "Who's not going to believe this place could catch fire by accident. It's a natural."

"It's full of holes," said Jay. "It doesn't work. Any cop will see right through it."

"It works well enough. Too perfect and people get suspicious. People like you." He shrugged and Jay saw his finger curl around the trigger of the M1.

He's getting ready.

"The cops will believe what they want to believe, and nothing's going to point to me playing Lazarus." He smiled. "They don't have lineups for dead men."

"Why?" asked Jay. "Why come back? Why risk everything when you had it all beat?"

Do it now, before your fucking hands burst into flame!
Wait.

Billy lifted his shoulders again. "It was all there. You would have put it together eventually. You would have woken up from a bad dream in the middle of the night and you would have figured it out, and I couldn't let that happen. You had to die; I knew that from the start." He took another step and Jay knew that time was running out. She lifted her hands an inch, testing the weight of the pipe. There had to be ten pounds on the gather. Now or never.

"So what's next for you, Billy?" She tensed the muscles in her shoulders and arms, setting her feet solidly, fractionally changing her grip on the pipe.

"A rest. A vacation." He smiled. "I thought Key West might be fun."

Bastard.

"And then you'll start again."

He nodded. "And then I'll start again."

"I can't let that happen, Billy, you know that."

"You can't stop me."

I have to.

He moved then, lifting the rifle at last. Jay pulled the blow-pipe out of the furnace, ten pounds of dripping molten glass, its core at more than two thousand degrees, turning in a blazing multihued oval on the end of a five-foot-long stainless-steel spear.

Without pause she rammed the pipe toward him, catching the barrel of the rifle, deflecting it by an inch or so, catching Billy off-balance. Jay jogged left, then took one long step as Billy stumbled toward her. She ducked under the rifle, tightening her hold on the pipe, knowing what was about to happen.

The hot glass wad on the end of the pipe touched the cotton face of the smiling Jerry Bear, and Billy's T-shirt burst into flames that raced up his chest toward his neck. The rifle seemed to fly out of his hand, a shot firing wildly, ricocheting off the cast-iron furnace and zinging off around the shop.

A split second later, the glass burned into Billy's flesh just below the hard bony knob of the xiphoid process, eating through his smooth skin and fat and muscle, sending up clouds of smoke and steam into the air, the glass chewing and searing into his abdomen, the awful smell and sound of it like someone cooking wet popcorn in rancid oil. He took a last, astonished breath into his already parboiled lungs and then his hair caught fire.

The ball of glass cooled as it cooked through Billy's flesh, but as it burned through to the liver and ruptured the falciform ligament, it was still over fifteen hundred degrees at the core, a small self-contained furnace of its own, ten times hotter than a blowtorch. Jay stood firm as Billy's momentum drove the pipe even deeper and the still-molten ball of glass touched both left and right lobes of his lungs and the base of his heart. Water boils at 212 degrees Fahrenheit and so did Billy. His major organs literally exploded as the glass touched them, hot steaming blood and tissue gouting from his gaping mouth in a final dying torrent.

Jay pulled back on the blowpipe, and the steel pole came free but the hot glass remained in Billy's chest, the weight of the cooling, lavalike mass burning and sputtering, still smoking as it oozed thick and still terribly hot down through his stomach, spleen, and kidneys. As Jay tossed the hot pipe aside, Billy dropped to his knees, his dark eyes already dead, then fell forward in a cloud of steam and smoke. The air in the shop was foul with his death. The whole thing had taken no more than ten seconds at the very most.

There wasn't even time for him to scream.

She stared down at him.

Was this what you really wanted, Billy?

Back to front, front to back. Role reversal, chaos?

You the willing victim and me, the willing executioner.

Jay stepped over what was left of Billy and walked through the door of the apartment. Without saying a word, she unbound Robin's hands, then pulled the strip of tape away from his mouth.

If you'd told me the truth maybe I would have done the same.

But that was a lie, too. Jay turned away, leaving him to undo the tape around his ankles, knowing that anything possible between them had gone forever. She crossed the shop, skirting the smoldering lump of Billy's corpse, and pushed up the big door, stepping out into the darkness. The moon was going down and the stars were brilliant specks in an infinite sheet of deep black glass.

Just like the night that Ricky Stiles died. All the stars.
Infinite choices and paths to take. Infinite destinies.

She stood there for a moment, letting the tears come at last, weeping for what might have been and what would never happen now, all of it too sad to contemplate. But standing there, she also felt something lift from her shoulders and her heart—a weight, a burden, and perhaps something else. Sudden knowledge, learned hard. The relief and pain of knowing that there was no place for her here, not in Robin's world, or even in the world of men like Jack Dane. She remembered her father, heard his voice as clear as the wind in the trees. Answering a child's question. In a boat on a lake, a long, long time ago.

"Why are people so different, Pop? Why can't they all be nice?"

"People are like eggs, kiddo. Some like 'em fried and some like 'em scrambled, and let's face it, child, some don't like 'em at all."

Jay wiped away her tears, smiled at the old joke from her past, and let out a long ragged sigh. She stepped down off the loading platform, suddenly realizing that her T-shirt was spattered with a drying cloud of Billy's blood. She'd go back to the house, change her clothes, warm up the coffee in the microwave, and make two calls. The first would be to 911, the second would be to Belle's B&B in Key West.

Time to go where I'm wanted.
Time to go home.